P9-AQX-284

F. Scott Fitzgerald

This Side of Paradise

... Well this side of Paradise! ...
There's little comfort in the wise.
—*Rupert Brooke*

Experience is the name so many
people give to their mistakes.
—*Oscar Wilde*

INTRODUCTION BY JAY PARINI

A SIGNET CLASSIC

SIGNET CLASSIC
Published by New American Library, a division of
Penguin Putnam Inc., 375 Hudson Street, New York,
New York 10014, U.S.A.
Penguin Books Ltd, 80 Strand,
London WC2R 0RL, England
Penguin Books Australia Ltd, Ringwood,
Victoria, Australia
Penguin Books Canada Ltd, 10 Alcorn Avenue,
Toronto, Ontario, Canada M4V 3B2
Penguin Books (N.Z.) Ltd, 182–190 Wairau Road,
Auckland 10, New Zealand

Penguin Books Ltd, Registered Offices:
Harmondsworth, Middlesex, England

Published by Signet Classic, an imprint of New American Library,
a division of Penguin Putnam Inc.

First Signet Classic Printing, January 1996
10 9 8 7 6

Introduction copyright © Jay Parini, 1996
All rights reserved

 REGISTERED TRADEMARK—MARCA REGISTRADA

Library of Congress Catalog Card Number: 95-69123

Printed in the United States of America

BOOKS ARE AVAILABLE AT QUANTITY DISCOUNTS WHEN USED TO PROMOTE
PRODUCTS OR SERVICES. FOR INFORMATION PLEASE WRITE TO PREMIUM MAR-
KETING DIVISION, PENGUIN PUTNAM INC., 375 HUDSON STREET, NEW YORK, NEW
YORK 10014.

F. SCOTT FITZGERALD was born in 1896 in St. Paul, Minnesota, and educated at various New England boarding schools and at Princeton. *This Side of Paradise,* his first novel, was published in 1920 and transformed him virtually overnight into a spokesman for his generation and a prophet of the "Jazz Age." That same year, he married Zelda Sayre, and the two became America's most notorious expatriates, dividing their time among New York, Paris, the Riviera, and Rome. Fitzgerald's greatest novel, *The Great Gatsby,* was published in 1925, and *Tender Is the Night* in 1934. After Scott and Zelda were forced by money and health problems to return to the States, Fitzgerald became a contract writer for a Hollywood movie studio and a prolific writer of short stories for magazines like the *Saturday Evening Post* and *Esquire.* He died in 1940 while working on his unfinished novel of Hollywood, *The Last Tycoon.* His other works include *Flappers and Philosophers* (1920), *The Beautiful and Damned* (1922), *Tales of the Jazz Age* (1922), *All the Sad Young Men* (1926), and *Taps at Reveille* (1935).

JAY PARINI, a poet and novelist, is Axinn Professor of English at Middlebury College. His books include the poetry collection *Anthracite Country,* the novel *The Last Station,* and *John Steinbeck: A Biography.*

Contents

Introduction

I was about nineteen when I first read F. Scott Fitzgerald's dazzling first novel, *This Side of Paradise*. A passage in which Amory Blaine, Fitzgerald's flagrantly autobiographical hero, bathes himself (quite literally) in the succulent atmosphere of Princeton University one spring night, has always stayed with me:

> The night mist fell. From the moon it rolled, clustered about the spires and towers, and then settled below them, so that the dreaming peaks were still in lofty aspiration toward the sky. Figures that dotted the day like ants now brushed along as shadowy ghosts, in and out of the foreground. The Gothic halls and cloisters were infinitely more mysterious as they loomed suddenly out of the darkness, outlined each by myriad faint squares of yellow light. Indefinitely from somewhere a bell boomed the quarter-hour, and Amory, pausing by the sun-dial, stretched himself out full length on the damp grass. The cool bathed his eyes and slowed the flight of time—time that had crept so insidiously through the lazy April afternoons, seemed so intangible in the long spring twilights. Evening after evening the senior singing had drifted over the campus in melancholy beauty, and through the shell of his undergraduate consciousness had broken a deep and reverent devotion to the gray walls and Gothic peaks and all they symbolized as warehouses of dead ages.

Fitzgerald's prose is powerfully overblown, but it edges toward the purest poetry in places: "Indefinitely from somewhere a bell boomed the quarter-hour" could be a line from T. S. Eliot. But the feeling of the passage has more in common with John Keats, the great English Romantic poet who died in his mid-twenties, having forged an aesthetic philosophy in which death is the mother of beauty. Death—the passing of time, "time that had crept so insidiously through the lazy April afternoons"—is what makes the fragrant spring night on the Princeton quad so heartbreakingly lovely.

The shimmering quality of Fitzgerald's writing in *This Side of Paradise* redeems what might otherwise seem to contemporary readers a disjointed novel about the coming-of-age of Amory Blaine, a spoiled preppie. Reflecting on the novel in 1938, eighteen years after its initial publication, a jaded Fitzgerald commented: "I think it is now one of the funniest books since 'Dorian Gray' in its utter spuriousness—and then, here and there, I find a page that is real and living." But this was the pronouncement of a jaded man who had lost everything: youth, his marriage (his wife, Zelda, had suffered a complete mental breakdown), his health (he was an alcoholic), even his public. It may well have pained him to remember those days, just before the Twenties began to roar, when he was the newly crowned King of American Fiction.

The Fitzgerald legend has become an indelible part of the landscape of modern literature. Born in St. Paul, Minnesota, in 1896, he grew up in a household riven by class differences. His affected, overbearing mother—who stands clearly behind Blaine's mother, Beatrice, in *This Side of Paradise*—was Mary McQuillan Fitzgerald, the eldest daughter of an Irish immigrant who had made a fortune in the wholesale grocery business. The McQuillans looked down on the genteel Fitzgeralds, who had squandered the money their ancestors once had in abundance. Fitzgerald's father, Edward Fitzgerald, was acutely conscious of his inability to make enough to support his wife in the style to which she had become accustomed, and it troubled his shy son to witness his futile attempts at business. Like Charles Dickens, whose father had gone bankrupt, Fitzgerald lived in constant fear of financial ruin, even after he became relatively wealthy through his writing.

Fitzgerald has a great deal in common with Amory Blaine. Like his fictional counterpart, he was sent to a Catholic school back East because of his Aunt Annabel McQuillan's benevolence. He attended the Newman School in Hackensack, New Jersey, an institution that resembles the fictional St. Regis, in Connecticut, where Amory Blaine is a student as the novel opens. At Newman, Fitzgerald began to separate from his domineering mother and develop a sense of himself; as he says of Blaine: "[St. Regis] had very painfully drilled Beatrice out of him and begun to lay down new and more conventional planking on the fundamental Amory."

The mentor figure in the novel, an avuncular priest called Monsignor Darcy, was closely modeled on Monsignor Sigourney Webster Fay, to whom the novel is dedicated. Fay made a profound impression on the young Scott, encouraging him to pursue his literary interests and recommending Princeton as the right university. Monsignor Darcy sends Blaine to Princeton as well, and he arrives with a heady desire to "be one of the gods of [his] class."

Fitzgerald is at his best in Book One of the novel, where he catches the evanescent flavor of life on an Ivy League campus just before the U.S. entry into World War I. In particular, he captures the driving ambition to succeed that a boy from an upwardly aspiring family from the Midwest would feel in the presence of so many sophisticated young men from the East. Like Blaine, Fitzgerald aspired to be counted among the "hot cats on top" at Princeton, and this meant joining one of the prestigious eating clubs (such as Cottage), writing for *The Tiger,* an undergraduate humor magazine, and participating in the yearly theatricals presented by the Triangle Club.

Princeton also meant, for both Blaine and Fitzgerald, the opportunity to form connections with the most promising minds of the new generation. Fitzgerald made many friends, including the writers John Peale Bishop and Edmund Wilson. Wilson, known as "the shy little scholar of Holder Court," was a class ahead of him; already an omnivorous reader, he would eventually become America's presiding intellectual, writing such influential books as *Axel's Castle* and *To the Finland Station*. He and Fitzgerald worked together on a musical comedy called *The Evil Eye*, which was performed by the Triangle Club in 1916, with the book by Wilson and the lyrics by Fitzgerald.

Frenetic social activity took its toll on Fitzgerald, who was never a dedicated student. He did miserably in his exams and was suspended from school for eight months. In a similar fashion, Blaine fails to pass an exam and is placed on probation, becoming one of the "conditioned men" who were not allowed to participate in the social life on campus because of their academic problems. Blaine clings desperately to his status as a Princeton undergraduate, believing that is where his dreams will be found. The glittering youth are there, with their prospects of European holidays, country club parties, beautiful women, and fun. Blaine wants all of this for himself.

Like any sensible young person, he also aspires to success in love, and his romantic affectations might be considered part of his charm. This was long before the era of "free love," of course; indeed, because of the Mann Act (1910), it was illegal for unmarried couples to "cohabit," even for one night. One of the central scenes in the second half of the novel concerns the near-arrest of Blaine for cohabitation when he takes the rap for a friend. (He is saved only because a nervous hotel manager wants to prevent a scandal.)

Blaine moves through a succession of romantic infatuations. First comes Isabelle Borgé, but she eventually strikes him as insubstantial, flighty, and annoying. (Borgé was lifted out of an early Fitzgerald story, "Babe in the Woods," name and all.) Blaine abandons her and takes up with Clara Page, a gorgeous widow with two small children. (She is also a distant cousin.) We soon discover that, despite her rare beauty, there is something stiff and lifeless about Clara, who Fitzgerald calls "the first fine woman [Amory Blaine] ever knew and one of the few good people who ever interested him." Their relationship is poignant but doomed. In many ways Clara Page is too good for the shallow, immature Blaine, although he and Fitzgerald seem not to know this.

Book One is aptly entitled "The Romantic Egotist," which was the original title for the novel. Amory Blaine is utterly self-absorbed, to a shocking degree egotistical. Although he plays with ideas and writes poetry, the life that interests him most is the sensuous one. He seeks a life filled with pretty women, lovely surroundings, good food and drink, and poetry. His attitude to serious events, such as the war in Europe, are characterized in this telling passage:

> The war began in the summer following his freshman year. Beyond a sporting interest in the German dash for Paris, the whole affair failed either to thrill or interest him. With the attitude he might have held toward an amusing melodrama he hoped it would be long and bloody. If it had not continued he would have felt like an irate ticket-holder at a prize-fight where the principals refused to mix it up.

One can see why the older generation, many of whom had suffered in this dreadful war, found Blaine's attitudes intolerable.

Alas, undergraduate life, and youth, are necessarily short-lived, and Book One ends on a melancholy note with Blaine's last, languorous day at Princeton. Fitzgerald writes: "Slowly and inevitably, yet with a sudden surge at the last, while Blaine talked and dreamed, war rolled swiftly up the beach and washed the sands where Princeton played." Blaine's college career is a dream that cannot be sustained; time, and the "real world," intervene. Thus Amory Blaine goes off to war.

The autobiographical elements of the story are worth noting. Fitzgerald himself dropped out of Princeton in his senior year to accept an army commission; it would be going too far to say he felt "patriotic," but his romantic nature responded to the notion of risking his life for his country, even though most of his more intellectual friends at Princeton were by this time against the war.

Before he left for basic training, Fitzgerald had completed the rough draft of the novel that became *This Side of Paradise*. He showed it to Professor Christian Gauss, who had become a mentor to all undergraduates with literary aspirations; Gauss read it carefully and returned it, urging Fitzgerald not to attempt to publish it. This blow did not crush the young novelist, much to his credit, and when he journeyed to Fort Leavenworth to begin his training, the manuscript was in his suitcase. He rewrote it thoroughly during the spring of 1918 and sent it to Scribner's, in New York, who refused it.

The war was winding down by now, and it soon became obvious that Fitzgerald was not going to fight in Europe. He was sent to Camp Sheridan, near Montgomery, Alabama, where he met and fell deeply in love with Zelda Sayre, the eighteen-year-old daughter of an eminent judge. Her brilliant red-gold hair and fiery nature appealed to the young officer, and he courted her assiduously. She was the prototype, for Fitzgerald, of "the Flapper," and he would write about Zelda again and again in many stories and novels, often combining her with some of the women he had met during his days at Princeton.

Book Two of *This Side of Paradise* is called "The Education of a Personage," elaborating on a distinction made by Monsignor Darcy between "a personality" and "a personage." A personality is insubstantial, he argues; it is superficial and flashy. The prelate urges Blaine to develop a "personage," which involves the slow gathering of "prestige and talent" through a process of maturation that is deliberate. As a man on a quest for excellence, Blaine must rid himself of any trace of personality; he must move from being overly self-conscious, even narcissistic, to something higher, selfless. Book Two of the novel portrays this quest, tracing the life of Amory Blaine through various developmental stages.

Book Two begins as Blaine returns from overseas, where not a great deal seems to have affected him. (One suspects that, because he never himself made it to Europe, Fitzgerald could not find anything to say about the war and wisely decided to skip ahead.) Blaine links up in New York with two Princeton buddies, Alec Connage and Tom D'Invilliers. He is soon drawn into the social swirl, which he loves. Landing a job in an advertising agency to make ends meet, Blaine pursues two key love affairs. First he meets Rosalind, the alluring sister of Alec Connage; this loose-tongued debutante is at the center of some of the novel's liveliest moments. She is based partly on a woman called Ginevra King, whom the author had courted frantically, in vain, while at Princeton, and partly on Zelda. Blaine adores her, but her recklessness unnerves him. He is disturbed when he sees her "doing things that even in his memory would have been impossible: eating three-o'clock, after-dance suppers in impossible cafés, talking of every side of life with an air half of earnestness, half of mockery, yet with a furtive excitement that Amory considered stood for a real moral letdown." Rosalind seems to adore Blaine too, but she cannot abide his lack of money. "I don't want to think of pots and kitchens and brooms," she explains in rejecting him. "I want to worry whether my legs will get slick and brown when I swim in the summer."

It appears that Fitzgerald, like Blaine, does not approve of Rosalind: one should have more on one's mind than getting a tan. On the other hand, he writes about the sweet young things who populate his novel with remarkable sincerity and considerable awe. The most obvious flaw of *This Side of Paradise* may be its lack of ironic perspective, although this flaw is also, in the contradictory way of art, the novel's greatest asset. The author's lack of cynicism is immensely appealing. In fact, too much irony would kill this story, which derives much of its interest from its naive tone.

Eleanor Savage is Blaine's next romantic affiliation, and she too recalls Zelda, whose self-destructiveness was legendary. Savage is much like her name: untamed, wild, unpredictable. She recites Verlaine and Poe to Blaine and declares herself an atheist. In one of the novel's tensest scenes, she insists on proving her mettle by riding a horse over a cliff; miraculously, she leaps from the horse just before it plunges over the cliff to destruction. Shortly after this terrible event, she confesses to Blaine that she has a "crazy streak" inherited from her mother, who went mad when she was eleven. Blaine knows only too well that he cannot link himself permanently with Eleanor Savage. She scares him, and he notes wryly that his "love [had] waned, slowly with the moon."

The novel's second half centers on the process by which Blaine becomes a fairly mature young man. Having created for himself a life that feels superficial and, at times, debauched, Blaine decides to reform. He comes to dislike the shallowness of those around him, and does not want to continue further in the vain pursuit of women, literary fame, and the sensuous life. He realizes that he is selfish, that he must extend himself to other people for his own good as well as theirs. He hopes to "attach a positive value to life."

The novel moves toward a rather hollow-sounding conclusion in which Amory Blaine is heard to say aloud: "This is the first time in my life I've argued Socialism. It's the only panacea I know. I'm restless. My whole generation is restless. I'm sick of a system where the richest man gets the most beautiful girl if he wants her, where the artist without an income has to sell his talents to a button manufacturer." There is more sour grapes than Socialism in this statement, but there is truth in one famous sentence: "My whole generation is restless."

"You are a lost generation," said Gertrude Stein to Ernest Hemingway a few years later. Fitzgerald in his way embodied this lost generation, and his first novel counts among the first examples of modern literature that expressed this lostness. The "restlessness" he detected among his contemporaries was one manifestation of that sense of loss. What was gone was a world where values were permanent and unquestioned. Now everything was up for grabs, and a young man like Blaine must find a value system all his own or drift to ruin in a world of glitter.

Fitzgerald captured the restlessness of his gereration brilliantly in *This Side of Paradise,* which became a sacred text for his generation. Having rewritten the book during his time in the army, he resubmitted it to Scribner's in 1919, with the working title of *The Romantic Egotist.* An editor there, a young man called Max Perkins, considered it promising and asked for more revisions. Delighted by this response, Fitzgerald retreated to his family home in St. Paul that summer and devoted himself to the manuscript, following Perkins' advice closely. It was accepted within two weeks of resubmission and published in the spring of 1920.

Few first novels ever win so many eager readers in such a short time. Twenty thousand copies were sold in the first week after publication, and by the end of the year—after nine printings—the novel had sold over forty-one thousand copies. That same year Fitzgerald also published his first book of short stories, *Flappers and Philosophers,* and the film rights to one of these stories, "Head and Shoulders," was sold to Hollywood. It was a thrilling time for him.

Only a week after the novel's publication, Fitzgerald married Zelda Sayre, and the Jazz Age was unofficially underway. But Zelda's instability, and Scott's alcholism, eventually took their toll, and these lives that began with such promise ended in waste, in tragedy. Their story has become a kind of cautionary tale. But *This Side of Paradise* is Fitzgerald before the fall: a novel of undeniable force and freshness.

It does not have anything like that perfection of form which makes *The Great Gatsby* one of the finest novels ever written by an American, but one sees in its pages the first awakening of a major talent. Fitzgerald's prose shimmers, lapses into absurdity and awkwardness, then shimmers again. The characters flash and fade. The plot tangles and snags. It appears at times that young Scott Fitzgerald threw everything into this book he could think of except the kitchen sink: poems, fragments of plays, philosophical ramblings, autobiographical notes, stories. Yet for all its flaws, a kind of truth permeates this novel, a likeness to the life of its time that cannot be denied.

Defending *This Side of Paradise* later in his life, Fitzgerald once remarked, "A lot of people thought it was a fake, and perhaps it was, and a lot of others thought it was a lie, which it was not." It was not a lie because Scott Fitzgerald lived the life captured in these pages, and its fragile beauty has not diminished after many decades.

—JAY PARINI

BOOK ONE

The Romantic Egotist

1

Amory, Son of Beatrice

AMORY BLAINE inherited from his mother every trait, except the stray inexpressible few, that made him worth while. His father, an ineffectual, inarticulate man with a taste for Byron and a habit of drowsing over the *Encyclopedia Britannica,* grew wealthy at thirty through the death of two elder brothers, successful Chicago brokers, and in the first flush of feeling that the world was his, went to Bar Harbor and met Beatrice O'Hara. In consequence, Stephen Blaine handed down to posterity his height of just under six feet and his tendency to waver at crucial moments, these two abstractions appearing in his son Amory. For many years he hovered in the background of his family's life, an unassertive figure with a face half-obliterated by lifeless, silky hair continually occupied in "taking care" of his wife, continually harassed by the idea that he didn't and couldn't understand her.

But Beatrice Blaine! There was a woman! Early pictures taken on her father's estate at Lake Geneva, Wisconsin, or in Rome at the Sacred Heart Convent—an educational extravagance that in her youth was only for the daughter of the exceptionally wealthy—showed the exquisite delicacy of her features, the consummate art and simplicity of her clothes. A brilliant education she had—her youth passed in renaissance glory, she was versed in the latest gossip of the Older Roman Families; known by name as a fabulously wealthy American girl to Cardinal Vitori and Queen Margherita and more subtle celebrities that one must have had some culture even to have heard of. She learned in England to prefer whiskey and soda to wine, and her small talk was broadened in two senses during a winter in Vienna. All in all

Beatrice O'Hara absorbed the sort of education that will
be quite impossible ever again; a tutelage measured by
the number of things and people one could be contemp-
tuous of and charming about; a culture rich in all arts
and traditions, barren of all ideas, in the last of those
days when the great gardener clipped the inferior roses
to produce one perfect bud.

In her less important moments she returned to America,
met Stephen Blaine and married him—this almost entirely
because she was a little bit weary, a little bit sad. Her
only child was carried through a tiresome season and
brought into the world on a spring day in ninety-six.

When Amory was five he was already a delightful
companion for her. He was an auburn-haired boy, with
great, handsome eyes which he would grow up to in
time, a facile imaginative mind and a taste for fancy
dress. From his fourth to his tenth year he *did* the country with his mother in her father's private car, from Cor-
onado, where his mother became so bored that she had
a nervous breakdown in a fashionable hotel, down to
Mexico City, where she took a mild, almost epidemic
consumption. This trouble pleased her, and later she
made use of it as an intrinsic part of her atmosphere—
especially after several astounding bracers.

So, while more or less fortunate little rich boys were
defying governesses on the beach at Newport, or being
spanked or tutored or read to from "Do and Dare," or
"Frank on the Lower Mississippi," Amory was biting
acquiescent bell-boys in the Waldorf, outgrowing a natural repugnance to chamber music and symphonies, and
deriving a highly specialized education from his mother.

"Amory."

"Yes, Beatrice." (Such a quaint name for his mother;
she encouraged it.)

"Dear, don't think of getting out of bed yet. I've always suspected that early rising in early life makes one
nervous. Clothilde is having your breakfast brought up."

"All right."

"I am feeling very old today, Amory," she would sigh,
her face a rare cameo of pathos, her voice exquisitely
modulated, her hands as facile as Bernhardt's. "My

nerves are on edge—on edge. We must leave this terrifying place tomorrow and go searching for sunshine."

Amory's penetrating green eyes would look out
through tangled hair at his mother. Even at this age he
had no illusions about her.

"Amory."

"Oh, *yes*."

"I want you to take a red-hot bath—as hot as you can
bear it, and just relax your nerves. You can read in the
tub if you wish."

She fed him sections of the "Fêtes Galantes" before
he was ten; at eleven he could talk glibly, if rather rem-
iniscently, of Brahms and Mozart and Beethoven. One
afternoon, when left alone in the hotel at Hot Springs,
he sampled his mother's apricot cordial, and as the taste
pleased him, he became quite tipsy. This was fun for a
while, but he essayed a cigarette in his exaltation, and
succumbed to a vulgar, plebeian reaction. Though this
incident horrified Beatrice, it also secretly amused her
and became part of what in a later generation would
have been termed her "line."

"This son of mine," he heard her tell a room full of
awestruck, admiring women one day, "is entirely sophisticated and quite charming—but delicate—we're all
delicate; *here*, you know." Her hand was radiantly outlined against her beautiful bosom; then sinking her voice
to a whisper, she told them of the apricot cordial. They
rejoiced, for she was a brave raconteuse, but many were
the keys turned in sideboard locks that night against the
possible defection of little Bobby or Barbara. . . .

These domestic pilgrimages were invariably in state;
two maids, the private car, or Mr. Blaine when available,
and very often a physician. When Amory had the
whooping-cough four disgusted specialists glared at
each other hunched around his bed; when he took scarlet
fever the number of attendants, including physicians and
nurses, totalled fourteen. However, blood being thicker
than broth, he was pulled through.

The Blaines were attached to no city. They were the
Blaines of Lake Geneva; they had quite enough relatives
to serve in place of friends, and an enviable standing

from Pasadena to Cape Cod. But Beatrice grew more and more prone to like only new acquaintances, as there were certain stories, such as the history of her constitution and its many amendments and her memories of her years abroad, that it was necessary for her to repeat at regular intervals. Like Freudian dreams, they must be thrown off, else they would sweep in and lay siege to her nerves. But Beatrice was critical about American women, especially the floating population of ex-Westerners.

"They have accents, my dear," she told Amory, "not Southern accents or Boston accents, not an accent attached to any locality, just an accent"—she became dreamy. "They pick up old, moth-eaten London accents that are down on their luck and have to be used by some one. They talk as an English butler might after several years in a Chicago grand opera company." She became almost incoherent—"Suppose—time in every Western woman's life—she feels her husband is prosperous enough for her to have—accent—they try to impress *me,* my dear—"

Though she thought of her body as a mass of frailties, she considered her soul quite as ill, and therefore important in her life. She had once been a Catholic, but discovering that priests were infinitely more attentive when she was in process of losing or regaining faith in Mother Church, she maintained an enchantingly wavering attitude. Often she deplored the bourgeois quality of the American Catholic clergy, and was quite sure that had she lived in the shadow of the great Continental cathedrals her soul would still be a thin flame on the mighty altar of Rome. Still, next to doctors, priests were her favorite sport.

"Ah, Bishop Wiston," she would declare, "I do not *want* to talk of myself. I can imagine the stream of hysterical women fluttering at your doors, beseeching you to be simpatico"—then after an interlude filled by the clergyman—"but my mood—is—oddly dissimilar."

Only to bishops and above did she divulge her clerical romance. When she had first returned to her country there had been a pagan, Swinburnian young man in Asheville, for whose passionate kisses and unsentimen-

tal conversations she had taken a decided penchant—
they had discussed the matter pro and con with an intellectual romancing quite devoid of soppiness. Eventually she had decided to marry for background, and the
young pagan from Asheville had gone through a spiritual crisis, joined the Catholic Church, and was
now—Monsignor Darcy.

"Indeed, Mrs. Blaine, he is still delightful company—
quite the cardinal's right-hand man."

"Amory will go to him one day, I know," breathed the
beautiful lady, "and Monsignor Darcy will understand
him as he understood me."

Amory became thirteen, rather tall and slender, and
more than ever on to his Celtic mother. He had tutored
occasionally—the idea being that he was to "keep up,"
at each place "taking up the work where he left off," yet
as no tutor ever found the place he left off, his mind was
still in very good shape. What a few more years of this
life would have made of him is problematical. However,
four hours out from land, Italy bound, with Beatrice, his
appendix burst, probably from too many meals in bed,
and after a series of frantic telegrams to Europe and
America, to the amazement of the passengers the great
ship slowly wheeled around and returned to New York
to deposit Amory at the pier. You will admit that if it
was not life it was magnificent.

After the operation Beatrice had a nervous breakdown
that bore a suspicious resemblance to delirium tremens,
and Amory was left in Minneapolis, destined to spend
the ensuing two years with his aunt and uncle. There the
crude, vulgar air of Western civilization first catches
him—in his underwear, so to speak.

A KISS FOR AMORY

His lip curled when he read it.

I am going to have a bobbing party, it said, on Thursday, December the seventeenth, at five o'clock, and I
would like it very much if you could come.
                              Yours truly,
R.S.V.P.   Myra St. Claire.

He had been two months in Minneapolis, and his chief struggle had been the concealing from "the other guys at school" how particularly superior he felt himself to be, yet this conviction was built upon shifting sands. He had shown off one day in French class (he was in senior French class) to the utter confusion of Mr. Reardon, whose accent Amory damned contemptuously, and to the delight of the class. Mr. Reardon, who had spent several weeks in Paris ten years before, took his revenge on the verbs, whenever he had his book open. But another time Amory showed off in history class, with quite disastrous results, for the boys there were his own age, and they shrilled innuendoes at each other all the following week:

"Aw—I b'lieve, doncherknow, the Umuricun revolution was *lawgely* an affair of the middul *clawses,*" or

"Washington came of very good blood—aw, quite good—I b'lieve."

Amory ingeniously tried to retrieve himself by blundering on purpose. Two years before he had commenced a history of the United States which, though it only got as far as the Colonial Wars, had been pronounced by his mother completely enchanting.

His chief disadvantage lay in athletics, but as soon as he discovered that it was the touchstone of power and popularity at school, he began to make furious, persistent efforts to excel in the winter sports, and with his ankles aching and bending in spite of his efforts, he skated valiantly around the Lorelei rink every afternoon, wondering how soon he would be able to carry a hockey stick without getting it inexplicably tangled in his skates.

The invitation to Miss Myra St. Claire's bobbing party spent the morning in his coat pocket, where it had an intense physical affair with a dusty piece of peanut brittle. During the afternoon he brought it to light with a sigh, and after some consideration and a preliminary draft in the back of Collar and Daniell's "First Year Latin," composed an answer:

My dear Miss St. Claire:
    Your truly charming envitation for the evening of next

Thursday evening was truly delightful to receive this morning. I will be charm and inchanted indeed to present my compliments on next Thursday evening.

Faithfully,

Amory Blaine.

On Thursday, therefore, he walked pensively along the slippery, shovel-scraped sidewalks, and came in sight of Myra's house, on the half-hour after five, a lateness which he fancied his mother would have favored. He waited on the doorstep with his eyes nonchalantly half-closed, and planned his entrance with precision. He would cross the floor, not too hastily, to Mrs. St. Claire, and say with exactly the correct modulation:

"My *dear* Mrs. St. Claire, I'm *frightfully* sorry to be late, but my maid"—he paused there and realized he would be quoting—"but my uncle and I had to see a fella—Yes, I've met your enchanting daughter at dancing-school."

Then he would shake hands, using that slight, half-foreign bow, with all the starchy little females, and nod to the fellas who would be standing 'round, paralyzed into rigid groups for mutual protection.

A butler (one of the three in Minneapolis) swung open the door. Amory stepped inside and divested himself of cap and coat. He was mildly surprised not to hear the shrill squawk of conversation from the next room, and he decided it must be quite formal. He approved of that—as he approved of the butler.

"Miss Myra," he said.

To his surprise the butler grinned horribly.

"Oh, yeah," he declared, "she's here." He was unaware that his failure to be cockney was ruining his standing. Amory considered him coldly.

"But," continued the butler, his voice rising unnecessarily, "she's the only one what *is* here. The party's gone."

Amory gasped in sudden horror.

"What?"

"She's been waitin' for Amory Blaine. That's you,

ain't it? Her mother says that if you showed up by five-thirty you two was to go after 'em in the Packard."

Amory's despair was crystallized by the appearance of Myra herself, bundled to the ears in a polo coat, her face plainly sulky, her voice pleasant only with difficulty.

" 'Lo, Amory."

" 'Lo, Myra." He had described the state of his vitality.

"Well—you *got* here, *anyways*."

"Well—I'll tell you. I guess you don't know about the auto accident," he romanced.

Myra's eyes opened wide.

"Who was it to?"

"Well," he continued desperately, "uncle'n aunt'n I."

"Was anyone *killed*?"

Amory paused and then nodded.

"Your uncle?"—alarm.

"Oh, no—just a horse—a sorta gray horse."

At this point the Erse butler snickered.

"Probably killed the engine," he suggested. Amory would have put him on the rack without a scruple.

"We'll go now," said Myra coolly. "You see, Amory, the bobs were ordered for five and everybody was here, so we couldn't wait—"

"Well, I couldn't help it, could I?"

"So mama said for me to wait till ha'past five. We'll catch the bob before it gets to the Minnehaha Club, Amory."

Amory's shredded poise dropped from him. He pictured the happy party jingling along snowy streets, the appearance of the limousine, the horrible public descent of him and Myra before sixty reproachful eyes, his apology—a real one this time. He sighed aloud.

"What?" inquired Myra.

"Nothing. I was just yawning. Are we going to *surely* catch up with 'em before they get there?" He was encouraging a faint hope that they might slip into the Minnehaha Club and meet the others there, be found in blasé seclusion before the fire and quite regain his lost attitude.

"Oh, sure Mike, we'll catch 'em all right—let's hurry."

He became conscious of his stomach. As they stepped into the machine he hurriedly slapped the paint of diplomacy over a rather box-like plan he had conceived. It was based upon some "trade-lasts" gleaned at dancing-school, to the effect that he was "awful good-looking and *English,* sort of."

"Myra," he said, lowering his voice and choosing his words carefully, "I beg a thousand pardons. Can you ever forgive me?"

She regarded him gravely, his intent green eyes, his mouth, that to her thirteen-year-old, arrow-collar taste was the quintessence of romance. Yes, Myra could forgive him very easily.

"Why—yes—sure."

He looked at her again, and then dropped his eyes. He had lashes.

"I'm awful," he said sadly. "I'm diff'runt. I don't know why I make faux pas. 'Cause I don't care, I s'pose." Then, recklessly: "I been smoking too much. I've got t'bacca heart."

Myra pictured an all-night tobacco debauch, with Amory pale and reeling from the effect of nicotined lungs. She gave a little gasp.

"Oh, *Amory,* don't smoke. You'll stunt your *growth*!"

"I don't care," he persisted gloomily. "I gotta. I got the habit. I've done a lot of things that if my family knew"—he hesitated, giving her imagination time to picture dark horrors—"I went to the burlesque show last week."

Myra was quite overcome. He turned the green eyes on her again.

"You're the only girl in town I like much," he exclaimed in a rush of sentiment. "You're simpatico."

Myra was not sure that she was, but it sounded stylish though vaguely improper.

Thick dusk had descended outside, and as the limousine made a sudden turn she was jolted against him; their hands touched.

"You shouldn't smoke, Amory," she whispered. "Don't you know that?"

He shook his head.

"Nobody cares."

Myra hesitated.

"*I* care."

Something stirred within Amory.

"Oh, yes, you do! You got a crush on Froggy Parker. I guess everybody knows that."

"No, I haven't," very slowly.

A silence, while Amory thrilled. There was something fascinating about Myra, shut away here cosily from the dim, chill air. Myra, a little bundle of clothes, with strands of yellow hair curling out from under her skating cap.

"Because I've got a crush, too—" He paused, for he heard in the distance the sound of young laughter and, peering through the frosted glass along the lamp-lit street, he made out the dark outline of the bobbing party. He must act quickly. He reached over with a violent, jerky effort, and clutched Myra's hand—her thumb, to be exact.

"Tell him to go to the Minnehaha straight," he whispered. "I wanta talk to you—I *got* to talk to you."

Myra made out the party ahead, had an instant vision of her mother, and then—alas for convention—glanced into the eyes beside.

"Turn down this side street, Richard, and drive straight to the Minnehaha Club!" she cried through the speaking tube. Amory sank back against the cushions with a sigh of relief.

"I can kiss her," he thought. "I'll bet I can. I'll *bet* I can!"

Overhead the sky was half crystaline, half misty, and the night around was chill and vibrant with rich tension. From the Country Club steps the roads stretched away, dark creases on the white blanket; huge heaps of snow lining the sides like the tracks of giant moles. They lingered for a moment on the steps, and watched the white holiday moon.

"Pale moons like that one"—Amory made a vague gesture—"make people mysterieuse. You look like a young witch with her cap off and her hair sorta mussed"—her hands clutched at her hair—"Oh, leave it, it looks good."

They drifted up the stairs and Myra led the way into the little den of his dreams, where a cosy fire was burning before a big sink-down couch. A few years later this was to be a great stage for Amory, a cradle for many an emotional crisis. Now they talked for a moment about bobbing parties.

"There's always a bunch of shy fellas," he commented, "sitting at the tail of the bob, sorta lurkin' an' whisperin' an' pushin' each other off. Then there's always some crazy cross-eyed girl"—he gave a terrifying imitation—"she's always talkin' *hard,* sorta, to the chaperon."

"You're such a funny boy," puzzled Myra.

"How d'y' mean?" Amory gave immediate attention, on his own ground at last.

"Oh—always talking about crazy things. Why don't you come skiing with Marylyn and I tomorrow?"

"I don't like girls in the daytime," he said shortly, and then, thinking this a bit abrupt, he added: "But I like you." He cleared his throat. "I like you first and second and third."

Myra's eyes became dreamy. What a story this would make to tell Marylyn! Here on the couch with this *wonderful*-looking boy—the little fire—the sense that they were alone in the great building—

Myra capitulated. The atmosphere was too appropriate.

"I like you the first twenty-five," she confessed, her voice trembling, "and Froggy Parker twenty-sixth."

Froggy had fallen twenty-five places in one hour. As yet he had not even noticed it.

But Amory, being on the spot, leaned over quickly and kissed Myra's cheek. He had never kissed a girl before, and he tasted his lips curiously, as if he had munched some new fruit. Then their lips brushed like young wild flowers in the wind.

"We're awful," rejoiced Myra gently. She slipped her hand into his, her head drooped against his shoulder. Sudden revulsion seized Amory, disgust, loathing for the whole incident. He desired frantically to be away, never to see Myra again, never to kiss any one; he became conscious of his face and hers, of their clinging hands, and he wanted to creep out of his body and hide somewhere safe out of sight, up in the corner of his mind.

"Kiss me again." Her voice came out of a great void.

"I don't want to," he heard himself saying. There was another pause.

"I don't want to!" he repeated passionately.

Myra sprang up, her cheeks pink with bruised vanity, the great bow on the back of her head trembling sympathetically.

"I hate you!" she cried. "Don't you ever dare to speak to me again!"

"What?" stammered Amory.

"I'll tell mama you kissed me! I will too! I will too! I'll tell mama, and she won't let me play with you!"

Amory rose and stared at her helplessly, as though she were a new animal of whose presence on the earth he had not heretofore been aware.

The door opened suddenly, and Myra's mother appeared on the threshold, fumbling with her lorgnette.

"Well," she began, adjusting it benignantly, "the man at the desk told me you two children were up here— How do you do, Amory."

Amory watched Myra and waited for the crash—but none came. The pout faded, the high pink subsided, and Myra's voice was placid as a summer lake when she answered her mother.

"Oh, we started so late, mama, that I thought we might as *well*—"

He heard from below the shrieks of laughter, and smelled the vapid odor of hot chocolate and tea-cakes as he silently followed mother and daughter downstairs. The sound of the graphophone mingled with the voices of many girls humming the air, and a faint glow was born and spread over him:

Casey-Jones—mounted to the cab-un
Casey-Jones—'th his orders in his hand.

Casey-Jones—mounted to the cab-un
Took his farewell journey to the prom-ised land.

SNAPSHOTS OF THE YOUNG EGOTIST

Amory spent nearly two years in Minneapolis. The
first winter he wore moccasins that were born yellow,
but after many applications of oil and dirt assumed their
mature color, a dirty, greenish brown; he wore a gray
plaid mackinaw coat, and a red toboggan cap. His dog,
Count Del Monte, ate the red cap, so his uncle gave him
a gray one that pulled down over his face. The trouble
with this one was that you breathed into it and your
breath froze; one day the darn thing froze his cheek. He
rubbed snow on his cheek, but it turned bluish-black just
the same.

The Count Del Monte ate a box of bluing once, but it
didn't hurt him. Later, however, he lost his mind and ran
madly up the street, bumping into fences, rolling in gut-
ters, and pursuing his eccentric course out of Amory's
life. Amory cried on his bed.
"Poor little Count," he cried. "Oh, *poor* little *Count*!"
After several months he suspected Count of a fine
piece of emotional acting.

Amory and Frog Parker considered that the greatest
line in literature occurred in Act III of "Arsene Lupin."
They sat in the first row at the Wednesday and Saturday matinées. The line was:
"If one can't be a great artist or a great soldier, the
next best thing is to be a great criminal."

Amory fell in love again, and wrote a poem. This was
it:

> Marylyn and Sallee,
> Those are the girls for me.
> Marylyn stands above
> Sallee in that sweet, deep love.

He was interested in whether McGovern of Minnesota would make the first or second All-American, how to do the card-pass, how to do the coin-pass, chameleon ties, how babies were born, and whether Three-finger Brown was really a better pitcher than Christy Mathewson.

Among other things he read: "For the Honor of the School," "Little Women" (twice), "Common Law," "Sapho," "Dangerous Dan McGrew," "The Broad Highway" (three times), "The Fall of the House of Usher," "Three Weeks," "Mary Ware, the Little Colonel's Chum," "Gunga Din," the Police Gazette, and Jim-Jam Jems.

He had all the Henty biasses in history, and was particularly fond of the cheerful murder stories of Mary Roberts Rinehart.

School ruined his French and gave him a distaste for standard authors. His masters considered him idle, unreliable and superficially clever.

He collected locks of hair from many girls. He wore the rings of several. Finally he could borrow no more rings, owing to his nervous habit of chewing them out of shape. This, it seemed, usually aroused the jealous suspicions of the next borrower.

All through the summer months Amory and Frog Parker went each week to the Stock Company. Afterward they would stroll home in the balmy air of August night, dreaming along Hennepin and Nicollet Avenues, through the gay crowd. Amory wondered how people could fail to notice that he was a boy marked for glory, and when faces of the throng turned toward him and ambiguous eyes stared into his, he assumed the most romantic of expressions and walked on the air cushions that lie on the asphalts of fourteen.

Always, after he was in bed, there were voices—indefinite, fading, enchanting—just outside his window, and before he fell asleep he would dream one of his favorite waking dreams, the one about becoming a great halfback, or the one about the Japanese invasion, when he was rewarded by being made the youngest general in the world. It was always the becoming he dreamed of, never the being. This, too, was quite characteristic of Amory.

CODE OF THE YOUNG EGOTIST

Before he was summoned back to Lake Geneva, he had appeared, shy but inwardly glowing, in his first long trousers, set off by a purple accordian tie and a "Belmont" collar with the edges unassailably meeting, purple socks, and handkerchief with a purple border peeping from his breast pocket. But more than that, he had formulated his first philosophy, a code to live by, which, as near as it can be named, was a sort of aristocratic egotism.

He had realized that his best interests were bound up with those of a certain variant, changing person, whose label, in order that his past might always be identified with him, was Amory Blaine. Amory marked himself a fortunate youth, capable of infinite expansion for good or evil. He did not consider himself a "strong char'c'ter," but relied on his facility (learn things sorta quick) and his superior mentality (read a lotta deep books). He was proud of the fact that he could never become a mechanical or scientific genius. From no other heights was he debarred.

Physically.—Amory thought that he was exceedingly handsome. He was. He fancied himself an athlete of possibilities and a supple dancer.

Socially.—Here his condition was, perhaps, most dangerous. He granted himself personality, charm, magnetism, poise, the power of dominating all contemporary males, the gift of fascinating all women.

Mentally.—Complete, unquestioned superiority.

Now a confession will have to be made. Amory had rather a Puritan conscience. Not that he yielded to it—later in life he almost completely slew it—but at fifteen it made him consider himself a great deal worse than

other boys ... unscrupulousness ... the desire to influence people in almost every way, even for evil ... a
certain coldness and lack of affection, amounting sometimes to cruelty ... a shifting sense of honor ... an un-
holy selfishness ... a puzzled, furtive interest in
everything concerning sex.

There was, also, a curious strain of weakness running
crosswise through his make-up ... a harsh phrase from
the lips of an older boy (older boys usually detested
him) was liable to sweep him off his poise into surly
sensitiveness, or timid stupidity ... he was a slave to his
own moods and he felt that though he was capable of
recklessness and audacity, he possessed neither courage,
perseverance, nor self-respect.

Vanity, tempered with self-suspicion if not self-
knowledge, a sense of people as automatons to his will,
a desire to "pass" as many boys as possible and get to
a vague top of the world ... with this background did
Amory drift into adolescence.

PREPARATORY TO THE GREAT ADVENTURE

The train slowed up with midsummer languor at Lake
Geneva, and Amory caught sight of his mother waiting
in her electric on the gravelled station drive. It was an
ancient electric, one of the early types, and painted gray.
The sight of her sitting there, slenderly erect, and of her
face, where beauty and dignity combined, melting to a
dreamy recollected smile, filled him with a sudden great
pride of her. As they kissed coolly and he stepped into
the electric, he felt a quick fear lest he had lost the req-
uisite charm to measure up to her.

"Dear boy—you're so tall ... look behind and see if
there's anything coming ..."

She looked left and right, she slipped cautiously into
a speed of two miles an hour, beseeching Amory to act
as sentinel; and at one busy crossing she made him get
out and run ahead to signal her forward like a traffic po-

liceman. Beatrice was what might be termed a careful driver.

"You *are* tall—but you're still very handsome—you've skipped the awkward age, or is that sixteen; perhaps it's fourteen or fifteen; I can never remember; but you've skipped it."

"Don't embarrass me," murmured Amory.

"But, my dear boy, what odd clothes! They look as if they were a *set*—don't they? Is your underwear purple, too?"

Amory grunted impolitely.

"You must go to Brooks' and get some really nice suits. Oh, we'll have a talk tonight or perhaps tomorrow night. I want to tell you about your heart—you've probably been neglecting your heart—and you don't *know*."

Amory thought how superficial was the recent overlay of his own generation. Aside from a minute shyness, he felt that the old cynical kinship with his mother had not been one bit broken. Yet for the first few days he wandered about the gardens and along the shore in a state of superloneliness, finding a lethargic content in smoking "Bull" at the garage with one of the chauffeurs.

The sixty acres of the estate were dotted with old and new summer houses and many fountains and white benches that came suddenly into sight from foliage-hung hiding-places; there was a great and constantly increasing family of white cats that prowled the many flower-beds and were silhouetted suddenly at night against the darkening trees. It was on one of the shadowy paths that Beatrice at last captured Amory, after Mr. Blaine had, as usual, retired for the evening to his private library. After reproving him for avoiding her, she took him for a long tête-à-tête in the moonlight. He could not reconcile himself to her beauty, that was mother to his own, the exquisite neck and shoulders, the grace of a fortunate woman of thirty.

"Amory, dear," she crooned softly, "I had such a strange, weird time after I left you."

"Did you, Beatrice?"

"When I had my last breakdown"—she spoke of it as a sturdy, gallant feat.

"The doctors told me"—her voice sang on a confidential note—"that if any man alive had done the consistent drinking that I have, he would have been physically *shattered,* my dear, and in his *grave*—long in his grave."

Amory winced, and wondered how this would have sounded to Froggy Parker.

"Yes," continued Beatrice tragically, "I had dreams—wonderful visions." She pressed the palms of her hands into her eyes. "I saw bronze rivers lapping marble shores, and great birds that soared through the air, parti-colored birds with iridescent plumage. I heard strange music and the flare of barbaric trumpets—what?"

Amory had snickered.

"What, Amory?"

"I said go on, Beatrice."

"That was all—it merely recurred and recurred—gardens that flaunted coloring against which this would be quite dull, moons that whirled and swayed, paler than winter moons, more golden than harvest moons—"

"Are you quite well now, Beatrice?"

"Quite well—as well as I will ever be. I am not understood, Amory. I know that can't express it to you, Amory, but—I am not understood."

Amory was quite moved. He put his arm around his mother, rubbing his head gently against her shoulder.

"Poor Beatrice—poor Beatrice."

"Tell me about *you,* Amory. Did you have two *horrible* years?"

Amory considered lying, and then decided against it.

"No, Beatrice. I enjoyed them. I adapted myself to the bourgeoisie. I became conventional." He surprised himself by saying that, and he pictured how Froggy would have gaped.

"Beatrice," he said suddenly, "I want to go away to school. Everybody in Minneapolis is going to go away to school."

Beatrice showed some alarm.

"But you're only fifteen."

"Yes, but everybody goes away to school at fifteen, and I *want* to, Beatrice."

On Beatrice's suggestion the subject was dropped for

the rest of the walk, but a week later she delighted him by saying:

"Amory, I have decided to let you have your way. If you still want to, you can go to school."

"Yes?"

"To St. Regis's in Connecticut."

Amory felt a quick excitement.

"It's being arranged," continued Beatrice. "It's better that you should go away. I'd have preferred you to have gone to Eton, and then to Christ Church, Oxford, but it seems impracticable now—and for the present we'll let the university question take care of itself."

"What are you going to do, Beatrice?"

"Heaven knows. It seems my fate to fret away my years in this country. Not for a second do I regret being American—indeed, I think that a regret typical of very vulgar people, and I feel sure we are the great coming nation—yet"—and she sighed—"I feel my life should have drowsed away close to an older, mellower civilization, a land of greens and autumnal browns—"

Amory did not answer, so his mother continued:

"My regret is that you haven't been abroad, but still, as you are a man, it's better that you should grow up here under the snarling eagle—is that the right term?"

Amory agreed that it was. She would not have appreciated the Japanese invasion.

"When do I go to school?"

"Next month. You'll have to start East a little early to take your examinations. After that you'll have a free week, so I want you to go up the Hudson and pay a visit."

"To who?"

"To Monsignor Darcy, Amory. He wants to see you. He went to Harrow and then to Yale—became a Catholic. I want him to talk to you—I feel he can be such a help—" She stroked his auburn hair gently. "Dear Amory, dear Amory—"

"Dear Beatrice—"

So early in September Amory, provided with "six suits summer underwear, six suits winter underwear, one sweater or T shirt, one jersey, one overcoat, winter, etc.," set out for New England, the land of schools.

There were Andover and Exeter with their memories of New England dead—large, college-like democracies; St. Mark's, Groton, St. Regis'—recruited from Boston and the Knickerbocker families of New York; St. Paul's, with its great rinks; Pomfret and St. George's, prosperous and well-dressed; Taft and Hotchkiss, which prepared the wealth of the Middle West for social success at Yale; Pawling, Westminster, Choate, Kent, and a hundred others; all milling out their well-set-up, conventional, impressive type, year after year; their mental stimulus the college entrance exams; their vague purpose set forth in a hundred circulars as "To impart a Thorough Mental, Moral, and Physical Training as a Christian Gentleman, to fit the boy for *meeting the problems of his day and generation,* and to give a solid foundation in the Arts and Sciences."

At St. Regis' Amory stayed three days and took his exams with a scoffing confidence, then doubling back to New York to pay his tutelary visit. The metropolis, barely glimpsed, made little impression on him, except for the sense of cleanliness he drew from the tall white buildings seen from a Hudson River steamboat in the early morning. Indeed, his mind was so crowded with dreams of athletic prowess at school that he considered this visit only as a rather tiresome prelude to the great adventure. This, however, it did not prove to be.

Monsignor Darcy's house was an ancient, rambling structure set on a hill overlooking the river, and there lived its owner, between his trips to all parts of the Roman Catholic world, rather like an exiled Stuart king waiting to be called to the rule of his land. Monsignor was forty-four then, and bustling—a trifle too stout for symmetry, with hair the color of spun gold, and a brilliant, enveloping personality. When he came into a room clad in his full purple regalia from thatch to toe, he resembled a Turner sunset, and attracted both admiration and attention. He had written two novels: one of them violently anti-Catholic, just before his conversion, and five years later another, in which he had attempted to

turn all his clever jibes against Catholics into even clev-
erer innuendoes against Episcopalians. He was intensely
ritualistic, startlingly dramatic, loved the idea of God
enough to be a celibate, and rather liked his neighbor.

Children adored him because he was like a child;
youth revelled in his company because he was still a
youth, and couldn't be shocked. In the proper land and
century he might have been a Richelieu—at present he
was a very moral, very religious (if not particularly pi-
ous) clergyman, making a great mystery about pulling
rusty wires, and appreciating life to the fullest, if not entirely enjoying it.

He and Amory took to each other at first sight—the
jovial, impressive prelate who could dazzle an embassy
ball, and the green-eyed, intent youth, in his first long
trousers, accepted in their own minds a relation of father
and son within a half-hour's conversation.

"My dear boy, I've been waiting to see you for years.
Take a big chair and we'll have a chat."

"I've just come from school—St. Regis', you know."

"So your mother says—a remarkable woman; have a
cigarette—I'm sure you smoke. Well, if you're like me,
you loathe all science and mathematics—"

Amory nodded vehemently.

"Hate 'em all. Like English and history."

"Of course. You'll hate school for a while, too, but
I'm glad you're going to St. Regis'."

"Why?"

"Because it's a gentleman's school, and democracy
won't hit you so early. You'll find plenty of that in college."

"I want to go to Princeton," said Amory. "I don't
know why, but I think of all Harvard men as sissies, like
I used to be, and all Yale men as wearing big blue
sweaters and smoking pipes."

Monsignor chuckled.

"I'm one, you know."

"Oh, you're different—I think of Princeton as being
lazy and good-looking and aristocratic—you know, like
a spring day. Harvard seems sort of indoors—"

"And Yale is November, crisp and energetic," finished Monsignor.

"That's it."

They slipped briskly into an intimacy from which they never recovered.

"I was for Bonnie Prince Charlie," announced Amory.

"Of course you were—and for Hannibal—"

"Yes, and for the Southern Confederacy." He was rather skeptical about being an Irish patriot—he suspected that being Irish was being somewhat common—but Monsignor assured him that Ireland was a romantic lost cause and Irish people quite charming, and that it should, by all means, be one of his principal biasses.

After a crowded hour which included several more cigarettes, and during which Monsignor learned, to his surprise but not to his horror, that Amory had not been brought up a Catholic, he announced that he had another guest. This turned out to be the Honorable Thornton Hancock, of Boston, ex-minister to The Hague, author of an erudite history of the Middle Ages and the last of a distinguished, patriotic, and brilliant family.

"He comes here for a rest," said Monsignor confidentially, treating Amory as a contemporary. "I act as an escape from the weariness of agnosticism, and I think I'm the only man who knows how his staid old mind is really at sea and longs for a sturdy spar like the Church to cling to."

Their first luncheon was one of the memorable events of Amory's early life. He was quite radiant and gave off a peculiar brightness and charm. Monsignor called out the best that he had thought by question and suggestion, and Amory talked with an ingenious brilliance of a thousand impulses and desires and repulsions and faiths and fears. He and Monsignor held the floor, and the older man, with his less receptive, less accepting, yet certainly not colder mentality, seemed content to listen and bask in the mellow sunshine that played between these two. Monsignor gave the effect of sunlight to many people; Amory gave it in his youth and, to some extent, when he was very much older, but never again was it quite so mutually spontaneous.

"He's a radiant boy," thought Thornton Hancock, who had seen the splendor of two continents and talked with Parnell and Gladstone and Bismarck—and afterward he added to Monsignor: "But his education ought not to be intrusted to a school or college."

But for the next four years the best of Amory's intellect was concentrated on matters of popularity, the intricacies of a university social system and American Society as represented by Biltmore Teas and Hot Springs golf links.

... In all, a wonderful week, that saw Amory's mind turned inside out, a hundred of his theories confirmed, and his joy of life crystallized to a thousand ambitions. Not that the conversation was scholastic—heaven forbid! Amory had only the vaguest idea as to what Bernard Shaw was—but Monsignor made quite as much out of "The Beloved Vagabond" and "Sir Nigel," taking good care that Amory never once felt out of his depth.

But the trumpets were sounding for Amory's preliminary skirmish with his own generation.

"You're not sorry to go, of course. With people like us our home is where we are not," said Monsignor.

"I *am* sorry—"

"No, you're not. No one person in the world is necessary to you or to me."

"Well—"

"Good-by."

THE EGOTIST DOWN

Amory's two years at St. Regis', though in turn painful and triumphant, had as little real significance in his own life as the American "prep" school, crushed as it is under the heel of the universities, has to American life in general. We have no Eton to create the self-consciousness of a governing class; we have, instead, clean, flaccid and innocuous preparatory schools.

He went all wrong at the start, was generally considered both conceited and arrogant, and universally detested. He played football intensely, alternating a reckless brilliancy with a tendency to keep himself as safe from hazard as decency would permit. In a wild panic he backed out of a fight with a boy his own size, to a chorus of scorn, and a week later, in desperation, picked a battle with another boy very much bigger, from which he emerged badly beaten, but rather proud of himself.

He was resentful against all those in authority over him, and this, combined with a lazy indifference toward his work, exasperated every master in school. He grew discouraged and imagined himself a pariah; took to sulking in corners and reading after lights. With a dread of being alone he attached a few friends, but since they were not among the élite of the school, he used them simply as mirrors of himself, audiences before which he might do that posing absolutely essential to him. He was unbearably lonely, desperately unhappy.

There were some few grains of comfort. Whenever Amory was submerged, his vanity was the last part to go below the surface, so he could still enjoy a comfortable glow when "Wookey-wookey," the deaf old house-keeper, told him that he was the best-looking boy she had ever seen. It had pleased him to be the lightest and youngest man on the first football squad; it pleased him when Doctor Dougall told him at the end of a heated conference that he could, if he wished, get the best marks in school. But Doctor Dougall was wrong. It was temperamentally impossible for Amory to get the best marks in school.

Miserable, confined to bounds, unpopular with both faculty and students—that was Amory's first term. But at Christmas he had returned to Minneapolis, tight-lipped and strangely jubilant.

"Oh, I was sort of fresh at first," he told Frog Parker patronizingly, "but I got along fine—lightest man on the squad. You ought to go away to school, Froggy. It's great stuff."

INCIDENT OF THE WELL-MEANING PROFESSOR

On the last night of his first term, Mr. Margotson, the senior master, sent word to study hall that Amory was to come to his room at nine. Amory suspected that advice was forthcoming, but he determined to be courteous, because this Mr. Margotson had been kindly disposed toward him.

His summoner received him gravely, and motioned him to a chair. He hemmed several times and looked consciously kind, as a man will when he knows he's on delicate ground.

"Amory," he began. "I've sent for you on a personal matter."

"Yes, sir."

"I've noticed you this year and I—I like you. I think you have in you the makings of a—a very good man."

"Yes, sir," Amory managed to articulate. He hated having people talk as if he were an admitted failure.

"But I've noticed," continued the older man blindly, "that you're not very popular with the boys."

"No, sir." Amory licked his lips.

"Ah—I thought you might not understand exactly what it was they—ah—objected to. I'm going to tell you, because I believe—ah—that when a boy knows his difficulties he's better able to cope with them—to conform to what others expect of him." He a-hemmed again with delicate reticence, and continued: "They seem to think that you're—ah—rather too fresh—"

Amory could stand no more. He rose from his chair, scarcely controlling his voice when he spoke.

"I know—oh, *don't* you s'pose I know." His voice rose. "I know what they think; do you s'pose you have to *tell* me." He paused. "I'm—I've got to go back now—hope I'm not rude—"

He left the room hurriedly. In the cool air outside, as he walked to his house, he exulted in his refusal to be helped.

"That *damn* old fool!" he cried wildly. "As if I didn't *know*!"

He decided, however, that this was a good excuse not to go back to study hall that night, so, comfortably couched up in his room, he munched Nabiscos and finished "The White Company."

INCIDENT OF THE WONDERFUL GIRL

There was a bright star in February. New York burst upon him on Washington's Birthday with the brilliance of a long-anticipated event. His glimpse of it as a vivid whiteness against a deep blue sky had left a picture of splendor that rivalled the dream cities in the Arabian Nights; but this time he saw it by electric light, and romance gleamed from the chariot-race sign on Broadway and from the women's eyes at the Astor, where he and young Paskert from St. Regis' had dinner. When they walked down the aisle of the theatre, greeted by the nervous twanging and discord of untuned violins and the sensuous, heavy fragrance of paint and powder, he moved in a sphere of epicurean delight. Everything enchanted him. The play was "The Little Millionaire," with George M. Cohan, and there was one stunning young brunette who made him sit with brimming eyes in the ecstasy of watching her dance.

> Oh—you—wonderful girl,
> What a wonderful girl you are—

sang the tenor, and Amory agreed silently, but passionately.

> All—your—wonderful words
> Thrill me through—

The violins swelled and quavered on the last notes, the girl sank to a crumpled butterfly on the stage, a great burst of clapping filled the house. Oh, to fall in love like that, to the languorous magic melody of such a tune!

The last scene was laid on a roof-garden, and the 'cellos sighed to the musical moon, while light adventure and facile froth-like comedy flitted back and forth in the calcium. Amory was on fire to be an habitué of roof-gardens, to meet a girl who should look like that—better, that very girl; whose hair would be drenched with golden moonlight, while at his elbow sparkling wine was poured by an unintelligible waiter. When the curtain fell for the last time he gave such a long sigh that the people in front of him twisted around and stared and said loud enough for him to hear:

"What a *remarkable*-looking boy!"

This took his mind off the play, and he wondered if he really did seem handsome to the population of New York.

Paskert and he walked in silence toward their hotel. The former was the first to speak. His uncertain fifteen-year-old voice broke in in a melancholy strain on Amory's musings:

"I'd marry that girl tonight."

There was no need to ask what girl he referred to.

"I'd be proud to take her home and introduce her to my people," continued Paskert.

Amory was distinctly impressed. He wished he had said it instead of Paskert. It sounded so mature.

"I wonder about actresses; are they all pretty bad?"

"No, *sir,* not by a darn sight," said the worldly youth with emphasis, "and I know that girl's as good as gold. I can tell."

They wandered on, mixing in the Broadway crowd, dreaming on the music that eddied out of the cafés. New faces flashed on and off like myriad lights, pale or rouged faces, tired, yet sustained by a weary excitement. Amory watched them in fascination. He was planning his life. He was going to live in New York, and be known at every restaurant and café, wearing a dress suit from early evening to early morning, sleeping away the dull hours of the forenoon.

"Yes, sir, I'd marry that girl tonight!"

HEROIC IN GENERAL TONE

October of his second and last year at St. Regis' was a high point in Amory's memory. The game with Groton was played from three of a snappy, exhilarating afternoon far into the crisp autumnal twilight, and Amory at quarterback, exhorting in wild despair, making impossible tackles, calling signals in a voice that had diminished to a hoarse, furious whisper, yet found time to revel in the blood-stained bandage around his head, and the straining, glorious heroism of plunging, crashing bodies and aching limbs. For those minutes courage flowed like wine out of the November dusk, and he was the eternal hero, one with the sea-rover on the prow of a Norse galley, one with Roland and Horatius, Sir Nigel and Ted Coy, scraped and stripped into trim and then flung by his own will into the breach, beating back the tide, hearing from afar the thunder of cheers ... finally bruised and weary, but still elusive, circling an end, twisting, changing pace, straight-arming ... falling behind the Groton goal with two men on his legs, in the only touchdown of the game.

THE PHILOSOPHY OF THE SLICKER

From the scoffing superiority of sixth-form year and success Amory looked back with cynical wonder on his status of the year before. He was changed as completely as Amory Blaine could ever be changed. Amory plus Beatrice plus two years in Minneapolis—these had been his ingredients when he entered St. Regis'. But the Minneapolis years were not a thick enough overlay to conceal the "Amory plus Beatrice" from the ferreting eyes of a boarding school, so St. Regis' had very painfully drilled Beatrice out of him, and had begun to lay down new and more conventional planking on the fundamental Amory. But both St. Regis' and Amory were unconscious of the fact that this fundamental Amory had not in himself changed. Those qualities for which he had

suffered, his moodiness, his tendency to pose, his laziness, and his love of playing the fool, were now taken as
a matter of course, recognized eccentricities in a star
quarterback, a clever actor, and the editor of the *St.
Regis Tattler*: it puzzled him to see impressionable small
boys imitating the very vanities that had not long ago
been contemptible weaknesses.

After the football season he slumped into dreamy content. The night of the pre-holiday dance he slipped away
and went early to bed for the pleasure of hearing the violin music cross the grass and come surging in at his
window. Many nights he lay there dreaming awake of
secret cafés in Montmartre, where ivory women delved
in romantic mysteries with diplomats and soldiers of
fortune, while orchestras played Hungarian waltzes and
the air was thick and exotic with intrigue and moonlight
and adventure. In the spring he read "L'Allegro," by request, and was inspired to lyrical outpourings on the
subject of Arcady and the pipes of Pan. He moved his
bed so that the sun would wake him at dawn, that he
might dress and go out to the archaic swing that hung
from an apple tree near the sixth-form house. Seating
himself in this he would pump higher and higher until
he got the effect of swinging into the wide air, into a
fairyland of piping satyrs and nymphs with the faces of
fair-haired girls he passed in the streets of Eastchester.
As the swing reached its highest point, Arcady really lay
just over the brow of a certain hill, where the brown
road dwindled out of sight in a golden dot.

He read voluminously all spring, the beginning of
his eighteenth year: "The Gentleman from Indiana,"
"The New Arabian Nights," "The Morals of Marcus Or-
deyne," "The Man Who Was Thursday," which he liked
without understanding; "Stover at Yale," that became
somewhat of a textbook; "Dombey and Son," because
he thought he really should read better stuff; Robert
Chambers, David Graham Phillips, and E. Phillips
Oppenheim complete, and a scattering of Tennyson and
Kipling. Of all his class work only "L'Allegro" and
some quality of rigid clarity in solid geometry stirred his
languid interest.

As June drew near, he felt the need of conversation to formulate his own ideas, and, to his surprise, found a co-philosopher in Rahill, the president of the sixth form. In many a talk, on the highroad or lying belly-down along the edge of the baseball diamond, or late at night with their cigarettes glowing in the dark, they threshed out the questions of school, and there was developed the term "slicker."

"Got tobacco?" whispered Rahill one night, putting his head inside the door five minutes after lights.

"Sure."

"I'm coming in."

"Take a couple of pillows and lie in the window-seat, why don't you."

Amory sat up in bed and lit a cigarette while Rahill settled for a conversation. Rahill's favorite subject was the respective futures of the sixth form, and Amory never tired of outlining them for his benefit.

"Ted Converse? 'At's easy. He'll fail his exams, tutor all summer at Harstrum's, get into Sheff with about four conditions, and flunk out in the middle of the freshman year. Then he'll go back West and raise hell for a year or so; finally his father will make him go into the paint business. He'll marry and have four sons, all bone heads. He'll always think St. Regis' spoiled him, so he'll send his sons to day school in Portland. He'll die of locomotor ataxia when he's forty-one, and his wife will give a baptizing stand or whatever you call it to the Presbyterian Church, with his name on it—"

"Hold up, Amory. That's too darned gloomy. How about yourself?"

"I'm in a superior class. You are, too. We're philosophers."

"I'm not."

"Sure you are. You've got a darn good head on you." But Amory knew that nothing in the abstract, no theory or generality, ever moved Rahill until he stubbed his toe upon the concrete minutiae of it.

"Haven't," insisted Rahill. "I let people impose on me here and don't get anything out of it. I'm the prey of my friends, damn it—do their lessons, get 'em out of trou-

ble, pay 'em stupid summer visits, and always entertain
their kid sisters; keep my temper when they get selfish
and *then* they think they pay me back by voting for me
and telling me I'm the 'big man' of St. Regis'. I want to
get where everybody does their own work and I can tell
people where to go. I'm tired of being nice to every
poor fish in school."

"You're not a slicker," said Amory suddenly.

"A what?"

"A slicker."

"What the devil's that?"

"Well, it's something that—that—there's a lot of
them. You're not one, and neither am I, though I am
more than you are."

"Who is one? What makes you one?"

Amory considered.

"Why—why, I suppose that the *sign* of it is when a
fellow slicks his hair back with water."

"Like Carstairs?"

"Yes—sure. He's a slicker."

They spent two evenings getting an exact definition.
The slicker was good-looking or *clean*-looking; he had
brains, social brains, that is, and he used all means on the
broad path of honesty to get ahead, be popular, admired,
and never in trouble. He dressed well, was particularly
neat in appearance, and derived his name from the fact
that his hair was inevitably worn short, soaked in water
or tonic, parted in the middle, and slicked back as the
current of fashion dictated. The slickers of that year had
adopted tortoise-shell spectacles as badges of their
slickerhood, and this made them so easy to recognize that
Amory and Rahill never missed one. The slicker seemed
distributed through school, always a little wiser and
shrewder than his contemporaries, managing some team
or other, and keeping his cleverness carefully concealed.

Amory found the slicker a most valuable classifica-
tion until his junior year in college, when the outline became so blurred and indeterminate that it had to be
subdivided many times, and became only a quality.
Amory's secret ideal had all the slicker qualifications,
but, in addition, courage and tremendous brains and

talents—also Amory conceded him a bizarre streak that was quite irreconcilable to the slicker proper.

This was a first real break from the hypocrisy of school tradition. The slicker was a definite element of success, differing intrinsically from the prep school "big man."

The Slicker	*The Big Man*
1. Clever sense of social values.	1. Inclined to stupidity and unconscious of social values.
2. Dresses well. Pretends that dress is superficial—but knows that it isn't.	2. Thinks dress is superficial, and is inclined to be careless about it.
3. Goes into such activities as he can shine in.	3. Goes out for everything from a sense of duty.
4. Gets to college and is, in a worldly way, successful.	4. Gets to college and has a problematical future. Feels lost without his circle, and always says that school days were happiest, after all. Goes back to school and makes speeches about what St. Regis' boys are doing.
5. Hair slicked.	5. Hair not slicked.

Amory had decided definitely on Princeton, even though he would be the only boy entering that year from St. Regis'. Yale had a romance and glamour from the tales of Minneapolis, and St. Regis' men who had been "tapped for Skull and Bones," but Princeton drew him most, with its atmosphere of bright colors and its alluring reputation as the pleasantest country club in America. Dwarfed by the menacing college exams, Amory's school days drifted into the past. Years afterward, when he went back to St. Regis', he seemed to have forgotten the successes of sixth-form year, and to be able to picture himself only as the unadjustable boy who had hurried down corridors, jeered at by his rabid contemporaries mad with common sense.

2

Spires and Gargoyles

At first Amory noticed only the wealth of sunshine creeping across the long greenswards, dancing on the leaded windowpanes, and swimming around the tops of spires and towers and battlemented walls. Gradually he realized that he was really walking up University Place, self-conscious about his suitcase, developing a new tendency to glare straight ahead when he passed any one. Several times he could have sworn that men turned to look at him critically. He wondered vaguely if there was something the matter with his clothes, and wished he had shaved that morning on the train. He felt unnecessarily stiff and awkward among these white-flannelled, bareheaded youths, who must be juniors and seniors, judging from the savoir faire with which they strolled.

He found that 12 University Place was a large, dilapidated mansion, at present apparently uninhabited, though he knew it housed usually a dozen freshmen. After a hurried skirmish with his landlady he sallied out on a tour of exploration, but he had gone scarcely a block when he became horribly conscious that he must be the only man in town who was wearing a hat. He returned hurriedly to 12 University, left his derby, and, emerging bareheaded, loitered down Nassau Street, stopping to investigate a display of athletic photographs in a store window, including a large one of Allenby, the football captain, and next attracted by the sign "Jigger Shop" over a confectionery window. This sounded familiar, so he sauntered in and took a seat on a high stool.

"Chocolate sundae," he told a colored person.

"Double chocolate jiggah? Anything else?"

"Why—yes."

"Bacon bun?"

"Why—yes."

He munched four of these, finding them of pleasing savor, and then consumed another double-chocolate jigger before ease descended upon him. After a cursory inspection of the pillowcases, leather pennants, and Gibson Girls that lined the walls, he left, and continued along Nassau Street with his hands in his pockets. Gradually he was learning to distinguish between upper classmen and entering men, even though the freshman cap would not appear until the following Monday. Those who were too obviously, too nervously at home were freshmen, for as each train brought a new contingent it was immediately absorbed into the hatless, white-shod, book-laden throng, whose function seemed to be to drift endlessly up and down the street, emitting great clouds of smoke from brand new pipes. By afternoon Amory realized that now the newest arrivals were taking him for an upper classman, and he tried conscientiously to look both pleasantly blasé and casually critical, which was as near as he could analyze the prevalent facial expression.

At five o'clock he felt the need of hearing his own voice, so he retreated to his house to see if any one else had arrived. Having climbed the rickety stairs he scrutinized his room resignedly, concluding that it was hopeless to attempt any more inspired decoration than class banners and tiger pictures. There was a tap at the door.

"Come in!"

A slim face with gray eyes and a humorous smile appeared in the doorway.

"Got a hammer?"

"No—sorry. Maybe Mrs. Twelve, or whatever she goes by, has one."

The stranger advanced into the room.

"You an inmate of this asylum?"

Amory nodded.

"Awful barn for the rent we pay."

Amory had to agree that it was.

"I thought of the campus," he said, "but they say

there's so few freshmen that they're lost. Have to sit around and study for something to do."

The gray-eyed man decided to introduce himself.

"My name's Holiday."

"Blaine's my name."

They shook hands with the fashionable low swoop. Amory grinned.

"Where'd you prep?"

"Andover—where did you?"

"St. Regis'."

"Oh, did you? I had a cousin there."

They discussed the cousin thoroughly, and then Holiday announced that he was to meet his brother for dinner at six.

"Come along and have a bite with us."

"All right."

At the Kenilworth Amory met Burne Holiday—he of the gray eyes was Kerry—and during a limpid meal of thin soup and anaemic vegetables they stared at the other freshmen, who sat either in small groups looking very ill at ease, or in large groups seeming very much at home.

"I hear Commons is pretty bad," said Amory.

"That's the rumor. But you've got to eat there—or pay anyways."

"Crime!"

"Imposition!"

"Oh, at Princeton you've got to swallow everything the first year. It's like a damned prep school."

Amory agreed.

"Lot of pep, though," he insisted. "I wouldn't have gone to Yale for a million."

"Me either."

"You going out for anything?" inquired Amory of the elder brother.

"Not me—Burne here is going out for the Prince—the Daily Princetonian, you know."

"Yes, I know."

"You going out for anything?"

"Why—yes. I'm going to take a whack at freshman football."

"Play at St. Regis'?"

"Some," admitted Amory depreciatingly, "but I'm getting so damned thin."

"You're not thin."

"Well, I used to be stocky last fall."

"Oh!"

After supper they attended the movies, where Amory was fascinated by the glib comments of a man in front of him, as well as by the wild yelling and shouting.

"Yoho!"

"Oh, honey–*baby*—you're so big and strong, but oh, so *gentle*!"

"Clinch!"

"Oh, *Clinch*!"

"Kiss her, kiss 'at lady, *quick*!"

"Oh-h-h——!"

A group began whistling "By the Sea," and the audience took it up noisily. This was followed by an indistinguishable song that included much stamping and then by an endless, incoherent dirge.

> Oh-h-h-h-h
> She works in a Jam Factoree
> And—that-may-be-all-right
> But you can't-fool-me
> For I know—DAMN—WELL
> That she DON'T-make-jam-all-night!
> Oh-h-h-h!

As they pushed out, giving and receiving curious impersonal glances, Amory decided that he liked the movies, wanted to enjoy them as the row of upper classmen in front had enjoyed them, with their arms along the backs of the seats, their comments Gaelic and caustic, their attitude a mixture of critical wit and tolerant amusement.

"Want a sundae—I mean a jigger?" asked Kerry.

"Sure."

They suppered heavily and then, still sauntering, eased back to 12.

"Wonderful night."

"It's a whiz."

"You men going to unpack?"

"Guess so. Come on, Burne."

Amory decided to sit for a while on the front steps, so he bade them good night.

The great tapestries of trees had darkened to ghosts back at the last edge of twilight. The early moon had drenched the arches with pale blue, and, weaving over the night, in and out of the gossamer rifts of moon, swept a song, a song with more than a hint of sadness, infinitely transient, infinitely regretful.

He remembered that an alumnus of the nineties had told him of one of Booth Tarkington's amusements: standing in mid-campus in the small hours and singing tenor songs to the stars, arousing mingled emotions in the couched undergraduates according to the sentiment of their moods.

Now, far down the shadowy line of University Place a white-clad phalanx broke the gloom, and marching figures, white-shirted, white-trousered, swung rhythmically up the street, with linked arms and heads thrown back:

> Going back—going back,
> Going—back—to—Nas-sau—Hall,
> Going back—going back—
> To the—Best—Old—Place—of—All
> Going back—going back,
> From all—this—earth-ly—ball,
> We'll—clear—the—track—as—we—go—back—
> Going—back—to—Nas-sau—Hall!

Amory closed his eyes as the ghostly procession drew near. The song soared so high that all dropped out except the tenors, who bore the melody triumphantly past the danger-point and relinquished it to the fantastic chorus. Then Amory opened his eyes, half afraid that sight would spoil the rich illusion of harmony.

He sighed eagerly. There at the head of the white platoon marched Allenby, the football captain, slim and defiant, as if aware that this year the hopes of the college rested on him, that his hundred-and-sixty pounds were expected to dodge to victory through the heavy blue and crimson lines.

Fascinated, Amory watched each rank of linked arms as it came abreast, the faces indistinct above the polo shirts, the voices blent in a paean of triumph—and then the procession passed through shadowy Campbell Arch, and the voices grew fainter as it wound eastward over the campus.

The minutes passed and Amory sat there very quietly. He regretted the rule that would forbid freshmen to be outdoors after curfew, for he wanted to ramble through the shadowy scented lanes, where Witherspoon brooded like a dark mother over Whig and Clio, her Attic children, where the black Gothic snake of Little curled down to Cuyler and Patton, these in turn flinging the mystery out over the placid slope rolling to the lake.

Princeton of the daytime filtered slowly into his consciousness—West and Reunion, redolent of the sixties, Seventy-nine Hall, brick-red and arrogant, Upper and Lower Pyne, aristocratic Elizabethan ladies not quite content to live among shopkeepers, and, topping all, climbing with clear blue aspiration, the great dreaming spires of Holder and Cleveland towers.

From the first he loved Princeton—its lazy beauty, its half-grasped significance, the wild moonlight revel of the rushes, the handsome, prosperous big-game crowds, and under it all the air of struggle that pervaded his class. From the day when, wild-eyed and exhausted, the jerseyed freshmen sat in the gymnasium and elected some one from Hill School class president, a Lawrence-ville celebrity vice-president, a hockey star from St. Paul's secretary, up until the end of sophomore year it never ceased, that breathless social system, that worship, seldom named, never really admitted, of the bogey "Big Man."

First it was schools, and Amory, alone from St. Regis', watched the crowds form and widen and form again; St. Paul's, Hill, Pomfret, eating at certain tacitly reserved tables in Commons, dressing in their own cor-

ners of the gymnasium, and drawing unconsciously
about them a barrier of the slightly less important but
socially ambitious to protect them from the friendly,
rather puzzled high school element. From the moment
he realized this Amory resented social barriers as artificial distinctions made by the strong to bolster up their
weak retainers and keep out the almost strong.

Having decided to be one of the gods of the class, he
reported for freshman football practice, but in the second week, playing quarterback, already paragraphed in
corners of the *Princetonian,* he wrenched his knee seriously enough to put him out for the rest of the season.
This forced him to retire and consider the situation.

"12 Univee" housed a dozen miscellaneous question
marks. There were three or four inconspicuous and quite
startled boys from Lawrenceville, two amateur wild men
from a New York private school (Kerry Holiday christened them the "plebeian drunks"), a Jewish youth, also
from New York, and, as compensation for Amory, the
two Holidays, to whom he took an instant fancy.

The Holidays were rumored twins, but really the dark-
haired one, Kerry, was a year older than his blond
brother, Burne. Kerry was tall, with humorous gray
eyes, and a sudden, attractive smile; he became at once
the mentor of the house, reaper of ears that grew too
high, censor of conceit, vendor of rare, satirical humor.
Amory spread the table of their future friendship with
all his ideas of what college should and did mean.
Kerry, not inclined as yet to take things seriously, chided
him gently for being curious at this inopportune time
about the intricacies of the social system, but liked him
and was both interested and amused.

Burne, fair-haired, silent, and intent, appeared in the
house only as a busy apparition, gliding in quietly at
night and off again in the early morning to get up his
work in the library—he was out for the *Princetonian,*
competing furiously against forty others for the coveted
first place. In December he came down with diphtheria,
and someone else won the competition, but, returning to
college in February, he dauntlessly went after the prize
again. Necessarily, Amory's acquaintance with him was

in the way of three-minute chats, walking to and from lectures, so he failed to penetrate Burne's one absorbing interest and find what lay beneath it.

Amory was far from contented. He missed the place he had won at St. Regis', the being known and admired, yet Princeton stimulated him, and there were many things ahead calculated to arouse the Machiavelli latent in him, could he but insert a wedge. The upper-class clubs, concerning which he had pumped a reluctant graduate during the previous summer, excited his curiosity: Ivy, detached and breathlessly aristocratic; Cottage, an impressive mélange of brilliant adventurers and well-dressed philanderers; Tiger Inn, broad-shouldered and athletic, vitalized by an honest elaboration of prep-school standards; Cap and Gown, anti-alcoholic, faintly religious and politically powerful; flamboyant Colonial; literary Quadrangle; and the dozen others, varying in age and position.

Anything which brought an under classman into too glaring a light was labelled with the damning brand of "running it out." The movies thrived on caustic comments, but the men who made them were generally running it out; talking of clubs was running it out; standing for anything very strongly, as, for instance, drinking parties or teetotalling, was running it out; in short, being personally conspicuous was not tolerated, and the influential man was the non-committal man, until at club elections in sophomore year every one should be sewed up in some bag for the rest of his college career.

Amory found that writing for the *Nassau Literary Magazine* would get him nothing, but that being on the board of the *Daily Princetonian* would get any one a good deal. His vague desire to do immortal acting with the English Dramatic Association faded out when he found that the most ingenious brains and talents were concentrated upon the Triangle Club, a musical comedy organization that every year took a great Christmas trip. In the meanwhile, feeling strangely alone and restless in Commons, with new desires and ambitions stirring in his mind, he let the first term go by between an envy of the embryo successes and a puzzled fretting with Kerry as to why they were not accepted immediately among the élite of the class.

Many afternoons they lounged in the windows of 12 Univee and watched the class pass to and from Commons, noting satellites already attaching themselves to the more prominent, watching the lonely grind with his hurried step and downcast eye, envying the happy security of the big school groups.

"We're the damned middle class, that's what!" he complained to Kerry one day as he lay stretched out on the sofa, consuming a family of Fatimas with contemplative precision.

"Well, why not? We came to Princeton so we could feel that way toward the small colleges—have it on 'em, more self-confidence, dress better, cut a swath——"

"Oh, it isn't that I mind the glittering caste system," admitted Amory. "I like having a bunch of hot cats on top, but gosh, Kerry, I've got to be one of them."

"But just now, Amory, you're only a sweaty bourgeois."

Amory lay for a moment without speaking.

"I won't be—long," he said finally. "But I hate to get anywhere by working for it. I'll show the marks, don't you know."

"Honorable scars." Kerry craned his neck suddenly at the street. "There's Langueduc, if you want to see what he looks like—and Humbird just behind."

Amory rose dynamically and sought the windows.

"Oh," he said, scrutinizing these worthies, "Humbird looks like a knockout, but this Langueduc—he's the rugged type, isn't he? I distrust that sort. All diamonds look big in the rough."

"Well," said Kerry, as the excitement subsided, "you're a literary genius. It's up to you."

"I wonder"—Amory paused—"if I could be. I honestly think so sometimes. That sounds like the devil, and I wouldn't say it to anybody except you."

"Well—go ahead. Let your hair grow and write poems like this guy D'Invilliers in the Lit."

Amory reached lazily at a pile of magazines on the table.

"Read his latest effort?"

"Never miss 'em. They're rare."

Amory glanced through the issue.

"Hello!" he said in surprise, "he's a freshman, isn't he?"

"Yeah."

"Listen to this! My God!

A serving lady speaks:
   Black velvet trails its folds over the day,
   White tapers, prisoned in their silver frames,
   Wave their thin flames like shadows in the wind,
   Pia, Pompia, come—come away—

"Now, what the devil does that mean?"

"It's a pantry scene."

Her toes are stiffened like a stork's in flight;
She's laid upon her bed, on the white sheets,
Her hands pressed on her smooth bust like a saint,
Bella Cunizza, come into the light!

"My gosh, Kerry, what in hell is it all about? I swear I don't get him at all, and I'm a literary bird myself."

"It's pretty tricky," said Kerry, "only you've got to think of hearses and stale milk when you read it. That isn't as pash as some of them."

Amory tossed the magazine on the table.

"Well," he sighed, "I sure am up in the air. I know I'm not a regular fellow, yet I loathe anybody else that isn't. I can't decide whether to cultivate my mind and be a great dramatist, or to thumb my nose at the Golden Treasury and be a Princeton slicker."

"Why decide?" suggested Kerry. "Better drift, like me. I'm going to sail into prominence on Burne's coattails."

"I can't drift—I want to be interested. I want to pull strings, even for somebody else, or be Princetonian chairman or Triangle president. I want to be admired, Kerry."

"You're thinking too much about yourself."

Amory sat up at this.

"No. I'm thinking about you, too. We've got to get out and mix around the class right now, when it's fun to be a snob. I'd like to bring a sardine to the prom in June, for instance, but I wouldn't do it unless I could be damn debonaire about it—introduce her to all the prize parlor-snakes, and the football captain, and all that simple stuff."

"Amory," said Kerry impatiently, "you're just going around in a circle. If you want to be prominent, get out and try for something; if you don't, just take it easy." He yawned. "Come on, let's let the smoke drift off. We'll go down and watch football practice."

Amory gradually accepted this point of view, decided that next fall would inaugurate his career, and relinquished himself to watching Kerry extract joy from 12 Univee.

They filled the Jewish youth's bed with lemon pie; they put out the gas all over the house every night by blowing into the jet in Amory's room, to the bewilderment of Mrs. Twelve and the local plumber; they set up the effects of the plebeian drunks—pictures, books, and furniture—in the bathroom, to the confusion of the pair, who hazily discovered the transposition on their return from a Trenton spree; they were disappointed beyond measure when the plebeian drunks decided to take it as a joke; they played red-dog and twenty-one and jackpot from dinner to dawn, and on the occasion of one man's birthday persuaded him to buy sufficient champagne for a hilarious celebration. The donor of the party having remained sober, Kerry and Amory accidentally dropped him down two flights of stairs and called, shame-faced and penitent, at the infirmary all the following week.

"Say, who are all these women?" demanded Kerry one day, protesting at the size of Amory's mail. "I've been looking at the postmarks lately—Farmington and Dobbs and Westover and Dana Hall—what's the idea?"

Amory grinned.

"All from the Twin Cities." He named them off. "There's Marylyn De Witt—she's pretty, got a car of her

own and that's damn convenient; there's Sally
Weatherby—she's getting too fat; there's Myra St.
Claire, she's an old flame, easy to kiss if you like it—"

"What line do you throw 'em?" demanded Kerry.
"I've tried everything, and the mad wags aren't even
afraid of me."

"You're the 'nice boy' type," suggested Amory.

"That's just it. Mother always feels the girl is safe if
she's with me. Honestly, it's annoying. If I start to hold
somebody's hand, they laugh at me, and *let* me, just as
if it wasn't part of them. As soon as I get hold of a hand
they sort of disconnect it from the rest of them."

"Sulk," suggested Amory. "Tell 'em you're wild and
have 'em reform you—go home furious—come back in
half an hour—startle 'em."

Kerry shook his head.

"No chance. I wrote a St. Timothy girl a really loving
letter last year. In one place I got rattled and said: 'My
God, how I love you!' She took a nail scissors, clipped
out the 'My God' and showed the rest of the letter all
over school. Doesn't work at all. I'm just 'good old
Kerry' and all that rot."

Amory smiled and tried to picture himself as "good
old Amory." He failed completely.

February dripped snow and rain, the cyclonic freshman mid-years passed, and life in 12 Univee continued
interesting if not purposeful. Once a day Amory indulged in a club sandwich, cornflakes, and Julienne po-
tatoes at "Joe's," accompanied usually by Kerry or Alec
Connage. The latter was a quiet, rather aloof slicker
from Hotchkiss, who lived next door and shared the
same enforced singleness as Amory, due to the fact that
his entire class had gone to Yale. "Joe's" was unaes-
thetic and faintly unsanitary, but a limitless charge account could be opened there, a convenience that Amory
appreciated. His father had been experimenting with
mining stocks and, in consequence, his allowance, while
liberal, was not at all what he had expected.

"Joe's" had the additional advantage of seclusion
from curious upper-class eyes, so at four each afternoon
Amory, accompanied by friend or book, went up to ex-

periment with his digestion. One day in March, finding that all the tables were occupied, he slipped into a chair opposite a freshman who bent intently over a book at the last table. They nodded briefly. For twenty minutes Amory sat consuming bacon buns and reading "Mrs. Warren's Profession" (he had discovered Shaw quite by accident while browsing in the library during mid-years); the other freshman, also intent on his volume, meanwhile did away with a trio of chocolate malted milks.

By and by Amory's eyes wandered curiously to his fellow-luncher's book. He spelled out the name and title upside down—"Marpessa," by Stephen Phillips. This meant nothing to him, his metrical education having been confined to such Sunday classics as "Come into the Garden, Maud," and what morsels of Shakespeare and Milton had been recently forced upon him.

Moved to address his vis-à-vis, he simulated interest in his book for a moment, and then exclaimed aloud as if involuntarily:

"Ha! Great stuff!"

The other freshman looked up and Amory registered artificial embarrassment.

"Are you referring to your bacon buns?" His cracked, kindly voice went well with the large spectacles and the impression of a voluminous keenness that he gave.

"No," Amory answered. "I was referring to Bernard Shaw." He turned the book around in explanation.

"I've never read any Shaw. I've always meant to." The boy paused and then continued: "Did you ever read Stephen Phillips, or do you like poetry?"

"Yes, indeed," Amory affirmed eagerly. "I've never read much of Phillips, though." (He had never heard of any Phillips except the late David Graham.)

"It's pretty fair, I think. Of course he's a Victorian." They sallied into a discussion of poetry, in the course of which they introduced themselves, and Amory's companion proved to be none other than "that awful highbrow, Thomas Parke D'Invilliers," who signed the passionate love-poems in the *Lit*. He was perhaps, nineteen, with stooped shoulders, pale blue eyes, and, as Amory could tell from his general appearance, without

much conception of social competition and such phenomena of absorbing interest. Still, he liked books, and
it seemed forever since Amory had met any one who
did; if only that St. Paul's crowd at the next table would
not mistake *him* for a bird, too, he would enjoy the en-
counter tremendously. They didn't seem to be noticing,
so he let himself go, discussed books by the dozens—
books he had read, read about, books he had never heard
of, rattling off lists of titles with the facility of a
Brentano's clerk. D'Invilliers was partially taken in and
wholly delighted. In a good-natured way he had almost
decided that Princeton was one part deadly Philistines
and one part deadly grinds, and to find a person who
could mention Keats without stammering, yet evidently
washed his hands, was rather a treat.

"Ever read any Oscar Wilde?" he asked.

"No. Who wrote it?"

"It's a man—don't you know?"

"Oh, surely." A faint chord was struck in Amory's
memory. "Wasn't the comic opera, 'Patience,' written
about him?"

"Yes, that's the fella. I've just finished a book of his,
'The Picture of Dorian Gray,' and I certainly wish you'd
read it. You'd like it. You can borrow it if you want to."

"Why, I'd like it a lot—thanks."

"Don't you want to come up to the room? I've got a
few other books."

Amory hesitated, glanced at the St. Paul's group—one
of them was the magnificent, exquisite Humbird—and
he considered how determinate the addition of this
friend would be. He never got to the stage of making
them and getting rid of them—he was not hard enough
for that—so he measured Thomas Parke D'Invilliers'
undoubted attractions and value against the menace of
cold eyes behind tortoise-rimmed spectacles that he fancied glared from the next table.

"Yes, I'll go."

So he found "Dorian Gray" and the "Mystic and
Somber Dolores" and the "Belle Dame sans Merci"; for
a month was keen on naught else. The world became
pale and interesting, and he tried hard to look at Prince-

ton through the satiated eyes of Oscar Wilde and Swinburne—or "Fingal O'Flaherty" and "Algernon Charles," as he called them in précieuse jest. He read enormously every night—Shaw, Chesterton, Barrie, Pinero, Yeats, Synge, Ernest Dowson, Arthur Symons, Keats, Sudermann, Robert Hugh Benson, the Savoy Operas—just a heterogeneous mixture, for he suddenly discovered that he had read nothing for years.

Tom D'Invilliers became at first an occasion rather than a friend. Amory saw him about once a week, and together they gilded the ceiling of Tom's room and decorated the walls with imitation tapestry, bought at an auction, tall candlesticks and figured curtains. Amory liked him for being clever and literary without effeminacy or affectation. In fact, Amory did most of the strutting and tried painfully to make every remark an epigram, than which, if one is content with ostensible epigrams, there are many feats harder. 12 Univee was amused. Kerry read "Dorian Gray" and simulated Lord Henry, following Amory about, addressing him as "Dorian" and pretending to encourage in him wicked fancies and attenuated tendencies to ennui. When he carried it into commons, to the amazement of the others at table, Amory became furiously embarrassed, and after that made epigrams only before D'Invilliers or a convenient mirror.

One day Tom and Amory tried reciting their own and Lord Dunsany's poems to the music of Kerry's graphophone.

"Chant!" cried Tom. "Don't recite. *Chant!*"

Amory, who was performing, looked annoyed, and claimed that he needed a record with less piano in it. Kerry thereupon rolled on the floor in stifled laughter.

"Put on 'Hearts and Flowers'!" he howled. "Oh, my Lord, I'm going to cast a kitten."

"Shut off the damn graphophone," Amory cried, rather red in the face. "I'm not giving an exhibition."

In the meanwhile Amory delicately kept trying to awaken a sense of the social system in D'Invilliers, for he knew that this poet was really more conventional than he, and needed merely watered hair, a smaller range of conversation, and a darker brown hat to become quite regular. But the liturgy of Livingstone collars and dark ties fell on heedless ears; in fact D'Invilliers faintly resented his efforts; so Amory confined himself to calls once a week, and brought him occasionally to 12 Univee. This caused mild titters among the other freshmen, who called them "Doctor Johnson and Boswell."

Alec Connage, another frequent visitor, liked him in a vague way, but was afraid of him as a highbrow. Kerry, who saw through his poetic patter to the solid, almost respectable depths within, was immensely amused and would have him recite poetry by the hour, while he lay with closed eyes on Amory's sofa and listened:

> Asleep or waking is it? for her neck,
> Kissed over close, wears yet a purple speck
>   Wherein the pained blood falters and goes out;
> Soft, and stung softly—fairer for a fleck.

"That's good," Kerry would say softly. "It pleases the elder Holiday. That's a great poet, I guess." Tom, delighted at an audience, would ramble through the "Poems and Ballads" until Kerry and Amory knew them almost as well as he.

Amory took to writing poetry on spring afternoons, in the gardens of the big estates near Princeton, while swans made effective atmosphere in the artificial pools, and slow clouds sailed harmoniously above the willows. May came too soon, and suddenly unable to bear walls, he wandered the campus at all hours through starlight and rain.

A DAMP SYMBOLIC INTERLUDE

The night mist fell. From the moon it rolled, clustered about the spires and towers, and then settled below them, so that the dreaming peaks were still in lofty aspiration toward the sky. Figures that dotted the day like ants now brushed along as shadowy ghosts, in and out of the foreground. The Gothic halls and cloisters were infinitely more mysterious as they loomed suddenly out of the darkness, outlined each by myriad faint squares of yellow light. Indefinitely from somewhere a bell boomed the quarter-hour, and Amory, pausing by the sundial, stretched himself out full length on the damp grass. The cool bathed his eyes and slowed the flight of time—time that had crept so insidiously through the lazy April afternoons, seemed so intangible in the long spring twilights. Evening after evening the senior singing had drifted over the campus in melancholy beauty, and through the shell of his undergraduate consciousness had broken a deep and reverent devotion to the gray walls and Gothic peaks and all they symbolized as warehouses of dead ages.

The tower that in view of his window sprang upward, grew into a spire, yearning higher until its uppermost tip was half invisible against the morning skies, gave him the first sense of the transiency and unimportance of the campus figures except as holders of the apostolic succession. He liked knowing that Gothic architecture, with its upward trend, was peculiarly appropriate to universities, and the idea became personal to him. The silent stretches of green, the quiet halls with an occasional late-burning scholastic light held his imagination in a strong grasp, and the chastity of the spire became a symbol of this perception.

"Damn it all," he whispered aloud, wetting his hands in the damp and running them through his hair. "Next year I work!" Yet he knew that where now the spirit of spires and towers made him dreamily acquiescent, it would then overawe him. Where now he realized only his own inconsequence, effort would make him aware of his own impotency and insufficiency.

The college dreamed on—awake. He felt a nervous excitement that might have been the very throb of its slow heart. It was a stream where he was to throw a stone whose faint ripple would be vanishing almost as it left his hand. As yet he had given nothing, he had taken nothing.

A belated freshman, his oilskin slicker rasping loudly,

slushed along the soft path. A voice from somewhere called the inevitable formula, "Stick out your head!" below an unseen window. A hundred little sounds of the current drifting on under the fog pressed in finally on his consciousness.

"Oh, *God*!" he cried suddenly, and started at the sound of his voice in the stillness. The rain dripped on. A minute longer he lay without moving, his hands clinched. Then he sprang to his feet and gave his clothes a tentative pat.

"I'm very damn wet!" he said aloud to the sundial.

HISTORICAL

The war began in the summer following his freshman year. Beyond a sporting interest in the German dash for Paris the whole affair failed either to thrill or interest him. With the attitude he might have held toward an amusing melodrama he hoped it would be long and bloody. If it had not continued he would have felt like an irate ticket holder at a prizefight where the principals refused to mix it up.

That was his total reaction.

"HA-HA HORTENSE!"

"All right, po*nies*!"

"Shake it up!"

"Hey, ponies—how about easing up on that crap game and shaking a mean hip?"

"Hey, *ponies*!"

The coach fumed helplessly, the Triangle Club president, glowering with anxiety, varied between furious bursts of authority and fits of temperamental lassitude, when he sat spiritless and wondered how the devil the show was ever going on tour by Christmas.

"All right. We'll take the pirate song."

The ponies took last drags at their cigarettes and

slumped into place; the leading lady rushed into the foreground, setting his hands and feet in an atmospheric mince; and as the coach clapped and stamped and tumped and da-da'd, they hashed out a dance.

A great, seething anthill was the Triangle Club. It gave a musical comedy every year, travelling with cast, chorus, orchestra, and scenery all through Christmas vacation. The play and music were the work of undergraduates, and the club itself was the most influential of institutions, over three hundred men competing for it every year.

Amory, after an easy victory in the first sophomore *Princetonian* competition, stepped into a vacancy of the cast as *Boiling Oil, a Pirate Lieutenant*. Every night for the last week they had rehearsed "Ha-Ha Hortense!" in the Casino, from two in the afternoon until eight in the morning, sustained by dark and powerful coffee, and sleeping in lectures through the interim. A rare scene, the Casino. A big, barnlike auditorium, dotted with boys as girls, boys as pirates, boys as babies; the scenery in the course of being violently set up; the spotlight man rehearsing by throwing weird shafts into angry eyes; over all the constant tuning of the orchestra or the cheerful tumpty-tump of a Triangle tune. The boy who writes the lyrics stands in the corner, biting a pencil, with twenty minutes to think of an encore; the business manager argues with the secretary as to how much money can be spent on "those damn milkmaid costumes"; the old graduate, president in ninety-eight, perches on a box and thinks how much simpler it was in his day.

How a Triangle show ever got off was a mystery, but it was a riotous mystery, anyway, whether or not one did enough service to wear a little gold Triangle on his watch-chain. "Ha-Ha Hortense!" was written over six times and had the names of nine collaborators on the programme. All Triangle shows started by being "something different—not just a regular musical comedy," but when the several authors, the president, the coach and the faculty committee finished with it, there remained just the old reliable Triangle show with the old reliable jokes and the star comedian who got expelled or sick or something just before the trip, and the dark-whiskered man in the pony ballet, who "absolutely won't shave twice a day, doggone it!"

There was one brilliant place in "Ha-Ha Hortense!" It is a Princeton tradition that whenever a Yale man who is a member of the widely advertised "Skull and Bones" hears the sacred name mentioned, he must leave the room. It is also a tradition that the members are invariably successful in later life, amassing fortunes or votes or coupons or whatever they choose to amass. Therefore, at each performance of "Ha-Ha Hortense!" half-a-dozen seats were kept from sale and occupied by six of the worst-looking vagabonds that could be hired from the streets, further touched up by the Triangle make-up man. At the moment in the show where *Firebrand, the Pirate Chief,* pointed at his black flag and said, "I am a Yale graduate—note my Skull and Bones!"—at this very moment the six vagabonds were instructed to rise *conspicuously* and leave the theatre with looks of deep melancholy and an injured dignity. It was claimed though never proved that on one occasion the hired Elis were swelled by one of the real thing.

They played through vacation to the fashionable of eight cities. Amory liked Louisville and Memphis best: these knew how to meet strangers, furnished extraordinary punch, and flaunted an astonishing array of feminine beauty. Chicago he approved for a certain verve that transcended its loud accent—however, it was a Yale town, and as the yale Glee Club was expected in a week the Triangle received only divided homage. In Baltimore, Princeton was at home, and every one fell in love. There was a proper consumption of strong waters all along the line; one man invariably went on the stage highly stimulated, claiming that his particular interpretation of the part required it. There were three private cars; however, no one slept except in the third car, which was called the "animal car," and where were herded the spectacled wind-jammers of the orchestra. Everything was so hurried that there was no time to be bored, but when they arrived in Philadelphia, with vacation nearly over, there was rest in getting out of the heavy atmosphere of flowers and grease paint, and the ponies took off their corsets with abdominal pains and sighs of relief.

When the disbanding came, Amory set out post haste for Minneapolis, for Sally Weatherby's cousin, Isabelle Borgé, was coming to spend the winter in Minneapolis while her parents went abroad. He remembered Isabelle only as a little girl with whom he had played sometimes when he first went to Minneapolis. She had gone to Baltimore to live—but since then she had developed a past.

Amory was in full stride, confident, nervous, and jubilant. Scurrying back to Minneapolis to see a girl he had known as a child seemed the interesting and romantic thing to do, so without compunction he wired his mother not to expect him ... sat in the train, and thought about himself for thirty-six hours.

"PETTING"

On the Triangle trip Amory had come into constant contact with the great current American phenomenon, the "petting party."

None of the Victorian mothers—and most of the mothers were Victorian—had any idea how casually their daughters were accustomed to be kissed. "*Servant*-girls are that way," says Mrs. Huston-Carmelite to her popular daughter. "They are kissed first and proposed to afterward."

But the Popular Daughter becomes engaged every six months between sixteen and twenty-two, when she arranges a match with young Hambell, of Cambell & Hambell, who fatuously considers himself her first love, and between engagements the P.D. (she is selected by the cut-in system at dances, which favors the survival of the fittest) has other sentimental last kisses in the moonlight, or the firelight, or the outer darkness.

Amory saw girls doing things that even in his memory would have been impossible: eating three-o'clock, after-dinner suppers in impossible cafés, talking of every side of life with an air half of earnestness, half of mockery, yet with a furtive excitement that Amory considered stood for a real moral letdown. But he never realized how widespread it was until he saw the cities between New York and Chicago as one vast juvenile intrigue.

Afternoon at the Plaza, with winter twilight hovering outside and faint drums downstairs ... they strut and fret in the lobby, taking another cocktail, scrupulously attired and waiting. Then the swinging doors revolve and three bundles of fur mince in. The theatre comes afterward; then a table at the Midnight Frolic—of course, mother will be along there, but she will serve only to make things more secretive and brilliant as she sits in solitary state at the deserted table and thinks such entertainments as this are not half so bad as they are painted, only rather wearying. But the P.D. is in love again ... it was odd, wasn't it?—that though there was so much room left in the taxi the P.D. and the boy from Williams were somehow crowded out and had to go in a separate car. Odd! Didn't you notice how flushed the P.D. was when she arrived just seven minutes late? But the P.D. "gets away with it."

The "belle" had become the "flirt," the "flirt" had become the "baby vamp." The "belle" had five or six callers every afternoon. If the P.D., by some strange accident, has two, it is made pretty uncomfortable for the one who hasn't a date with her. The "belle" was surrounded by a dozen men in the intermissions between dances. Try to find the P.D. between dances, just *try* to find her.

The same girl ... deep in an atmosphere of jungle music and the questioning of moral codes. Amory found it rather fascinating to feel that any popular girl he met before eight he might quite possibly kiss before twelve.

"Why on earth are we here?" he asked the girl with the green combs one night as they sat in some one's limousine, outside the Country Club in Louisville.

"I don't know. I'm just full of the devil."

"Let's be frank—we'll never see each other again. I wanted to come out here with you because I thought you were the best-looking girl in sight. You really don't care whether you ever see me again, do you?"

"No—but is this your line for every girl? What have I done to deserve it?"

"And you didn't feel tired dancing or want a cigarette or any of the things you said? You just wanted to be——"

"Oh, let's go in," she interrupted, "if you want to *analyze*. Let's not *talk* about it."

When the hand-knit, sleeveless jerseys were stylish, Amory, in a burst of inspiration, named them "petting shirts." The named travelled from coast to coast on the lips of parlor-snakes and P.D.'s.

DESCRIPTIVE

Amory was now eighteen years old, just under six feet tall and exceptionally, but not conventionally, handsome. He had rather a young face, the ingenuousness of which was marred by the penetrating green eyes, fringed with long dark eyelashes. He lacked somehow that intense animal magnetism that so often accompanies beauty in men or women; his personality seemed rather a mental thing, and it was not in his power to turn it on and off like a water faucet. But people never forgot his face.

ISABELLE

She paused at the top of the staircase. The sensations attributed to divers on spring-boards, leading ladies on opening nights, and lumpy, husky young men on the day of the Big Game, crowded through her. She should have descended to a burst of drums or a discordant blend of themes from "Thais" and "Carmen." She had never been so curious about her appearance, she had never been so satisfied with it. She had been sixteen years old for six months.

"Isabelle!" called her cousin Sally from the doorway of the dressing-room.

"I'm ready." She caught a slight lump of nervousness in her throat.

"I had to send back to the house for another pair of slippers. It'll be just a minute."

Isabelle started toward the dressing-room for a last peek in the mirror, but something decided her to stand there and gaze down the broad stairs of the Minnehaha Club. They curved tantalizingly, and she could catch just a glimpse of two pairs of masculine feet in the hall below. Pump-shod in uniform black, they gave no hint of identity, but she wondered eagerly if one pair were attached to Amory Blaine. This young man, not as yet encountered, had nevertheless taken up a considerable part of her day—the first day of her arrival. Coming up in the machine from the station, Sally had volunteered, amid a rain of question, comment, revelation, and exaggeration:

"You remember Amory Blaine, of *course*. Well, he's simply mad to see you again. He's stayed over a day from college, and he's coming tonight. He's heard so much about you—says he remembers your eyes."

This had pleased Isabelle. It put them on equal terms, although she was quite capable of staging her own romances, with or without advance advertising. But following her happy tremble of anticipation, came a sinking sensation that made her ask:

"How do you mean he's heard about me? What sort of things?"

Sally smiled. She felt rather in the capacity of a showman with her more exotic cousin.

"He knows you're—you're considered beautiful and all that"—she paused—"and I guess he knows you've been kissed."

At this Isabelle's little fist had clinched suddenly under the fur robe. She was accustomed to be thus followed by her desperate past, and it never failed to rouse in her the same feeling of resentment; yet—in a strange town it was an advantageous reputation. She was a "Speed," was she? Well—let them find out.

Out of the window Isabelle watched the snow glide by in the frosty morning. It was ever so much colder here than in Baltimore; she had not remembered; the glass of the side door was iced, the windows were shirred with snow in the corners. Her mind played still with one subject. Did *he* dress like that boy there, who walked calmly down a bustling business street, in moccasins and winter-carnival costume? How very *Western*! Of course he wasn't that way: he went to Princeton, was a sophomore or something. Really she had no distinct idea of him. An ancient snapshot she had preserved in an old kodak book had impressed her by the big eyes (which he had probably grown up to by now). However, in the last month, when her winter visit to Sally had been decided on, he had assumed the proportions of a worthy adversary. Children, most astute of matchmakers, plot their campaigns quickly, and Sally had played a clever correspondence sonata to Isabelle's excitable temperament. Isabelle had been for some time capable of very strong, if very transient emotions. . . .

They drew up at a spreading, white-stone building, set back from the snowy street. Mrs. Weatherby greeted her warmly and her various younger cousins were produced from the corners where they skulked politely. Isabelle met them tactfully. At her best she allied all with whom she came in contact—except older girls and some women. All the impressions she made were conscious. The half-dozen girls she renewed acquaintance with that morning were all rather impressed and as much by her direct personality as by her reputation. Amory Blaine was an open subject. Evidently a bit light of love, neither popular nor unpopular—every girl there seemed to have had an affair with him at some time or other, but no one volunteered any really useful information. He was going to fall for her. . . . Sally had published that information to her young set and they were retailing it back to Sally as fast as they set eyes on Isabelle. Isabelle resolved secretly that she would, if necessary, *force* herself to like him—she owed it to Sally. Suppose she were terribly disappointed. Sally had painted him in such glowing colors—he was good-looking, "sort of dis-

tinguished, when he wants to be," had a line, and was
properly inconstant. In fact, he summed up all the romance that her age and environment led her to desire.
She wondered if those were his dancing shoes that fox-
trotted tentatively around the soft rug below.

All impressions and, in fact, all ideas were extremely
kaleidoscopic to Isabelle. She had that curious mixture
of the social and the artistic temperaments found often
in two classes, society women and actresses. Her education or, rather, her sophistication, had been absorbed
from the boys who had dangled on her favor; her tact
was instinctive, and her capacity for love-affairs was
limited only by the number of the susceptible within
telephone distance. Flirt smiled from her large black-
brown eyes and shone through her intense physical magnetism.

So she waited at the head of the stairs that evening
while slippers were fetched. Just as she was growing impatient, Sally came out of the dressing-room, beaming
with her accustomed good nature and high spirits, and
together they descended to the floor below, while the
shifting searchlight of Isabelle's mind flashed on two
ideas: she was glad she had high color tonight, and she
wondered if he danced well.

Downstairs, in the club's great room, she was surrounded for a moment by the girls she had met in the afternoon, then she heard Sally's voice repeating a cycle
of names, and found herself bowing to a sextet of black
and white, terribly stiff, vaguely familiar figures. The
name Blaine figured somewhere, but at first she could
not place him. A very confused, very juvenile moment
of awkward backings and bumpings followed, and ev-
eryone found himself talking to the person he least desired to. Isabelle manoeuvered herself and Froggy
Parker, freshman at Harvard, with whom she had once
played hopscotch, to a seat on the stairs. A humorous
reference to the past was all she needed. The things Isabelle could do socially with one idea were remarkable.
First, she repeated it rapturously in an enthusiastic contralto with a soupçon of Southern accent; then she held
it off at a distance and smiled at it—her wonderful

smile; then she delivered it in variations and played a sort of mental catch with it, all this in the nominal form of dialogue. Froggy was fascinated and quite unconscious that this was being done, not for him, but for the green eyes that glistened under the shining carefully watered hair, a little to her left, for Isabelle had discovered Amory. As an actress even in the fullest flush of her own conscious magnetism gets a deep impression of most of the people in the front row, so Isabelle sized up her antagonist. First, he had auburn hair, and from her feeling of disappointment she knew that she had expected him to be dark and of garter-advertisement slenderness.... For the rest, a faint flush and a straight, romantic profile; the effect set off by a close-fitting dress suit and a silk ruffled shirt of the kind that women still delight to see men wear, but men were just beginning to get tired of.

During this inspection Amory was quietly watching.

"Don't *you* think so?" she said suddenly, turning to him, innocent-eyed.

There was a stir, and Sally led the way over to their table. Amory struggled to Isabelle's side, and whispered:

"You're my dinner partner, you know. We're all coached for each other."

Isabelle gasped—this was rather right in line. But really she felt as if a good speech had been taken from the star and given to a minor character.... She mustn't lose the leadership a bit. The dinner-table glittered with laughter at the confusion of getting places and then curious eyes were turned on her, sitting near the head. She was enjoying this immensely, and Froggy Parker was so engrossed with the added sparkle of her rising color that he forgot to pull out Sally's chair, and fell into a dim confusion. Amory was on the other side, full of confidence and vanity, gazing at her in open admiration. He began directly, and so did Froggy:

"I've heard a lot about you since you wore braids——"

"Wasn't it funny this afternoon——"

Both stopped. Isabelle turned to Amory shyly. Her

face was always enough answer for any one, but she decided to speak.

"How—from whom?"

"From everybody—for all the years since you've been away." She blushed appropriately. On her right Froggy was *hors de combat* already, although he hadn't quite realized it.

"I'll tell you what I remembered about you all these years," Amory continued. She leaned slightly toward him and looked modestly at the celery before her. Froggy sighed—he knew Amory, and the situations that Amory seemed born to handle. He turned to Sally and asked her if she was going away to school next year. Amory opened with grape-shot.

"I've got an adjective that just fits you." This was one of his favorite starts—he seldom had a word in mind, but it was a curiosity provoker, and he could always produce something complimentary if he got in a tight corner.

"Oh—what?" Isabelle's face was a study in enraptured curiosity.

Amory shook his head.

"I don't know you very well yet."

"Will you tell me—afterward?" she half whispered.

He nodded.

"We'll sit out."

Isabelle nodded.

"Did any one ever tell you, you have keen eyes?" she said.

Amory attempted to make them look even keener. He fancied, but he was not sure, that her foot had just touched his under the table. But it might possibly have been only the table leg. It was so hard to tell. Still it thrilled him. He wondered quickly if there would be any difficulty in securing the little den upstairs.

BABES IN THE WOODS

Isabelle and Amory were distinctly not innocent, nor were they particularly brazen. Moreover, amateur standing had very little value in the game they were playing, a game that would presumably be her principal study for years to come. She had begun as he had, with good looks and an excitable temperament, and the rest was the result of accessible popular novels and dressing room conversation culled from a slightly older set. Isabelle had walked with an artificial gait at nine and a half, and when her eyes, wide and starry, proclaimed the ingenue most. Amory was proportionately less deceived. He waited for the mask to drop off, but at the same time he did not question her right to wear it. She, on her part, was not impressed by his studied air of blasé sophistication. She had lived in a larger city and had slightly an advantage in range. But she accepted his pose—it was one of the dozen little conventions of this kind of affair. He was aware that he was getting this particular favor now because she had been coached; he knew that he stood for merely the best game in sight, and that he would have to improve his opportunity before he lost his advantage. So they proceeded with an infinite guile that would have horrified her parents.

After the dinner the dance began ... smoothly. Smoothly?—boys cut in on Isabelle every few feet and then squabbled in the corners with: "You might let me get more than an inch!" and "She didn't like it either—she told me so next time I cut in." It was true—she told every one so, and gave every hand a parting pressure that said: "You know that your dances are *making* my evening."

But time passed, two hours of it, and the less subtle beaux had better learned to focus their pseudo-passionate glances elsewhere, for eleven o'clock found Isabelle and Amory sitting on the couch in the little den off the reading-room upstairs. She was conscious that they were a handsome pair, and seemed to belong dis-

tinctively in this seclusion, while lesser lights fluttered
and chattered downstairs.

Boys who passed the door looked in enviously—girls
who passed only laughed and frowned and grew wise
within themselves.

They had now reached a very definite stage. They had
traded accounts of their progress since they had met last,
and she had listened to much she had not heard before.
He was a sophomore, was on the *Princetonian* board,
hoped to be chairman in senior year. He learned that
some of the boys she went with in Baltimore were "terrible speeds" and came to dances in states of artificial
stimulation; most of them were twenty or so, and drove
alluring red Stutzes. A good half seemed to have already
flunked out of various schools and colleges, but some of
them bore athletic names that made him look at her ad-
miringly. As a matter of fact, Isabelle's closer acquaintance with the universities was just commencing. She
had bowing acquaintance with a lot of young men who
thought she was a "pretty kid—worth keeping an eye
on." But Isabelle strung the names into a fabrication of
gayety that would have dazzled a Viennese nobleman.
Such is the power of young contralto voices on sink-
down sofas.

He asked her if she thought he was conceited. She
said there was a difference between conceit and self-
confidence. She adored self-confidence in men.

"Is Froggy a good friend of yours?" she asked.

"Rather—why?"

"He's a bum dancer."

Amory laughed.

"He dances as if the girl were on his back instead of
in his arms."

She appreciated this.

"You're awfully good at sizing people up."

Amory denied this painfully. However, he sized up
several people for her. Then they talked about hands.

"You've got awfully nice hands," she said. "They
look as if you played the piano. Do you?"

I have said they had reached a very definite stage—

nay, more, a very critical stage. Amory had stayed over a day to see her, and his train left at twelve-eighteen that night. His trunk and suitcase awaited him at the station; his watch was beginning to hang heavy in his pocket.

"Isabelle," he said suddenly, "I want to tell you something." They had been talking lightly about "that funny look in her eyes," and Isabelle knew from the change in his manner what was coming—indeed, she had been wondering how soon it would come. Amory reached above their heads and turned out the electric light, so that they were in the dark, except for the red glow that fell through the door from the reading-room lamps. Then he began:

"I don't know whether or not you know what you— what I'm going to say. Lordy, Isabelle—this *sounds* like a line, but it isn't."

"I know," said Isabelle softly.

"Maybe we'll never meet again like this—I have darned hard luck sometimes." He was leaning away from her on the other arm of the lounge, but she could see his eyes plainly in the dark.

"You'll meet me again—silly." There was just the slightest emphasis on the last word—so that it became almost a term of endearment. He continued a bit huskily:

"I've fallen for a lot of people—girls—and I guess you have, too—boys, I mean, but, honestly, you—" he broke off suddenly and leaned forward, chin on his hands: "Oh, what's the use—you'll go your way and I suppose I'll go mine."

Silence for a moment. Isabelle was quite stirred; she wound her handkerchief into a tight ball, and by the faint light that streamed over her, dropped it deliberately on the floor. Their hands touched for an instant, but neither spoke. Silences were becoming more frequent and more delicious. Outside another stray couple had come up and were experimenting on the piano in the next room. After the usual preliminary of "chop-sticks," one of them started "Babes in the Woods" and a light tenor carried the words into the den:

> Give me your hand—
> I'll understand
> We're off to slumberland.

Isabelle hummed it softly and trembled as she felt Amory's hand close over hers.

"Isabelle," he whispered. "You know I'm mad about you. You *do* give a darn about me."

"Yes."

"How much do you care—do you like any one better?"

"No." He could scarcely hear her, although he bent so near that he felt her breath against his cheek.

"Isabelle, I'm going back to college for six long months, and why shouldn't we—if I could only just have one thing to remember you by——"

"Close the door. . . ." Her voice had just stirred so that he half wondered whether she had spoken at all. As he swung the door softly shut, the music seemed quivering just outside.

> Moonlight is bright,
> Kiss me good night.

What a wonderful song, she thought—everything was wonderful tonight, most of all this romantic scene in the den, with their hands clinging and the inevitable looming charmingly close. The future vista of her life seemed an unending succession of scenes like this: under moonlight and pale starlight, and in the backs of warm limousines and in low, cosey roadsters stopped under sheltering trees—only the boy might change, and this one was *so* nice. He took her hand softly. With a sudden movement he turned it and, holding it to his lips, kissed the palm.

"Isabelle!" His whisper blended in the music, and they seemed to float nearer together. Her breath came faster. "Can't I kiss you, Isabelle—Isabelle?" Lips half parted, she turned her head to him in the dark. Suddenly the ring of voices, the sound of running footsteps surged toward them. Quick as a flash Amory reached up and turned on the light, and when the door opened and three boys, the wrathy and dance-craving Froggy among them, rushed in, he was turning over the magazines on the table, while she sat without moving, serene and un-embarrassed, and even greeted them with a welcoming smile. But her heart was beating wildly, and she felt somehow as if she had been deprived.

It was evidently over. There was a clamor for a dance, there was a glance that passed between them—on his side despair, on hers regret, and then the evening went on, with the reassured beaux and the eternal cutting in.

At quarter to twelve Amory shook hands with her gravely, in the midst of a small crowd assembled to wish him good-speed. For an instant he lost his poise, and she felt a bit rattled when a satirical voice from a concealed wit cried:

"Take her outside, Amory!" As he took her hand he pressed it a little, and she returned the pressure as she had done to twenty hands that evening—that was all.

At two o'clock back at the Weatherbys' Sally asked her if she and Amory had had a "time" in the den. Isa-belle turned to her quietly. In her eyes was the light of the idealist, the inviolate dreamer of Joan-like dreams.

"No," she answered. "I don't do that sort of thing any more; he asked me to, but I said no."

As she crept in bed she wondered what he'd say in his special delivery tomorrow. He had such a good-looking mouth—would she ever——?

"Fourteen angels were watching o'er them," sang Sally sleepily from the next room.

"Damn!" muttered Isabelle, punching the pillow into a luxurious lump and exploring the cold sheets cau-tiously. "Damn!"

CARNIVAL

Amory, by way of the *Princetonian,* had arrived. The minor snobs, finely balanced thermometers of success, warmed to him as the club elections grew nigh, and he and Tom were visited by groups of upper classmen who arrived awkwardly, balanced on the edge of the furniture and talked of all subjects except the one of absorbing interest. Amory was amused at the intent eyes upon him, and, in case the visitors represented some club in which he was not interested, took great pleasure in shocking them with unorthodox remarks.

"Oh, let me see—" he said one night to a flabbergasted delegation, "what club do you represent?"

With visitors from Ivy and Cottage and Tiger Inn he played the "nice, unspoilt, ingenuous boy" very much at ease and quite unaware of the object of the call.

When the fatal morning arrived, early in March, and the campus became a document in hysteria, he slid smoothly into Cottage with Alec Connage and watched his suddenly neurotic class with much wonder.

There were fickle groups that jumped from club to club; there were friends of two or three days who announced tearfully and wildly that they must join the same club, nothing should separate them; there were snarling disclosures of long-hidden grudges as the Suddenly Prominent remembered snubs of freshman year. Unknown men were elevated into importance when they received certain coveted bids; others who were considered "all set" found that they had made unexpected enemies, felt themselves stranded and deserted, talked wildly of leaving college.

In his own crowd Amory saw men kept out for wearing green hats, for being "a damn tailor's dummy," for having "too much pull in heaven," for getting drunk one night "not like a gentleman, by God," or for unfathomable secret reasons known to no one but the wielders of the black balls.

This orgy of sociability culminated in a gigantic party at the Nassau Inn, where punch was dispensed from immense bowls, and the whole downstairs became a delirious, circulating, shouting pattern of faces and voices.

"Hi, Dibby—'gratulations!"

"Goo' boy, Tom, you got a good bunch in Cap."

"Say, Kerry——"

"Oh, Kerry—I hear you went Tiger with all the weightlifters!"

"Well, I didn't go Cottage—the parlor-snakes' delight."

"They say Overton fainted when he got his Ivy bid— Did he sign up the first day?—oh, *no*. Tore over to Murray-Dodge on a bicycle—afraid it was a mistake."

"How'd you get into Cap—you old roué?"

" 'Gratulations!"

" 'Gratulations yourself. Hear you got a good crowd."

When the bar closed, the party broke up into groups and streamed, singing, over the snow-clad campus, in a weird delusion that snobbishness and strain were over at last, and that they could do what they pleased for the next two years.

Long afterward Amory thought of sophomore spring as the happiest time of his life. His ideas were in tune with life as he found it; he wanted no more than to drift and dream and enjoy a dozen new-found friendships through the April afternoons.

Alec Connage came into his room one morning and woke him up into the sunshine and peculiar glory of Campbell Hall shining in the window.

"Wake up, Original Sin, and scrape yourself together. Be in front of Renwick's in half an hour. Somebody's got a car." He took the bureau cover and carefully deposited it, with its load of small articles, upon the bed.

"Where'd you get the car?" demanded Amory cynically.

"Sacred trust, but don't be a critical goopher or you can't go!"

"I think I'll sleep," Amory said calmly, resettling himself and reaching beside the bed for a cigarette.

"Sleep!"

"Why not? I've got a class at eleven-thirty."

"You damned gloom! Of course, if you don't want to go to the coast——"

With a bound Amory was out of bed, scattering the bureau cover's burden on the floor. The coast ... he hadn't seen it for years, since he and his mother were on their pilgrimage.

"Who's going?" he demanded as he wiggled into his B. V. D.'s.

"Oh, Dick Humbird and Kerry Holiday and Jesse Ferrenby and—oh about five or six. Speed it up, kid!"

In ten minutes Amory was devouring cornflakes in Renwick's, and at nine-thirty they bowled happily out of town, headed for the sands of Deal Beach.

"You see," said Kerry, "the car belongs down there. In fact, it was stolen from Asbury Park by persons unknown, who deserted it in Princeton and left for the West. Heartless Humbird here got permission from the city council to deliver it."

"Anybody got any money?" suggested Ferrenby, turning around from the front seat.

There was an emphatic negative chorus.

"That makes it interesting."

"Money—what's money? We can sell the car."

"Charge him salvage or something."

"How're we going to get food?" asked Amory.

"Honestly," answered Kerry, eying him reprovingly, "do you doubt Kerry's ability for three short days? Some people have lived on nothing for years at a time. Read the Boy Scout Monthly."

"Three days," Amory mused, "and I've got classes."

"One of the days is the Sabbath."

"Just the same, I can only cut six more classes, with over a month and a half to go."

"Throw him out!"

"It's a long walk back."

"Amory, you're running it out, if I may coin a new phrase."

"Hadn't you better get some dope on yourself, Amory?"

Amory subsided resignedly and drooped into a contemplation of the scenery. Swinburne seemed to fit in somehow.

> For, winter's rains and ruins are over,
> And all the season of snows and sins;
> The days dividing lover and lover,
> The light that loses, the night that wins;

And time remembered is grief forgotten,
And frosts are slain and flowers begotten,
And in green underwood and cover
Blossom by blossom the spring begins.
The full streams feed on flower of——

"What's the matter, Amory? Amory's thinking about poetry, about the pretty birds and flowers. I can see it in his eye."

"No, I'm not," he lied. "I'm thinking about the *Princetonian*. I ought to make up tonight; but I can telephone back, I suppose."

"Oh," said Kerry respectfully, "these important men——"

Amory flushed and it seemed to him that Ferrenby, a defeated competitor, winced a little. Of course, Kerry was only kidding, but he really mustn't mention the *Princetonian*.

It was a halcyon day, and as they neared the shore and the salt breezes scurried by, he began to picture the ocean and long, level stretches of sand and red roofs over blue sea. Then they hurried through the little town and it all flashed upon his consciousness to a mighty paean of emotion. . . .

"Oh, good Lord! *Look* at it!" he cried.

"What?"

"Let me out, quick—I haven't seen it for eight years! Oh, gentlefolk, stop the car!"

"What an odd child!" remarked Alec.

"I do believe he's a bit eccentric."

The car was obligingly drawn up at a curb, and Amory ran for the boardwalk. First, he realized that the sea was blue and that there was an enormous quantity of it, and that it roared and roared—really all the banalities about the ocean that one could realize, but if any one had told him then that these things were banalities, he would have gaped in wonder.

"Now we'll get lunch," ordered Kerry, wandering up with the crowd. "Come on, Amory, tear yourself away and get practical."

"We'll try the best hotel first," he went on, "and thence and so forth."

They strolled along the boardwalk to the most imposing hostelry in sight, and, entering the dining-room, scattered about a table.

"Eight Bronxes," commanded Alec, "and a club sandwich with Juliennes. The food for one. Hand the rest around."

Amory ate little, having seized a chair where he could watch the sea and feel the rock of it. When luncheon was over they sat and smoked quietly.

"What's the bill?"

Some one scanned it.

"Eight twenty-five."

"Rotten overcharge. We'll give them two dollars and one for the waiter. Kerry, collect the small change."

The waiter approached, and Kerry gravely handed him a dollar, tossed two dollars on the check, and turned away. They sauntered leisurely toward the door, pursued in a moment by the suspicious Ganymede.

"Some mistake, sir."

Kerry took the bill and examined it critically.

"No mistake!" he said, shaking his head gravely, and, tearing it into four pieces, he handed the scraps to the waiter, who was so dumfounded that he stood motionless and expressionless while they walked out.

"Won't he send after us?"

"No," said Kerry; "for a minute he'll think we're the proprietor's sons or something; then he'll look at the check again and call the manager, and in the meantime——"

They left the car at Asbury and street-car'd to Allenhurst, where they investigated the crowded pavilions for beauty. At four there were refreshments in a lunchroom, and this time they paid an even smaller per cent on the total cost; something about the appearance and savoir faire of the crowd made the thing go, and they were not pursued.

"You see, Amory, we're Marxian Socialists," explained Kerry. "We don't believe in property and we're putting it to the great test."

"Night will descend," Amory suggested.

"Watch, and put your trust in Holiday."

They became jovial about five-thirty and, linking arms, strolled up and down the boardwalk in a row, chanting a monotonous ditty about the sad sea waves. Then Kerry saw a face in the crowd that attracted him and, rushing off, reappeared in a moment with one of the homeliest girls Amory had ever set eyes on. Her pale mouth extended from ear to ear, her teeth projected in a solid wedge, and she had little, squinty eyes that peeped ingratiatingly over the side sweep of her nose. Kerry presented them formally.

"Name of Kaluka, Hawaiian queen! Let me present Messrs. Connage, Sloane, Humbird, Ferrenby, and Blaine."

The girl bobbed courtesies all around. Poor creature; Amory supposed she had never before been noticed in her life—possibly she was half-witted. While she accompanied them (Kerry had invited her to supper) she said nothing which could discountenance such a belief.

"She prefers her native dishes," said Alec gravely to the waiter, "but any coarse food will do."

All through supper he addressed her in the most respectful language, while Kerry made idiotic love to her on the other side, and she giggled and grinned. Amory was content to sit and watch the by-play, thinking what a light touch Kerry had and how he could transform the barest incident into a thing of curve and contour. They all seemed to have the spirit of it more or less, and it was a relaxation to be with them. Amory usually liked men individually, yet feared them in crowds unless the crowd was around *him*. He wondered how much each one contributed to the party, for there was somewhat of a spiritual tax levied. Alec and Kerry were the life of it, but not quite the centre. Somehow the quiet Humbird, and Sloane, with his impatient superciliousness, were the centre.

Dick Humbird had, ever since freshman year, seemed to Amory a perfect type of aristocrat. He was slender but well-built—black curly hair, straight features, and rather a dark skin. Everything he said sounded intangi-

bly appropriate. He possessed infinite courage, an aver-
agely good mind, and a sense of honor with a clear
charm and *noblesse oblige* that varied it from righteousness. He could dissipate without going to pieces, and
even his most bohemian adventures never seemed "running it out." People dressed like him, tried to talk as he
did. . . . Amory decided that he probably held the world
back, but he wouldn't have changed him. . . .

He differed from the healthy type that was essentially
middle class—he never seemed to perspire. Some people couldn't be familiar with a chauffeur without having
it returned; Humbird could have lunched at Sherry's
with a colored man, yet people would have somehow
known that it was all right. He was not a snob, though
he knew only half his class. His friends ranged from the
highest to the lowest, but it was impossible to "cultivate" him. Servants worshipped him, and treated him
like a god. He seemed the eternal example of what the
upper class tries to be.

"He's like those pictures in the Illustrated London
News of the English officers who have been killed,"
Amory had said to Alec.

"Well," Alec had answered, "if you want to know the
shocking truth, his father was a grocery clerk who made
a fortune in Tacoma real estate and came to New York
ten years ago."

Amory had felt a curious sinking sensation.

This present type of party was made possible by the
surging together of the class after club elections—as if
to make a last desperate attempt to know itself, to keep
together, to fight off the tightening spirit of the clubs. It
was a letdown from the conventional heights they had
all walked so rigidly.

After supper they saw Kaluka to the boardwalk, and
then strolled back along the beach to Asbury. The evening sea was a new sensation, for all its color and mellow age was gone, and it seemed the bleak waste that
made the Norse sagas sad; Amory thought of Kipling's

The Beaches of Lukannon—before the sealers came!

It was still a music, though, infinitely sorrowful.

Ten o'clock found them penniless. They had suppered greatly on their last eleven cents and, singing, strolled up through the casinos and lighted arches on the boardwalk, stopping to listen approvingly to all band concerts. In one place Kerry took up a collection for the French War Orphans which netted a dollar and twenty cents, and with this they bought some brandy in case they caught cold in the night. They finished the day in a moving-picture show and went into solemn systematic roars of laughter at an ancient comedy, to the startled annoyance of the rest of the audience. Their entrance was distinctly strategic, for each man as he entered pointed reproachfully at the one just behind him. Sloane, bringing up the rear, disclaimed all knowledge and responsibility as soon as the others were scattered inside; then as the irate ticket-taker rushed in he followed nonchalantly.

They reassembled later by the Casino and made arrangements for the night. Kerry wormed permission from the watchman to sleep on the platform and, having collected a huge pile of rugs from the booths to serve as mattresses and blankets, they talked until midnight, and then fell into a dreamless sleep, though Amory tried hard to stay awake and watch that marvelous moon settle on the sea.

So they progressed for two happy days, up and down the shore by streetcar or machine, or by shoe-leather on the crowded boardwalk; sometimes eating with the wealthy, more frequently dining frugally at the expense of an unsuspecting restaurateur. They had their photos taken, eight poses, in a quick-development store. Kerry insisted on grouping them as a "varsity" football team, and then as a tough gang from the East Side, with their coats inside out, and himself sitting in the middle on a cardboard moon. The photographer probably has them yet—at least they never called for them. The weather was perfect, and again they slept outside, and again Amory fell unwillingly asleep.

Sunday broke stolid and respectable, and even the sea seemed to mumble and complain, so they returned to

Princeton via Fords of transient farmers, and broke up with colds in their heads, but otherwise none the worse for wandering.

Even more than in the year before, Amory neglected his work, not deliberately but lazily and through a multitude of other interests. Co-ordinate geometry and the melancholy hexameters of Corneille and Racine held forth small allurements, and even psychology, which he had eagerly awaited, proved to be a dull subject full of muscular reactions and biological phrases rather than the study of personality and influence. That was a noon class, and it always sent him dozing. Having found that "subjective and objective, sir," answered most of the questions, he used the phrase on all occasions, and it became the class joke when, a query being levelled at him, he was nudged awake by Ferrenby or Sloane to gasp it out.

Mostly there were parties—to Orange or the Shore, more rarely to New York and Philadelphia, though one night they marshalled fourteen waitresses out of Childs' and took them to ride down Fifth Avenue on top of an autobus. They all cut more classes than were allowed, which meant an additional course the following year, but spring was too rare to let anything interfere with their colorful ramblings. In May Amory was elected to the Sophomore Prom Committee, and when after a long evening's discussion with Alec they made out a tentative list of class probabilities for the senior council, they placed themselves among the surest. The senior council was composed presumably of the eighteen most representative seniors, and in view of Alec's football managership and Amory's chance of nosing out Burne Holiday as *Princetonian* chairman, they seemed fairly justified in this presumption. Oddly enough, they both placed D'Invilliers as among the possibilities, a guess that a year before the class would have gaped at.

All through the spring Amory had kept up an intermittent correspondence with Isabelle Borgé, punctuated by violent squabbles and chiefly enlivened by his attempts to find new words for love. He discovered Isabelle to be discreetly and aggravatingly unsentimental in letters, but

he hoped against hope that she would prove not too exotic a bloom to fit the large spaces of spring as she had
fitted the den in the Minnehaha Club. During May he
wrote thirty-page documents almost nightly, and sent
them to her in bulky envelopes exteriorly labelled
"Part I" and "Part II."

"Oh, Alec, I believe I'm tired of college," he said
sadly, as they walked the dusk together.

"I think I am, too, in a way."

"All I'd like would be a little home in the country,
some warm country, and a wife, and just enough to do
to keep from rotting."

"Me, too."

"I'd like to quit."

"What does your girl say?"

"Oh!" Amory gasped in horror. "She wouldn't *think*
of marrying . . . that is, not now. I mean the future, you
know."

"My girl would. I'm engaged."

"Are you really?"

"Yes. Don't say a word to anybody, please, but I am.
I may not come back next year."

"But you're only twenty! Give up college?"

"Why, Amory, you were saying a minute ago——"

"Yes," Amory interrupted, "but I was just wishing. I
wouldn't think of leaving college. It's just that I feel so
sad these wonderful nights. I sort of feel they're never
coming again, and I'm not really getting all I could out
of them. I wish my girl lived here. But marry—not a
chance. Especially as father says the money isn't forthcoming as it used to be."

"What a waste these nights are!" agreed Alec.

But Amory sighed and made use of the nights. He had
a snapshot of Isabelle, enshrined in an old watch, and at
eight almost every night he would turn off all the lights
except the desk lamp and, sitting by the open windows
with the picture before him, write her rapturous letters.

　　. . . Oh, it's so hard to write you what I really *feel*
when I think about you so much; you've gotten to mean
to me a dream that I can't put on paper any more. Your

last letter came and it was wonderful! I read it over about six times, especially the *last* part, but I do wish, sometimes, you'd be more frank and tell me what you really do think of me, yet your last letter was too good to be true, and I can hardly wait until June! Be sure and be able to come to the prom. It'll be fine, I think, and I want to bring you just at the end of a wonderful year. I often think over what you said on that night and wonder how much you meant. If it were any one but you—but you see I thought you were fickle that first time I saw you and you are so popular and everything that I can't imagine your really liking me best.

Oh, Isabelle, dear—it's a wonderful night. Somebody is playing "Love Moon" on a mandolin far across the campus, and the music seems to bring you into the window. Now he's playing "Good-by, Boys, I'm Through," and how well it suits me. For I am through with everything. I have decided never to take a cocktail again, and I know I'll never again fall in love—I couldn't—you've been too much a part of my days and nights to ever let me think of another girl. I meet them all the time and they don't interest me. I'm not pretending to be blasé, because it's not that. It's just that I'm in love. Oh, dearest Isabelle (somehow I can't call you just Isabelle, and I'm afraid I'll come out with the "dearest" before your family this June), you've got to come to the prom, and then I'll come up to your house for a day and everything'll be perfect. . . .

And so on in an eternal monotone that seemed to both of them infinitely charming, infinitely new.

June came and the days grew so hot and lazy that they could not worry even about exams, but spent dreamy evenings on the court of Cottage, talking of long subjects until the sweep of country toward Stony Brook became a blue haze and the lilacs were white around tennis courts, and words gave way to silent cigarettes. . . . Then down deserted Prospect and along McCosh with song everywhere around them, up to the hot joviality of Nassau Street.

Tom D'Invilliers and Amory walked late in those days. A gambling fever swept through the sophomore class and they bent over the bones till three o'clock many a sultry night. After one session they came out of Sloane's room to find the dew fallen and the stars old in the sky.

"Let's borrow bicycles and take a ride," Amory suggested.

"All right. I'm not a bit tired and this is almost the last night of the year, really, because the prom stuff starts Monday."

They found two unlocked bicycles in Holder Court and rode out about half-past three along the Lawrenceville Road.

"What are you going to do this summer, Amory?"

"Don't ask me—same old things, I suppose. A month or two in Lake Geneva—I'm counting on you to be there in July, you know—then there'll be Minneapolis, and that means hundreds of summer hops, parlorsnaking, getting bored— But oh, Tom," he added suddenly, "hasn't this year been slick!"

"No," declared Tom emphatically, a new Tom, clothed by Brooks, shod by Franks, "I've won this game, but I feel as if I never want to play another. You're all right— you're a rubber ball, and somehow it suits you, but I'm sick of adapting myself to the local snobbishness of this corner of the world. I want to go where people aren't barred because of the color of their neckties and the roll of their coats."

"You can't, Tom," argued Amory, as they rolled along through the scattering night; "wherever you go now you'll always unconsciously apply these standards of 'having it' or 'lacking it.' For better or worse we've stamped you; you're a Princeton type!"

"Well, then," complained Tom, his cracked voice rising plaintively, "why do I have to come back at all? I've learned all that Princeton has to offer. Two years more of mere pedantry and lying around a club aren't going to help. They're just going to disorganize me, conventionalize me completely. Even now I'm so spineless that I wonder how I get away with it."

"Oh, but you're missing the real point, Tom," Amory interrupted. "You've just had your eyes opened to the snobbishness of the world in a rather abrupt manner. Princeton invariably gives the thoughtful man a social sense."

"You consider you taught me that, don't you?" he asked quizzically, eying Amory in the half dark.

Amory laughed quietly.

"Didn't I?"

"Sometimes," he said slowly, "I think you're my bad angel. I might have been a pretty fair poet."

"Come on, that's rather hard. You chose to come to an Eastern college. Either your eyes were opened to the mean scrambling quality of people, or you'd have gone through blind, and you'd hate to have done that—been like Marty Kaye."

"Yes," he agreed, "you're right. I wouldn't have liked it. Still, it's hard to be made a cynic at twenty."

"I was born one," Amory murmured. "I'm a cynical idealist." He paused and wondered if that meant anything.

They reached the sleeping school of Lawrenceville, and turned to ride back.

"It's good, this ride, isn't it?" Tom said presently.

"Yes; it's a good finish, it's knock-out; everything's good tonight. Oh, for a hot, languorous summer and Isabelle!"

"Oh, you and your Isabelle! I'll bet she's a simple one . . . let's say some poetry."

So Amory declaimed "The Ode to a Nightingale" to the bushes they passed.

"I'll never be a poet," said Amory as he finished. "I'm not enough of a sensualist really; there are only a few obvious things that I notice as primarily beautiful: women, spring evenings, music at night, the sea; I don't catch the subtle things like 'silver-snarling trumpets.' I may turn out an intellectual, but I'll never write anything but mediocre poetry."

They rode into Princeton as the sun was making colored maps of the sky behind the graduate school, and hurried to the refreshment of a shower that would have to serve in place of sleep. By noon the bright-costumed alumni crowded the streets with their bands and choruses, and in the tents there was great reunion under the orange and black banners that curled and strained in the wind. Amory looked long at one house which bore the legend "Sixty-nine." There a few gray-haired men sat and talked quietly while the classes swept by in panorama of life.

UNDER THE ARC-LIGHT

Then tragedy's emerald eyes glared suddenly at Amory over the edge of June. On the night after his ride to Lawrenceville a crowd sallied to New York in quest of adventure, and started back to Princeton about twelve o'clock in two machines. It had been a gay party and different stages of sobriety were represented. Amory was in the car behind; they had taken the wrong road and lost the way, and so were hurrying to catch up.

It was a clear night and the exhilaration of the road went to Amory's head. He had the ghost of two stanzas of a poem forming in his mind. . . .

> So the gray car crept nightward in the dark and there was no life stirred as it went by. . . . As the still ocean paths before the shark in starred and glittering waterways, beauty-high, the moon-swathed trees divided, pair on pair, while flapping nightbirds cried across the air. . . .
> A moment by an inn of lamps and shades, a yellow inn under a yellow moon—then silence, where crescendo laughter fades . . . the car swung out again to the winds of June, mellowed the shadows where the distance grew, then crushed the yellow shadows into blue. . . .

They jolted to a stop, and Amory peered up, startled. A woman was standing beside the road, talking to Alec at the wheel. Afterward he remembered the harpy effect that her old kimono gave her, and the cracked hollowness of her voice as she spoke:

"You Princeton boys?"

"Yes."

"Well, there's one of you killed here, and two others about dead."

"My God!"

"Look!" She pointed and they gazed in horror. Under the full light of a roadside arc-light lay a form, face downward in a widening circle of blood.

They sprang from the car. Amory thought of the back of that head—that hair—that hair ... and then they turned the form over.

"It's Dick—Dick Humbird!"

"Oh, Christ!"

"Feel his heart!"

Then the insistent voice of the old crone in a sort of croaking triumph:

"He's quite dead, all right. The car turned over. Two of the men that weren't hurt just carried the others in, but this one's no use."

Amory rushed into the house and the rest followed with a limp mass that they laid on the sofa in the shoddy little front parlor. Sloane, with his shoulder punctured, was on another lounge. He was half delirious, and kept calling something about a chemistry lecture at 8:10.

"I don't know what happened," said Ferrenby in a strained voice. "Dick was driving and he wouldn't give up the wheel; we told him he'd been drinking too much—then there was this damn curve—oh, my *God*! ..." He threw himself face downward on the floor and broke into dry sobs.

The doctor had arrived, and Amory went over to the couch, where some one handed him a sheet to put over the body. With a sudden hardness, he raised one of the hands and let it fall back inertly. The brow was cold but the face not expressionless. He looked at the shoe-laces—Dick had tied them that morning. *He* had tied them—and now he was this heavy white mass. All that remained of the charm and personality of the Dick Humbird he had known—oh, it was all so horrible and unaristocratic and close to the earth. All tragedy has that strain of the grotesque and squalid—so useless, futile ... the way animals die.... Amory was reminded of a cat that had lain horribly mangled in some alley of his childhood.

"Some one go to Princeton with Ferrenby."

Amory stepped outside the door and shivered slightly at the late night wind—a wind that stirred a broken fender on the mass of bent metal to a plaintive, tinny sound.

CRESCENDO!

The next day, by a merciful chance, passed in a whirl. When Amory was by himself his thoughts zigzagged inevitably to the picture of that red mouth yawning incongruously in the white face, but with a determined effort he piled present excitement upon the memory of it and shut it coldly away from his mind.

Isabelle and her mother drove into town at four, and they rode up smiling Prospect Avenue, through the gay crowd, to have tea at Cottage. The clubs had their annual dinners that night, so at seven he loaned her to a freshman and arranged to meet her in the gymnasium at eleven, when the upper classmen were admitted to the freshman dance. She was all he had expected, and he was happy and eager to make that night the center of every dream. At nine the upper classes stood in front of the clubs as the freshman torchlight parade rioted past, and Amory wondered if the dress-suited groups against the dark, stately backgrounds and under the flare of the torches made the night as brilliant to the staring, cheering freshman as it had been to him the year before.

The next day was another whirl. They lunched in a gay party of six in a private dining-room at the club, while Isabelle and Amory looked at each other tenderly over the fried chicken and knew that their love was to be eternal. They danced away the prom until five, and the stags cut in on Isabelle with joyous abandon, which grew more and more enthusiastic as the hour grew late, and their wines, stored in overcoat pockets in the coat room, made old weariness wait until another day. The stag line is a most homogeneous mass of men. It fairly sways with a single soul. A dark-haired beauty dances by and there is a half-gasping sound as the ripple surges forward and some one sleeker than the rest darts out and cuts in. Then when the six-foot girl (brought by Kaye in your class, and to whom he has been trying to introduce you all evening) gallops by, the line surges back and the groups face about and become intent on far corners of the hall, for Kaye, anxious and perspiring, appears, elbowing through the crowd in search of familiar faces.

"I say, old man, I've got an awfully nice——"

"Sorry, Kaye, but I'm set for this one. I've got to cut in on a fella."

"Well, the next one?"

"What—ah—er—I swear I've got to go cut in—look me up when she's got a dance free."

It delighted Amory when Isabelle suggested that they leave for a while and drive around in her car. For a delicious hour that passed too soon they glided the silent roads about Princeton and talked from the surface of their hearts in shy excitement. Amory felt strangely ingenuous and made no attempt to kiss her.

Next day they rode up through the Jersey country, had luncheon in New York, and in the afternoon went to see a problem play at which Isabelle wept all through the second act, rather to Amory's embarrassment—though it filled him with tenderness to watch her. He was tempted to lean over and kiss away her tears, and she slipped her hand into his under cover of darkness to be pressed softly.

Then at six they arrived at the Borgés' summer place on Long Island, and Amory rushed upstairs to change into a dinner coat. As he put in his studs he realized that he was enjoying life as he would probably never enjoy it again. Everything was hallowed by the haze of his own youth. He had arrived, abreast of the best in his generation at Princeton. He was in love and his love was returned. Turning on all the lights, he looked at himself in the mirror, trying to find in his own face the qualities that made him see more clearly than the great crowd of people, that made him decide firmly, and able to influence and follow his own will. There was little in his life now that he would have changed. . . . Oxford might have been a bigger field.

Silently he admired himself. How conveniently well he looked, and how well a dinner coat became him. He stepped into the hall and then waited at the top of the stairs, for he heard footsteps coming. It was Isabelle, and from the top of her shining hair to her little golden slippers she had never seemed so beautiful.

"Isabelle!" he cried, half involuntarily, and held out his arms. As in the story-books, she ran into them, and on that half-minute, as their lips first touched, rested the high point of vanity, the crest of his young egotism.

3

The Egotist Considers

"OUCH! Let me go!"

He dropped his arms to his sides.

"What's the matter?"

"Your shirt stud—it hurt me—look!" She was looking down at her neck, where a little blue spot about the size of a pea marred its pallor.

"Oh, Isabelle," he reproached himself, "I'm a goopher. Really, I'm sorry—I shouldn't have held you so close."

She looked up impatiently.

"Oh, Amory, of course you couldn't help it, and it didn't hurt much; but what *are* we going to do about it?"

"*Do* about it?" he asked. "Oh—that spot; it'll disappear in a second."

"It isn't," she said, after a moment of concentrated gazing, "it's still there—and it looks like Old Nick—oh, Amory, what'll we do! It's *just* the height of your shoulder."

"Massage it," he suggested, repressing the faintest inclination to laugh.

She rubbed it delicately with the tips of her fingers, and then a tear gathered in the corner of her eye, and slid down her cheek.

"Oh, Amory," she said despairingly, lifting up a most pathetic face, "I'll just make my whole neck *flame* if I rub it. What'll I do?"

A quotation sailed into his head and he couldn't resist repeating it aloud.

All the perfumes of Arabia will not whiten this little hand.

She looked up and the sparkle of the tear in her eye
was like ice.

"You're not very sympathetic."

Amory mistook her meaning.

"Isabelle, darling, I think it'll——"

"Don't touch me!" she cried. "Haven't I enough on
my mind and you stand there and *laugh*!"

Then he slipped again.

"Well, it *is* funny, Isabelle, and we were talking the
other day about a sense of humor being——"

She was looking at him with something that was not
a smile, rather the faint, mirthless echo of a smile, in the
corners of her mouth.

"Oh, shut up!" she cried suddenly, and fled down the
hallway toward her room. Amory stood there, covered
with remorseful confusion.

"Damn!"

When Isabelle reappeared she had thrown a light wrap
about her shoulders, and they descended the stairs in a
silence that endured through dinner.

"Isabelle," he began rather testily, as they arranged
themselves in the car, bound for a dance at the Greenwich Country Club, "you're angry, and I'll be, too, in a
minute. Let's kiss and make up."

Isabelle considered glumly.

"I hate to be laughed at," she said finally.

"I won't laugh any more. I'm not laughing, now,
am I?"

"You did."

"Oh, don't be so darned feminine."

Her lips curled slightly.

"I'll be anything I want."

Amory kept his temper with difficulty. He became
aware that he had not an ounce of real affection for Isabelle, but her coldness piqued him. He wanted to kiss
her, kiss her a lot, because then he knew he could leave
in the morning and not care. On the contrary, if he didn't
kiss her, it would worry him. . . . It would interfere
vaguely with his idea of himself as a conqueror. It
wasn't dignified to come off second best, *pleading,* with
a doughty warrior like Isabelle.

Perhaps she suspected this. At any rate, Amory watched the night that should have been the consummation of romance glide by with great moths overhead and the heavy fragrance of roadside gardens, but without those broken words, those little sighs. . . .

Afterward they supped on ginger ale and devil's food in the pantry, and Amory announced a decision.

"I'm leaving early in the morning."

"Why?"

"Why not?" he countered.

"There's no need."

"However, I'm going."

"Well, if you insist on being ridiculous—"

"Oh, don't put it that way," he objected.

"—just because I won't let you kiss me. Do you think——"

"Now, Isabelle," he interrupted, "you know it's not that—even suppose it is. We've reached the stage where we either ought to kiss—or—or—nothing. It isn't as if you were refusing on moral grounds."

She hesitated.

"I really don't know what to think about you," she began, in a feeble, perverse attempt at conciliation. "You're so funny."

"How?"

"Well, I thought you had a lot of self-confidence and all that; remember you told me the other day that you could do anything you wanted, or get anything you wanted?"

Amory flushed. He *had* told her a lot of things.

"Yes."

"Well, you didn't seem to feel so self-confident to-night. Maybe you're just plain conceited."

"No, I'm not," he hesitated. "At Princeton——"

"Oh, you and Princeton! You'd think that was the world, the way you talk! Perhaps you *can* write better than anybody else on your old Princetonian; maybe the freshmen *do* think you're important——"

"You don't understand——"

"Yes, I do," she interrupted. "I *do,* because you're always talking about yourself and I used to like it; now I don't."

"Have I tonight?"

"That's just the point," insisted Isabelle. "You got all upset tonight. You just sat and watched my eyes. Besides, I have to think all the time I'm talking to you—you're so critical."

"I make you think, do I?" Amory repeated with a touch of vanity.

"You're a nervous strain"—this emphatically—"and when you analyze every little emotion and instinct I just don't have 'em."

"I know." Amory admitted her point and shook his head helplessly.

"Let's go." She stood up.

He rose abstractedly and they walked to the foot of the stairs.

"What train can I get?"

"There's one about 9:11 if you really must go."

"Yes, I've got to go, really. Good night."

"Good night."

They were at the head of the stairs, and as Amory turned into his room he thought he caught just the faintest cloud of discontent in her face. He lay awake in the darkness and wondered how much he cared—how much of his sudden unhappiness was hurt vanity—whether he was, after all, temperamentally unfitted for romance.

When he awoke, it was with a glad flood of consciousness. The early wind stirred the chintz curtains at the windows and he was idly puzzled not to be in his room at Princeton with his school football picture over the bureau and the Triangle Club on the wall opposite. Then the grandfather's clock in the hall outside struck eight, and the memory of the night before came to him. He was out of bed, dressing, like the wind; he must get out of the house before he saw Isabelle. What had seemed a melancholy happening now seemed a tiresome anticlimax. He was dressed at half past, so he sat down by the window; felt that the sinews of his heart were twisted somewhat more than he had thought. What an ironic mockery the morning seemed!—bright and sunny, and full of the smell of the garden; hearing Mrs. Borgé's voice in the sun-parlor below, he wondered where was Isabelle.

There was a knock at the door.

"The car will be around at ten minutes of nine, sir."

He returned to his contemplation of the outdoors, and began repeating over and over, mechanically, a verse from Browning, which he had once quoted to Isabelle in a letter:

> Each life unfulfilled, you see;
>   It hangs still, patchy and scrappy:
> We have not sighed deep, laughed free,
>   Starved, feasted, despaired,—been happy.

But his life would not be unfulfilled. He took a sombre satisfaction in thinking that perhaps all along she had been nothing except what he had read into her; that this was her high point, that no one else would ever make her think. Yet that was what she had objected to in him; and Amory was suddenly tired of thinking, thinking!

"Damn her!" he said bitterly, "she's spoiled my year!"

THE SUPERMAN GROWS CARELESS

On a dusty day in September Amory arrived in Princeton and joined the sweltering crowd of conditioned men who thronged the streets. It seemed a stupid way to commence his upper-class years, to spend four hours a morning in the stuffy room of a tutoring school, imbibing the infinite boredom of conic sections. Mr. Rooney, pander to the dull, conducted the class and smoked innumerable Pall Malls as he drew diagrams and worked equations from six in the morning until midnight.

"Now, Langueduc, if I used that formula, where would my A point be?"

Langueduc lazily shifts his six-foot-three of football material and tries to concentrate.

"Oh—ah—I'm damned if I know, Mr. Rooney."

"Oh, why of course, of course you can't *use* that formula. *That's* what I wanted you to say."

"Why, sure, of course."

"Do you see why?"

"You bet—I suppose so."

"If you don't see, tell me. I'm here to show you."

"Well, Mr. Rooney, if you don't mind, I wish you'd go over that again."

"Gladly. Now here's 'A' ..."

The room was a study in stupidity—two huge stands for paper, Mr. Rooney in his shirt-sleeves in front of them, and slouched around on chairs, a dozen men: Fred Sloane, the pitcher, who absolutely *had* to get eligible; "Slim" Langueduc, who would beat Yale this fall, if only he could muster a poor fifty per cent; McDowell, gay young sophomore, who thought it was quite a sporting thing to be tutoring here with all these prominent athletes.

"Those poor birds who haven't a cent to tutor and have to study during the term are the ones I pity," he announced to Amory one day, with a flaccid camaraderie in the droop of the cigarette from his pale lips. "I should think it would be such a bore, there's so much else to do in New York during the term. I suppose they don't know what they miss, anyhow." There was such an air of "you and I" about Mr. McDowell that Amory very nearly pushed him out of the open window when he said this. . . . Next February his mother would wonder why he didn't make a club and increase his allowance ... simple little nut. . . .

Through the smoke and the air of solemn, dense earnestness that filled the room would come the inevitable helpless cry:

"I don't get it! Repeat that, Mr. Rooney!" Most of them were so stupid or careless that they wouldn't admit when they didn't understand, and Amory was of the latter. He found it impossible to study conic sections; something in their calm and tantalizing respectability breathing defiantly through Mr. Rooney's fetid parlors distorted their equations into insoluble anagrams. He made a last night's effort with the proverbial wet towel, and then blissfully took the exam, wondering unhappily why all the color and ambition of the spring before had faded out. Somehow, with the defection of Isabelle the idea of undergraduate success had loosed its grasp on his imagination, and he contemplated a possible failure to pass off his condition with equanimity, even though it would arbitrarily mean his removal from the *Princetonian* board and the slaughter of his chances for the Senior Council.

There was always his luck.

He yawned, scribbled his honor pledge on the cover, and sauntered from the room.

"If you don't pass it," said the newly arrived Alec as they sat on the window-seat of Amory's room and mused upon a scheme of wall decoration, "you're the world's worst goopher. Your stock will go down like an elevator at the club and on the campus."

"Oh, hell, I know it. Why rub it in?"

"'Cause you deserve it. Anybody that'd risk what you were in line for *ought* to be ineligible for *Princetonian* chairman."

"Oh, drop the subject," Amory protested. "Watch and wait and shut up. I don't want every one at the club asking me about it, as if I were a prize potato being fattened for a vegetable show."

One evening a week later Amory stopped below his own window on the way to Renwick's, and, seeing a light, called up:

"Oh, Tom, any mail?"

Alec's head appeared against the yellow square of light.

"Yes, your result's here."

His heart clamored violently.

"What is it, blue or pink?"

"Don't know. Better come up."

He walked into the room and straight over to the table, and then suddenly noticed that there were other people in the room.

" 'Lo, Kerry." He was most polite. "Ah, men of Princeton." They seemed to be mostly friends, so he picked up the envelope marked "Registrar's Office," and weighed it nervously.

"We have here quite a slip of paper."

"Open it, Amory."

"Just to be dramatic, I'll let you know that if it's blue, my name is withdrawn from the editorial board of the *Prince*, and my short career is over."

He paused, and then saw for the first time Ferrenby's eyes, wearing a hungry look and watching him eagerly. Amory returned the gaze pointedly.

"Watch my face, gentlemen, for the primitive emotions."

He tore it open and held the slip up to the light.

"Well?"

"Pink or blue?"

"Say what it is."

"We're all ears, Amory."

"Smile or swear—or something."

There was a pause . . . a small crowd of seconds swept by . . . then he looked again and another crowd went on into time.

"Blue as the sky, gentlemen. . . ."

AFTERMATH

What Amory did that year from early September to late in the spring was so purposeless and inconsecutive that it seems scarcely worth recording. He was, of course, immediately sorry for what he had lost. His philosophy of success had tumbled down upon him, and he looked for the reasons.

"Your own laziness," said Alec later.

"No—something deeper than that. I've begun to feel that I was meant to lose this chance."

"They're rather off you at the club, you know; every man that doesn't come through makes our crowd just so much weaker."

"I hate that point of view."

"Of course, with a little effort you could still stage a comeback."

"No—I'm through—as far as ever being a power in college is concerned."

"But, Amory, honestly, what makes me the angriest isn't the fact that you won't be chairman of the *Prince* and on the Senior Council, but just that you didn't get down and pass that exam."

"Not me," said Amory slowly; "I'm mad at the concrete thing. My own idleness was quite in accord with my system, but the luck broke."

"Your system broke, you mean."

"Maybe."

"Well, what are you going to do? Get a better one quick, or just bum around for two more years as a has-been?"

"I don't know yet . . ."

"Oh, Amory, buck up!"

"Maybe."

Amory's point of view, though dangerous, was not far from the true one. If his reactions to his environment could be tabulated, the chart would have appeared like this, beginning with his earliest years:

1. The fundamental Amory.
2. Amory plus Beatrice.
3. Amory plus Beatrice plus Minneapolis.

Then St. Regis' had pulled him to pieces and started him over again:

4. Amory plus St. Regis'.
5. Amory plus St. Regis' plus Princeton.

That had been his nearest approach to success through conformity. The fundamental Amory, idle, imaginative, rebellious, had been nearly snowed under. He had conformed, he had succeeded, but as his imagination was neither satisfied nor grasped by his own success, he had listlessly, half-accidentally chucked the whole thing and become again:

6. The fundamental Amory.

FINANCIAL

His father died quietly and inconspicuously at Thanksgiving. The incongruity of death with either the beauties of Lake Geneva or with his mother's dignified, reticent attitude diverted him, and he looked at the funeral with an amused tolerance. He decided that burial was after all preferable to cremation, and he smiled at his old boyhood choice, slow oxidation in the top of a tree. The day after the ceremony he was amusing himself in the great library by sinking back on a couch in graceful mortuary attitudes, trying to determine whether he would, when his day came, be found with his arms crossed piously over his chest (Monsignor Darcy had once advocated this posture as being the most distinguished), or with his hands clasped behind his head, a more pagan and Byronic attitude.

What interested him much more than the final departure of his father from things mundane was a tricornered conversation among Beatrice, Mr. Barton, of Barton and Krogman, their lawyers, and himself, that took place several days after the funeral. For the first time he came into actual cognizance of the family finances, and realized what a tidy fortune had once been under his father's management. He took a ledger labelled "1906" and ran through it rather carefully. The total expenditure that year had come to something over one hundred and ten thousand dollars. Forty thousand of this had been Beatrice's own income, and there had been no attempt to account for it: it was all under the heading, "Drafts, checks, and letters of credit forwarded to Beatrice Blaine." The dispersal of the rest was rather minutely itemized: the taxes and improvements on the Lake Geneva estate had come to almost nine thousand dollars;

the general up-keep, including Beatrice's electric and a French car, bought that year, was over thirty-five thousand dollars. The rest was fully taken care of, and there were invariably items which failed to balance on the right side of the ledger.

In the volume for 1912 Amory was shocked to discover the decrease in the number of bond holdings and the great drop in the income. In the case of Beatrice's money this was not so pronounced, but it was obvious that his father had devoted the previous year to several unfortunate gambles in oil. Very little of the oil had been burned, but Stephen Blaine had been rather badly singed. The next year and the next and the next showed similar decreases, and Beatrice had for the first time begun using her own money for keeping up the house. Yet her doctor's bill for 1913 had been over nine thousand dollars.

About the exact state of things Mr. Barton was quite vague and confused. There had been recent investments, the outcome of which was for the present problematical, and he had an idea there were further speculations and exchanges concerning which he had not been consulted.

It was not for several months that Beatrice wrote Amory the full situation. The entire residue of the Blaine and O'Hara fortunes consisted of the place at Lake Geneva and approximately a half million dollars, invested now in fairly conservative six-per-cent holdings. In fact, Beatrice wrote that she was putting the money into railroad and street-car bonds as fast as she could conveniently transfer it.

I am quite sure, she wrote to Amory, that if there is one thing we can be positive of, it is that people will not stay in one place. This Ford person has certainly made the most of that idea. So I am instructing Mr. Barton to specialize on such things as Northern Pacific and these Rapid Transit Companies, as they call the street-cars. I shall never forgive myself for not buying Bethlehem Steel. I've heard the most fascinating stories. You must go into finance, Amory. I'm sure you would revel in it. You start as a messenger or a teller, I believe, and from that you go up—almost indefinitely. I'm sure if I were a man I'd love the handling of money; it has become quite a senile passion with me. Before I get any farther I want to discuss something. A Mrs. Bispam, an overcordial little lady whom I met at a tea the other day, told me that her son, he is at Yale, wrote her that all the boys there wore their summer underwear all during the winter, and also went about with their heads wet and in low shoes on the coldest days. Now, Amory, I don't know whether that is a fad at Princeton too, but I don't want you to be so foolish. It not only inclines a young man to pneumonia and infantile paralysis, but to all forms of lung trouble, to which you are particularly inclined. You cannot experiment with your health. I have found that out. I will not make myself ridiculous as some mothers no doubt do, by insisting that you wear overshoes, though I remember one Christmas you wore them around constantly without a single buckle latched, making such a curious swishing sound, and you refused to buckle them because it was not the thing to do. The very next Christmas you would not wear even rubbers, though I begged you. You are nearly twenty years old now, dear, and I can't be with you constantly to find whether you are doing the sensible thing.

This has been a very practical letter. I warned you in my last that the lack of money to do the things one wants to makes one quite prosy and domestic, but there is still plenty for everything if we are not too extravagant. Take care of yourself, my dear boy, and do try to write at least once a week, because I imagine all sorts of horrible things if I don't hear from you.

                    Affectionately,   MOTHER.

FIRST APPEARANCE OF THE TERM "PERSONAGE"

Monsignor Darcy invited Amory up to the Stuart palace on the Hudson for a week at Christmas, and they had enormous conversations around the open fire. Monsignor was growing a trifle stouter and his personality had expanded even with that, and Amory felt both rest and security in sinking into a squat, cushioned chair and joining him in the middle-aged sanity of a cigar.

"I've felt like leaving college, Monsignor."

"Why?"

"All my career's gone up in smoke; you think it's petty and all that, but——"

"Not at all petty. I think it's most important. I want to hear the whole thing. Everything you've been doing since I saw you last."

Amory talked, he went thoroughly into the destruction of his egotistic highways, and in a half-hour the listless quality had left his voice.

"What would you do if you left college?" asked Monsignor.

"Don't know. I'd like to travel, but of course this tiresome war prevents that. Anyways, mother would hate not having me graduate. I'm just at sea. Kerry Holiday wants me to go over with him and join the Lafayette Escadrille."

"You know you wouldn't like to go."

"Sometimes I would—tonight I'd go in a second."

"Well, you'd have to be very much more tired of life than I think you are. I know you."

"I'm afraid you do," agreed Amory reluctantly. "It just seemed an easy way out of everything—when I think of another useless, draggy year."

"Yes, I know; but to tell you the truth, I'm not worried about you; you seem to me to be progressing perfectly naturally."

"No," Amory objected. "I've lost half my personality in a year."

"Not a bit of it!" scoffed Monsignor. "You've lost a great amount of vanity and that's all."

"Lordy! I feel, anyway, as if I'd gone through another fifth form at St. Regis's."

"No." Monsignor shook his head. "That was a misfortune; this has been a good thing. Whatever worth while comes to you, won't be through the channels you were searching last year."

"What could be more unprofitable than my present lack of pep?"

"Perhaps in itself . . . but you're developing. This has given you time to think and you're casting off a lot of your old luggage about success and the superman and all. People like us can't adopt whole theories, as you did. If we can do the next thing, and have an hour a day to think in, we can accomplish marvels, but as far as any high-handed scheme of blind dominance is concerned— we'd just make asses of ourselves."

"But, Monsignor, I can't do the next thing."

"Amory, between you and me, I have only just learned to do it myself. I can do the one hundred things beyond the next thing, but I stub my toe on that, just as you stubbed your toe on mathematics this fall."

"Why do we have to do the next thing? It never seems the sort of thing I should do."

"We have to do it because we're not personalities, but personages."

"That's a good line—what do you mean?"

"A personality is what you thought you were, what this Kerry and Sloane you tell me of evidently are. Personality is a physical matter almost entirely; it lowers the people it acts on—I've seen it vanish in a long sickness. But while a personality is active, it overrides 'the next thing.' Now a personage, on the other hand, gathers. He is never thought of apart from what he's done. He's a bar on which a thousand things have been hung—glittering things sometimes, as ours are, but he uses those things with a cold mentality back of them."

"And several of my most glittering possessions had fallen off when I needed them." Amory continued the simile eagerly.

"Yes, that's it; when you feel that your garnered prestige and talents and all that are hung out, you need never bother about anybody; you can cope with them without difficulty."

"But, on the other hand, if I haven't my possessions, I'm helpless!"

"Absolutely."

"That's certainly an idea."

"Now you've a clean start—a start Kerry or Sloane can constitutionally never have. You brushed three of four ornaments down, and, in a fit of pique, knocked off the rest of them. The thing now is to collect some new ones, and the farther you look ahead in the collecting the better. But remember, do the next thing!"

"How clear you can make things!"

So they talked, often about themselves, sometimes of philosophy and religion, and life as respectively a game or a mystery. The priest seemed to guess Amory's thoughts before they were clear in his own head, so closely related were their minds in form and groove.

"Why do I make lists?" Amory asked him one night. "Lists of all sorts of things?"

"Because you're a mediaevalist," Monsignor answered. "We both are. It's the passion for classifying and finding a type."

"It's a desire to get something definite."

"It's the nucleus of scholastic philosophy."

"I was beginning to think I was grown eccentric till I came up here. It was a pose, I guess."

"Don't worry about that; for you not posing may be the biggest pose of all. Pose——"

"Yes?"

"But do the next thing."

After Amory returned to college he received several letters from Monsignor which gave him more egotistic food for consumption.

I am afraid that I gave you too much assurance of your inevitable safety, and you must remember that I did that through faith in your springs of effort; not in the silly conviction that you will arrive without struggle. Some nuances of character you will have to take for granted in yourself, though you must be careful in confessing them to others. You are unsentimental, almost incapable of affection, astute without being cunning and vain without being proud.

Don't let yourself feel worthless; often through life you will really be at your worst when you seem to think best of yourself; and don't worry about losing your "personality," as you persist in calling it; at fifteen you had the radiance of early morning, at twenty you will begin to have the melancholy brilliance of the moon, and when you are my age you will give out, as I do, the genial golden warmth of 4 P.M.

If you write me letters, please let them be natural ones. Your last, that dissertation on architecture, was perfectly awful—so "highbrow" that I picture you living in an intellectual and emotional vacuum; and beware of trying to classify people too definitely into types; you will find that all through their youth they will persist annoyingly in jumping from class to class, and by pasting a supercilious label on every one you meet you are merely packing a Jack-in-the-box that will spring up and leer at you when you begin to come into really antagonistic contact with the world. An idealization of some such a man as Leonardo da Vinci would be a more valuable beacon to you at present.

You are bound to go up and down, just as I did in my youth, but do keep your clarity of mind, and if fools or sages dare to criticise don't blame yourself too much.

You say that convention is all that really keeps you straight in this "woman proposition"; but it's more than that, Amory; it's the fear that what you begin you can't stop; you would run amuck, and I know whereof I speak; it's that half-miraculous sixth sense by which you detect evil, it's the half-realized fear of God in your heart.

Whatever your metier proves to be—religion, architecture, literature—I'm sure you would be much safer anchored to the Church, but I won't risk my influence by arguing with you even though I am secretly sure that the "black chasm of Romanism" yawns beneath you. Do write me soon.

With affectionate regards,

THAYER DARCY.

Even Amory's reading paled during this period; he delved further into the misty side streets of literature: Huysmans, Walter Pater, Theophile Gautier, and the racier sections of Rabelais, Boccaccio, Petronius, and Suetonius. One week, through general curiosity, he inspected the private libraries of his classmates and found Sloane's as typical as any: sets of Kipling, O. Henry, John Fox, Jr., and Richard Harding Davis; "What Every Middle-Aged Woman Ought to Know," "The Spell of the Yukon"; a "gift" copy of James Whitcomb Riley, an assortment of battered, annotated schoolbooks, and, finally, to his surprise, one of his own late discoveries, the collected poems of Rupert Brooke.

Together with Tom D'Invilliers, he sought among the lights of Princeton for some one who might found the Great American Poetic Tradition.

The undergraduate body itself was rather more interesting that year than had been the entirely Philistine Princeton of two years before. Things had livened surprisingly, though at the sacrifice of much of the spontaneous charm of freshman year. In the old Princeton they would never have discovered Tanaduke Wylie. Tanaduke was a sophomore, with tremendous ears and a way of saying, "The earth swirls down through the ominous moons of preconsidered generations!" that made them vaguely wonder why it did not sound quite clear, but never question that it was the utterance of a supersoul. At least so Tom and Amory took him. They told him in all earnestness that he had a mind like Shelley's, and featured his ultrafree free verse and prose poetry in the *Nassau Literary Magazine*. But Tanaduke's genius absorbed the many colors of the age, and he took to the Bohemian life, to their great disappointment. He talked of Greenwich Village now instead of "noon-swirled moons," and met winter muses, unacademic, and cloistered by Forty-second Street and Broadway, instead of the Shelleyan dream-children with whom he had regaled their expectant appreciation. So they surrendered Tanaduke to the futurists, deciding that he and his flaming ties would do better there. Tom gave him the final advice that he should stop writing for two years and read the complete works of Alexander Pope four times, but on Amory's suggestion that Pope for Tanaduke was like foot-ease for stomach trouble, they withdrew in laughter, and called it a coin's toss whether this genius was too big or too petty for them.

Amory rather scornfully avoided the popular professors who dispensed easy epigrams and thimblefuls of Chartreuse to groups of admirers every night. He was disappointed, too, at the air of general uncertainty on every subject that seemed linked with the pedantic temperament; his opinions took shape in a miniature satire called "In a Lecture-Room," which he persuaded Tom to print in the *Nassau Lit.*

Good-morning, Fool ...
                    Three times a week
You hold us helpless while you speak,
Teasing our thirsty souls with the
Sleek 'yeas' of your philosophy ...
Well, here we are, your hundred sheep,
Tune up, play on, pour forth ... we sleep ...
You are a student, so they say;
You hammered out the other day
A syllabus, from what we know
Of some forgotten folio;
You'd sniffled through an era's must,
Filling your nostrils up with dust,
And then, arising from your knees,
Published, in one gigantic sneeze ...
But here's a neighbor on my right,
An Eager Ass, considered bright;
Asker of questions.... How he'll stand,
With earnest air and fidgy hand,
After this hour, telling you
He sat all night and burrowed through
Your book.... Oh, you'll be coy and he
Will simulate precosity,
And pedants both, you'll smile and smirk,
And leer, and hasten back to work....

'Twas this day week, sir, you returned
A theme of mine, from which I learned
(Through various comment on the side
Which you had scrawled) that I defied
The highest rules of criticism
For cheap and careless witticism....
'Are you quite sure that this could be?'
                    And
'Shaw is no authority!'
But Eager Ass, with what he's sent,
Plays havoc with your best per cent.
Still—still I meet you here and there ...
When Shakespeare's played you hold a chair,
And some defunct, moth-eaten star
Enchants the mental prig you are ...

A radical comes down and shocks
The atheistic orthodox?—
You're representing Common Sense,
Mouth open, in the audience.
And, sometimes, even chapel lures
That conscious tolerance of yours,
That broad and beaming view of truth
(Including Kant and General Booth ...)
And so from shock to shock you live,
A hollow, pale affirmative ...

The hour's up ... and roused from rest
One hundred children of the blest
Cheat you a word or two with feet
That down the noisy aisle-ways beat ...
Forget on narrow-minded earth
The Mighty Yawn that gave you birth.

In April, Kerry Holiday left college and sailed for France to enroll in the Lafayette Escadrille. Amory's envy and admiration of this step was drowned in an experience of his own to which he never succeeded in giving an appropriate value, but which, nevertheless, haunted him for three years afterward.

THE DEVIL

Healy's they left at twelve and taxied to Bistolary's. There were Axia Marlowe and Phoebe Column, from the Summer Garden show, Fred Sloane and Amory. The evening was so very young that they felt ridiculous with surplus energy, and burst into the café like Dionysian revellers.

"Table for four in the middle of the floor," yelled Phoebe. "Hurry, old dear, tell 'em we're here!"

"Tell 'em to play 'Admiration'!" shouted Sloane. "You two order; Phoebe and I are going to shake a wicked calf," and they sailed off in a muddled crowd. Axia and Amory, acquaintances of an hour, jostled behind a waiter to a table at a point of vantage; there they took seats and watched.

"There's Findle Marbotson, from New Haven!" she cried above the uproar. "'Lo, Findle! Whoo-ee!"

"Oh, Axia!" he shouted in salutation. "C'mon over to our table."

"No!" Amory whispered.

"Can't do it, Findle; I'm with somebody else! Call me up tomorrow about one o'clock!"

Findle, a nondescript man-about-Bisty's, answered incoherently and turned back to the brilliant blonde whom he was endeavoring to steer around the room.

"There's a natural damn fool," commented Amory.

"Oh, he's all right. Here's the old jitney waiter. If you ask me, I want a double Daiquiri."

"Make it four."

The crowd whirled and changed and shifted. They were mostly from the colleges, with a scattering of the male refuse of Broadway, and women of two types, the higher of which was the chorus girl. On the whole it was a typical crowd, and their party as typical as any. About three-fourths of the whole business was for effect and therefore harmless, ended at the door of the café, soon enough for the five-o'clock train back to Yale or Princeton; about one-fourth continued on into the dimmer hours and gathered strange dust from strange places. Their party was scheduled to be one of the harmless kind. Fred Sloane and Phoebe Column were old friends; Axia and Amory new ones. But strange things are prepared even in the dead of night, and the unusual, which lurks least in the café, home of the prosaic and inevitable, was preparing to spoil for him the waning romance of Broadway. The way it took was so inexpressibly terrible, so unbelievable, that afterward he never thought of it as experience; but it was a scene from a misty tragedy, played far behind the veil, and that it meant something definite he knew.

About one o'clock they moved to Maxim's, and two found them in Devinière's. Sloane had been drinking consecutively and was in a state of unsteady exhilaration, but Amory was quite tiresomely sober; they had run across none of those ancient, corrupt buyers of champagne who usually assisted their New York parties.

They were just through dancing and were making their way back to their chairs when Amory became aware that someone at a nearby table was looking at him. He turned and glanced casually . . . a middle-aged man dressed in a brown sack suit, it was, sitting a little apart at a table by himself and watching their party intently. At Amory's glance he smiled faintly. Amory turned to Fred, who was just sitting down.

"Who's that pale fool watching us?" he complained indignantly.

"Where?" cried Sloane. "We'll have him thrown out!" He rose to his feet and swayed back and forth, clinging to his chair. "Where is he?"

Axia and Phoebe suddenly leaned and whispered to each other across the table, and before Amory realized it they found themselves on their way to the door.

"Where now?"

"Up to the flat," suggested Phoebe. "We've got brandy and fizz—and everything's slow down here tonight."

Amory considered quickly. He hadn't been drinking, and decided that if he took no more, it would be reasonably discreet for him to trot along in the party. In fact, it would be, perhaps, the thing to do in order to keep an eye on Sloane, who was not in a state to do his own thinking. So he took Axia's arm and, piling intimately into a taxicab, they drove out over the hundreds and drew up at a tall, white-stone apartment-house. . . . Never would he forget that street. . . . It was a broad street, lined on both sides with just such tall, whitestone buildings, dotted with dark windows; they stretched along as far as the eye could see, flooded with a bright moonlight that gave them a calcium pallor. He imagined each one to have an elevator and a colored hall-boy and a key-rack; each one to be eight stories high and full of three and four room suites. He was rather glad to walk into the cheeriness of Phoebe's living-room and sink onto a sofa, while the girls went rummaging for food.

"Phoebe's great stuff," confided Sloane, sotto voce.

"I'm only going to stay half an hour," Amory said sternly. He wondered if it sounded priggish.

"Hell y' say," protested Sloane. "We're here now—don't le's rush."

"I don't like this place," Amory said sulkily, "and I don't want any food."

Phoebe reappeared with sandwiches, brandy bottle, siphon, and four glasses.

"Amory, pour 'em out," she said, "and we'll drink to Fred Sloane, who has a rare, distinguished edge."

"Yes," said Axia, coming in, "and Amory. I like Amory." She sat down beside him and laid her yellow head on his shoulder.

"I'll pour," said Sloane; "you use siphon, Phoebe."

They filled the tray with glasses.

"Ready, here she goes!"

Amory hesitated, glass in hand.

There was a minute while temptation crept over him like a warm wind, and his imagination turned to fire, and he took the glass from Phoebe's hand. That was all; for at the second that his decision came, he looked up and saw, ten yards from him, the man who had been in the café, and with his jump of astonishment the glass fell from his uplifted hand. There the man half sat, half leaned against a pile of pillows on the corner divan. His face was cast in the same yellow wax as in the café, neither the dull, pasty color of a dead man—rather a sort of virile pallor—nor unhealthy, you'd have called it; but like a strong man who'd worked in a mine or done night shifts in a damp climate. Amory looked him over carefully and later he could have drawn him after a fashion, down to the merest details. His mouth was the kind that is called frank, and he had steady gray eyes that moved slowly from one to the other of their group, with just the shade of a questioning expression. Amory noticed his hands; they weren't fine at all, but they had versatility and a tenuous strength . . . they were nervous hands that sat lightly along the cushions and moved constantly with little jerky openings and closings. Then, suddenly, Amory perceived the feet, and with a rush of blood to the head he realized he was afraid. The feet were all wrong . . . with a sort of wrongness that he felt rather than knew. . . . It was like weakness in a good woman, or blood on satin; one of those terrible incongruities that shake little things in the back of the brain. He wore no shoes, but, instead, a sort of half moccasin, pointed, though, like the shoes they wore in the fourteenth century, and with the little ends curling up. They were a darkish brown and his toes seemed to fill them to the end.... They were unutterably terrible....

He must have said something, or looked something, for Axia's voice came out of the void with a strange goodness.

"Well, look at Amory! Poor old Amory's sick—old head going 'round?"

"Look at that man!" cried Amory, pointing toward the corner divan.

"You mean that purple zebra!" shrieked Axia facetiously. "Ooo-ee! Amory's got a purple zebra watching him!"

Sloane laughed vacantly.

"Ole zebra gotcha, Amory?"

There was a silence.... The man regarded Amory quizzically.... Then the human voices fell faintly on his ear:

"Thought you weren't drinking," remarked Axia sardonically, but her voice was good to hear; the whole divan that held the man was alive; alive like heat waves over asphalt, like wriggling worms....

"Come back! Come back!" Axia's arm fell on his. "Amory, dear, you aren't going, Amory!" He was half-way to the door.

"Come on, Amory, stick 'th us!"

"Sick, are you?"

"Sit down a second!"

"Take some water."

"Take a little brandy...."

The elevator was close, and the colored boy was half asleep, paled to a livid bronze ... Axia's beseeching voice floated down the shaft. Those feet ... those feet ...

As they settled to the lower floor the feet came into view in the sickly electric light of the paved hall.

IN THE ALLEY

Down the long street came the moon, and Amory turned his back on it and walked. Ten, fifteen steps away sounded the footsteps. They were like a slow dripping, with just the slightest insistence in their fall. Amory's shadow lay, perhaps, ten feet ahead of him, and soft shoes was presumably that far behind. With the instinct of a child Amory edged in under the blue darkness of the white buildings, cleaving the moonlight for haggard seconds, once bursting into a slow run with clumsy stumblings. After that he stopped suddenly; he must keep hold, he thought. His lips were dry and he licked them.

If he met any one good—were there any good people left in the world or did they all live in white apartment-houses now? Was every one followed in the moonlight? But if he met some one good who'd know what he meant and hear this damned scuffle . . . then the scuffling grew suddenly nearer, and a black cloud settled over the moon. When again the pale sheen skimmed the cornices, it was almost beside him, and Amory thought he heard a quiet breathing. Suddenly he realized that the footsteps were not behind, had never been behind, they were ahead and he was not eluding but following . . . following. He began to run, blindly, his heart knocking heavily, his hands clinched. Far ahead a black dot showed itself, resolved slowly into a human shape. But Amory was beyond that now; he turned off the street and darted into an alley, narrow and dark and smelling of old rottenness. He twisted down a long, sinuous blackness, where the moonlight was shut away except for tiny glints and patches . . . then suddenly sank panting into a corner by a fence, exhausted. The steps ahead stopped, and he could hear them shift slightly with a continuous motion, like waves around a dock.

He put his face in his hands and covered eyes and ears as well as he could. During all this time it never occurred to him that he was delirious or drunk. He had a sense of reality such as material things could never give him. His intellectual content seemed to submit passively to it, and it fitted like a glove everything that had ever preceded it in his life. It did not muddle him. It was like a problem whose answer he knew on paper, yet whose solution he was unable to grasp. He was far beyond horror. He had sunk through the thin surface of that, now moved in a region where the feet and the fear of white walls were real, living things, things he must accept. Only far inside his soul a little fire leaped and cried that something was pulling him down, trying to get him inside a door and slam it behind him. After that door was slammed there would be only footfalls and white buildings in the moonlight, and perhaps he would be one of the footfalls.

During the five or ten minutes he waited in the shadow of the fence, there was somehow this fire ... that was as near as he could name it afterward. He remembered calling aloud:

"I want someone stupid. Oh, send someone stupid!" This to the black fence opposite him, in whose shadows the footsteps shuffled ... shuffled. He supposed "stupid" and "good" had become somehow intermingled through previous association. When he called thus it was not an act of will at all—will had turned him away from the moving figure in the street; it was almost instinct that called, just the pile on pile of inherent tradition or some wild prayer from way over the night. Then something clanged like a low gong struck at a distance, and before his eyes a face flashed over the two feet, a face pale and distorted with a sort of infinite evil that twisted it like flame in the wind; *but he knew, for the half instant that the gong tanged and hummed, that it was the face of Dick Humbird.*

Minutes later he sprang to his feet, realizing dimly that there was no more sound, and that he was alone in the graying alley. It was cold, and he started on a steady run for the light that showed the street at the other end.

AT THE WINDOW

It was late morning when he woke and found the telephone beside his bed in the hotel tolling frantically, and remembered that he had left word to be called at eleven. Sloane was snoring heavily, his clothes in a pile by his bed. They dressed and ate breakfast in silence, and then sauntered out to get some air. Amory's mind was working slowly, trying to assimilate what had happened and separate from the chaotic imagery that stacked his memory the bare shreds of truth. If the morning had been cold and gray he could have grasped the reins of the past in an instant, but it was one of those days that New York gets sometimes in May, when the air on Fifth Avenue is a soft, light wine. How much or how little Sloane remembered Amory did not care to know; he apparently had none of the nervous tension that was gripping Amory and forcing his mind back and forth like a shrieking saw.

Then Broadway broke upon them, and with the babel of noise and the painted faces a sudden sickness rushed over Amory.

"For God's sake, let's go back! Let's get off of this— this place!"

Sloane looked at him in amazement.

"What do you mean?"

"This street, it's ghastly! Come on! let's get back to the Avenue!"

"Do you mean to say," said Sloane stolidly, "that 'cause you had some sort of indigestion that made you act like a maniac last night, you're never coming on Broadway again?"

Simultaneously Amory classed him with the crowd, and he seemed no longer Sloane of the debonair humor and the happy personality, but only one of the evil faces that whirled along the turbid stream.

"Man!" he shouted so loud that the people on the corner turned and followed them with their eyes, "it's filthy, and if you can't see it, you're filthy, too!"

"I can't help it," said Sloane doggedly. "What's the

matter with you? Old remorse getting you? You'd be in a fine state if you'd gone through with our little party."

"I'm going, Fred," said Amory slowly. His knees were shaking under him, and he knew that if he stayed another minute on this street he would keel over where he stood. "I'll be at the Vanderbilt for lunch." And he strode rapidly off and turned over to Fifth Avenue. Back at the hotel he felt better, but as he walked into the barber-shop, intending to get a head massage, the smell of the powders and tonics brought back Axia's sidelong, suggestive smile, and he left hurriedly. In the doorway of his room a sudden blackness flowed around him like a divided river.

When he came to himself he knew that several hours had passed. He pitched onto the bed and rolled over on his face with a deadly fear that he was going mad. He wanted people, people, some one sane and stupid and good. He lay for he knew not how long without moving. He could feel the little hot veins on his forehead standing out, and his terror had hardened on him like plaster. He felt he was passing up again through the thin crust of horror, and now only could he distinguish the shadowy twilight he was leaving. He must have fallen asleep again, for when he next recollected himself he had paid the hotel bill and was stepping into a taxi at the door. It was raining torrents.

On the train for Princeton he saw no one he knew, only a crowd of fagged-looking Philadelphians. The presence of a painted woman across the aisle filled him with a fresh burst of sickness and he changed to another car, tried to concentrate on an article in a popular magazine. He found himself reading the same paragraphs over and over, so he abandoned this attempt and leaning over wearily pressed his hot forehead against the damp window-pane. The car, a smoker, was hot and stuffy with most of the smells of the state's alien population; he opened a window and shivered against the cloud of fog that drifted in over him. The two hours' ride were like days, and he nearly cried aloud with joy when the towers of Princeton loomed up beside him and the yellow squares of light filtered through the blue rain.

Tom was standing in the centre of the room, pensively relighting a cigar-stub. Amory fancied he looked rather relieved on seeing him.

"Had a hell of a dream about you last night," came in the cracked voice through the cigar smoke. "I had an idea you were in some trouble."

"Don't tell me about it!" Amory almost shrieked. "Don't say a word; I'm tired and pepped out."

Tom looked at him queerly and then sank into a chair and opened his Italian notebook. Amory threw his coat and hat on the floor, loosened his collar, and took a Wells novel at random from the shelf. "Wells is sane," he thought, "and if he won't do I'll read Rupert Brooke."

Half an hour passed. Outside the wind came up, and Amory started as the wet branches moved and clawed with their fingernails at the window-pane. Tom was deep in his work, and inside the room only the occasional scratch of a match or the rustle of leather as they shifted in their chairs broke the stillness. Then like a zigzag of lightning came the change. Amory sat bolt upright, frozen cold in his chair. Tom was looking at him with his mouth dropping, eyes fixed.

"God help us!" Amory cried.

"Oh, my heavens!" shouted Tom, "look behind!" Quick as a flash Amory whirled around. He saw nothing but the dark window-pane.

"It's gone now," came Tom's voice after a second in a still terror. "Something was looking at you."

Trembling violently, Amory dropped into his chair again.

"I've got to tell you," he said. "I've had one hell of an experience. I think I've—I've seen the devil or—something like him. What face did you just see?—or no," he added quickly, "don't tell me!"

And he gave Tom the story. It was midnight when he finished, and after that, with all lights burning, two sleepy, shivering boys read to each other from "The

New Machiavelli," until dawn came up out of
Witherspoon Hall, and the *Princetonian* fell against the
door, and the May birds hailed the sun on last night's
rain.

4

Narcissus Off Duty

DURING Princeton's transition period, that is, during Amory's last two years there, while he saw it change and broaden and live up to its Gothic beauty by better means than night parades, certain individuals arrived who stirred it to its plethoric depths. Some of them had been freshmen, and wild freshmen, with Amory; some were in the class below; and it was in the beginning of his last year and around small tables at the Nassau Inn that they began questioning aloud the institutions that Amory and countless others before him had questioned so long in secret. First, and partly by accident, they struck on certain books, a definite type of biographical novel that Amory christened "quest" books. In the "quest" book the hero set off in life armed with the best weapons and avowedly intending to use them as such weapons are usually used, to push their possessors ahead as selfishly and blindly as possible, but the heroes of the "quest" books discovered that there might be a more magnificent use for them. "None Other Gods," "Sinister Street," and "The Research Magnificent" were examples of such books; it was the last of these three that gripped Burne Holiday and made him wonder in the beginning of senior year how much it was worth while being a diplomatic autocrat around his club on Prospect Avenue and basking in the high lights of class office. It was distinctly through the channels of aristocracy that Burne found his way. Amory, through Kerry, had had a vague drifting acquaintance with him, but not until January of senior year did their friendship commence.

"Heard the latest?" said Tom, coming in late one drizzly evening with that triumphant air he always wore after a successful conversational bout.

"No. Somebody flunked out? Or another ship sunk?"

"Worse than that. About one-third of the junior class are going to resign from their clubs."

"What!"

"Actual fact!"

"Why!"

"Spirit of reform and all that. Burne Holiday is behind it. The club presidents are holding a meeting tonight to see if they can find a joint means of combating it."

"Well, what's the idea of the thing?"

"Oh, clubs injurious to Princeton democracy; cost a lot; draw social lines, take time; the regular line you get sometimes from disappointed sophomores. Woodrow thought they should be abolished and all that."

"But this is the real thing?"

"Absolutely. I think it'll go through."

"For Pete's sake, tell me more about it."

"Well," began Tom, "it seems that the idea developed simultaneously in several heads. I was talking to Burne awhile ago, and he claims that it's a logical result if an intelligent person thinks long enough about the social system. They had a 'discussion crowd' and the point of abolishing the clubs was brought up by some one— everybody there leaped at it—it had been in each one's mind, more or less, and it just needed a spark to bring it out."

"Fine! I swear I think it'll be most entertaining. How do they feel up at Cap and Gown?"

"Wild, of course. Every one's been sitting and arguing and swearing and getting mad and getting sentimental and getting brutal. It's the same at all the clubs; I've been the rounds. They get one of the radicals in the corner and fire questions at him."

"How do the radicals stand up?"

"Oh, moderately well. Burne's a damn good talker, and so obviously sincere that you can't get anywhere with him. It's so evident that resigning from his club means so much more to him than preventing it does to us that I felt futile when I argued; finally took a position that was brilliantly neutral. In fact, I believe Burne thought for a while that he'd converted me."

"And you say almost a third of the junior class are going to resign?"

"Call it a fourth and be safe."

"Lord—who'd have thought it possible!"

There was a brisk knock at the door, and Burne himself came in.

"Hello, Amory—hello, Tom."

Amory rose.

" 'Evening, Burne. Don't mind if I seem to rush; I'm going to Renwick's."

Burne turned to him quickly.

"You probably know what I want to talk to Tom about, and it isn't a bit private. I wish you'd stay."

"I'd be glad to." Amory sat down again, and as Burne perched on a table and launched into argument with Tom, he looked at this revolutionary more carefully than he ever had before. Broad-browed and strong-chinned, with a fineness in the honest gray eyes that were like Kerry's, Burne was a man who gave an immediate impression of bigness and security—stubborn, that was evident, but his stubbornness wore no stolidity, and when he had talked for five minutes Amory knew that this keen enthusiasm had in it no quality of diletantism.

The intense power Amory felt later in Burne Holiday differed from the admiration he had had for Humbird. This time it began as purely a mental interest. With other men whom he had thought as primarily first-class, he had been attracted first by their personalities, and in Burne he missed that immediate magnetism to which he usually swore allegience. But that night Amory was struck by Burne's intense earnestness, a quality he was accustomed to associate only with the dread stupidity, and by the great enthusiasm that struck dead chords in his heart. Burne stood vaguely for a land Amory hoped he was drifting toward—and it was almost time that land was in sight. Tom and Amory and Alec had reached an impasse; never did they seem to have new experiences in common, for Tom and Alec had been as blindly busy with their committees and boards as Amory had been

blindly idling, and the things they had for dissection—
college, contemporary personality and the like—they
had hashed and rehashed for many a frugal conversational meal.

That night they discussed the clubs until twelve, and,
in the main, they agreed with Burne. To the roommates
it did not seem such a vital subject as it had in the two
years before, but the logic of Burne's objections to the
social system dovetailed so completely with everything
they had thought, that they questioned rather than argued, and envied the sanity that enabled this man to
stand out so against all traditions.

Then Amory branched off and found that Burne was
deep in other things as well. Economics had interested
him and he was turning socialist. Pacifism played in the
back of his mind, and he read *The Masses* and Lyof
Tolstoi faithfully.

"How about religion?" Amory asked him.

"Don't know. I'm in a muddle about a lot of things—
I've just discovered that I've a mind, and I'm starting to
read."

"Read what?"

"Everything. I have to pick and choose, of course, but
mostly things to make me think. I'm reading the four
gospels now, and the 'Varieties of Religious Experience.' "

"What chiefly started you?"

"Wells, I guess, and Tolstoi, and a man named
Edward Carpenter. I've been reading for over a year
now—on a few lines, on what I consider the essential
lines."

"Poetry?"

"Well, frankly, not what you call poetry, or for your
reasons—you two write, of course, and look at things
differently. Whitman is the man that attracts me."

"Whitman?"

"Yes; he's a definite ethical force."

"Well, I'm ashamed to say that I'm a blank on the
subject of Whitman. How about you, Tom?"

Tom nodded sheepishly.

"Well," continued Burne, "you may strike a few

poems that are tiresome, but I mean the mass of his
work. He's tremendous—like Tolstoi. They both look
things in the face, and, somehow, different as they are,
stand for somewhat the same things."

"You have me stumped, Burne," Amory admitted.
"I've read 'Anna Karénina' and the 'Kreutzer Sonata' of
course, but Tolstoi is mostly in the original Russian as
far as I'm concerned."

"He's the greatest man in hundreds of years," cried
Burne enthusiastically. "Did you ever see a picture of
that shaggy old head of his?"

They talked until three, from biology to organized religion, and when Amory crept shivering into bed it was
with his mind aglow with ideas and a sense of shock
that some one else had discovered the path he might
have followed. Burne Holiday was so evidently
developing—and Amory had considered that he was
doing the same. He had fallen into a deep cynicism over
what had crossed his path, plotted the imperfectability
of man and read Shaw and Chesterton enough to keep
his mind from the edges of decadence—now suddenly
all his mental processes of the last year and a half
seemed stale and futile—a petty consummation of himself . . . and like a sombre background lay that incident
of the spring before, that filled half his nights with a
dreary terror and made him unable to pray. He was not
even a Catholic, yet that was the only ghost of a code
that he had, the gaudy, ritualistic, paradoxical Catholicism whose prophet was Chesterton, whose claqueurs
were such reformed rakes of literature as Huysmans and
Bourget, whose American sponsor was Ralph Adams
Cram, with his adulation of thirteenth-century
cathedrals—a Catholicism which Amory found convenient and ready-made, without priest or sacraments or
sacrifice.

He could not sleep, so he turned on his reading-lamp
and, taking down the "Kreutzer Sonata," searched it
carefully for the germs of Burne's enthusiasm. Being
Burne was suddenly so much realler than being clever.
Yet he sighed . . . here were other possible clay feet.

He thought back through two years, of Burne as a hurried, nervous freshman, quite submerged in his brother's personality. Then he remembered an incident of sophomore year, in which Burne had been suspected of the leading role.

Dean Hollister had been heard by a large group arguing with a taxi-driver, who had driven him from the junction. In the course of the altercation the dean remarked that he "might as well buy the taxicab." He paid and walked off, but next morning he entered his private office to find the taxicab itself in the space usually occupied by his desk, bearing a sign which read "Property of Dean Hollister. Bought and Paid for." . . . It took two expert mechanics half a day to dissemble it into its minutest parts and remove it, which only goes to prove the rare energy of sophomore humor under efficient leadership.

Then again, that very fall, Burne had caused a sensation. A certain Phyllis Styles, an intercollegiate promtrotter, had failed to get her yearly invitation to the Harvard-Princeton game.

Jesse Ferrenby had brought her to a smaller game a few weeks before, and had pressed Burne into service—to the ruination of the latter's misogyny.

"Are you coming to the Harvard game?" Burne had asked indiscreetly, merely to make conversation.

"If you ask me," cried Phyllis quickly.

"Of course I do," said Burne feebly. He was unversed in the arts of Phyllis, and was sure that this was merely a vapid form of kidding. Before an hour had passed he knew that he was indeed involved. Phyllis had pinned him down and served him up, informed him the train she was arriving by, and depressed him thoroughly. Aside from loathing Phyllis, he had particularly wanted to stag that game and entertain some Harvard friends.

"She'll see," he informed a delegation who arrived in his room to josh him. "This will be the last game she ever persuades any young innocent to take her to!"

"But, Burne—why did you *invite* her if you didn't want her?"

"Burne, you *know* you're secretly mad about her— that's the *real* trouble."

"What can *you* do, Burne? What can *you* do against Phyllis?"

But Burne only shook his head and muttered threats which consisted largely of the phrase: "She'll see, she'll see!"

The blithesome Phyllis bore her twenty-five summers gayly from the train, but on the platform a ghastly sight met her eyes. There were Burne and Fred Sloane arrayed at the last dot like the lurid figures on college posters. They had bought flaring suits with huge peg-top trousers and gigantic padded shoulders. On their heads were rakish college hats, pinned up in front and sporting bright orange-and-black bands, while from their celluloid collars blossomed flaming orange ties. They wore black arm-bands with orange "P's," and carried canes flying Princeton pennants, the effect completed by socks and peeping handkerchiefs in the same color motifs. On a clanking chain they led a large, angry tom-cat, painted to represent a tiger.

A good half of the station crowd was already staring at them, torn between horrified pity and riotous mirth, and as Phyllis, with her svelte jaw dropping, approached, the pair bent over and emitted a college cheer in loud, far-carrying voices, thoughtfully adding the name "Phyllis" to the end. She was vociferously greeted and escorted enthusiastically across the campus, followed by half a hundred village urchins—to the stifled laughter of hundreds of alumni and visitors, half of whom had no idea that this was a practical joke, but thought that Burne and Fred were two varsity sports showing their girl a collegiate time.

Phyllis's feelings as she was paraded by the Harvard and Princeton stands, where sat dozens of her former devotees, can be imagined. She tried to walk a little ahead, she tried to walk a little behind—but they stayed close, that there should be no doubt whom she was with, talking in loud voices of their friends on the football team, until she could almost hear her acquaintances whispering:

"Phyllis Styles must be *awfully hard up* to have to come with *those two*."

That had been Burne, dynamically humorous, fundamentally serious. From that root had blossomed the energy that he was now trying to orient with progress....

So the weeks passed and March came and the clay feet that Amory looked for failed to appear. About a hundred juniors and seniors resigned from their clubs in a final fury of righteousness, and the clubs in helplessness turned upon Burne their finest weapon: ridicule. Every one who knew him liked him—but what he stood for (and he began to stand for more all the time) came under the lash of many tongues, until a frailer man than he would have been snowed under.

"Don't you mind losing prestige?" asked Amory one night. They had taken to exchanging calls several times a week.

"Of course I don't. What's prestige, at best?"

"Some people say that you're just a rather original politician."

He roared with laughter.

"That's what Fred Sloane told me today. I suppose I have it coming."

One afternoon they dipped into a subject that had interested Amory for a long time—the matter of the bearing of physical attributes on a man's make-up. Burne had gone into the biology of this, and then:

"Of course health counts—a healthy man has twice the chance of being good," he said.

"I don't agree with you—I don't believe in 'muscular Christianity.' "

"I do—I believe Christ had great physical vigor."

"Oh, no," Amory protested. "He worked too hard for that. I imagine that when he died he was a broken-down man—and the great saints haven't been strong."

"Half of them have."

"Well, even granting that, I don't think health has anything to do with goodness; of course, it's valuable to a great saint to be able to stand enormous strains, but this fad of popular preachers rising on their toes in simulated virility, bellowing that calisthenics will save the world—no, Burne, I can't go that."

"Well, let's waive it—we won't get anywhere, and besides I haven't quite made up my mind about it myself. Now, here's something I *do* know—personal appearance has a lot to do with it."

"Coloring?" Amory asked eagerly.

"Yes."

"That's what Tom and I figured," Amory agreed. "We took the year-books for the last ten years and looked at the pictures of the senior council. I know you don't think much of that august body, but it does represent success here in a general way. Well, I suppose only about thirty-five per cent of every class here are blonds, are really light—yet *two-thirds* of every senior council are light. We looked at pictures of ten years of them, mind you; that means that out of every *fifteen* light-haired men in the senior class *one* is on the senior council, and of the dark-haired men it's only one in *fifty*."

"It's true," Burne agreed. "The light-haired man *is* a higher type, generally speaking. I worked the thing out with the Presidents of the United States once, and found that way over half of them were light-haired—yet think of the preponderant number of brunettes in the race."

"People unconsciously admit it," said Amory. "You'll notice a blond person is *expected* to talk. If a blond girl doesn't talk we call her a 'doll'; if a light-haired man is silent he's considered stupid. Yet the world is full of 'dark silent men' and 'languorous brunettes' who haven't a brain in their heads, but somehow are never accused of the dearth."

"And the large mouth and broad chin and rather big nose undoubtedly make the superior face."

"I'm not so sure." Amory was all for classical features.

"Oh, yes—I'll show you," and Burne pulled out of his desk a photographic collection of heavily bearded, shaggy celebrities—Tolstoi, Whitman, Carpenter, and others.

"Aren't they wonderful?"

Amory tried politely to appreciate them, and gave up laughingly.

"Burne, I think they're the ugliest-looking crowd I ever came across. They look like an old man's home."

"Oh, Amory, look at that forehead on Emerson; look at Tolstoi's eyes." His tone was reproachful.

Amory shook his head.

"No! Call them remarkable-looking or anything you want—but ugly they certainly are."

Unabashed, Burne ran his hand lovingly across the spacious foreheads, and piling up the pictures put them back in his desk.

Walking at night was one of his favorite pursuits, and one night he persuaded Amory to accompany him.

"I hate the dark," Amory objected. "I didn't use to— except when I was particularly imaginative, but now, I really do—I'm a regular fool about it."

"That's useless, you know."

"Quite possibly."

"We'll go east," Burne suggested, "and down that string of roads through the woods."

"Doesn't sound very appealing to me," admitted Amory reluctantly, "but let's go."

They set off at a good gait, and for an hour swung along in a brisk argument until the lights of Princeton were luminous white blots behind them.

"Any person with any imagination is bound to be afraid," said Burne earnestly. "And this very walking at night is one of the things I was afraid about. I'm going to tell you why I can walk anywhere now and not be afraid."

"Go on," Amory urged eagerly. They were striding toward the woods, Burne's nervous, enthusiastic voice warming to his subject.

"I used to come out here alone at night, oh, three months ago, and I always stopped at that cross-road we just passed. There were the woods looming up ahead, just as they do now, there were dogs howling and the shadows and no human sound. Of course, I peopled the woods with everything ghastly, just like you do; don't you?"

"I do," Amory admitted.

"Well, I began analyzing it—my imagination persisted in sticking horrors into the dark—so I stuck my imagination into the dark instead, and let it look out at me—I let it play stray dog or escaped convict or ghost, and then saw myself coming along the road. That made it all right—as it always makes everything all right to project yourself completely into another's place. I knew that if I were the dog or the convict or the ghost I wouldn't be a menace to Burne Holiday any more than he was a menace to me. Then I thought of my watch. I'd better go back and leave it and then essay the woods. No; I decided, it's better on the whole that I should lose a watch than that I should turn back—and I did go into them—not only followed the road through them, but walked into them until I wasn't frightened any more— did it until one night I sat down and dozed off in there; then I knew I was through being afraid of the dark."

"Lordy," Amory breathed. "I couldn't have done that. I'd have come out half-way, and the first time an automobile passed and made the dark thicker when its lamps disappeared, I'd have come in."

"Well," Burne said suddenly, after a few moments' silence, "we're half-way through, let's turn back."

On the return he launched into a discussion of will.

"It's the whole thing," he asserted. "It's the one dividing line between good and evil. I've never met a man who led a rotten life and didn't have a weak will."

"How about great criminals?"

"They're usually insane. If not, they're weak. There is no such thing as a strong, sane criminal."

"Burne, I disagree with you altogether; how about the superman?"

"Well?"

"He's evil, I think, yet he's strong and sane."

"I've never met him. I'll bet, though, that he's stupid or insane."

"I've met him over and over and he's neither. That's why I think you're wrong."

"I'm sure I'm not—and so I don't believe in imprisonment except for the insane."

On this point Amory could not agree. It seemed to him that life and history were rife with the strong criminal, keen, but often self-deluding; in politics and business one found him and among the old statesmen and kings and generals; but Burne never agreed and their courses began to split on that point.

Burne was drawing farther and farther away from the world about him. He resigned the vice-presidency of the senior class and took to reading and walking as almost his only pursuits. He voluntarily attended graduate lectures in philosophy and biology, and sat in all of them with a rather pathetically intent look in his eyes, as if waiting for something the lecturer would never quite come to. Sometimes Amory would see him squirm in his seat; and his face would light up; he was on fire to debate a point.

He grew more abstracted on the street and was even accused of becoming a snob, but Amory knew it was nothing of the sort, and once when Burne passed him four feet off, absolutely unseeingly, his mind a thousand miles away, Amory almost choked with the romantic joy of watching him. Burne seemed to be climbing heights where others would be forever unable to get a foothold.

"I tell you," Amory declared to Tom, "he's the first contemporary I've ever met whom I'll admit is my superior in mental capacity."

"It's a bad time to admit it—people are beginning to think he's odd."

"He's way over their heads—you know you think so yourself when you talk to him—Good Lord, Tom, you *used* to stand out against 'people.' Success has completely conventionalized you."

Tom grew rather annoyed.

"What's he trying to do—be excessively holy?"

"No! not like anybody you've ever seen. Never enters the Philadelphian Society. He has no faith in that rot. He doesn't believe that public swimming-pools and a kind word in time will right the wrongs of the world; moreover, he takes a drink whenever he feels like it."

"He certainly is getting in wrong."

"Have you talked to him lately?"

"No."

"Then you haven't any conception of him."

The argument ended nowhere, but Amory noticed

more than ever how the sentiment toward Burne had changed on the campus.

"It's odd," Amory said to Tom one night when they had grown more amicable on the subject, "that the people who violently disapprove of Burne's radicalism are distinctly the Pharisee class—I mean they're the best-educated men in college—the editors of the papers, like yourself and Ferrenby, the younger professors.... The illiterate athletes like Langueduc think he's getting eccentric, but they just say, 'Good old Burne has got some queer ideas in his head,' and pass on—the Pharisee class—Gee! they ridicule him unmercifully."

The next morning he met Burne hurrying along McCosh walk after a recitation.

"Whither bound, Tsar?"

"Over to the *Prince* office to see Ferrenby," he waved a copy of the morning's *Princetonian* at Amory. "He wrote this editorial."

"Going to flay him alive?"

"No—but he's got me all balled up. Either I've misjudged him or he's suddenly become the world's worst radical."

Burne hurried on, and it was several days before Amory heard an account of the ensuing conversation. Burne had come into the editor's sanctum displaying the paper cheerfully.

"Hello, Jesse."

"Hello there, Savonarola."

"I just read your editorial."

"Good boy—didn't know you stooped that low."

"Jesse, you startled me."

"How so?"

"Aren't you afraid the faculty'll get after you if you pull this irreligious stuff?"

"What?"

"Like this morning."

"What the devil—that editorial was on the coaching system."

"Yes, but that quotation——"

Jesse sat up.

"What quotation?"

"You know: 'He who is not with me is against me.' "

"Well—what about it?"

Jesse was puzzled but not alarmed.

"Well, you say here—let me see." Burne opened the paper and read: "*He who is not with me is against me, as that gentleman said who was notoriously capable of only coarse distinctions and puerile generalities.*' "

"What of it?" Ferrenby began to look alarmed. "Oliver Cromwell said it, didn't he? or was it Washington, or one of the saints? Good Lord, I've forgotten."

Burne roared with laughter.

"Oh, Jesse, oh, good, kind Jesse."

"Who said it, for Pete's sake?"

"Well," said Burne, recovering his voice, "St. Matthew attributes it to Christ."

"My God!" cried Jesse, and collapsed backward into the waste-basket.

AMORY WRITES A POEM

The weeks tore by. Amory wandered occasionally to New York on the chance of finding a new shining green autobus, that its stick-of-candy glamour might penetrate his disposition. One day he ventured into a stock-company revival of a play whose name was faintly familiar. The curtain rose—he watched casually as a girl entered. A few phrases rang in his ear and touched a faint chord of memory. Where—? When—?

Then he seemed to hear a voice whispering beside him, a very soft, vibrant voice: "Oh, I'm such a poor little fool; *do* tell me when I do wrong."

The solution came in a flash and he had a quick, glad memory of Isabelle.

He found a blank space on his programme, and began to scribble rapidly:

Here in the figured dark I watch once more,
  There, with the curtain, roll the years away;
Two years of years—there was an idle day
  Of ours, when happy endings didn't bore

Our unfermented souls; I could adore
Your eager face beside me, wide-eyed, gay,
Smiling a repertoire while the poor play
Reached me as a faint ripple reaches shore.

Yawning and wondering an evening through,
I watch alone ... and chatterings, of course,
Spoil the one scene which, somehow, did have charms;
You wept a bit, and I grew sad for you
Right here! Where Mr. X defends divorce
And what's-her-name falls fainting in his arms.

STILL CALM

"Ghosts are such dumb things," said Alec, "they're slow-witted. I can always outguess a ghost."

"How?" asked Tom.

"Well, it depends where. Take a bedroom, for example. If you use *any* discretion a ghost can never get you in a bedroom."

"Go on, s'pose you think there's maybe a ghost in your bedroom—what measures do you take on getting home at night?" demanded Amory, interested.

"Take a stick," answered Alec, with ponderous reverence, "one about the length of a broom-handle. Now, the first thing to do is to get the room *cleared*—to do this you rush with your eyes closed into your study and turn on the lights—next, approaching the closet, carefully run the stick in the door three or four times. Then, if nothing happens, you can look in. *Always, always* run the stick in viciously first—*never* look first!"

"Of course, that's the ancient Celtic school," said Tom gravely.

"Yes—but they usually pray first. Anyway, you use this method to clear the closets and also for behind all doors——"

"And the bed," Amory suggested.

"Oh, Amory, no!" cried Alec in horror. "That isn't the way—the bed requires different tactics—let the bed alone, as you value your reason—if there is a ghost in the room and that's only about a third of the time, it is *almost always* under the bed."

"Well—" Amory began.

Alec waved him into silence.

"Of *course* you never look. You stand in the middle of the floor and before he knows what you're going to do make a sudden leap for the bed—never walk near the bed; to a ghost your ankle is your most vulnerable part—once in bed, you're safe; he may lie around under the bed all night, but you're safe as daylight. If you still have doubts pull the blanket over your head."

"All that's very interesting, Tom."

"Isn't it?" Alec beamed proudly. "All my own, too— the Sir Oliver Lodge of the new world."

Amory was enjoying college immensely again. The sense of going forward in a direct, determined line had come back; youth was stirring and shaking out a few new feathers. He had even stored enough surplus energy to sally into a new pose.

"What's the idea of all this 'distracted' stuff, Amory?" asked Alec one day, and then as Amory pretended to be cramped over his book in a daze: "Oh, don't try to act Burne, the mystic, to me."

Amory looked up innocently.

"What?"

"What?" mimicked Alec. "Are you trying to read yourself into a rhapsody with—let's see the book."

He snatched it; regarded it derisively.

"Well?" said Amory a little stiffly.

" 'The Life of St. Teresa,' " read Alec aloud. "Oh, my gosh!"

"Say, Alec."

"What?"

"Does it bother you?"

"Does what bother me?"

"My acting dazed and all that?"

"Why, no—of course it doesn't *bother* me."

"Well, then, don't spoil it. If I enjoy going around telling people guilelessly that I think I'm a genius, let me do it."

"You're getting a reputation for being eccentric," said Alec, laughing, "if that's what you mean."

Amory finally prevailed, and Alec agreed to accept his face value in the presence of others if he was allowed rest periods when they were alone; so Amory "ran it out" at a great rate, bringing the most eccentric characters to dinner, wild-eyed grad students, preceptors with strange theories of God and government, to the cynical amazement of the supercilious Cottage Club.

As February became slashed by sun and moved cheerfully into March, Amory went several times to spend weekends with Monsignor; once he took Burne, with great success, for he took equal pride and delight in displaying them to each other. Monsignor took him several times to see Thornton Hancock, and once or twice to the house of a Mrs. Lawrence, a type of Rome-haunting American whom Amory liked immediately.

Then one day came a letter from Monsignor, which appended an interesting P.S.:

> Do you know, it ran, that your third cousin, Clara Page, widowed six months and very poor, is living in Philadelphia? I don't think you've ever met her, but I wish, as a favor to me, you'd go to see her. To my mind, she's rather a remarkable woman, and just about your age.

Amory sighed and decided to go, as a favor. . . .

CLARA

She was immemorial. . . . Amory wasn't good enough for Clara, Clara of ripply golden hair, but then no man was. Her goodness was above the prosy morals of the husband-seeker, apart from the dull literature of female virtue.

Sorrow lay lightly around her, and when Amory found her in Philadelphia he thought her steely blue eyes held only happiness; a latent strength, a realism, was brought to its fullest development by the facts that she was compelled to face. She was alone in the world, with two small children, little money, and, worst of all, a host of friends. He saw her that winter in Philadelphia entertaining a houseful of men for an evening, when he knew she had not a servant in the house except the little colored girl guarding the babies overhead. He saw one of the greatest libertines in that city, a man who was habitually drunk and notorious at home and abroad, sitting opposite her for an evening, discussing *girls' boarding-schools* with a sort of innocent excitement. What a twist Clara had to her mind! She could make fascinating and almost brilliant conversation out of the thinnest air that ever floated through a drawing-room.

The idea that the girl was poverty-stricken had appealed to Amory's sense of situation. He arrived in Philadelphia expecting to be told that 921 Ark Street was in a miserable lane of hovels. He was even disappointed when it proved to be nothing of the sort. It was an old house that had been in her husband's family for years. An elderly aunt, who objected to having it sold, had put ten years' taxes with a lawyer and pranced off to Honolulu, leaving Clara to struggle with the heating-problem as best she could. So no wild-haired woman with a hungry baby at her breast and a sad Amelia-like look greeted him. Instead, Amory would have thought from his reception that she had not a care in the world.

A calm virility and a dreamy humor, marked contrasts to her level-headedness—into these moods she slipped sometimes as a refuge. She could do the most prosy things (though she was wise enough never to stultify herself with such "household arts" as *knitting* and *embroidery*), yet immediately afterward pick up a book and let her imagination rove as a formless cloud with the wind. Deepest of all in her personality was the golden radiance that she diffused around her. As an open fire in a dark room throws romance and pathos into the quiet faces at its edge, so she cast her lights and shadows around the rooms that held her, until she made of her prosy old uncle a man of quaint and meditative charm, metamorphosed the stray telegraph boy into a Puck-like creature of delightful originality. At first this quality of hers somehow irritated Amory. He considered his own uniqueness sufficient, and it rather embarrassed him when she tried to read new interests into him for the benefit of what other adorers were present. He felt as if a polite but insistent stage-manager were attempting to make him give a new interpretation of a part he had conned for years.

But Clara talking, Clara telling a slender tale of a hat-pin and an inebriated man and herself. . . . People tried afterward to repeat her anecdotes but for the life of them they could make them sound like nothing whatever. They gave her a sort of innocent attention and the best smiles many of them had smiled for long; there were few tears in Clara, but people smiled misty-eyed at her.

Very occasionally Amory stayed for little half-hours after the rest of the court had gone, and they would have bread and jam and tea late in the afternoon or "maple-sugar lunches," as she called them, at night.

"You *are* remarkable, aren't you!" Amory was becoming trite from where he perched in the centre of the dining-room table one six o'clock.

"Not a bit," she answered. She was searching out napkins in the sideboard. "I'm really most humdrum and commonplace. One of those people who have no interest in anything but their children."

"Tell that to somebody else," scoffed Amory. "You know you're perfectly effulgent." He asked her the one thing that he knew might embarrass her. It was the remark that the first bore made to Adam.

"Tell me about yourself." And she gave the answer that Adam must have given.

"There's nothing to tell."

But eventually Adam probably told the bore all the things he thought about at night when the locusts sang in the sandy grass, and he must have remarked patronizingly how *different* he was from Eve, forgetting how different she was from him . . . at any rate, Clara told Amory much about herself that evening. She had had a harried life from sixteen on, and her education had stopped sharply with her leisure. Browsing in her library, Amory found a tattered gray book out of which

fell a yellow sheet that he impudently opened. It was a
poem that she had written at school about a gray convent wall on a gray day, and a girl with her cloak blown
by the wind sitting atop of it and thinking about the
many-colored world. As a rule such sentiment bored
him, but this was done with so much simplicity and atmosphere, that it brought a picture of Clara to his mind,
of Clara on such a cool, gray day with her keen blue
eyes staring out, trying to see her tragedies come marching over the gardens outside. He envied that poem. How
he would have loved to have come along and seen her
on the wall and talked nonsense or romance to her,
perched above him in the air. He began to be frightfully
jealous of everything about Clara: of her past, of her babies, of the men and women who flocked to drink deep
of her cool kindness and rest their tired minds as at an
absorbing play.

"*Nobody* seems to bore you," he objected.

"About half the world do," she admitted, "but I think
that's a pretty good average, don't you?" and she turned
to find something in Browning that bore on the subject.
She was the only person he ever met who could look up
passages and quotations to show him in the middle of
the conversation, and yet not be irritating to distraction.
She did it constantly, with such a serious enthusiasm
that he grew fond of watching her golden hair bent over
a book, brow wrinkled ever so little at hunting her sentence.

Through early March he took to going to Philadelphia
for weekends. Almost always there was someone else
there and she seemed not anxious to see him alone, for
many occasions presented themselves when a word from
her would have given him another delicious half-hour of
adoration. But he fell gradually in love and began to
speculate wildly on marriage. Though this design flowed
through his brain even to his lips, still he knew afterward that the desire had not been deeply rooted. Once
he dreamt that it had come true and woke up in a cold
panic, for in his dream she had been a silly, flaxen
Clara, with the gold gone out of her hair and platitudes
falling insipidly from her changeling tongue. But she

was the first fine woman he ever knew and one of the
few good people who ever interested him. She made her
goodness such an asset. Amory had decided that most
good people either dragged theirs after them as a liabil-
ity, or else distorted it to artificial geniality, and of
course there were the ever-present prig and Pharisee—
(but Amory never included *them* as being among the
saved).

ST. CECILIA

> Over her gray and velvet dress,
>   Under her molten, beaten hair,
> Color of rose in mock distress
>   Flushes and fades and makes her fair;
> Fills the air from her to him
>   With light and languor and little sighs,
> Just so subtly he scarcely knows . . .
>   Laughing lightning, color of rose.

"Do you like me?"

"Of course I do," said Clara seriously.

"Why?"

"Well, we have some qualities in common. Things
that are spontaneous in each of us—or were originally."

"You're implying that I haven't used myself very
well?"

Clara hesitated.

"Well, I can't judge. A man, of course, has to go
through a lot more, and I've been sheltered."

"Oh, don't stall, please, Clara," Amory interrupted;
"but do talk about me a little, won't you?"

"Surely, I'd adore to." She didn't smile.

"That's sweet of you. First answer some questions.
Am I painfully conceited?"

"Well—no, you have tremendous vanity, but it'll
amuse the people who notice its preponderance."

"I see."

"You're really humble at heart. You sink to the third
hell of depression when you think you've been slighted.
In fact, you haven't much self-respect."

"Centre of target twice, Clara. How do you do it? You never let me say a word."

"Of course not—I can never judge a man while he's talking. But I'm not through; the reason you have so little real self-confidence, even though you gravely announce to the occasional philistine that you think you're a genius, is that you've attributed all sorts of atrocious faults to yourself and are trying to live up to them. For instance, you're always saying that you are a slave to high-balls."

"But I am, potentially."

"And you say you're a weak character, that you've no will."

"Not a bit of will—I'm a slave to my emotions, to my likes, to my hatred of boredom, to most of my desires——"

"You are not!" She brought one little fist down onto the other. "You're a slave, a bound helpless slave to one thing in the world, your imagination."

"You certainly interest me. If this isn't boring you, go on."

"I notice that when you want to stay over an extra day from college you go about it in a sure way. You never decide at first while the merits of going or staying are fairly clear in your mind. You let your imagination shinny on the side of your desires for a few hours, and then you decide. Naturally your imagination, after a little freedom, thinks up a million reasons why you should stay, so your decision when it comes isn't true. It's biassed."

"Yes," objected Amory, "but isn't it lack of will-power to let my imagination shinny on the wrong side?"

"My dear boy, there's your big mistake. This has nothing to do with will-power; that's a crazy, useless word, anyway; you lack judgment—the judgment to decide at once when you know your imagination will play you false, given half a chance."

"Well, I'll be darned!" exclaimed Amory in surprise, "that's the last thing I expected."

Clara didn't gloat. She changed the subject immediately. But she had started him thinking and he believed she was partly right. He felt like a factory-owner who after accusing a clerk of dishonesty finds that his own son, in the office, is changing the books once a week. His poor, mistreated will that he had been holding up to the scorn of himself and his friends, stood before him innocent, and his judgment walked off to prison with the unconfinable imp, imagination, dancing in mocking glee beside him. Clara's was the only advice he ever asked without dictating the answer himself—except, perhaps, in his talks with Monsignor Darcy.

How he loved to do any sort of thing with Clara! Shopping with her was a rare, epicurean dream. In every store where she had ever traded she was whispered about as the beautiful Mrs. Page.

"I'll bet she won't stay single long."

"Well, don't scream it out. She ain't lookin' for no advice."

"Ain't she beautiful!"

> (Enter a floor-walker—silence till he moves forward, smirking.)

"Society person, ain't she?"

"Yeah, but poor now, I guess; so they say."

"Gee! girls, *ain't* she some kid!"

And Clara beamed on all alike. Amory believed that tradespeople gave her discounts, sometimes to her knowledge and sometimes without it. He knew she dressed very well, had always the best of everything in the house, and was inevitably waited upon by the head floor-walker at the very least.

Sometimes they would go to church together on Sunday and he would walk beside her and revel in her cheeks moist from the soft water in the new air. She was very devout, always had been, and God knows what heights she attained and what strength she drew down to herself when she knelt and bent her golden hair into the stained-glass light.

"St. Cecilia," he cried aloud one day, quite involuntarily, and the people turned and peered, and the priest paused in his sermon and Clara and Amory turned to fiery red.

That was the last Sunday they had, for he spoiled it all that night. He couldn't help it.

They were walking through the March twilight where it was as warm as June, and the joy of youth filled his soul so that he felt he must speak.

"I think," he said and his voice trembled, "that if I lost faith in you I'd lose faith in God."

She looked at him with such a startled face that he asked her the matter.

"Nothing," she said slowly, "only this: five men have said that to me before, and it frightens me."

"Oh, Clara, is that your fate!"

She did not answer.

"I suppose love to you is—" he began.

She turned like a flash.

"I have never been in love."

They walked along, and he realized slowly how much she had told him . . . never in love. . . . She seemed suddenly a daughter of light alone. His entity dropped out of her plane and he longed only to touch her dress with almost the realization that Joseph must have had of Mary's eternal significance. But quite mechanically he heard himself saying:

"And I love you—any latent greatness that I've got is . . . oh, I can't talk, but Clara, if I come back in two years in a position to marry you——"

She shook her head.

"No," she said; "I'd never marry again. I've got my two children and I want myself for them. I like you—I like all clever men, you more than any—but you know me well enough to know that I'd never marry a clever man—" She broke off suddenly.

"Amory."

"What?"

"You're not in love with me. You never wanted to marry me, did you?"

"It was the twilight," he said wonderingly. "I didn't feel as though I were speaking aloud. But I love you—or adore you—or worship you——"

"There you go—running through your catalogue of emotions in five seconds."

He smiled unwillingly.

"Don't make me out such a light-weight, Clara; you *are* depressing sometimes."

"You're not a light-weight, of all things," she said intently, taking his arm and opening wide her eyes—he could see their kindliness in the fading dusk. "A light-weight is an eternal nay."

"There's so much spring in the air—there's so much lazy sweetness in your heart."

She dropped his arm.

"You're all fine now, and I feel glorious. Give me a cigarette. You've never seen me smoke, have you? Well, I do, about once a month."

And then that wonderful girl and Amory raced to the corner like two mad children gone wild with pale-blue twilight.

"I'm going to the country for tomorrow," she announced, as she stood panting, safe beyond the flare of the corner lamppost. "These days are too magnificent to miss, though perhaps I feel them more in the city."

"Oh, Clara!" Amory said; "what a devil you could have been if the Lord had just bent your soul a little the other way!"

"Maybe," she answered; "but I think not. I'm never really wild and never have been. That little outburst was pure spring."

"And you are, too," said he.

They were walking along now.

"No—you're wrong again, how can a person of your own self-reputed brains be so constantly wrong about me? I'm the opposite of everything spring ever stood for. It's unfortunate, if I happen to look like what pleased some soppy old Greek sculptor, but I assure you that if it weren't for my face I'd be a quiet nun in the convent without"—then she broke into a run and her raised voice floated back to him as he followed—"my precious babies, which I must go back and see."

She was the only girl he ever knew with whom he could understand how another man might be preferred. Often Amory met wives whom he had known as debutantes, and looking intently at them imagined that he found something in their faces which said:

"Oh, if I could only have gotten *you*!" Oh, the enormous conceit of the man!

But that night seemed a night of stars and singing and Clara's bright soul still gleamed on the ways they had trod.

"*Golden, golden is the air*—" he chanted to the little pools of water. . . . "*Golden is the air, golden notes from golden mandolins, golden frets of golden violins, fair, oh, wearily fair. . . . Skeins from braided basket, mortals may not hold; oh, what young extravagant God, who would know or ask it? . . . who could give such gold . . .*"

AMORY IS RESENTFUL

Slowly and inevitably, yet with a sudden surge at the last, while Amory talked and dreamed, war rolled swiftly up the beach and washed the sands where Princeton played. Every night the gymnasium echoed as platoon after platoon swept over the floor and shuffled out the basket-ball markings. When Amory went to Washington the next week-end he caught some of the spirit of crisis which changed to repulsion in the Pullman car coming back, for the berths across from him were occupied by stinking aliens—Greeks, he guessed, or Russians. He thought how much easier patriotism had been to a homogeneous race, how much easier it would have been to fight as the Colonies fought, or as the Confederacy fought. And he did no sleeping that night, but listened to the aliens guffaw and snore while they filled the car with the heavy scent of latest America.

In Princeton every one bantered in public and told themselves privately that their deaths at least would be heroic. The literary students read Rupert Brooke passionately; the lounge-lizards worried over whether the government would permit the English-cut uniform for officers; a few of the hopelessly lazy wrote to the obscure branches of the War Department, seeking an easy commission and a soft berth.

Then, after a week, Amory saw Burne and knew at once that argument would be futile—Burne had come out as a pacifist. The socialist magazines, a great smattering of Tolstoi, and his own intense longing for a cause that would bring out whatever strength lay in him, had finally decided him to preach peace as a subjective ideal.

"When the German army entered Belgium," he began, "if the inhabitants had gone peaceably about their business, the German army would have been disorganized in——"

"I know," Amory interrupted, "I've heard it all. But I'm not going to talk propaganda with you. There's a chance that you're right—but even so we're hundreds of years before the time when non-resistance can touch us as a reality."

"But, Amory, listen——"

"Burne, we'd just argue——"

"Very well."

"Just one thing—I don't ask you to think of your family or friends, because I know they don't count a picayune with you beside your sense of duty—but, Burne, how do you know that the magazines you read and the societies you join and these idealists you meet aren't just plain *German*?"

"Some of them are, of course."

"How do you know they aren't *all* pro-German—just a lot of weak ones—with German-Jewish names."

"That's the chance, of course," he said slowly. "How much or how little I'm taking this stand because of propaganda I've heard, I don't know; naturally I think that it's my most innermost conviction—it seems a path spread before me just now."

Amory's heart sank.

"But think of the cheapness of it—no one's really going to martyr you for being a pacifist—it's just going to throw you in with the worst——"

"I doubt it," he interrupted.

"Well, it all smells of Bohemian New York to me."

"I know what you mean, and that's why I'm not sure I'll agitate."

"You're one man, Burne—going to talk to people who won't listen—with all God's given you."

"That's what Stephen must have thought many years ago. But he preached his sermon and they killed him. He probably thought as he was dying what a waste it all was. But you see, I've always felt that Stephen's death was the thing that occurred to Paul on the road to Damascus, and sent him to preach the word of Christ all over the world."

"Go on."

"That's all—this is my particular duty. Even if right now I'm just a pawn—just sacrificed. God! Amory— you don't think *I* like the Germans!"

"Well, I can't say anything else—I get to the end of all the logic about non-resistance, and there, like an excluded middle, stands the huge spectre of man as he is and always will be. And this spectre stands right beside the one logical necessity of Tolstoi's, and the other logical necessity of Nietzsche's—" Amory broke off suddenly. "When are you going?"

"I'm going next week."

"I'll see you, of course."

As he walked away it seemed to Amory that the look in his face bore a great resemblance to that in Kerry's when he had said good-by under Blair Arch two years before. Amory wondered unhappily why he could never go into anything with the primal honesty of those two.

"Burne's a fanatic," he said to Tom, "and he's dead wrong and, I'm inclined to think, just an unconscious pawn in the hands of anarchistic publishers and German-paid rag wavers—but he haunts me—just leaving everything worth while——"

Burne left in a quietly dramatic manner a week later. He sold all his possessions and came down to the room to say good-by, with a battered old bicycle, on which he intended to ride to his home in Pennsylvania.

"Peter the Hermit bidding farewell to Cardinal Richelieu," suggested Alec, who was lounging in the window-seat as Burne and Amory shook hands.

But Amory was not in the mood for that, and as he saw Burne's long legs propel his ridiculous bicycle out of sight beyond Alexander Hall, he knew he was going to have a bad week. Not that he doubted the war—Germany stood for everything repugnant to him; for materialism and the direction of tremendous licentious force; it was just that Burne's face stayed in his memory and he was sick of the hysteria he was beginning to hear.

"What on earth is the use of suddenly running down Goethe," he declared to Alec and Tom. "Why write books to prove he started the war—or that that stupid, overestimated Schiller is a demon in disguise?"

"Have you ever read anything of theirs?" asked Tom shrewdly.

"No," Amory admitted.

"Neither have I," he said laughing.

"People will shout," said Alec quietly, "but Goethe's on his same old shelf in the library—to bore any one that wants to read him!"

Amory subsided, and the subject dropped.

"What are you going to do, Amory?"

"Infantry or aviation, I can't make up my mind—I hate mechanics, but then of course aviation's the thing for me——"

"I feel as Amory does," said Tom. "Infantry or aviation—aviation sounds like the romantic side of the war, of course—like cavalry used to be, you know; but like Amory I don't know a horsepower from a piston-rod."

Somehow Amory's dissatisfaction with his lack of enthusiasm culminated in an attempt to put the blame for the whole war on the ancestors of his generation ... all the people who cheered for Germany in 1870. ... All the materialists rampant, all the idolizers of German science and efficiency. So he sat one day in an English lecture and heard "Locksley Hall" quoted and fell into a brown study with contempt for Tennyson and all he stood for—for he took him as a representative of the Victorians.

> Victorians, Victorians, who never learned to weep
> Who sowed the bitter harvest that your children go to
> reap——

scribbled Amory in his note-book. The lecture was saying something about Tennyson's solidity and fifty heads were bent to take notes. Amory turned over to a fresh page and began scrawling again.

> They shuddered when they found what Mr. Darwin was
> about,
> They shuddered when the waltz came in and Newman
> hurried out——

But the waltz came in much earlier; he crossed that out. "And entitled *A Song in the Time of Order*," came the professor's voice, droning far away. "Time of Order"— Good Lord! Everything crammed in the box and the Victorians sitting on the lid smiling serenely.... With Browning in his Italian villa crying bravely: "All's for the best." Amory scribbled again.

> You knelt up in the temple and he bent to hear you pray,
> You thanked him for your "glorious gains"—reproached
> him for "Cathay."

Why could he never get more than a couplet at a time? Now he needed something to rhyme with:

> You would keep Him straight with science, tho He had
> gone wrong before ...

Well, anyway....

> You met your children in your home—"I've fixed it
> up!" you cried,
> Took your fifty years of Europe, and then virtuously—
> died.

"That was to a great extent Tennyson's idea," came the lecturer's voice. "Swinburne's *Song in the Time of*

Order might well have been Tennyson's title. He idealized order against chaos, against waste."

At last Amory had it. He turned over another page and scrawled vigorously for the twenty minutes that was left of the hour. Then he walked up to the desk and deposited a page torn out of his note-book.

"Here's a poem to the Victorians, sir," he said coldly.

The professor picked it up curiously while Amory backed rapidly through the door.

Here is what he had written:

> Songs in the time of order
>   You left for us to sing,
>   Proofs with excluded middles,
>   Answers to life in rhyme,
> Keys of the prison warder
>   And ancient bells to ring,
>   Time was the end of riddles,
>   We were the end of time . . .
>
> Here were domestic oceans
>   And a sky that we might reach,
>   Guns and a guarded border,
>   Gantlets—but not to fling,
> Thousands of old emotions
>   And a platitude for each,
>   Songs in the time of order—
>   And tongues, that we might sing.

THE END OF MANY THINGS

Early April slipped by in a haze—a haze of long evenings on the club veranda with the graphophone playing "Poor Butterfly" inside . . . for "Poor Butterfly" had been the song of that last year. The war seemed scarcely to touch them and it might have been one of the senior springs of the past, except for the drilling every other afternoon, yet Amory realized poignantly that this was the last spring under the old régime.

"This is the great protest against the superman," said Amory.

"I suppose so," Alec agreed.

"He's absolutely irreconcilable with any Utopia. As long as he occurs, there's trouble and all the latent evil that makes a crowd list and sway when he talks."

"And of course all that he is is a gifted man without a moral sense."

"That's all. I think the worst thing to contemplate is this—it's all happened before, how soon will it happen again? Fifty years after Waterloo Napoleon was as much a hero to English school children as Wellington. How do we know our grandchildren won't idolize Von Hindenburg the same way?"

"What brings it about?"

"Time, damn it, and the historian. If we could only learn to look on evil *as* evil, whether it's clothed in filth or monotony or magnificence."

"God! Haven't we raked the universe over the coals for four years?"

Then the night came that was to be the last. Tom and Amory, bound in the morning for different training-camps, paced the shadowy walks as usual and seemed still to see around them the faces of the men they knew.

"The grass is full of ghosts tonight."

"The whole campus is alive with them."

They paused by Little and watched the moon rise, to make silver of the slate roof of Dodd and blue the rustling trees.

"You know," whispered Tom, "what we feel now is the sense of all the gorgeous youth that has rioted through here in two hundred years."

A last burst of singing flooded up from Blair Arch—broken voices for some long parting.

"And what we leave here is more than this class; it's the whole heritage of youth. We're just one generation—we're breaking all the links that seemed to bind us here to top-booted and high-stocked generations. We've walked arm and arm with Burr and Light-Horse Harry Lee through half these deep-blue nights."

"That's what they are," Tom tangented off, "deep blue—a bit of color would spoil them, make them exotic. Spires, against a sky that's a promise of dawn, and blue light on the slate roofs—it hurts . . . rather——"

"Good-by, Aaron Burr," Amory called toward deserted Nassau Hall, "you and I knew strange corners of life."

His voice echoed in the stillness.

"The torches are out," whispered Tom. "Ah, Messalina, the long shadows are building minarets on the stadium——"

For an instant the voices of freshman year surged around them and then they looked at each other with faint tears in their eyes.

"Damn!"

"Damn!"

The last light fades and drifts across the land—the low, long land, the sunny land of spires; the ghosts of evening tune again their lyres and wander singing in a plaintive band down the long corridors of trees; pale fires echo the night from tower top to tower: Oh, sleep that dreams, and dream that never tires, press from the petals of the lotus flower something of this to keep, the essence of an hour.

No more to wait the twilight of the moon in this sequestered vale of star and spire, for one eternal morning of desire passes to time and earthly afternoon. Here, Heraclitus, did you find in fire and shifting things the prophecy you hurled down the dead years; this midnight my desire will see, shadowed among the embers, furled in flame, the splendor and the sadness of the world.

INTERLUDE

May, 1917—
February, 1919

A letter dated January, 1918, written by Monsignor Darcy to Amory, who is a second lieutenant in the 171st Infantry, Port of Embarkation, Camp Mills, Long Island.

MY DEAR BOY:—

All you need tell me of yourself is that you still are; for the rest I merely search back in a restive memory, a thermometer that records only fevers, and match you with what I was at your age. But men will chatter and you and I will still shout our futilities to each other across the stage until the last silly curtain falls plump! upon our bobbing heads. But you are starting the spluttering magic-lantern show of life with much the same array of slides as I had, so I need to write you if only to shriek the colossal stupidity of people. . . .

This is the end of one thing: for better or worse you will never again be quite the Amory Blaine that I knew, never again will we meet as we have met, because your generation is growing hard, much harder than mine ever grew, nourished as they were on the stuff of the nineties.

Amory, lately I reread Æschylus and there in the divine irony of the "Agamemnon" I find the only answer to this bitter age—all the world tumbled about our ears, and the closest parallel ages back in that hopeless resignation. There are times when I think of the men out there as Roman legionaries, miles from their corrupt city, stemming back the hordes . . . hordes a little more menacing, after all, than the corrupt city . . . another blind blow at the race, furies that we passed with ovations years ago, over whose corpses we bleated triumphantly all through the Victorian era. . . .

And afterward an out-and-out materialistic world—

and the Catholic Church. I wonder where you'll fit in. Of one thing I'm sure—Celtic you'll live and Celtic you'll die; so if you don't use heaven as a continual referendum for your ideas you'll find earth a continual recall to your ambitions.

Amory, I've discovered suddenly that I'm an old man. Like all old men, I've had dreams sometimes and I'm going to tell you of them. I've enjoyed imagining that you were my son, that perhaps when I was young I went into a state of coma and begat you, and when I came to, had no recollection of it . . . it's the paternal instinct, Amory—celibacy goes deeper than the flesh. . . .

Sometimes I think that the explanation of our deep resemblance is some common ancestor, and I find that the only blood that the Darcys and the O'Haras have in common is that of the O'Donahues . . . Stephen was his name, I think. . . .

When the lightning strikes one of us it strikes both: you had hardly arrived at the port of embarkation when I got my papers to start for Rome, and I am waiting every moment to be told where to take ship. Even before you get this letter I shall be on the ocean; then will come your turn. You went to war as a gentleman should, just as you went to school and college, because it was the thing to do. It's better to leave the blustering and tremulo-heroism to the middle classes; they do it so much better.

Do you remember that week-end last March when you brought Burne Holiday from Princeton to see me? What a magnificent boy he is! It gave me a frightful shock afterward when you wrote that he thought me splendid; how could he be so deceived? Splendid is the one thing that neither you nor I are. We are many other things—we're extraordinary, we're clever, we could be said, I suppose, to be brilliant. We can attract people, we can make atmosphere, we can almost lose our Celtic souls in Celtic subtleties, we can almost always have our own way; but splendid—rather not!

I am going to Rome with a wonderful dossier and letters of introduction that cover every capital in Europe, and there will be "no small stir" when I get there. How I wish you were with me! This sounds like a rather cynical paragraph, not at all the sort of thing that a middle-aged clergyman should write to a youth about to depart

for the war; the only excuse is that the middle-aged clergyman is talking to himself. There are deep things in us
and you know what they are as well as I do. We have
great faith, though yours at present is uncrystallized; we
have a terrible honesty that all our sophistry cannot de-
stroy and, above all, a childlike simplicity that keeps us
from ever being really malicious.

I have written a keen for you which follows. I am sorry
your cheeks are not up to the description I have written of
them, but you will smoke and read all night—

At any rate here it is:

A Lament for a Foster Son, and He Going to the War
          Against the King of Foreign.

Ochone
He is gone from me the son of my mind
    And he in his golden youth like Angus Oge
Angus of the bright birds
    And his mind strong and subtle like the mind of Cuchulin
    on Muirtheme.

Awirra sthrue
His brow is as white as the milk of the cows of Maeve
    And his cheeks like the cherries of the tree
And it bending down to Mary and she feeding the Son of
    God.

Aveelia Vrone
His hair is like the golden collar of the Kings at Tara
    And his eyes like the four gray seas of Erin.
And they swept with the mists of rain.

Mavrone go Gudyo
He to be in the joyful and red battle
    Amongst the chieftains and they doing great deeds of
    valor
His life to go from him
    It is the chords of my own soul would be loosed.

A Vich Deelish
My heart is in the heart of my son
    And my life is in his life surely
A man can be twice young
    In the life of his sons only.

Jia du Vaha Alanav
May the Son of God be above him and beneath him, before
    him and behind him
  May the King of the elements cast a mist over the eyes
      of the King of Foreign,
May the Queen of the Graces lead him by the hand the way
      he can go through the midst of his enemies and they
      not seeing him

May Patrick of the Gael and Collumb of the Churches and
      the five thousand Saints of Erin be better than a shield
      to him
And he got into the fight.
  Och Ochone.

Amory—Amory—I feel, somehow, that this is all; one or
both of us is not going to last out this war. . . . I've been trying
to tell you how much this reincarnation of myself in you has
meant in the last few years . . . curiously alike we are . . . curiously unlike.

  Good-by, dear boy, and God be with you.

                                        THAYER DARCY.

EMBARKING AT NIGHT

Amory moved forward on the deck until he found a
stool under an electric light. He searched in his pocket
for note-book and pencil and then began to write,
slowly, laboriously:

  We leave tonight . . .
    Silent, we filled the still, deserted street,
      A column of dim gray,
    And ghosts rose startled at the muffled beat
      Along the moonless way;
    The shadowy shipyards echoed to the feet
      That turned from night and day.

    And so we linger on the windless decks,
      See on the spectre shore
    Shades of a thousand days, poor gray-ribbed
      wrecks . . .

Oh, shall we then deplore
Those futile years!
See how the sea is white!
The clouds have broken and the heavens burn
To hollow highways, paved with gravelled light
The churning of the waves about the stern
Rises to one voluminous nocturne,
. . . We leave tonight.

A letter from Amory, headed "Brest, January 11th, 1919," to Lieutenant T. P. D'Invilliers, Camp Gordon, Ga.

DEAR BAUDELAIRE:—

We meet in Manhattan on the 30th of this very mo.; we then proceed to take a very sporty apartment, you and I and Alec, who is at me elbow as I write. I don't know what I'm going to do but I have a vague dream of going into politics. Why is it that the pick of the young Englishmen from Oxford and Cambridge go into politics and in the U.S.A. we leave it to the muckers?—raised in the ward, educated in the assembly and sent to Congress, fat-paunched bundles of corruption, devoid of "both ideas and ideals" as the debaters used to say. Even forty years ago we had good men in politics, but we, we are brought up to pile up a million and "show what we are made of." Sometimes I wish I'd been an Englishman; American life is so damned dumb and stupid and healthy.

Since poor Beatrice died I'll probably have a little money, but very darn little. I can forgive mother almost everything except the fact that in a sudden burst of religiosity toward the end, she left half of what remained to be spent in stained-glass windows and seminary endowments. Mr. Barton, my lawyer, writes me that my thousands are mostly in street railways and that the said Street R.R.s are losing money because of the five-cent fares. Imagine a salary list that gives $350 a month to a man that can't read and write!—yet I believe in it, even though I've seen what was once a sizable fortune melt away between speculation, extravagance, the democratic administration, and the income tax—modern, that's me all over, Mabel.

At any rate we'll have really knock-out rooms—you can get a job on some fashion magazine, and Alec can go into the Zinc Company or whatever it is that his people own—he's looking over my shoulder and he says it's a brass company, but I don't think it matters much, do you? There's probably as much corruption in zinc-made money as brass-made money. As for the well-known Amory, he would write immortal literature if he were sure enough about anything to risk telling any one else about it. There is no more dangerous gift to posterity than a few cleverly turned platitudes.

Tom, why don't you become a Catholic? Of course to be a good one you'd have to give up those violent intrigues you used to tell me about, but you'd write better poetry if you were linked up to tall golden candlesticks and long, even chants, and even if the American priests are rather bourgeois, as Beatrice used to say, still you need only go to the sporty churches, and I'll introduce you to Monsignor Darcy who really is a wonder.

Kerry's death was a blow, so was Jesse's to a certain extent. And I have a great curiosity to know what queer corner of the world has swallowed Burne. Do you suppose he's in prison under some false name? I confess that the war instead of making me orthodox, which is the correct reaction, has made me a passionate agnostic. The Catholic Church has had its wings clipped so often lately that its part was timidly negligible, and they haven't any good writers any more. I'm sick of Chesterton.

I've only discovered one soldier who passed through the much-advertised spiritual crisis, like this fellow, Donald Hankey, and the one I knew was already studying for the ministry, so he was ripe for it. I honestly think that's all pretty much rot, though it seemed to give sentimental comfort to those at home; and may make fathers and mothers appreciate their children. This crisis-inspired religion is rather valueless and fleeting at best. I think four men have discovered Paris to one that discovered God.

But us—you and me and Alec—oh, we'll get a Jap butler and dress for dinner and have wine on the table and lead a contemplative, emotionless life until we decide to use machine-guns with the property owners—or throw bombs with the Bolshevik. God! Tom, I hope something happens. I'm restless as the devil and have a horror of getting fat or falling in love and growing domestic.

The place at Lake Geneva is now for rent but when I

land I'm going West to see Mr. Barton and get some details. Write me care of the Blackstone, Chicago.

S'ever, dear Boswell,
SAMUEL JOHNSON.

BOOK TWO

The Education of
a Personage

1

The Débutante

The time is February. The place is a large, dainty bed-
room in the Connage house on Sixty-eighth Street,
New York. A girl's room: pink walls and curtains and
a pink bedspread on a cream-colored bed. Pink and
cream are the motifs of the room, but the only article
of furniture in full view is a luxurious dressing-table
with a glass top and a three-sided mirror. On the
walls there is an expensive print of "Cherry Ripe," a
few polite dogs by Landseer, and the "King of the
Black Isles," by Maxfield Parrish.
Great disorder consisting of the following items: (1)
seven or eight empty cardboard boxes, with tissue-
paper tongues hanging panting from their mouths; (2)
an assortment of street dresses mingled with their sis-
ters of the evening, all upon the table, all evidently
new; (3) a roll of tulle, which has lost its dignity and
wound itself tortuously around everything in sight,
and (4) upon the two small chairs, a collection of lin-
gerie that beggars description. One would enjoy see-
ing the bill called forth by the finery displayed and
one is possessed by a desire to see the princess for
whose benefit— Look! There's some one! Disappoint-
ment! This is only a maid hunting for something—she
lifts a heap from a chair— Not there; another heap,
the dressing-table, the chiffonier drawers. She brings
to light several beautiful chemises and an amazing
pajama but this does not satisfy her—she goes out.
An indistinguishable mumble from the next room.
Now we are getting warm. This is Alec's mother, Mrs.
Connage, ample, dignified, rouged to the dowager
point and quite worn out. Her lips move significantly

*as she looks for IT. Her search is less thorough than
the maid's but there is a touch of fury in it, that quite
makes up for its sketchiness. She stumbles on the tulle
and her "damn" is quite audible. She retires, empty-
handed.*

*More chatter outside and a girl's voice, a very spoiled
voice, says: "Of all the stupid people——"*

*After a pause a third seeker enters, not she of the
spoiled voice, but a younger edition. This is Cecelia
Connage, sixteen, pretty, shrewd, and constitutionally
good-humored. She is dressed for the evening in a
gown the obvious simplicity of which probably bores
her. She goes to the nearest pile, selects a small pink
garment and holds it up appraisingly.*

CECELIA: Pink?

ROSALIND: *(Outside)* Yes!

CECELIA: *Very* snappy?

ROSALIND: Yes!

CECELIA: I've got it!

> *(She sees herself in the mirror of the dressing-table
> and commences to shimmy enthusiastically.)*

ROSALIND: *(Outside)* What are you doing—trying it
on?

> *(CECELIA ceases and goes out carrying the garment
> at the right shoulder.*
>
> *From the other door, enters ALEC CONNAGE. He
> looks around quickly and in a huge voice shouts:
> Mama! There is a chorus of protest from next
> door and encouraged he starts toward it, but is
> repelled by another chorus.)*

ALEC: So *that's* where you all are! Amory Blaine is
here.

CECELIA: *(Quickly)* Take him down-stairs.

ALEC: Oh, he *is* down-stairs.

MRS. CONNAGE: Well, you can show him where his
room is. Tell him I'm sorry that I can't meet him now.

ALEC: He's heard a lot about you all. I wish you'd
hurry. Father's telling him all about the war and he's
restless. He's sort of temperamental.

> *(This last suffices to draw CECELIA into the room.)*

CECELIA. *(Seating herself high upon lingerie)* How do you mean—temperamental? You used to say that about him in letters.

ALEC: Oh, he writes stuff.

CECELIA: Does he play the piano?

ALEC: Don't think so.

CECELIA: *(Speculatively)* Drink?

ALEC: Yes—nothing queer about him.

CECELIA: Money?

ALEC: Good Lord—ask him, he used to have a lot, and he's got some income now.

(MRS. CONNAGE appears.)

MRS. CONNAGE: Alec, of course we're glad to have any friend of yours——

ALEC: You certainly ought to meet Amory.

MRS. CONNAGE: Of course, I want to. But I think it's so childish of you to leave a perfectly good home to go and live with two other boys in some impossible apartment. I hope it isn't in order that you can all drink as much as you want. *(She pauses.)* He'll be a little neglected tonight. This is Rosalind's week, you see. When a girl comes out, she needs *all* the attention.

ROSALIND: *(Outside)* Well, then prove it by coming here and hooking me.

(MRS. CONNAGE goes.)

ALEC: Rosalind hasn't changed a bit.

CECELIA: *(In a lower tone)* She's awfully spoiled.

ALEC: She'll meet her match tonight.

CECELIA: Who—Mr. Amory Blaine?

(ALEC nods.)

CECELIA: Well, Rosalind has still to meet the man she can't outdistance. Honestly, Alec, she treats men terribly. She abuses them and cuts them and breaks dates with them and yawns in their faces—and they come back for more.

ALEC: They love it.

CECELIA: They hate it. She's a—she's a sort of vampire, I think—and she can make girls do what she wants usually—only she hates girls.

ALEC: Personality runs in our family.

CECELIA: *(Resignedly)* I guess it ran out before it got to me.

ALEC: Does Rosalind behave herself?

CECELIA: Not particularly well. Oh, she's average—smokes sometimes, drinks punch, frequently kissed—Oh, yes—common knowledge—one of the effects of the war, you know.

(Emerges MRS. CONNAGE.)

MRS. CONNAGE: Rosalind's almost finished so I can go down and meet your friend.

(ALEC and his mother go out.)

ROSALIND: *(Outside)* Oh, mother——

CECELIA: Mother's gone down.

(And now ROSALIND enters. ROSALIND is—utterly ROSALIND. She is one of those girls who need never make the slightest effort to have men fall in love with them. Two types of men seldom do: dull men are usually afraid of her cleverness and intellectual men are usually afraid of her beauty. All others are hers by natural prerogative.

If ROSALIND could be spoiled the process would have been complete by this time, and as a matter of fact, her disposition is not all it should be; she wants what she wants when she wants it and she is prone to make every one around her pretty miserable when she doesn't get it—but in the true sense she is not spoiled. Her fresh enthusiasm, her will to grow and learn, her endless faith in the inexhaustibility of romance, her courage and fundamental honesty—these things are not spoiled.

There are long periods when she cordially loathes her whole family. She is quite unprincipled; her philosophy is carpe diem for herself and laissez-faire for others. She loves shocking stories: she has that coarse streak that usually goes with natures that are both fine and big. She wants people to like her, but if they do not it never worries her or changes her.

She is by no means a model character.

The education of all beautiful women is the knowl-

edge of men. ROSALIND *had been disappointed in man after man as individuals, but she had great faith in man as a sex. Women she detested. They represented qualities that she felt and despised in herself—incipient meanness, conceit, cowardice, and petty dishonesty. She once told a roomful of her mother's friends that the only excuse for women was the necessity for a disturbing element among men. She danced exceptionally well, drew cleverly but hastily, and had a startling facility with words, which she used only in love-letters.*

But all criticism of ROSALIND *ends in her beauty. There was that shade of glorious yellow hair, the desire to imitate which supports the dye industry. There was the eternal kissable mouth, small, slightly sensual, and utterly disturbing. There were gray eyes and an unimpeachable skin with two spots of vanishing color. She was slender and athletic, without underdevelopment, and it was a delight to watch her move about a room, walk along a street, swing a golf club, or turn a "cart-wheel."*

A last qualification—her vivid, instant personality escaped that conscious, theatrical quality that AMORY *had found in* ISABELLE. MONSIGNOR DARCY *would have been quite up a tree whether to call her a personality or a personage. She was perhaps the delicious, inexpressible, once-in-a-century blend.*

On the night of her début she is, for all her strange, stray wisdom, quite like a happy little girl. Her mother's maid has just done her hair, but she has decided impatiently that she can do a better job herself. She is too nervous just now to stay in one place. To that we owe her presence in this littered room. She is going to speak. ISABELLE'S *alto tones had been like a violin, but if you could hear* ROSALIND, *you would say her voice was musical as a waterfall.*

ROSALIND: Honestly, there are only two costumes in

the world that I really enjoy being in— *(Combing her hair at the dressing-table.)* One's a hoop skirt with pantaloons; the other's a one-piece bathing-suit. I'm quite charming in both of them.

CECELIA: Glad you're coming out?

ROSALIND: Yes; aren't you?

CECELIA: *(Cynically)* You're glad so you can get married and live on Long Island with the *fast younger married set*. You want life to be a chain of flirtation with a man for every link.

ROSALIND: *Want* it to be one! You mean I've *found* it one.

CECELIA: Ha!

ROSALIND: Cecelia, darling, you don't know what a trial it is to be—like me. I've got to keep my face like steel in the street to keep men from winking at me. If I laugh hard from a front row in the theatre, the comedian plays to me for the rest of the evening. If I drop my voice, my eyes, my handkerchief at a dance, my partner calls me up on the 'phone every day for a week.

CECELIA: It must be an awful strain.

ROSALIND: The unfortunate part is that the only men who interest me at all are the totally ineligible ones. Now—if I were poor I'd go on the stage.

CECELIA: Yes, you might as well get paid for the amount of acting you do.

ROSALIND: Sometimes when I've felt particularly radiant I've thought, why should this be wasted on one man?

CECELIA: Often when you're particularly sulky, I've wondered why it should all be wasted on just one family. *(Getting up.)* I think I'll go down and meet Mr. Amory Blaine. I like temperamental men.

ROSALIND: There aren't any. Men don't know how to be really angry or really happy—and the ones that do, go to pieces.

CECELIA: Well, I'm glad I don't have all your worries. I'm engaged.

ROSALIND: *(With a scornful smile)* Engaged? Why, you little lunatic! If mother heard you talking like that she'd send you off to boarding school, where you belong.

CECELIA: You won't tell her, though, because I know things I could tell—and you're too selfish!

ROSALIND: *(A little annoyed)* Run along, little girl! Who are you engaged to, the iceman? the man that keeps the candy-store?

CECELIA: Cheap wit—good-by, darling, I'll see you later.

ROSALIND: Oh, be *sure* and do that—you're *such* a help.

> *(Exit CECELIA. ROSALIND finishes her hair and rises, humming. She goes up to the mirror and starts to dance in front of it on the soft carpet. She watches not her feet, but her eyes—never casually but always intently, even when she smiles. The door suddenly opens and then slams behind* AMORY, *very cool and handsome as usual. He melts into instant confusion.)*

HE: Oh, I'm sorry. I thought——

SHE: *(Smiling radiantly)* Oh, you're Amory Blaine, aren't you?

HE: *(Regarding her closely)* And you're Rosalind?

SHE: I'm going to call you Amory—oh, come in—it's all right—mother'll be right in—*(under her breath)* unfortunately.

HE: *(Gazing around)* This is sort of a new wrinkle for me.

SHE: This is No Man's Land.

HE: This is where you—you—*(pause)*

SHE: Yes—all those things. *(She crosses to the bureau.)* See, here's my rouge—eye pencils.

HE: I didn't know you were that way.

SHE: What did you expect?

HE: I thought you'd be sort of—sort of—sexless, you know, swim and play golf.

SHE: Oh, I do—but not in business hours.

HE: Business?

SHE: Six to two—strictly.

HE: I'd like to have some stock in the corporation.

SHE: Oh, it's not a corporation—it's just "Rosalind,

Unlimited." Fifty-one shares, name, good-will, and everything goes at $25,000 a year.

HE: *(Disapprovingly)* Sort of a chilly proposition.

SHE: Well, Amory, you don't mind—do you? When I meet a man that doesn't bore me to death after two weeks, perhaps it'll be different.

HE: Odd, you have the same point of view on men that I have on women.

SHE: I'm not really feminine, you know—in my mind.

HE: *(Interested)* Go on.

SHE: No, you—you go on—you've made me talk about myself. That's against the rules.

HE: Rules?

SHE: My own rules—but you— Oh, Amory, I hear you're brilliant. The family expects *so* much of you.

HE: How encouraging!

SHE: Alec said you'd taught him to think. Did you? I didn't believe any one could.

HE: No. I'm really quite dull.

　　(He evidently doesn't intend this to be taken seriously.)

SHE: Liar.

HE: I'm—I'm religious—I'm literary. I've—I've even written poems.

SHE: Vers libre—splendid! *(She declaims.)*

> The trees are green,
> The birds are singing in the trees,
> The girl sips her poison
> The bird flies away the girl dies.

HE: *(Laughing)* No, not that kind.

SHE: *(Suddenly)* I like you.

HE: Don't.

SHE: Modest too——

HE: I'm afraid of you. I'm always afraid of a girl—until I've kissed her.

SHE: *(Emphatically)* My dear boy, the war is over.

HE: So I'll always be afraid of you.

SHE: *(Rather sadly)* I suppose you will.

　　(A slight hesitation on both their parts.)

He: *(After due consideration)* Listen. This is a frightful thing to ask.

She: *(Knowing what's coming)* After five minutes.

He: But will you—kiss me? Or are you afraid?

She: I'm never afraid—but your reasons are so poor.

He: Rosalind, I really *want* to kiss you.

She: So do I.

    (They kiss— definitely and thoroughly.)

He: *(After a breathless second)* Well, is your curiosity satisfied?

She: Is yours?

He: No, it's only aroused.

    (He looks it.)

She: *(Dreamily)* I've kissed dozens of men. I suppose I'll kiss dozens more.

He: *(Abstractedly)* Yes, I suppose you could—like that.

She: Most people like the way I kiss.

He: *(Remembering himself)* Good Lord, yes. Kiss me once more, Rosalind.

She: No—my curiosity is generally satisfied at one.

He: *(Discouraged)* Is that a rule?

She: I make rules to fit the cases.

He: You and I are somewhat alike—except that I'm years older in experience.

She: How old are you?

He: Almost twenty-three. You?

She: Nineteen—just.

He: I suppose you're the product of a fashionable school.

She: No—I'm fairly raw material. I was expelled from Spence—I've forgotten why.

He: What's your general trend?

She: Oh, I'm bright, quite selfish, emotional when aroused, fond of admiration——

He: *(Suddenly)* I don't want to fall in love with you——

She: *(Raising her eyebrows)* Nobody asked you to.

He: *(Continuing coldly)* But I probably will. I love your mouth.

She: Hush! Please don't fall in love with my mouth—

hair, eyes, shoulders, slippers—but *not* my mouth. Everybody falls in love with my mouth.

HE: It's quite beautiful.

SHE: It's too small.

HE: No it isn't—let's see.

(He kisses her again with the same thoroughness.)

SHE: *(Rather moved)* Say something sweet.

HE: *(Frightened)* Lord help me.

SHE: *(Drawing away)* Well, don't—if it's so hard.

HE: Shall we pretend? So soon?

SHE: We haven't the same standards of time as other people.

HE: Already it's—other people.

SHE: Let's pretend.

HE: No—I can't—it's sentiment.

SHE: You're not sentimental?

HE: No, I'm romantic—a sentimental person thinks things will last—a romantic person hopes against hope that they won't. Sentiment is emotional.

SHE: And you're not? *(With her eyes half-closed.)* You probably flatter yourself that that's a superior attitude.

HE: Well—Rosalind, Rosalind, don't argue—kiss me again.

SHE: *(Quite chilly now)* No—I have no desire to kiss you.

HE: *(Openly taken aback)* You wanted to kiss me a minute ago.

SHE: This is now.

HE: I'd better go.

SHE: I suppose so.

(He goes toward the door.)

SHE: Oh!

(He turns.)

SHE: *(Laughing)* Score—Home Team: One hundred—Opponents: Zero.

(He starts back.)

SHE: *(Quickly)* Rain—no game.

(He goes out.)

(She goes quietly to the chiffonier, takes out a cigarette-case and hides it in the side drawer of a desk. Her mother enters, note-book in hand.)

MRS. CONNAGE: Good—I've been wanting to speak to you alone before we go down-stairs.

ROSALIND: Heavens! you frighten me!

MRS. CONNAGE: Rosalind, you've been a very expensive proposition.

ROSALIND: (*Resignedly*) Yes.

MRS. CONNAGE: And you know your father hasn't what he once had.

ROSALIND: (*Making a wry face*) Oh, please don't talk about money.

MRS. CONNAGE: You can't do anything without it. This is our last year in this house—and unless things change Cecelia won't have the advantages you've had.

ROSALIND: (*Impatiently*) Well—what is it?

MRS. CONNAGE: So I ask you to please mind me in several things I've put down in my note-book. The first one is: don't disappear with young men. There may be a time when it's valuable, but at present I want you on the dance-floor where I can find you. There are certain men I want to have you meet and I don't like finding you in some corner of the conservatory exchanging silliness with any one—or listening to it.

ROSALIND: (*Sarcastically*) Yes, listening to it *is* better.

MRS. CONNAGE: And don't waste a lot of time with the college set—little boys nineteen and twenty years old. I don't mind a prom or a football game, but staying away from advantageous parties to eat in little cafés down-town with Tom, Dick, and Harry——

ROSALIND: (*Offering her code, which is, in its way, quite as high as her mother's*) Mother, it's done—you can't run everything now the way you did in the early nineties.

MRS. CONNAGE: (*Paying no attention*) There are several bachelor friends of your father's that I want you to meet tonight—youngish men.

ROSALIND: (*Nodding wisely*) About forty-five?

MRS. CONNAGE: (*Sharply*) Why not?

ROSALIND: Oh, *quite* all right—they know life and are so adorably tired looking (*shakes her head*)—but they *will* dance.

MRS. CONNAGE: I haven't met Mr. Blaine—but I don't

think you'll care for him. He doesn't sound like a money-maker.

ROSALIND: Mother, I never *think* about money.

MRS. CONNAGE: You never keep it long enough to think about it.

ROSALIND: *(Sighs)* Yes, I suppose some day I'll marry a ton of it—out of sheer boredom.

MRS. CONNAGE: *(Referring to note-book)* I had a wire from Hartford. Dawson Ryder is coming up. Now there's a young man I like, and he's floating in money. It seems to me that since you seem tired of Howard Gillespie you might give Mr. Ryder some encouragement. This is the third time he's been up in a month.

ROSALIND: How did you know I was tired of Howard Gillespie?

MRS. CONNAGE: The poor boy looks so miserable every time he comes.

ROSALIND: That was one of those romantic, pre-battle affairs. They're all wrong.

MRS. CONNAGE: *(Her say said)* At any rate, make us proud of you tonight.

ROSALIND: Don't you think I'm beautiful?

MRS. CONNAGE: You know you are.

(From down-stairs is heard the moan of a violin being tuned, the roll of a drum. MRS. CONNAGE turns quickly to her daughter.)

MRS. CONNAGE: Come!

ROSALIND: One minute!

(Her mother leaves. ROSALIND goes to the glass where she gazes at herself with great satisfaction. She kisses her hand and touches her mirrored mouth with it. Then she turns out the lights and leaves the room. Silence for a moment. A few chords from the piano, the discreet patter of faint drums, the rustle of new silk, all blend on the staircase outside and drift in through the partly opened door. Bundled figures pass in the lighted hall. The laughter heard below becomes doubled and multiplied. Then some one comes in, closes the door, and switches on the lights. It is CECELIA. She goes to the chiffonier, looks in the

drawers, hesitates—then to the desk whence she takes the cigarette-case and extracts one. She lights it and then, puffing and blowing, walks toward the mirror.)

CECELIA: *(In tremendously sophisticated accents)* Oh, yes, coming out is *such* a farce nowadays, you know. One really plays around so much before one is seventeen, that it's positively anticlimax. *(Shaking hands with a visionary middle-aged nobleman.)* Yes, your grace—I b'lieve I've heard my sister speak of you. Have a puff—they're very good. They're—they're Coronas. You don't smoke? What a pity! The king doesn't allow it, I suppose. Yes, I'll dance.

(So she dances around the room to a tune from downstairs, her arms outstretched to an imaginary partner, the cigarette waving in her hand.)

SEVERAL HOURS LATER

The corner of a den down-stairs, filled by a very comfortable leather lounge. A small light is on each side above, and in the middle, over the couch hangs a painting of a very old, very dignified gentleman, period 1860. Outside the music is heard in a fox-trot.

ROSALIND *is seated on the lounge and on her left is* HOWARD GILLESPIE, *a vapid youth of about twenty-four. He is obviously very unhappy, and she is quite bored.*

GILLESPIE: *(Feebly)* What do you mean I've changed. I feel the same toward you.

ROSALIND: But you don't look the same to me.

GILLESPIE: Three weeks ago you used to say that you liked me because I was so blasé, so indifferent—I still am.

ROSALIND: But not about me. I used to like you because you had brown eyes and thin legs.

GILLESPIE: *(Helplessly)* They're still thin and brown. You're a vampire, that's all.

ROSALIND: The only thing I know about vamping is what's on the piano score. What confuses men is that

I'm perfectly natural. I used to think you were never jealous. Now you follow me with your eyes wherever I go.

GILLESPIE: I love you.

ROSALIND: *(Coldly)* I know it.

GILLESPIE: And you haven't kissed me for two weeks. I had an idea that after a girl was kissed she was—was—won.

ROSALIND: Those days are over. I have to be won all over again every time you see me.

GILLESPIE: Are you serious?

ROSALIND: About as usual. There used to be two kinds of kisses: First when girls were kissed and deserted; second, when they were engaged. Now there's a third kind, where the man is kissed and deserted. If Mr. Jones of the nineties bragged he'd kissed a girl, every one knew he was through with her. If Mr. Jones of 1919 brags the same every one knows it's because he can't kiss her any more. Given a decent start any girl can beat a man nowadays.

GILLESPIE: Then why do you play with men?

ROSALIND: *(Leaning forward confidentially)* For that first moment, when he's interested. There is a moment—Oh, just before the first kiss, a whispered word—something that makes it worth while.

GILLESPIE: And then?

ROSALIND: Then after that you make him talk about himself. Pretty soon he thinks of nothing but being alone with you—he sulks, he won't fight, he doesn't want to play— Victory!

(Enter DAWSON RYDER, twenty-six, handsome, wealthy, faithful to his own, a bore perhaps, but steady and sure of success.)

RYDER: I believe this is my dance, Rosalind.

ROSALIND: Well, Dawson, so you recognize me. Now I know I haven't got too much paint on. Mr. Ryder, this is Mr. Gillespie.

(They shake hands and GILLESPIE leaves, tremendously downcast.)

RYDER: Your party is certainly a success.

ROSALIND: Is it—I haven't seen it lately. I'm weary— Do you mind sitting out a minute?

RYDER: Mind—I'm delighted. You know I loathe this "rushing" idea. See a girl yesterday, today, tomorrow.

ROSALIND: Dawson!

RYDER: What?

ROSALIND: I wonder if you know you love me.

RYDER: *(Startled)* What— Oh—you know you're remarkable!

ROSALIND: Because you know I'm an awful proposition. Any one who marries me will have his hands full. I'm mean—mighty mean.

RYDER: Oh, I wouldn't say that.

ROSALIND: Oh, yes, I am—especially to the people nearest to me. *(She rises.)* Come, let's go. I've changed my mind and I want to dance. Mother is probably having a fit.

(Exeunt. Enter ALEC *and* CECELIA.*)*

CECELIA: Just my luck to get my own brother for an intermission.

ALEC: *(Gloomily)* I'll go if you want me to.

CECELIA: Good heavens, no—with whom would I begin the next dance? *(Sighs.)* There's no color in a dance since the French officers went back.

ALEC: *(Thoughtfully)* I don't want Amory to fall in love with Rosalind.

CECELIA: Why, I had an idea that that was just what you did want.

ALEC: I did, but since seeing these girls—I don't know. I'm awfully attached to Amory. He's sensitive and I don't want him to break his heart over somebody who doesn't care about him.

CECELIA: He's very good looking.

ALEC: *(Still thoughtfully)* She won't marry him, but a girl doesn't have to marry a man to break his heart.

CECELIA: What does it? I wish I knew the secret.

ALEC: Why, you cold-blooded little kitty. It's lucky for some that the Lord gave you a pug nose.

(Enter MRS. CONNAGE.*)*

MRS. CONNAGE: Where on earth is Rosalind?

ALEC: *(Brilliantly)* Of course you've come to the best people to find out. She'd naturally be with us.

MRS. CONNAGE: Her father has marshalled eight bachelor millionaires to meet her.

ALEC: You might form a squad and march through the halls.

MRS. CONNAGE: I'm perfectly serious—for all I know she may be at the Cocoanut Grove with some football player on the night of her début. You look left and I'll——

ALEC: *(Flippantly)* Hadn't you better send the butler through the cellar?

MRS. CONNAGE: *(Perfectly serious)* Oh, you don't think she'd be there?

CECELIA: He's only joking, mother.

ALEC: Mother had a picture of her tapping a keg of beer with some high hurdler.

MRS. CONNAGE: Let's look right away.

(They go out. ROSALIND *comes in with* GILLESPIE.*)*

GILLESPIE: Rosalind—Once more I ask you. Don't you care a blessed thing about me?

*(*AMORY *walks in briskly.)*

AMORY: My dance.

ROSALIND: Mr. Gillespie, this is Mr. Blaine.

GILLESPIE: I've met Mr. Blaine. From Lake Geneva, aren't you?

AMORY: Yes.

GILLESPIE: *(Desperately)* I've been there. It's in the—the Middle West, isn't it?

AMORY: *(Spicily)* Approximately. But I always felt that I'd rather be provincial hot-tamale than soup without seasoning.

GILLESPIE: What!

AMORY: Oh, no offense.

*(*GILLESPIE *bows and leaves.)*

ROSALIND: He's too much *people.*

AMORY: I was in love with a *people* once.

ROSALIND: So?

AMORY: Oh, yes—her name was Isabelle—nothing at all to her except what I read into her.

ROSALIND: What happened?

AMORY: Finally I convinced her that she was smarter than I was—then she threw me over. Said I was critical and impractical, you know.

ROSALIND: What do you mean impractical?

AMORY: Oh—drive a car, but can't change a tire.

ROSALIND: What are you going to do?

AMORY: Can't say—run for President, write——

ROSALIND: Greenwich Village?

AMORY: Good heavens, no—I said write—not drink.

ROSALIND: I like business men. Clever men are usually so homely.

AMORY: I feel as if I'd known you for ages.

ROSALIND: Oh, are you going to commence the "pyramid" story?

AMORY: No—I was going to make it French. I was Louis XIV and you were one of my—my— *(Changing his tone.)* Suppose—we fell in love.

ROSALIND: I've suggested pretending.

AMORY: If we did it would be very big.

ROSALIND: Why?

AMORY: Because selfish people are in a way terribly capable of great loves.

ROSALIND: *(Turning her lips up)* Pretend.

(Very deliberately they kiss.)

AMORY: I can't say sweet things. But you *are* beautiful.

ROSALIND: Not that.

AMORY: What then?

ROSALIND: *(Sadly)* Oh, nothing—only I want sentiment, real sentiment—and I never find it.

AMORY: I never find anything else in the world—and I loathe it.

ROSALIND: It's so hard to find a male to gratify one's artistic taste.

(Some one has opened a door and the music of a waltz surges into the room. ROSALIND rises.)

ROSALIND: Listen! they're playing "Kiss Me Again."

(He looks at her)

AMORY: Well?

ROSALIND: Well?

AMORY: *(Softly—the battle lost)* I love you.

ROSALIND: I love you—now.
(They kiss.)
AMORY: Oh, God, what have I done?
ROSALIND: Nothing. Oh, don't talk. Kiss me again.
AMORY: I don't know why or how, but I love you—
from the moment I saw you.
ROSALIND: Me too—I—I—oh, tonight's tonight.
(Her brother strolls in, starts and then in a loud
voice says: "Oh, excuse me," and goes.)
ROSALIND: *(Her lips scarcely stirring)* Don't let me
go—I don't care who knows what I do.
AMORY: Say it!
ROSALIND: I love you—now. *(They part.)* Oh—I am
very youthful, thank God—and rather beautiful, thank
God—and happy, thank God, thank God— *(She pauses*
and then, in an odd burst of prophecy, adds) Poor
Amory!
(He kisses her again.)

KISMET

Within two weeks Amory and Rosalind were deeply
and passionately in love. The critical qualities which
had spoiled for each of them a dozen romances were
dulled by the great wave of emotion that washed over
them.

"It may be an insane love-affair," she told her anxious
mother, "but it's not inane."

The wave swept Amory into an advertising agency
early in March, where he alternated between astonishing
bursts of rather exceptional work and wild dreams of becoming suddenly rich and touring Italy with Rosalind.

They were together constantly, for lunch, for dinner,
and nearly every evening—always in a sort of breathless
hush, as if they feared that any minute the spell would
break and drop them out of this paradise of rose and
flame. But the spell became a trance, seemed to increase
from day to day; they began to talk of marrying in
July—in June. All life was transmitted into terms of

their love, all experience, all desires, all ambitions, were nullified—their senses of humor crawled into corners of sleep; their former love-affairs seemed faintly laughable and scarcely regretted juvenilia.

For the second time in his life Amory had had a complete bouleversement and was hurrying into line with his generation.

A LITTLE INTERLUDE

Amory wandered slowly up the avenue and thought of the night as inevitably his—the pageantry and carnival of rich dusk and dim streets ... it seemed that he had closed the book of fading harmonies at last and stepped into the sensuous vibrant walks of life. Everywhere these countless lights, this promise of a night of streets and singing—he moved in a half-dream through the crowd as if expecting to meet Rosalind hurrying toward him with eager feet from every corner.... How the unforgettable faces of dusk would blend to hers, the myriad footsteps, a thousand overtures, would blend to her footsteps; and there would be more drunkenness than wine in the softness of her eyes on his. Even his dreams now were faint violins drifting like summer sounds upon the summer air.

The room was in darkness except for the faint glow of Tom's cigarette where he lounged by the open window. As the door shut behind him, Amory stood a moment with his back against it.

"Hello, Benvenuto Blaine. How went the advertising business today?"

Amory sprawled on a couch.

"I loathed it as usual!" The momentary vision of the bustling agency was displaced quickly by another picture.

"My God! She's wonderful!"

Tom sighed.

"I can't tell you," repeated Amory, "just how wonderful she is. I don't want you to know. I don't want any one to know."

Another sigh came from the window—quite a resigned sigh.

"She's life and hope and happiness, my whole world now."

He felt the quiver of a tear on his eyelid.

"Oh, *Golly,* Tom!"

BITTER SWEET

"Sit like we do," she whispered.

He sat in the big chair and held out his arms so that she could nestle inside them.

"I knew you'd come tonight," she said softly, "like summer, just when I needed you most ... darling ... darling ..."

His lips moved lazily over her face.

"You *taste* so good," he sighed.

"How do you mean, lover?"

"Oh, just sweet, just sweet ..." He held her closer.

"Amory," she whispered, "when you're ready for me I'll marry you."

"We won't have much at first."

"Don't!" she cried. "It hurts when you reproach yourself for what you can't give me. I've got your precious self—and that's enough for me."

"Tell me ..."

"You know, don't you? Oh, you know."

"Yes, but I want to hear you say it."

"I love you, Amory, with all my heart."

"Always, will you?"

"All my life— Oh, Amory——"

"What?"

"I want to belong to you. I want your people to be my people. I want to have your babies."

"But I haven't any people."

"Don't laugh at me, Amory. Just kiss me."

"I'll do what you want," he said.

"No, I'll do what *you* want. We're *you*—not me. Oh, you're so much a part, so much all of me . . ."

He closed his eyes.

"I'm so happy that I'm frightened. Wouldn't it be awful if this was—was the high point? . . ."

She looked at him dreamily.

"Beauty and love pass, I know. . . . Oh, there's sadness, too. I suppose all great happiness is a little sad. Beauty means the scent of roses and then the death of roses——"

"Beauty means the agony of sacrifice and the end of agony. . . ."

"And, Amory, we're beautiful, I know. I'm sure God loves us——"

"He loves you. You're his most precious possession."

"I'm not his, I'm yours. Amory, I belong to you. For the first time I regret all the other kisses; now I know how much a kiss can mean."

Then they would smoke and he would tell her about his day at the office—and where they might live. Sometimes, when he was particularly loquacious, she went to sleep in his arms, but he loved that Rosalind—all Rosalinds—as he had never in the world loved any one else. Intangibly fleeting, unrememberable hours.

AQUATIC INCIDENT

One day Amory and Howard Gillespie meeting by accident down-town took lunch together, and Amory heard a story that delighted him. Gillespie after several cocktails was in a talkative mood; he began by telling Amory that he was sure Rosalind was slightly eccentric.

He had gone with her on a swimming party up in Westchester County, and some one mentioned that Annette Kellerman had been there one day on a visit and had dived from the top of the rickety, thirty-foot summer-house. Immediately Rosalind insisted that Howard should climb up with her to see what it looked like.

A minute later, as he sat and dangled his feet on the

edge, a form shot by him; Rosalind, her arms spread in a beautiful swan dive, had sailed through the air into the clear water.

"Of course *I* had to go, after that—and I nearly killed myself. I thought I was pretty good to even try it. Nobody else in the party tried it. Well, afterward Rosalind had the nerve to ask me why I stooped over when I dove. 'It didn't make it any easier,' she said, 'it just took all the courage out of it.' I ask you, what can a man do with a girl like that? Unnecessary, I call it."

Gillespie failed to understand why Amory was smiling delightedly all through lunch. He thought perhaps he was one of these hollow optimists.

FIVE WEEKS LATER

Again the library of the Connage house. ROSALIND *is alone, sitting on the lounge staring very moodily and unhappily at nothing. She has changed perceptibly—she is a trifle thinner for one thing; the light in her eyes is not so bright; she looks easily a year older. Her mother comes in, muffled in an opera-cloak. She takes in* ROSALIND *with a nervous glance.*

MRS. CONNAGE: Who is coming tonight?

   (ROSALIND *fails to hear her, at least takes no notice.*)

MRS. CONNAGE: Alec is coming up to take me to this Barrie play, "Et tu, Brutus." *(She perceives that she is talking to herself.)* Rosalind! I asked you who is coming tonight?

ROSALIND: *(Starting)* Oh—what—oh—Amory——

MRS. CONNAGE: *(Sarcastically)* You have so *many* admirers lately that I couldn't imagine *which* one. (ROSALIND *doesn't answer.*) Dawson Ryder is more patient than I thought he'd be. You haven't given him an evening this week.

ROSALIND: *(With a very weary expression that is quite new to her face.)* Mother—please——

MRS. CONNAGE: Oh, *I* won't interfere. You've already

wasted over two months on a theoretical genius who hasn't a penny to his name, but *go* ahead, waste your life on him. *I* won't interfere.

ROSALIND: *(As if repeating a tiresome lesson)* You know he has a little income—and you know he's earning thirty-five dollars a week in advertising——

MRS. CONNAGE: And it wouldn't buy your clothes. *(She pauses but* ROSALIND *makes no reply.)* I have your best interests at heart when I tell you not to take a step you'll spend your days regretting. It's not as if your father could help you. Things have been hard for him lately and he's an old man. You'd be dependent absolutely on a dreamer, a nice, well-born boy, but a dreamer—merely *clever. (She implies that this quality in itself is rather vicious.)*

ROSALIND: For heaven's sake, mother——

(A maid appears, announces Mr. Blaine who follows immediately. AMORY'S *friends have been telling him for ten days that he "looks like the wrath of God," and he does. As a matter of fact he has not been able to eat a mouthful in the last thirty-six hours.)*

AMORY: Good evening, Mrs. Connage.

MRS. CONNAGE: *(Not unkindly)* Good evening, Amory.

(AMORY and ROSALIND exchange glances—and ALEC comes in. ALEC'S attitude throughout has been neutral. He believes in his heart that the marriage would make AMORY mediocre and ROSALIND miserable, but he feels a great sympathy for both of them.)

ALEC: Hi, Amory!

AMORY: Hi, Alec! Tom said he'd meet you at the theatre.

ALEC: Yeah, just saw him. How's the advertising today? Write some brilliant copy?

AMORY: Oh, it's about the same. I got a raise—*(Every one looks at him rather eagerly)*—of two dollars a week. *(General collapse.)*

MRS. CONNAGE: Come, Alec, I hear the car.

(A good night, rather chilly in sections. After MRS. CONNAGE *and* ALEC *go out there is a pause.*

ROSALIND *still stares moodily at the fireplace.*
AMORY *goes to her and puts his arm around her.*)
AMORY: Darling girl.

(They kiss. Another pause and then she seizes his hand, covers it with kisses and holds it to her breast.)

ROSALIND: *(Sadly)* I love your hands, more than anything. I see them often when you're away from me—so tired; I know every line of them. Dear hands!

(Their eyes meet for a second and then she begins to cry—a tearless sobbing.)

AMORY: Rosalind!

ROSALIND: Oh, we're so darned pitiful!

AMORY: Rosalind!

ROSALIND: Oh, I want to die!

AMORY: Rosalind, another night of this and I'll go to pieces. You've been this way four days now. You've got to be more encouraging or I can't work or eat or sleep. *(He looks around helplessly as if searching for new words to clothe an old, shop-worn phrase.)* We'll have to make a start. I *like* having to make a start together. *(His forced hopefulness fades as he sees her unresponsive.)* What's the matter? *(He gets up suddenly and starts to pace the floor.)* It's Dawson Ryder, that's what it is. He's been working on your nerves. You've been with him every afternoon for a week. People come and tell me they've seen you together, and I have to smile and nod and pretend it hasn't the slightest significance for me. And you won't tell me anything as it develops.

ROSALIND: Amory, if you don't sit down I'll scream.

AMORY: *(Sitting down suddenly beside her)* Oh, Lord.

ROSALIND: *(Taking his hand gently)* You know I love you, don't you?

AMORY: Yes.

ROSALIND: You know I'll always love you——

AMORY: Don't talk that way; you frighten me. It sounds as if we weren't going to have each other. *(She cries a little and rising from the couch goes to the armchair.)* I've felt all afternoon that things were worse. I nearly went wild down at the office—couldn't write a line. Tell me everything.

ROSALIND: There's nothing to tell, I say. I'm just nervous.

AMORY: Rosalind, you're playing with the idea of marrying Dawson Ryder.

ROSALIND: *(After a pause)* He's been asking me to all day.

AMORY: Well, he's got his nerve!

ROSALIND: *(After another pause)* I like him.

AMORY: Don't say that. It hurts me.

ROSALIND: Don't be a silly idiot. You know you're the only man I've ever loved, ever will love.

AMORY: *(Quickly)* Rosalind, let's get married—next week.

ROSALIND: We can't.

AMORY: Why not?

ROSALIND: Oh, we can't. I'd be your squaw—in some horrible place.

AMORY: We'll have two hundred and seventy-five dollars a month all told.

ROSALIND: Darling, I don't even do my own hair, usually.

AMORY: I'll do it for you.

ROSALIND: *(Between a laugh and a sob)* Thanks.

AMORY: Rosalind, you *can't* be thinking of marrying some one else. Tell me! You leave me in the dark. I can help you fight it out if you'll only tell me.

ROSALIND: It's just—us. We're pitiful, that's all. The very qualities I love you for are the ones that will always make you a failure.

AMORY: *(Grimly)* Go on.

ROSALIND: Oh—it *is* Dawson Ryder. He's so reliable, I almost feel that he'd be a—a background.

AMORY: You don't love him.

ROSALIND: I know, but I respect him, and he's a good man and a strong one.

AMORY: *(Grudgingly)* Yes—he's that.

ROSALIND: Well—here's one little thing. There was a little poor boy we met in Rye Tuesday afternoon—and, oh, Dawson took him on his lap and talked to him and promised him an Indian suit—and next day he remembered and bought it—and, oh, it was so sweet and I couldn't help thinking he'd be so nice to—to our children—take care of them—and I wouldn't have to worry.

AMORY: *(In despair)* Rosalind! Rosalind!

ROSALIND: *(With a faint roguishness)* Don't look so consciously suffering.

AMORY: What power we have of hurting each other!

ROSALIND: *(Commencing to sob again)* It's been so perfect—you and I. So like a dream that I'd longed for and never thought I'd find. The first real unselfishness I've ever felt in my life. And I can't see it fade out in a colorless atmosphere!

AMORY: It won't—it won't!

ROSALIND: I'd rather keep it as a beautiful memory—tucked away in my heart.

AMORY: Yes, women can do that—but not men. I'd remember always, not the beauty of it while it lasted, but just the bitterness, the long bitterness.

ROSALIND: Don't!

AMORY: All the years never to see you, never to kiss you, just a gate shut and barred—you don't dare be my wife.

ROSALIND: No—no—I'm taking the hardest course, the strongest course. Marrying you would be a failure and I never fail—if you don't stop walking up and down I'll scream!

(Again he sinks despairingly onto the lounge.)

AMORY: Come over here and kiss me.

ROSALIND: No.

AMORY: Don't you *want* to kiss me?

ROSALIND: Tonight I want you to love me calmly and coolly.

AMORY: The beginning of the end.

ROSALIND: *(With a burst of insight)* Amory, you're young. I'm young. People excuse us now for our poses and vanities, for treating people like Sancho and yet getting away with it. They excuse us now. But you've got a lot of knocks coming to you——

AMORY: And you're afraid to take them with me.

ROSALIND: No, not that. There was a poem I read

somewhere—you'll say Ella Wheeler Wilcox and laugh—but listen:

> For this is wisdom—to love and live,
> To take what fate or the gods may give,
> To ask no question, to make no prayer,
> To kiss the lips and caress the hair,
> Speed passion's ebb as we greet its flow,
> To have and to hold, and, in time—let go.

AMORY: But we haven't had.

ROSALIND: Amory, I'm yours—you know it. There have been times in the last month I'd have been completely yours if you'd said so. But I can't marry you and ruin both our lives.

AMORY: We've got to take our chance for happiness.

ROSALIND: Dawson says I'd learn to love him.

(AMORY with his head sunk in his hands does not move. The life seems suddenly gone out of him.)

ROSALIND: Lover! Lover! I can't do with you, and I can't imagine life without you.

AMORY: Rosalind, we're on each other's nerves. It's just that we're both high-strung, and this week——

(His voice is curiously old. She crosses to him and taking his face in her hands, kisses him.)

ROSALIND: I can't, Amory. I can't be shut away from the trees and flowers, cooped up in a little flat, waiting for you. You'd hate me in a narrow atmosphere. I'd make you hate me.

(Again she is blinded by sudden uncontrolled tears.)

AMORY: Rosalind——

ROSALIND: Oh, darling, go— Don't make it harder! I can't stand it——

AMORY: *(His face drawn, his voice strained)* Do you know what you're saying? Do you mean forever?

(There is a difference somehow in the quality of their suffering.)

ROSALIND: Can't you see——

AMORY: I'm afraid I can't if you love me. You're afraid of taking two years' knocks with me.

ROSALIND: I wouldn't be the Rosalind you love.

AMORY: *(A little hysterically)* I can't give you up! I can't, that's all! I've got to have you!

ROSALIND: *(A hard note in her voice)* You're being a baby now.

AMORY: *(Wildly)* I don't care! You're spoiling our lives!

ROSALIND: I'm doing the wise thing, the only thing.

AMORY: Are you going to marry Dawson Ryder?

ROSALIND: Oh, don't ask me. You know I'm old in some ways—in others—well, I'm just a little girl. I like sunshine and pretty things and cheerfulness—and I dread responsibility. I don't want to think about pots and kitchens and brooms. I want to worry whether my legs will get slick and brown when I swim in the summer.

AMORY: And you love me.

ROSALIND: That's just why it has to end. Drifting hurts too much. We can't have any more scenes like this.

(She draws his ring from her finger and hands it to him. Their eyes blind again with tears.)

AMORY: *(His lips against her wet cheek)* Don't! Keep it, please—oh, don't break my heart!

(She presses the ring softly into his hand.)

ROSALIND: *(Brokenly)* You'd better go.

AMORY: Good-by——

(She looks at him once more, with infinite longing, infinite sadness.)

ROSALIND: Don't ever forget me, Amory——

AMORY: Good-by——

(He goes to the door, fumbles for the knob, finds it—she sees him throw back his head—and he is gone. Gone—she half starts from the lounge and then sinks forward on her face into the pillows.)

ROSALIND: Oh, God, I want to die! *(After a moment she rises and with her eyes closed feels her way to the door. Then she turns and looks once more at the room. Here they had sat and dreamed: that tray she had so often filled with matches for him; that shade that they had discreetly lowered one long Sunday afternoon. Misty-*

eyed she stands and remembers; she speaks aloud.) Oh,
Amory, what have I done to you?

> *(And deep under the aching sadness that will pass
> in time, Rosalind feels that she has lost some-
> thing, she knows not what, she knows not why.)*

2

Experiments in Convalescence

THE Knickerbocker Bar, beamed upon by Maxfield Parrish's jovial, colorful "Old King Cole," was well crowded. Amory stopped in the entrance and looked at his wrist-watch; he wanted particularly to know the time, for something in his mind that catalogued and classified liked to chip things off cleanly. Later it would satisfy him in a vague way to be able to think "that thing ended at exactly twenty minutes after eight on Thursday, June 10, 1919." This was allowing for the walk from her house—a walk concerning which he had afterward not the faintest recollection.

He was in rather grotesque condition: two days of worry and nervousness, of sleepless nights, of untouched meals, culminating in the emotional crisis and Rosalind's abrupt decision—the strain of it had drugged the foreground of his mind into a merciful coma. As he fumbled clumsily with the olives at the free-lunch table, a man approached and spoke to him, and the olives dropped from his nervous hands.

"Well, Amory . . ."

It was some one he had known at Princeton; he had no idea of the name.

"Hello, old boy—" he heard himself saying.

"Name's Jim Wilson—you've forgotten."

"Sure, you bet, Jim. I remember."

"Going to reunion?"

"You know!" Simultaneously he realized that he was not going to reunion.

"Get overseas?"

Amory nodded, his eyes staring oddly. Stepping back

to let some one pass, he knocked the dish of olives to a crash on the floor.

"Too bad," he muttered. "Have a drink?"

Wilson, ponderously diplomatic, reached over and slapped him on the back.

"You've had plenty, old boy."

Amory eyed him dumbly until Wilson grew embarrassed under the scrutiny.

"Plenty, hell!" said Amory finally. "I haven't had a drink to-day."

Wilson looked incredulous.

"Have a drink or not?" cried Amory rudely.

Together they sought the bar.

"Rye high."

"I'll just take a Bronx."

Wilson had another; Amory had several more. They decided to sit down. At ten o'clock Wilson was displaced by Carling, class of '15. Amory, his head spinning gorgeously, layer upon layer of soft satisfaction setting over the bruised spots of his spirit, was discoursing volubly on the war.

"'S a mental was'e," he insisted with owl-like wisdom. "Two years my life spent inalleshual vacuity. Los' idealism, got be physical anmal," he shook his fist expressively at Old King Cole, "got be Prussian 'bout ev'thing, women 'specially. Use' be straight 'bout women college. Now don' givadam." He expressed his lack of principle by sweeping a seltzer bottle with a broad gesture to noisy extinction on the floor, but this did not interrupt his speech. "Seek pleasure where find it for tomorrow die. 'At's philos'phy for me now on."

Carling yawned, but Amory, waxing brilliant, continued:

"Use' wonder 'bout things—people satisfied compromise, fif'y-fif'y att'tude on life. Now don' wonder, don' wonder—" He became so emphatic in impressing on Carling the fact that he didn't wonder that he lost the thread of his discourse and concluded by announcing to the bar at large that he was a "physcal anmal."

"What are you celebrating, Amory?"

Amory leaned forward confidentially.

"Cel'brating blowmylife. Great moment blow my life. Can't tell you 'bout it——"

He heard Carling addressing a remark to the bartender:

"Give him a bromo-seltzer."

Amory shook his head indignantly.

"None that stuff!"

"But listen, Amory, you're making yourself sick. You're white as a ghost."

Amory considered the question. He tried to look at himself in the mirror but even by squinting up one eye could only see as far as the row of bottles behind the bar.

"Like som'n solid. We go get some—some salad."

He settled his coat with an attempt at nonchalance, but letting go of the bar was too much for him, and he slumped against a chair.

"We'll go over to Shanley's," suggested Carling, offering an elbow.

With this assistance Amory managed to get his legs in motion enough to propel him across Forty-second Street.

Shanley's was very dim. He was conscious that he was talking in a loud voice, very succinctly and convincingly, he thought, about a desire to crush people under his heel. He consumed three club sandwiches, devouring each as though it were no larger than a chocolate-drop. Then Rosalind began popping into his mind again, and he found his lips forming her name over and over. Next he was sleepy, and he had a hazy, listless sense of people in dress suits, probably waiters, gathering around the table. . . .

. . . He was in a room and Carling was saying something about a knot in his shoe-lace.

"Nemmine," he managed to articulate drowsily. "Sleep in 'em. . . ."

STILL ALCOHOLIC

He awoke laughing and his eyes lazily roamed his surroundings, evidently a bedroom and bath in a good hotel. His head was whirring and picture after picture was forming and blurring and melting before his eyes, but beyond the desire to laugh he had no entirely conscious reaction. He reached for the 'phone beside his bed.

"Hello—what hotel is this—?

"Knickerbocker? All right, send up two rye highballs——"

He lay for a moment and wondered idly whether they'd send up a bottle or just two of those little glass containers. Then, with an effort, he struggled, out of bed and ambled into the bathroom.

When he emerged, rubbing himself lazily with a towel, he found the bar boy with the drinks and had a sudden desire to kid him. On reflection he decided that this would be undignified, so he waved him away.

As the new alcohol tumbled into his stomach and warmed him, the isolated pictures began slowly to form a cinema reel of the day before. Again he saw Rosalind curled weeping among the pillows, again he felt her tears against his cheek. Her words began ringing in his ears: "Don't ever forget me, Amory—don't ever forget me——"

"Hell!" he faltered aloud, and then he choked and collapsed on the bed in a shaken spasm of grief. After a minute he opened his eyes and regarded the ceiling.

"Damned fool!" he exclaimed in disgust, and with a voluminous sigh rose and approached the bottle. After another glass he gave way loosely to the luxury of tears. Purposely he called up into his mind little incidents of the vanished spring, phrased to himself emotions that would make him react even more strongly to sorrow.

"We were so happy," he intoned dramatically, "so very happy." Then he gave way again and knelt beside the bed, his head half-buried in the pillow.

"My own girl—my own— Oh——"

He clenched his teeth so that the tears streamed in a flood from his eyes.

"Oh . . . my baby girl, all I had, all I wanted! . . . Oh, my girl, come back, come back! I need you . . . need you . . . we're so pitiful . . . just misery we brought each other. . . . She'll be shut away from me. . . . I can't see her; I can't be her friend. It's got to be that way—it's got to be——"

And then again:

"We've been so happy, so very happy. . . ."

He rose to his feet and threw himself on the bed in an ecstasy of sentiment, and then lay exhausted while he realized slowly that he had been very drunk the night before, and that his head was spinning again wildly. He laughed, rose, and crossed again to Lethe. . . .

At noon he ran into a crowd in the Biltmore bar, and the riot began again. He had a vague recollection afterward of discussing French poetry with a British officer who was introduced to him as "Captain Corn, of his Majesty's Foot," and he remembered attempting to recite "Clair de Lune" at luncheon; then he slept in a big, soft chair until almost five o'clock when another crowd found and woke him; there followed an alcoholic dressing of several temperaments for the ordeal of dinner. They selected theatre tickets at Tyson's for a play that had a four-drink programme—a play with two monotonous voices, with turbid, gloomy scenes, and lighting effects that were hard to follow when his eyes behaved so amazingly. He imagined afterward that it must have been "The Jest.". . .

. . . Then the Cocoanut Grove, where Amory slept again on a little balcony outside. Out in Shanley's, Yonkers, he became almost logical, and by a careful control of the number of high-balls he drank, grew quite lucid and garrulous. He found that the party consisted of five men, two of whom he knew slightly; he became righteous about paying his share of the expense and insisted in a loud voice on arranging everything then and there to the amusement of the tables around him. . . .

Some one mentioned that a famous cabaret star was at the next table, so Amory rose and, approaching gallantly, introduced himself . . . this involved him in an argument, first with her escort and then with the headwaiter—Amory's attitude being a lofty and exaggerated courtesy . . . he consented, after being confronted with irrefutable logic, to being led back to his own table.

"Decided to commit suicide," he announced suddenly.

"When? Next year?"

"Now. Tomorrow morning. Going to take a room at the Commodore, get into a hot bath and open a vein."

"He's getting morbid!"

"You need another rye, old boy!"

"We'll all talk it over tomorrow."

But Amory was not to be dissuaded, from argument at least.

"Did you ever get that way?" he demanded confidentially fortaccio.

"Sure!"

"Often?"

"My chronic state."

This provoked discussion. One man said that he got so depressed sometimes that he seriously considered it. Another agreed that there was nothing to live for. "Captain Corn," who had somehow rejoined the party, said that in his opinion it was when one's health was bad that one felt that way most. Amory's suggestion was that they should each order a Bronx, mix broken glass in it, and drink it off. To his relief no one applauded the idea, so having finished his high-ball, he balanced his chin in his hand and his elbow on the table—a most delicate, scarcely noticeable sleeping position, he assured himself—and went into a deep stupor. . . .

He was awakened by a woman clinging to him, a pretty woman, with brown, disarranged hair and dark blue eyes.

"Take me home!" she cried.

"Hello!" said Amory, blinking.

"I like you," she announced tenderly.

"I like you too."

He noticed that there was a noisy man in the background and that one of his party was arguing with him.

"Fella I was with's a damn fool," confided the blue-eyed woman. "I hate him. I want to go home with you."

"You drunk?" queried Amory with intense wisdom.

She nodded coyly.

"Go home with him," he advised gravely. "He brought you."

At this point the noisy man in the background broke away from his detainers and approached.

"Say!" he said fiercely. "I brought this girl out here and you're butting in!"

Amory regarded him coldly, while the girl clung to him closer.

"You let go that girl!" cried the noisy man.

Amory tried to make his eyes threatening.

"You go to hell!" he directed finally, and turned his attention to the girl.

"Love first sight," he suggested.

"I love you," she breathed and nestled close to him. She *did* have beautiful eyes.

Some one leaned over and spoke in Amory's ear.

"That's just Margaret Diamond. She's drunk and this fellow here brought her. Better let her go."

"Let him take care of her, then!" shouted Amory furiously. "I'm no W.Y.C.A. worker, am I?—am I?"

"Let her go!"

"It's *her* hanging on, damn it! Let her hang!"

The crowd around the table thickened. For an instant a brawl threatened, but a sleek waiter bent back Margaret Diamond's fingers until she released her hold on Amory, whereupon she slapped the waiter furiously in the face and flung her arms about her raging original escort.

"Oh, Lord!" cried Amory.

"Let's go!"

"Come on, the taxis are getting scarce!"

"Check, waiter."

"C'mon, Amory. Your romance is over."

Amory laughed.

"You don't know how true you spoke. No idea. 'At's the whole trouble."

AMORY ON THE LABOR QUESTION

Two mornings later he knocked at the president's door at Bascome and Barlow's advertising agency.

"Come in!"

Amory entered unsteadily.

" 'Morning, Mr. Barlow."

Mr. Barlow brought his glasses to the inspection and set his mouth slightly ajar that he might better listen.

"Well, Mr. Blaine. We haven't seen you for several days."

"No," said Amory. "I'm quitting."

"Well—well—this is——"

"I don't like it here."

"I'm sorry. I thought our relations had been quite—ah—pleasant. You seemed to be a hard worker—a little inclined perhaps to write fancy copy——"

"I just got tired of it," interrupted Amory rudely. "It didn't matter a damn to me whether Harebell's flour was any better than any one else's. In fact, I never ate any of it. So I got tired of telling people about it—oh, I know I've been drinking——"

Mr. Barlow's face steeled by several ingots of expression.

"You asked for a position——"

Amory waved him to silence.

"And I think I was rottenly underpaid. Thirty-five dollars a week—less than a good carpenter."

"You had just started. You'd never worked before," said Mr. Barlow coolly.

"But it took about ten thousand dollars to educate me where I could write your darned stuff for you. Anyway, as far as length of service goes, you've got stenographers here you've paid fifteen a week for five years."

"I'm not going to argue with you, sir," said Mr. Barlow rising.

"Neither am I. I just wanted to tell you I'm quitting."

They stood for a moment looking at each other impassively and then Amory turned and left the office.

A LITTLE LULL

Four days after that he returned at last to the apartment. Tom was engaged on a book review for *The New Democracy* on the staff of which he was employed. They regarded each other for a moment in silence.

"Well?"

"Well?"

"Good Lord, Amory, where'd you get the black eye—and the jaw?"

Amory laughed.

"That's a mere nothing."

He peeled off his coat and bared his shoulders.

"Look here!"

Tom emitted a low whistle.

"What hit you?"

Amory laughed again.

"Oh, a lot of people. I got beaten up. Fact." He slowly replaced his shirt. "It was bound to come sooner or later and I wouldn't have missed it for anything."

"Who was it?"

"Well, there were some waiters and a couple of sailors and a few stray pedestrians, I guess. It's the strangest feeling. You ought to get beaten up just for the experience of it. You fall down after a while and everybody sort of slashes in at you before you hit the ground—then they kick you."

Tom lighted a cigarette.

"I spent a day chasing you all over town, Amory. But you always kept a little ahead of me. I'd say you've been on some party."

Amory tumbled into a chair and asked for a cigarette.

"You sober now?" asked Tom quizzically.

"Pretty sober. Why?"

"Well, Alec has left. His family had been after him to go home and live, so he——"

A spasm of pain shook Amory.

"Too bad."

"Yes, it is too bad. We'll have to get some one else if we're going to stay here. The rent's going up."

"Sure. Get anybody. I'll leave it to you, Tom."

Amory walked into his bedroom. The first thing that met his glance was a photograph of Rosalind that he had intended to have framed, propped up against a mirror on his dresser. He looked at it unmoved. After the vivid mental pictures of her that were his portion at present, the portrait was curiously unreal. He went back into the study.

"Got a cardboard box?"

"No," answered Tom, puzzled. "Why should I have? Oh, yes—there may be one in Alec's room."

Eventually Amory found what he was looking for and, returning to his dresser, opened a drawer full of letters, notes, part of a chain, two little handkerchiefs, and some snap-shots. As he transferred them carefully to the box his mind wandered to some place in a book where the hero, after preserving for a year a cake of his lost love's soap, finally washed his hands with it. He laughed and began to hum "After you've gone" . . . ceased abruptly . . .

The string broke twice, and then he managed to secure it, dropped the package into the bottom of his trunk, and having slammed the lid returned to the study.

"Going out?" Tom's voice held an undertone of anxiety.

"Uh-huh."

"Where?"

"Couldn't say, old keed."

"Let's have dinner together."

"Sorry. I told Sukey Brett I'd eat with him."

"Oh."

"By-by."

Amory crossed the street and had a high-ball; then he walked to Washington Square and found a top seat on a bus. He disembarked at Forty-third Street and strolled to the Biltmore bar.

"Hi, Amory!"

"What'll you have?"

"Yoho! Waiter!"

TEMPERATURE NORMAL

The advent of prohibition with the "thirsty-first" put a sudden stop to the submerging of Amory's sorrows, and when he awoke one morning to find that the old bar-to-bar days were over, he had neither remorse for the past three weeks nor regret that their repetition was impossible. He had taken the most violent, if the weakest, method to shield himself from the stabs of memory, and while it was not a course he would have prescribed for others, he found in the end that it had done its business: he was over the first flush of pain.

Don't misunderstand! Amory had loved Rosalind as he would never love another living person. She had taken the first flush of his youth and brought from his unplumbed depths tenderness that had surprised him, gentleness and unselfishness that he had never given to another creature. He had later love-affairs, but of a different sort: in those he went back to that, perhaps, more typical frame of mind, in which the girl became the mirror of a mood in him. Rosalind had drawn out what was more than passionate admiration; he had a deep, undying affection for Rosalind.

But there had been, near the end, so much dramatic tragedy, culminating in the arabesque nightmare of his three weeks' spree, that he was emotionally worn out. The people and surroundings that he remembered as being cool or delicately artificial, seemed to promise him a refuge. He wrote a cynical story which featured his father's funeral and despatched it to a magazine, receiving in return a check for sixty dollars and a request for more of the same tone. This tickled his vanity, but inspired him to no further effort.

He read enormously. He was puzzled and depressed by "A Portrait of the Artist as a Young Man"; intensely interested by "Joan and Peter" and "The Undying Fire," and rather surprised by his discovery through a critic named Mencken of several excellent American novels: "Vandover and the Brute," "The Damnation of Theron Ware," and "Jennie Gerhardt." Mackenzie, Chesterton,

Galsworthy, Bennett, had sunk in his appreciation from sagacious, life-saturated geniuses to merely diverting contemporaries. Shaw's aloof clarity and brilliant consistency and the gloriously intoxicated efforts of H. G. Wells to fit the key of romantic symmetry into the elusive lock of truth, alone won his rapt attention.

He wanted to see Monsignor Darcy, to whom he had written when he landed, but he had not heard from him; besides he knew that a visit to Monsignor would entail the story of Rosalind, and the thought of repeating it turned him cold with horror.

In his search for cool people he remembered Mrs. Lawrence, a very intelligent, very dignified lady, a convert to the church, and a great devotee of Monsignor's.

He called her on the 'phone one day. Yes, she remembered him perfectly; no, Monsignor wasn't in town, was in Boston she thought; he'd promised to come to dinner when he returned. Couldn't Amory take luncheon with her?

"I thought I'd better catch up, Mrs. Lawrence," he said rather ambiguously when he arrived.

"Monsignor was here just last week," said Mrs. Lawrence regretfully. "He was very anxious to see you, but he'd left your address at home."

"Did he think I'd plunged into Bolshevism?" asked Amory, interested.

"Oh, he's having a frightful time."

"Why?"

"About the Irish Republic. He thinks it lacks dignity."

"So?"

"He went to Boston when the Irish President arrived and he was greatly distressed because the receiving committee, when they rode in an automobile, *would* put their arms around the President."

"I don't blame him."

"Well, what impressed you more than anything while you were in the army? You look a great deal older."

"That's from another, more disastrous battle," he answered, smiling in spite of himself. "But the army—let me see—well, I discovered that physical courage depends to a great extent on the physical shape a man is in. I found that I was as brave as the next man—it used to worry me before."

"What else?"

"Well, the idea that men can stand anything if they get used to it, and the fact that I got a high mark in the psychological examination."

Mrs. Lawrence laughed. Amory was finding it a great relief to be in this cool house on Riverside Drive, away from more condensed New York and the sense of people expelling great quantities of breath into a little space. Mrs. Lawrence reminded him vaguely of Beatrice, not in temperament, but in her perfect grace and dignity. The house, its furnishings, the manner in which dinner was served, were in immense contrast to what he had met in the great places on Long Island, where the servants were so obtrusive that they had positively to be bumped out of the way, or even in the houses of more conservative "Union Club" families. He wondered if this air of symmetrical restraint, this grace, which he felt was continental, was distilled through Mrs. Lawrence's New England ancestry or acquired in long residence in Italy or Spain.

Two glasses of sauterne at luncheon loosened his tongue, and he talked, with what he felt was something of his old charm, of religion and literature and the menacing phenomena of the social order. Mrs. Lawrence was ostensibly pleased with him, and her interest was especially in his mind; he wanted people to like his mind again—after a while it might be such a nice place in which to live.

"Monsignor Darcy still thinks that you're his reincarnation, that your faith will eventually clarify."

"Perhaps," he assented. "I'm rather pagan at present. It's just that religion doesn't seem to have the slightest bearing on life at my age."

When he left her house he walked down Riverside Drive with a feeling of satisfaction. It was amusing to discuss again such subjects as this young poet, Stephen Vincent Benét, or the Irish Republic. Between the rancid accusations of Edward Carson and Justice Cohalan he

had completely tired of the Irish question; yet there had
been a time when his own Celtic traits were pillars of
his personal philosophy.

There seemed suddenly to be much left in life, if only
this revival of old interests did not mean that he was
backing away from it again—backing away from life itself.

RESTLESSNESS

"I'm très old and très bored, Tom," said Amory one
day, stretching himself at ease in the comfortable
window-seat. He always felt most natural in a recum-
bent position.

"You used to be entertaining before you started to
write," he continued. "Now you save any idea that you
think would do to print."

Existence had settled back to an ambitionless normal-
ity. They had decided that with economy they could still
afford the apartment, which Tom, with the domesticity
of an elderly cat, had grown fond of. The old English
hunting prints on the wall were Tom's, and the large tapestry by courtesy, a relic of decadent days in college,
and the great profusion of orphaned candlesticks and the
carved Louis XV chair in which no one could sit more
than a minute without acute spinal disorders—Tom
claimed that this was because one was sitting in the lap
of Montespan's wraith—at any rate, it was Tom's furniture that decided them to stay.

They went out very little: to an occasional play, or to
dinner at the Ritz or the Princeton Club. With prohibition the great rendezvous had received their death
wounds; no longer could one wander to the Biltmore bar
at twelve or five and find congenial spirits, and both
Tom and Amory had outgrown the passion for dancing
with mid-Western or New Jersey debbies at the Club-de-
Vingt (nick-named the "Club de Gink") or the Plaza
Rose Room—besides even that required several cocktails "to come down to the intellectual level of the

women present," as Amory had once put it to a horrified matron.

Amory had lately received several alarming letters from Mr. Barton—the Lake Geneva house was too large to be easily rented; the best rent obtainable at present would serve this year to little more than pay for the taxes and necessary improvements; in fact, the lawyer suggested that the whole property was simply a white elephant on Amory's hands. Nevertheless, even though it might not yield a cent for the next three years, Amory decided with a vague sentimentality that for the present, at any rate, he would not sell the house.

This particular day on which he announced his ennui to Tom had been quite typical. He had risen at noon, lunched with Mrs. Lawrence, and then ridden abstractedly homeward atop one of his beloved buses.

"Why shouldn't you be bored," yawned Tom. "Isn't that the conventional frame of mind for the young man of your age and condition?"

"Yes," said Amory speculatively, "but I'm more than bored; I'm restless."

"Love and war did for you."

"Well," Amory considered, "I'm not sure that the war itself had any great effect on either you or me—but it certainly ruined the old backgrounds, sort of killed individualism out of our generation."

Tom looked up in surprise.

"Yes it did," insisted Amory. "I'm not sure it didn't kill it out of the whole world. Oh, Lord, what a pleasure it used to be to dream I might be a really great dictator or writer or religious or political leader—and now even a Leonardo da Vinci or Lorenzo de Medici couldn't be a real old-fashioned bolt in the world. Life is too huge and complex. The world is so overgrown that it can't lift its own fingers, and I was planning to be such an important finger——"

"I don't agree with you," Tom interrupted. "There never were men placed in such egotistic positions since—oh, since the French Revolution."

Amory disagreed violently.

"You're mistaking this period when every nut is an

individualist for a period of individualism. Wilson has only been powerful when he has represented; he's had to compromise over and over again. Just as soon as Trotsky and Lenin take a definite, consistent stand they'll become two-minute figures like Kerensky. Even Foch hasn't half the significance of Stonewall Jackson. War used to be the most individualistic pursuit of man, and yet the popular heroes of the war had neither authority nor responsibility: Guynemer and Sergeant York. How could a schoolboy make a hero of Pershing? A big man has no time really to do anything but just sit and be big."

"Then you don't think there will be any more permanent world heroes?"

"Yes—in history—not in life. Carlyle would have difficulty getting material for a new chapter on 'The Hero as a Big Man.' "

"Go on. I'm a good listener to-day."

"People try so hard to believe in leaders now, pitifully hard. But we no sooner get a popular reformer or politician or soldier or writer or philosopher—a Roosevelt, a Tolstoi, a Wood, a Shaw, a Nietzsche, than the crosscurrents of criticism wash him away. My Lord, no man can stand prominence these days. It's the surest path to obscurity. People get sick of hearing the same name over and over."

"Then you blame it on the press?"

"Absolutely. Look at you; you're on *The New Democracy,* considered the most brilliant weekly in the country, read by the men who do things and all that. What's your business? Why, to be as clever, as interesting, and as brilliantly cynical as possible about every man, doctrine, book, or policy that is assigned you to deal with. The more strong lights, the more spiritual scandal you can throw on the matter, the more money they pay you, the more the people buy the issue. You, Tom d'Invilliers, a blighted Shelley, changing, shifting, clever, unscrupulous, represent the critical consciousness of the race— Oh, don't protest, I know the stuff. I used to write book reviews in college; I considered it rare sport to refer to the latest honest, conscientious effort to propound a theory or a remedy as a 'welcome addition to our light summer reading.' Come on now, admit it."

Tom laughed, and Amory continued triumphantly.

"We *want* to believe. Young students try to believe in older authors, constituents try to believe in their Congressmen, countries try to believe in their statesmen, but they *can't*. Too many voices, too much scattered, illogical, ill-considered criticism. It's worse in the case of newspapers. Any rich, unprogressive old party with that particularly grasping, acquisitive form of mentality known as financial genius can own a paper that is the intellectual meat and drink of thousands of tired, hurried men, men too involved in the business of modern living to swallow anything but predigested food. For two cents the voter buys his politics, prejudices, and philosophy. A year later there is a new political ring or a change in the paper's ownership, consequence: more confusion, more contradiction, a sudden inrush of new ideas, their tempering, their distillation, the reaction against them——"

He paused only to get his breath.

"And that is why I have sworn not to put pen to paper until my ideas either clarify or depart entirely; I have quite enough sins on my soul without putting dangerous, shallow epigrams into people's heads; I might cause a poor, inoffensive capitalist to have a vulgar liaison with a bomb, or get some innocent little Bolshevik tangled up with a machine-gun bullet——"

Tom was growing restless under this lampooning of his connection with *The New Democracy*.

"What's all this got to do with your being bored?"

Amory considered that it had much to do with it.

"How'll I fit in?" he demanded. "What am I for? To propagate the race? According to the American novels we are led to believe that the 'healthy American boy' from nineteen to twenty-five is an entirely sexless animal. As a matter of fact, the healthier he is the less that's true. The only alternative to letting it get you is some violent interest. Well, the war is over; I believe too much in the responsibilities of authorship to write just now; and business, well, business speaks for itself. It has no connection with anything in the world that I've ever been interested in, except a slim, utilitarian connection with economics. What I'd see of it, lost in a clerk-ship, for the next and best ten years of my life would have the intellectual content of an industrial movie."

"Try fiction," suggested Tom.

"Trouble is I get distracted when I start to write stories—get afraid I'm doing it instead of living—get thinking maybe life is waiting for me in the Japanese gardens at the Ritz or at Atlantic City or on the lower East Side.

"Anyway," he continued, "I haven't the vital urge. I wanted to be a regular human being but the girl couldn't see it that way."

"You'll find another."

"God! Banish the thought. Why don't you tell me that 'if the girl had been worth having she'd have waited for you'? No, sir, the girl really worth having won't wait for anybody. If I thought there'd be another I'd lose my remaining faith in human nature. Maybe I'll play—but Rosalind was the only girl in the wide world that could have held me."

"Well," yawned Tom, "I've played confidant a good hour by the clock. Still, I'm glad to see you're beginning to have violent views again on something."

"I am," agreed Amory reluctantly. "Yet when I see a happy family it makes me sick at my stomach——"

"Happy families try to make people feel that way," said Tom cynically.

TOM THE CENSOR

There were days when Amory listened. These were when Tom, wreathed in smoke, indulged in the slaughter of American literature. Words failed him.

"Fifty thousand dollars a year," he would cry. "My God! Look at them, look at them—Edna Ferber, Gouverneur Morris, Fannie Hurst, Mary Roberts Rinehart—not producing among 'em one story or novel that will last ten years. This man Cobb—I don't think he's either clever or amusing—and what's more, I don't think very many people do, except the editors. He's just groggy with advertising. And—oh Harold Bell Wright oh Zane Grey——"

"They try."

"No, they don't even try. Some of them *can* write, but they won't sit down and do one honest novel. Most of them *can't* write, I'll admit. I believe Rupert Hughes tries to give a real, comprehensive picture of American life, but his style and perspective are barbarous. Ernest Poole and Dorothy Canfield try but they're hindered by their absolute lack of any sense of humor; but at least they crowd their work instead of spreading it thin. Every author ought to write every book as if he were going to be beheaded the day he finished it."

"Is that *double entente*?"

"Don't slow me up! Now there's a few of 'em that seem to have some cultural background, some intelligence and a good deal of literary felicity but they just simply won't write honestly; they'd all claim there was no public for good stuff. Then why the devil is it that Wells, Conrad, Galsworthy, Shaw, Bennett, and the rest depend on America for over half their sales?"

"How does little Tommy like the poets?"

Tom was overcome. He dropped his arms until they swung loosely beside the chair and emitted faint grunts.

"I'm writing a satire on 'em now, calling it 'Boston Bards and Hearst Reviewers.' "

"Let's hear it," said Amory eagerly.

"I've only got the last few lines done."

"That's very modern. Let's hear 'em, if they're funny."

Tom produced a folded paper from his pocket and read aloud, pausing at intervals so that Amory could see that it was free verse:

> So
> Walter Arensberg,
> Alfred Kreymborg,
> Carl Sandburg,
> Louis Untermeyer,

Eunice Tietjens,
Clara Shanafelt,
James Oppenheim,
Maxwell Bodenheim,
Richard Glaenzer,
Scharmel Iris,
Conrad Aiken,
I place your names here
So that you may live
If only as names,
Sinuous, mauve-colored names,
In the juvenilia
Of my collected editions.

Amory roared.

"You win the iron pansy. I'll buy you a meal on the arrogance of the last two lines."

Amory did not entirely agree with Tom's sweeping damnation of American novelists and poets. He enjoyed both Vachel Lindsay and Booth Tarkington, and admired the conscientious, if slender, artistry of Edgar Lee Masters.

"What I hate is this idiotic drivel about 'I am God—I am man—I ride the winds—I look through the smoke—I am the life sense.'"

"It's ghastly!"

"And I wish American novelists would give up trying to make business romantically interesting. Nobody wants to read about it, unless it's crooked business. If it was an entertaining subject they'd buy the life of James J. Hill and not one of these long office tragedies that harp along on the significance of smoke——"

"And gloom," said Tom. "That's another favorite, though I'll admit the Russians have the monopoly. Our specialty is stories about little girls who break their spines and get adopted by grouchy old men because they smile so much. You'd think we were a race of cheerful cripples and that the common end of the Russian peasant was suicide——"

"Six o'clock," said Amory, glancing at his wrist-watch. "I'll buy you a grea' big dinner on the strength of the juvenilia of your collected editions."

LOOKING BACKWARD

July sweltered out with a last hot week, and Amory in another surge of unrest realized that it was just five months since he and Rosalind had met. Yet it was already hard for him to visualize the heart-whole boy who had stepped off the transport, passionately desiring the adventure of life. One night while the heat, overpowering and enervating, poured into the windows of his room he struggled for several hours in a vague effort to immortalize the poignancy of that time.

The February streets, wind-washed by night, blow full of strange half-intermittent damps, bearing on wasted walks in shining sight wet snow plashed into gleams under the lamps, like golden oil from some divine machine, in an hour of thaw and stars.

Strange damps—full of the eyes of many men, crowded with life borne in upon a lull.... Oh, I was young, for I could turn again to you, most finite and most beautiful, and taste the stuff of half-remembered dreams, sweet and new on your mouth.

... There was a tanging in the midnight air—silence was dead and sound not yet awoken— Life cracked like ice!—one brilliant note and there, radiant and pale, you stood ... and spring had broken. (The icicles were short upon the roofs and the changeling city swooned.)

Our thoughts were frosty mist along the eaves; our two ghosts kissed, high on the long, mazed wires—eerie half-laughter echoes here and leaves only a fatuous sigh for young desires; regret has followed after things she loved, leaving the great husk.

ANOTHER ENDING

In mid-August came a letter from Monsignor Darcy, who had evidently just stumbled on his address:

MY DEAR BOY:—

Your last letter was quite enough to make me worry

about you. It was not a bit like yourself. Reading between the lines I should imagine that your engagement
to this girl is making you rather unhappy, and I see you
have lost all the feeling of romance that you had before
the war. You make a great mistake if you think you can
be romantic without religion. Sometimes I think that
with both of us the secret of success, when we find it,
is the mystical element in us: something flows into us
that enlarges our personalities, and when it ebbs out our
personalities shrink; I should call your last two letters
rather shrivelled. Beware of losing yourself in the personality of another being, man or woman.

His Eminence Cardinal O'Neill and the Bishop of
Boston are staying with me at present, so it is hard for
me to get a moment to write, but I wish you would
come up here later if only for a weekend. I go to
Washington this week.

What I shall do in the future is hanging in the balance. Absolutely between ourselves I should not be surprised to see the red hat of a cardinal descend upon my
unworthy head within the next eight months. In any
event, I should like to have a house in New York or
Washington where you could drop in for week-ends.

Amory, I'm very glad we're both alive; this war could
easily have been the end of a brilliant family. But in re-
gard to matrimony, you are now at the most dangerous
period of your life. You might marry in haste and repent
at leisure, but I think you won't. From what you write
me about the present calamitous state of your finances,
what you want is naturally impossible. However, if I
judge you by the means I usually choose, I should say
that there will be something of an emotional crisis
within the next year.

Do write me. I feel annoyingly out of date on you.

With greatest affection,

THAYER DARCY.

Within a week after the receipt of this letter their little
household fell precipitously to pieces. The immediate
cause was the serious and probably chronic illness of
Tom's mother. So they stored the furniture, gave instruc-
tions to sublet and shook hands gloomily in the Pennsylvania Station. Amory and Tom seemed always to be
saying good-by.

Feeling very much alone, Amory yielded to an impulse and set off southward, intending to join Monsignor in Washington. They missed connections by two hours, and, deciding to spend a few days with an ancient, remembered uncle, Amory journeyed up through the luxuriant fields of Maryland into Ramilly County. But instead of two days his stay lasted from mid-August nearly through September, for in Maryland he met Eleanor.

3

Young Irony

FOR YEARS afterward when Amory thought of Eleanor he seemed still to hear the wind sobbing around him and sending little chills into the places beside his heart. The night when they rode up the slope and watched the cold moon float through the clouds, he lost a further part of him that nothing could restore; and when he lost it he lost also the power of regretting it. Eleanor was, say, the last time that evil crept close to Amory under the mask of beauty, the last weird mystery that held him with wild fascination and pounded his soul to flakes.

With her his imagination ran riot and that is why they rode to the highest hill and watched an evil moon ride high, for they knew then that they could see the devil in each other. But Eleanor—did Amory dream her? Afterward their ghosts played, yet both of them hoped from their souls never to meet. Was it the infinite sadness of her eyes that drew him or the mirror of himself that he found in the gorgeous clarity of her mind? She will have no other adventure like Amory, and if she reads this she will say:

"And Amory will have no other adventure like me."

Nor will she sigh, any more than he would sigh.

Eleanor tried to put it on paper once:

The fading things we only know
   We'll have forgotten . . .
      Put away . . .
Desires that melted with the snow,
   And dreams begotten
      This today:
The sudden dawns we laughed to greet,

That all could see, that none could share,
Will be but dawns ... and if we meet
We shall not care.

Dear ... not one tear will rise for this ...
A little while hence
No regret
Will stir for a remembered kiss—
Not even silence,
When we've met,
Will give old ghosts a waste to roam,
Or stir the surface of the sea ...
If gray shapes drift beneath the foam
We shall not see.

They quarrelled dangerously because Amory maintained that *sea* and *see* couldn't possibly be used as a rhyme. And then Eleanor had part of another verse that she couldn't find a beginning for:

... But wisdom passes ... still the years
Will feed us wisdom.... Age will go
Back to the old— For all our tears
We shall not know.

Eleanor hated Maryland passionately. She belonged to the oldest of the old families of Ramilly County and lived in a big, gloomy house with her grandfather. She had been born and brought up in France.... I see I am starting wrong. Let me begin again.

Amory was bored, as he usually was in the country. He used to go for far walks by himself—and wander along reciting "Ulalume" to the corn-fields, and congratulating Poe for drinking himself to death in that atmosphere of smiling complacency. One afternoon he had strolled for several miles along a road that was new to him, and then through a wood on bad advice from a colored woman ... losing himself entirely. A passing storm decided to break out, and to his great impatience the sky grew black as pitch and the rain began to splatter down through the trees, become suddenly furtive and ghostly. Thunder rolled with menacing crashes up the valley and scattered through the woods in intermittent batteries. He stumbled blindly on, hunting for a way out, and finally, through webs of twisted branches, caught sight of a rift in the trees where the unbroken lightning showed open country. He rushed to the edge of the woods and then hesitated whether or not to cross the fields and try to reach the shelter of the little house marked by a light far down the valley. It was only half past five, but he could see scarcely ten steps before him, except when the lightning made everything vivid and grotesque for great sweeps around.

Suddenly a strange sound fell on his ears. It was a song, in a low, husky voice, a girl's voice, and whoever was singing was very close to him. A year before he might have laughed, or trembled; but in his restless mood he only stood and listened while the words sank into his consciousness:

> Les sanglots longs
> Des violins
>   De l'automne
> Blessent mon cœur
> D'une langueur
>   Monotone.

The lightning split the sky, but the song went on without a quaver. The girl was evidently in the field and the voice seemed to come vaguely from a haystack about twenty feet in front of him.

Then it ceased; ceased and began again in a weird chant that soared and hung and fell and blended with the rain:

> Tout suffocant
> Et blême quand
>   Sonne l'heure
> Je me souviens
> Des jours anciens
>   Et je pleure. . . .

"Who the devil is there in Ramilly County," muttered Amory aloud, "who would deliver Verlaine in an extemporaneous tune to a soaking haystack?"

"Somebody's there!" cried the voice unalarmed. "Who are you?—Manfred, St. Christopher, or Queen Victoria?"

"I'm Don Juan!" Amory shouted on impulse, raising his voice above the noise of the rain and the wind.

A delighted shriek came from the haystack.

"I know who you are—you're the blond boy that likes 'Ulalume'—I recognize your voice."

"How do I get up?" he cried from the foot of the haystack, whither he had arrived, dripping wet. A head appeared over the edge—it was so dark that Amory could just make out a patch of damp hair and two eyes that gleamed like a cat's.

"Run back!" came the voice, "and jump and I'll catch your hand—no, not there—on the other side."

He followed directions and as he sprawled up the side, knee-deep in hay, a small, white hand reached out, gripped his, and helped him onto the top.

"Here you are, Juan," cried she of the damp hair. "Do you mind if I drop the Don?"

"You've got a thumb like mine!" he exclaimed.

"And you're holding my hand, which is dangerous without seeing my face." He dropped it quickly.

As if in answer to his prayers came a flash of lightning and he looked eagerly at her who stood beside him on the soggy haystack, ten feet above the ground. But she had covered her face and he saw nothing but a slender figure, dark, damp, bobbed hair, and the small white hands with the thumbs that bent back like his.

"Sit down," she suggested politely, as the dark closed in on them. "If you'll sit opposite me in this hollow you can have half of the raincoat, which I was using as a water-proof tent until you so rudely interrupted me."

"I was asked," Amory said joyfully; "you asked me—you know you did."

"Don Juan always manages that," she said, laughing, "but I shan't call you that any more, because you've got reddish hair. Instead you can recite 'Ulalume' and I'll be Psyche, your soul."

Amory flushed, happily invisible under the curtain of wind and rain. They were sitting opposite each other in a slight hollow in the hay with the raincoat spread over most of them, and the rain doing for the rest. Amory was trying desperately to see Psyche, but the lightning refused to flash again, and he waited impatiently. Good Lord! supposing she wasn't beautiful—supposing she was forty and pedantic—heavens! Suppose, only suppose, she was mad. But he knew the last was unworthy. Here had Providence sent a girl to amuse him just as it sent Benvenuto Cellini men to murder, and he was wondering if she was mad, just because she exactly filled his mood.

"I'm not," she said.

"Not what?"

"Not mad. I didn't think you were mad when I first saw you, so it isn't fair that you should think so of me."

"How on earth——"

As long as they knew each other Eleanor and Amory could be "on a subject" and stop talking with the definite thought of it in their heads, yet ten minutes later speak aloud and find that their minds had followed the same channels and led them each to a parallel idea, an idea that others would have found absolutely unconnected with the first.

"Tell me," he demanded, leaning forward eagerly, "how do you know about 'Ulalume'—how did you know the color of my hair? What's your name? What were you doing here? Tell me all at once!"

Suddenly the lightning flashed in with a leap of overreaching light and he saw Eleanor, and looked for the first time into those eyes of hers. Oh, she was magnificent—pale skin, the color of marble in starlight, slender brows, and eyes that glittered green as emeralds in the blinding glare. She was a witch, of perhaps nineteen, he judged, alert and dreamy and with the tell-tale white line over her upper lip that was a weakness and a delight. He sank back with a gasp against the wall of hay.

"Now you've seen me," she said calmly, "and I suppose you're about to say that my green eyes are burning into your brain."

"What color is your hair?" he asked intently. "It's bobbed, isn't it?"

"Yes, it's bobbed. I don't know what color it is," she answered, musing, "so many men have asked me. It's medium, I suppose— No one ever looks long at my hair. I've got beautiful eyes, though, haven't I. I don't care what you say, I have beautiful eyes."

"Answer my question, Madeline."

"Don't remember them all—besides my name isn't Madeline, it's Eleanor."

"I might have guessed it. You *look* like Eleanor—you have that Eleanor look. You know what I mean."

There was a silence as they listened to the rain.

"It's going down my neck, fellow lunatic," she offered finally.

"Answer my questions."

"Well—name of Savage, Eleanor; live in big old house mile down road; nearest living relation to be notified, grandfather—Ramilly Savage; height, five feet four inches; number on watch-case, 3077 W; nose, delicate aquiline, temperament, uncanny——"

"And me," Amory interrupted, "where did you see me?"

"Oh, you're one of *those* men," she answered haughtily, "must lug old self into conversation. Well, my boy, I was behind a hedge sunning myself one day last week, and along comes a man saying in a pleasant, conceited way of talking:

> "And now when the night was senescent"
> (says he)
> "And the star dials pointed to morn
> At the end of the path a liquescent"
> (says he)
> "And nebulous lustre was born."

So I poked my eyes up over the hedge, but you had started to run, for some unknown reason, and so I saw but the back of your beautiful head. 'Oh!' says I, 'there's a man for whom many of us might sigh,' and I continued in my best Irish——"

"All right," Amory interrupted. "Now go back to yourself."

"Well, I will. I'm one of those people who go through the world giving other people thrills, but getting few myself except those I read into men on such nights as these. I have the social courage to go on the stage, but not the energy; I haven't the patience to write books; and I never met a man I'd marry. However, I'm only eighteen."

The storm was dying down softly and only the wind kept up its ghostly surge and made the stack lean and gravely settle from side to side. Amory was in a trance. He felt that every moment was precious. He had never met a girl like this before—she would never seem quite the same again. He didn't at all feel like a character in a play, the appropriate feeling in an unconventional situation—instead, he had a sense of coming home.

"I have just made a great decision," said Eleanor after another pause, "and that is why I'm here, to answer another of your questions. I have just decided that I don't believe in immortality."

"Really! how banal!"

"Frightfully so," she answered, "but depressing with a stale, sickly depression, nevertheless. I came out here to get wet—like a wet hen; wet hens always have great clarity of mind," she concluded.

"Go on," Amory said politely.

"Well—I'm not afraid of the dark, so I put on my slicker and rubber boots and came out. You see I was always afraid, before, to say I didn't believe in God—because the lightning might strike me—but here I am and it hasn't, of course, but the main point is that this time I wasn't any more afraid of it than I had been when I was a Christian Scientist, like I was last year. So now I know I'm a materialist and I was fraternizing with the hay when you came out and stood by the woods, scared to death."

"Why, you little wretch—" cried Amory indignantly. "Scared of what?"

"Yourself!" she shouted, and he jumped. She clapped her hands and laughed. "See—see! Conscience—kill it like me! Eleanor Savage, materiologist—no jumping, no staring, come early——"

"But I *have* to have a soul," he objected. "I can't be rational—and I won't be molecular."

She leaned toward him, her burning eyes never leaving his own and whispered with a sort of romantic finality:

"I thought so, Juan, I feared so—you're sentimental. You're not like me. I'm a romantic little materialist."

"I'm not sentimental—I'm as romantic as you are. The idea, you know, is that the sentimental person thinks things will last—the romantic person has a desperate confidence that they won't." (This was an ancient distinction of Amory's.)

"Epigrams. I'm going home," she said sadly. "Let's get off the haystack and walk to the cross-roads."

They slowly descended from their perch. She would not let him help her down and motioning him away arrived in a graceful lump in the soft mud where she sat for an instant, laughing at herself. Then she jumped to her feet and slipped her hand into his, and they tip-toed across the fields, jumping and swinging from dry spot to dry spot. A transcendent delight seemed to sparkle in every pool of water, for the moon had risen and the storm had scurried away into western Maryland. When Eleanor's arm touched his he felt his hands grow cold with deadly fear lest he should lose the shadow brush with which his imagination was painting wonders of her. He watched her from the corners of his eyes as ever he did when he walked with her—she was a feast and a folly and he wished it had been his destiny to sit forever on a haystack and see life through her green eyes. His paganism soared that night and when she faded out like a gray ghost down the road, a deep singing came out of the fields and filled his way homeward. All night the summer moths flitted in and out of Amory's window; all night large looming sounds swayed in mystic revery through the silver grain—and he lay awake in the clear darkness.

SEPTEMBER

Amory selected a blade of grass and nibbled at it scientifically.

"I never fall in love in August or September," he proffered.

"When then?"

"Christmas or Easter. I'm a liturgist."

"Easter!" She turned up her nose. "Huh! Spring in corsets!"

"Easter *would* bore spring, wouldn't she? Easter has her hair braided, wears a tailored suit."

Bind on thy sandals, oh, thou most fleet.
Over the splendor and speed of thy feet——

quoted Eleanor softly, and then added: "I suppose Hallowe'en is a better day for autumn than Thanksgiving."

"Much better—and Christmas Eve does very well for winter, but summer . . ."

"Summer has no day," she said. "We can't possibly have a summer love. So many people have tried that the name's become proverbial. Summer is only the unfulfilled promise of spring, a charlatan in place of the warm balmy nights I dream of in April. It's a sad season of life without growth. . . . It has no day."

"Fourth of July," Amory suggested facetiously.

"Don't be funny!" she said, raking him with her eyes.

"Well, what could fulfill the promise of spring?"

She thought a moment.

"Oh, I suppose heaven would, if there was one," she said finally, "a sort of pagan heaven—you ought to be a materialist," she continued irrelevantly.

"Why?"

"Because you look a good deal like the pictures of Rupert Brooke."

To some extent Amory tried to play Rupert Brooke as long as he knew Eleanor. What he said, his attitude toward life, toward her, toward himself, were all reflexes of the dead Englishman's literary moods. Often she sat in the grass, a lazy wind playing with her short hair, her voice husky as she ran up and down the scale from Grantchester to Waikiki. There was something most passionate in Eleanor's reading aloud. They seemed nearer, not only mentally, but physically, when they read, than when she was in his arms, and this was often, for they fell half into love almost from the first. Yet was Amory capable of love now? He could, as always, run through the emotions in a half hour, but even while they revelled in their imaginations, he knew that neither of them could care as he had cared once before—I suppose that was why they turned to Brooke, and Swinburne, and Shelley. Their chance was to make everything fine and finished and rich and imaginative; they must bend tiny golden tentacles from his imagination to hers, that would take the place of the great, deep love that was never so near, yet never so much of a dream.

One poem they read over and over; Swinburne's "Triumph of Time," and four lines of it rang in his memory afterward on warm nights when he saw the fireflies among dusky tree trunks and heard the low drone of many frogs. Then Eleanor seemed to come out of the night and stand by him, and he heard her throaty voice, with its tone of a fleecy-headed drum, repeating:

> Is it worth a tear, is it worth an hour,
> To think of things that are well outworn;
> Of fruitless husks and fugitive flower,
> The dream foregone and the deed foreborne?

They were formally introduced two days later, and his aunt told him her history. The Ramillys were two: old Mr. Ramilly and his granddaughter, Eleanor. She had lived in France with a restless mother whom Amory imagined to have been very like his own, on whose death she had come to America, to live in Maryland. She had gone to Baltimore first to stay with a bachelor uncle, and there she insisted on being a débutante at the age of seventeen. She had a wild winter and arrived in the country in March, having quarrelled frantically with all her Baltimore relatives, and shocked them into fiery

protest. A rather fast crowd had come out, who drank
cocktails in limousines and were promiscuously conde-
scending and patronizing toward older people, and
Eleanor with an esprit that hinted strongly of the boule-
vards, led many innocents still redolent of St. Timothy's
and Farmington, into paths of Bohemian naughtiness.
When the story came to her uncle, a forgetful cavalier of
a more hypocritical era, there was a scene, from which
Eleanor emerged, subdued but rebellious and indignant,
to seek haven with her grandfather who hovered in the
country on the near side of senility. That's as far as her
story went; she told him the rest herself, but that was
later.

Often they swam and as Amory floated lazily in the
water he shut his mind to all thoughts except those of
hazy soap-bubble lands where the sun splattered through
wind-drunk trees. How could any one possibly think or
worry, or do anything except splash and dive and loll
there on the edge of time while the flower months
failed. Let the days move over—sadness and memory
and pain recurred outside, and here, once more, before
he went on to meet them he wanted to drift and be
young.

There were days when Amory resented that life had
changed from an even progress along a road stretching
ever in sight, with the scenery merging and blending,
into a succession of quick, unrelated scenes—two years
of sweat and blood, that sudden absurd instinct for pa-
ternity that Rosalind had stirred; the half-sensual, half-
neurotic quality of this autumn with Eleanor. He felt that
it would take all time, more than he could ever spare, to
glue these strange cumbersome pictures into the scrap-
book of his life. It was all like a banquet where he sat
for this half-hour of his youth and tried to enjoy brilliant
epicurean courses.

Dimly he promised himself a time where all should be
welded together. For months it seemed that he had alternated between being borne along a stream of love or
fascination, or left in an eddy, and in the eddies he had
not desire to think, rather to be picked up on a wave's
top and swept along again.

"The despairing, dying autumn and our love—how well they harmonize!" said Eleanor sadly one day as they lay dripping by the water.

"The Indian summer of our hearts—" he ceased.

"Tell me," she said finally, "was she light or dark?"

"Light."

"Was she more beautiful than I am?"

"I don't know," said Amory shortly.

One night they walked while the moon rose and poured a great burden of glory over the garden until it seemed fairyland with Amory and Eleanor, dim phantasmal shapes, expressing eternal beauty and curious elfin love moods. Then they turned out of the moonlight into the trellised darkness of a vine-hung pagoda, where there were scents so plaintive as to be nearly musical.

"Light a match," she whispered. "I want to see you." Scratch! Flare!

The night and the scarred trees were like scenery in a play, and to be there with Eleanor, shadowy and unreal, seemed somehow oddly familiar. Amory thought how it was only the past that ever seemed strange and unbelievable. The match went out.

"It's black as pitch."

"We're just voices now," murmured Eleanor, "little lonesome voices. Light another."

"That was my last match."

Suddenly he caught her in his arms.

"You *are* mine—you know you're mine!" he cried wildly . . . the moonlight twisted in through the vines and listened . . . the fireflies hung upon their whispers as if to win his glance from the glory of their eyes.

THE END OF SUMMER

"No wind is stirring in the grass; not one wind stirs . . . the water in the hidden pools, as glass, fronts the full moon and so inters the golden token in its icy mass," chanted Eleanor to the trees that skeletoned the body of the night. "Isn't it ghostly here? If you can hold your horse's feet up, let's cut through the woods and find the hidden pools."

"It's after one, and you'll get the devil," he objected, "and I don't know enough about horses to put one away in the pitch dark."

"Shut up, you old fool," she whispered irrelevantly, and, leaning over, she patted him lazily with her riding-crop. "You can leave your old plug in our stable and I'll send him over tomorrow."

"But my uncle has got to drive me to the station with this old plug at seven o'clock."

"Don't be a spoilsport—remember, you have a tendency toward wavering that prevents you from being the entire light of my life."

Amory drew his horse up close beside, and, leaning toward her, grasped her hand.

"Say I am—*quick,* or I'll pull you over and make you ride behind me."

She looked up and smiled and shook her head excitedly.

"Oh, do!—or rather, don't! Why are all the exciting things so uncomfortable, like fighting and exploring and skiing in Canada? By the way, we're going to ride up Harper's Hill. I think that comes in our programme about five o'clock.

"You little devil," Amory growled. "You're going to make me stay up all night and sleep in the train like an immigrant all day tomorrow, going back to New York."

"Hush! some one's coming along the road—let's go! *Whoo-ee-oop!*" And with a shout that probably gave the belated traveller a series of shivers, she turned her horse into the woods and Amory followed slowly, as he had followed her all day for three weeks.

The summer was over, but he had spent the days in watching Eleanor, a graceful, facile Manfred, build herself intellectual and imaginative pyramids while she revelled in the artificialities of the temperamental teens and they wrote poetry at the dinner-table.

When Vanity kissed Vanity, a hundred happy Junes ago, he pondered o'er her breathlessly, and, that all men might ever know, he rhymed her eyes with life and death:

"Thru Time I'll save my love!" he said . . . yet Beauty vanished with his breath, and, with her lovers, she was dead . . .

—Ever his wit and not her eyes, ever his art and not her hair:

"Who'd learn a trick in rhyme, be wise and pause before his sonnet there" . . . So all my words, however true, might sing you to a thousandth June, and no one ever know that you were Beauty for an afternoon.

So he wrote one day, when he pondered how coldly we thought of the "Dark Lady of the Sonnets," and how little we remembered her as the great man wanted her remembered. For what Shakespeare *must* have desired, to have been able to write with such divine despair, was that the lady should live . . . and now we have no real interest in her. . . . The irony of it is that if he had cared *more* for the poem than for the lady the sonnet would be only obvious, imitative rhetoric and no one would ever have read it after twenty years. . . .

This was the last night Amory ever saw Eleanor. He was leaving in the morning and they had agreed to take a long farewell trot by the cold moonlight. She wanted to talk, she said—perhaps the last time in her life that she could be rational (she meant pose with comfort). So they had turned into the woods and rode for half an hour with scarcely a word, except when she whispered "Damn!" at a bothersome branch—whispered it as no other girl was ever able to whisper it. Then they started up Harper's Hill, walking their tired horses.

"Good Lord! It's quiet here!" whispered Eleanor; "much more lonesome than the woods."

"I hate woods," Amory said, shuddering. "Any kind of foliage or underbrush at night. Out here it's so broad and easy on the spirit."

"The long slope of a long hill."

"And the cold moon rolling moonlight down it."

"And thee and me, last and most important."

It was quiet that night—the straight road they followed up to the edge of the cliff knew few footsteps at any time. Only an occasional Negro cabin, silver-gray in the rock-ribbed moonlight, broke the long line of bare ground; behind lay the black edge of the woods like a dark frosting on white cake, and ahead the sharp, high horizon. It was much colder—so cold that it settled on them and drove all the warm nights from their minds.

"The end of summer," said Eleanor softly. "Listen to the beat of our horses' hoofs—'tump-tump-tump-a-tump.' Have you ever been feverish and had all noises divide into 'tump-tump-tump' until you could swear eternity was divisible into so many tumps? That's the way I feel—old horses go tump-tump. . . . I guess that's the only thing that separates horses and clocks from us. Human beings can't go 'tump-tump-tump' without going crazy."

The breeze freshened and Eleanor pulled her cape around her and shivered.

"Are you very cold?" asked Amory.

"No, I'm thinking about myself—my black old inside self, the real one, with the fundamental honesty that keeps me from being absolutely wicked by making me realize my own sins."

They were riding up close by the cliff and Amory gazed over. Where the fall met the ground a hundred feet below, a black stream made a sharp line, broken by tiny glints in the swift water.

"Rotten, rotten old world," broke out Eleanor suddenly, "and the wretchedest thing of all is me—oh, *why* am I a girl? Why am I not a stupid—? Look at you; you're stupider than I am, not much, but some, and you can lope about and get bored and then lope somewhere else, and you can play around with girls without being involved in meshes of sentiment, and you can do anything and be justified—and here am I with the brains to do everything, yet tied to the sinking ship of future matrimony. If I were born a hundred years from now, well and good, but now what's in store for me—I have to marry, that goes without saying. Who? I'm too bright for most men, and yet I have to descend to their level and let them patronize my intellect in order to get their attention. Every year that I don't marry I've got less

chance for a first-class man. At the best I can have my
choice from one or two cities and, of course, I have to
marry into a dinner-coat.

"Listen," she leaned close again, "I like clever men and
good-looking men, and, of course, no one cares more for
personality than I do. Oh, just one person in fifty has any
glimmer of what sex is. I'm hipped on Freud and all that,
but it's rotten that every bit of *real* love in the world is
ninety-nine per cent passion and one little soupcon of
jealousy." She finished as suddenly as she began.

"Of course, you're right," Amory agreed. "It's a
rather unpleasant overpowering force that's part of the
machinery under everything. It's like an actor that lets
you see his mechanics! Wait a minute till I think this
out. . . ."

He paused and tried to get a metaphor. They had
turned the cliff and were riding along the road about
fifty feet to the left.

"You see every one's got to have some cloak to throw
around it. The mediocre intellects, Plato's second class,
use the remnants of romantic chivalry diluted with Victorian sentiment—and we who consider ourselves the
intellectuals cover it up by pretending that it's another
side of us, has nothing to do with our shining brains; we
pretend that the fact that we realize it is really absolving
us from being a prey to it. But the truth is that sex is
right in the middle of our purest abstractions, so close
that it obscures vision. . . . I can kiss you now and
will. . . ." He leaned toward her in his saddle, but she
drew away.

"I can't—I can't kiss you now—I'm more sensitive."

"You're more stupid then," he declared rather impatiently. "Intellect is no protection from sex any more
than convention is . . ."

"What is?" she fired up. "The Catholic Church or the
maxims of Confucius?"

Amory looked up, rather taken aback.

"That's your panacea, isn't it?" she cried. "Oh, you're
just an old hypocrite, too. Thousands of scowling priests
keeping the degenerate Italians and illiterate Irish re-
pentant with gabble-gabble about the sixth and ninth

commandments. It's just all cloaks, sentiment and spiritual rouge and panaceas. I'll tell you there *is* no God, not even a definite abstract goodness; so it's all got to be worked out for the individual by the individual here in high white foreheads like mine, and you're too much the prig to admit it." She let go her reins and shook her little fists at the stars.

"If there's a God let him strike me—strike me!"

"Talking about God again after the manner of atheists," Amory said sharply. His materialism, always a thin cloak, was torn to shreds by Eleanor's blasphemy. . . . She knew it and it angered him that she knew it.

"And like most intellectuals who don't find faith convenient," he continued coldly, "like Napoleon and Oscar Wilde and the rest of your type, you'll yell loudly for a priest on your death-bed."

Eleanor drew her horse up sharply and he reined in beside her.

"Will I?" she said in a queer voice that scared him. "Will I? Watch! *I'm going over the cliff!*" And before he could interfere she had turned and was riding breakneck for the end of the plateau.

He wheeled and started after her, his body like ice, his nerves in a vast clangor. There was no chance of stopping her. The moon was under a cloud and her horse would step blindly over. Then some ten feet from the edge of the cliff she gave a sudden shriek and flung herself sideways—plunged from her horse and, rolling over twice, landed in a pile of brush five feet from the edge. The horse went over with a frantic whinny. In a minute he was by Eleanor's side and saw that her eyes were open.

"Eleanor!" he cried.

She did not answer, but her lips moved and her eyes filled with sudden tears.

"Eleanor, are you hurt?"

"No; I don't think so," she said faintly, and then began weeping.

"My horse dead?"

"Good God—Yes!"

"Oh!" she wailed. "I thought I was going over. I didn't know——"

He helped her gently to her feet and boosted her onto his saddle. So they started homeward; Amory walking and she bent forward on the pommel, sobbing bitterly.

"I've got a crazy streak," she faltered, "twice before I've done things like that. When I was eleven mother went—went mad—stark raving crazy. We were in Vienna——"

All the way back she talked haltingly about herself, and Amory's love waned slowly with the moon. At her door they started from habit to kiss good night, but she could not run into his arms, nor were they stretched to meet her as in the week before. For a minute they stood there, hating each other with a bitter sadness. But as Amory had loved himself in Eleanor, so now what he hated was only a mirror. Their poses were strewn about the pale dawn like broken glass. The stars were long gone and there were left only the little sighing gusts of wind and the silences between . . . but naked souls are poor things ever, and soon he turned homeward and let new lights come in with the sun.

A POEM THAT ELEANOR SENT AMORY
SEVERAL YEARS LATER

Here, Earth-born, over the lilt of the water,
    Lisping its music and bearing a burden of light,
Bosoming day as a laughing and radiant daughter . . .
    Here we may whisper unheard, unafraid of the night.
Walking alone . . . was it splendor, or what, we were
bound with,
    Deep in the time when summer lets down her hair?
Shadows we loved and the patterns they covered the
ground with
    Tapestries, mystical, faint in the breathless air.

That was the day . . . and the night for another story,
    Pale as a dream and shadowed with pencilled trees—
Ghosts of the stars came by who had sought for glory,
    Whispered to us of peace in the plaintive breeze,

Whispered of old dead faiths that the day had shattered,
   Youth the penny that bought delight of the moon;
That was the urge that we knew and the language that
mattered
   That was the debt that we paid to the usurer June.

Here, deepest of dreams, by the waters that bring not
   Anything back of the past that we need not know,
What if the light is but sun and the little streams sing
not,
   We are together, it seems ... I have loved you so ...
What did the last night hold, with the summer over,
   Drawing us back to the home in the changing glade?
What leered out of the dark in the ghostly clover?
   God! ... till you stirred in your sleep ... and were
wild afraid ...

Well ... we have passed ... we are chronicle now to the
eerie.
   Curious metal from meteors that failed in the sky;
Earth-born the tireless is stretched by the water, quite
weary,
   Close to this ununderstandable changeling that's I ...
Fear is an echo we traced to Security's daughter;
   Now we are faces and voices ... and less, too soon,
Whispering half-love over the lilt of the water ...
   Youth the penny that bought delight of the moon.

A POEM AMORY SENT TO ELEANOR AND WHICH HE CALLED "SUMMER STORM"

Faint winds, and a song fading and leaves falling,
Faint winds, and far away a fading laughter ...
And the rain and over the fields a voice calling ...
Our gray blown cloud scurries and lifts above,
Slides on the sun and flutters there to waft her
Sisters on. The shadow of a dove
Falls on the cote, the trees are filled with wings;
And down the valley through the crying trees
The body of the darker storm flies; brings
With its new air the breath of sunken seas
And slender tenuous thunder ...

                                        But I wait . . .
Wait for the mists and for the blacker rain—
Heavier winds that stir the veil of fate,
Happier winds that pile her hair;
                    Again
They tear me, teach me, strew the heavy air
Upon me, winds that I know, and storm.

There was a summer every rain was rare;
There was a season every wind was warm. . . .
And now you pass me in the mist   your hair
Rain-blown about you, damp lips curved once more
In that wild irony, that gay despair
That made you old when we have met before;
Wraith-like you drift on out before the rain,
Across the fields, blown with the stemless flowers,
With your old hopes, dead leaves and loves again—
Dim as a dream and wan with all old hours
(Whispers will creep into the growing dark . . .
Tumult will die over the trees)
                    Now night
Tears from her wetted breast the splattered blouse
Of day, glides down the dreaming hills, tear-bright,
To cover with her hair the eerie green . . .
Love for the dusk . . . Love for the glistening after;
Quiet the trees to their last tops . . . serene . . .

Faint winds, and far away a fading laughter . . .

4

The Supercilious Sacrifice

ATLANTIC CITY. Amory paced the board walk at day's end, lulled by the everlasting surge of changing waves, smelling the half-mournful odor of the salt breeze. The sea, he thought, had treasured its memories deeper than the faithless land. It seemed still to whisper of Norse galleys ploughing the water world under raven-figured flags, of the British dreadnoughts, gray bulwarks of civilization steaming up through the fog of one dark July into the North Sea.

"Well—Amory Blaine!"

Amory looked down into the street below. A low racing car had drawn to a stop and a familiar cheerful face protruded from the driver's seat.

"Come on down, goopher!" cried Alec.

Amory called a greeting and descending a flight of wooden steps approached the car. He and Alec had been meeting intermittently, but the barrier of Rosalind lay always between them. He was sorry for this; he hated to lose Alec.

"Mr. Blaine, this is Miss Waterson, Miss Wayne, and Mr. Tully."

"How d'y do?"

"Amory," said Alec exuberantly, "if you'll jump in we'll take you to some secluded nook and give you a wee jolt of Bourbon."

Amory considered.

"That's an idea."

"Step in—move over, Jill, and Amory will smile very handsomely at you."

Amory squeezed into the back seat beside a gaudy, vermilion-lipped blonde.

"Hello, Doug Fairbanks," she said flippantly. "Walking for exercise or hunting for company?"

"I was counting the waves," replied Amory gravely. "I'm going in for statistics."

"Don't kid me, Doug."

When they reached an unfrequented side street Alec stopped the car among deep shadows.

"What you doing down here these cold days, Amory?" he demanded, as he produced a quart of Bourbon from under the fur rug.

Amory avoided the question. Indeed, he had had no definite reason for coming to the coast.

"Do you remember that party of ours, sophomore year?" he asked instead.

"Do I? When we slept in the pavilions up in Asbury Park—"

"Lord, Alec! It's hard to think that Jesse and Dick and Kerry are all three dead."

Alec shivered.

"Don't talk about it. These dreary fall days depress me enough."

Jill seemed to agree.

"Doug here is sorta gloomy anyways," she commented. "Tell him to drink deep—it's good and scarce these days."

"What I really want to ask you, Amory, is where you are—"

"Why, New York, I suppose—"

"I mean tonight, because if you haven't got a room yet you'd better help me out."

"Glad to."

"You see, Tully and I have two rooms with bath between at the Rainer, and he's got to go back to New York. I don't want to have to move. Question is, will you occupy one of the rooms?"

Amory was willing, if he could get in right away.

"You'll find the key in the office; the rooms are in my name."

Declining further locomotion or further stimulation, Amory left the car and sauntered back along the board walk to the hotel.

He was in an eddy again, a deep, lethargic gulf, without desire to work or write, love or dissipate. For the first time in his life he rather longed for death to roll over his generation, obliterating their petty fevers and struggles and exultations. His youth seemed never so vanished as now in the contrast between the utter loneliness of this visit and that riotous, joyful party of four years before. Things that had been the merest commonplaces of his life then, deep sleep, the sense of beauty around him, all desire, had flown away and the gaps they left were filled only with the great listlessness of his disillusion.

"To hold a man a woman has to appeal to the worst in him." This sentence was the thesis of most of his bad nights, of which he felt this was to be one. His mind had already started to play variations on the subject. Tireless passion, fierce jealousy, longing to possess and crush—these alone were left of all his love for Rosalind; these remained to him as payment for the loss of his youth—bitter calomel under the thin sugar of love's exaltation.

In his room he undressed and wrapping himself in blankets to keep out the chill October air drowsed in an armchair by the open window.

He remembered a poem he had read months before:

Oh staunch old heart who toiled so long for me,
I waste my years sailing along the sea—

Yet he had no sense of waste, no sense of the present hope that waste implied. He felt that life had rejected him.

"Rosalind! Rosalind!" He poured the words softly into the half-darkness until she seemed to permeate the room; the wet salt breeze filled his hair with moisture; the rim of a moon seared the sky and made the curtains dim and ghostly. He fell asleep.

When he awoke it was very late and quiet. The blanket had slipped partly off his shoulders and he touched his skin to find it damp and cold.

Then he became aware of a tense whispering not ten feet away.

He became rigid.

"Don't make a sound!" It was Alec's voice. *"Jill—do you hear me?"*

"Yes—" breathed very low, very frightened. They were in the bathroom.

Then his ears caught a louder sound from somewhere along the corridor outside. It was a mumbling of men's voices and a repeated muffled rapping. Amory threw off the blankets and moved close to the bathroom door.

"My God!" came the girl's voice again. "You'll have to let them in."

"Sh!"

Suddenly a steady, insistent knocking began at Amory's hall door and simultaneously out of the bathroom came Alec, followed by the vermilion-lipped girl. They were both clad in pajamas.

"Amory!" an anxious whisper.

"What's the trouble?"

"It's house detectives. My God, Amory—they're just looking for a test-case—"

"Well, better let them in."

"You don't understand. They can get me under the Mann Act."

The girl followed him slowly, a rather miserable, pathetic figure in the darkness.

Amory tried to plan quickly.

"You make a racket and let them in your room," he suggested anxiously, "and I'll get her out by this door."

"They're here too, though. They'll watch this door."

"Can't you give a wrong name?"

"No chance. I registered under my own name; besides, they'd trail the auto license number."

"Say you're married."

"Jill says one of the house detectives knows her."

The girl had stolen to the bed and tumbled upon it; lay there listening wretchedly to the knocking which had grown gradually to a pounding. Then came a man's voice, angry and imperative:

"Open up or we'll break the door in!"

In the silence when this voice ceased Amory realized that there were other things in the room besides people

. . . over and around the figure crouched on the bed there
hung an aura, gossamer as a moonbeam, tainted as stale,
weak wine, yet a horror, diffusively brooding already
over the three of them . . . and over by the window
among the stirring curtains stood something else, fea-
tureless and indistinguishable, yet strangely familiar. . . .
Simultaneously two great cases presented themselves
side by side to Amory; all that took place in his mind,
then, occupied in actual time less than ten seconds.

The first fact that flashed radiantly on his comprehen-
sion was the great impersonality of sacrifice—he perceived that what we call love and hate, reward and
punishment, had no more to do with it than the date of
the month. He quickly recapitulated the story of a sacrifice he had heard of in college: a man had cheated in an
examination; his roommate in a gust of sentiment had
taken the entire blame—due to the shame of it the innocent one's entire future seemed shrouded in regret and
failure, capped by the ingratitude of the real culprit. He
had finally taken his own life—years afterward the facts
had come out. At the time the story had both puzzled
and worried Amory. Now he realized the truth; that sacrifice was no purchase of freedom. It was like a great
elective office, it was like an inheritance of power—to
certain people at certain times an essential luxury, carry-
ing with it not a guarantee but a responsibility, not a security but an infinite risk. Its very momentum might
drag him down to ruin—the passing of the emotional
wave that made it possible might leave the one who
made it high and dry forever on an island of despair.

. . . Amory knew that afterward Alec would secretly
hate him for having done so much for him. . . .

. . . All this was flung before Amory like an opened
scroll, while ulterior to him and speculating upon him
were those two breathless, listening forces: the gossamer
aura that hung over and about the girl and that familiar
thing by the window.

Sacrifice by its very nature was arrogant and impersonal; sacrifice should be eternally supercilious.

Weep not for me but for thy children.

That—thought Amory—would be somehow the way God would talk to me.

Amory felt a sudden surge of joy and then like a face in a motion-picture the aura over the bed faded out; the dynamic shadow by the window, that was as near as he could name it, remained for the fraction of a moment and then the breeze seemed to lift it swiftly out of the room. He clinched his hands in quick ecstatic excitement . . . the ten seconds were up. . . .

"Do what I say, Alec—do what I say. Do you understand?"

Alec looked at him dumbly—his face a tableau of anguish.

"You have a family," continued Amory slowly. "You have a family and it's important that you should get out of this. Do you hear me?" He repeated clearly what he had said. "Do you hear me?"

"I hear you." The voice was curiously strained, the eyes never for a second left Amory's.

"Alec, you're going to lie down here. If any one comes in you act drunk. You do what I say—if you don't I'll probably take a paste at you."

There was another moment while they stared at each other. Then Amory went briskly to the bureau and, taking his pocketbook, beckoned peremptorily to the girl. He heard one word from Alec that sounded like "penitentiary," then he and Jill were in the bathroom with the door bolted behind them.

"You're here with me," he said sternly. "You've been with me all evening."

She nodded, gave a little half cry.

In a second he had the door of the other room open and three men entered. There was an immediate flood of electric light and he stood there blinking.

"You've been playing a little too dangerous a game, young man!"

Amory laughed.

"Well?"

The leader of the trio nodded authoritatively at a burly man in a check suit.

"All right, Olson."

"I got you, Mr. O'May," said Olson, nodding. The other two took a curious glance at their quarry and then withdrew, closing the door angrily behind them.

The burly man regarded Amory contemptuously.

"Didn't you ever hear of the Mann Act? Coming down here with her," he indicated the girl with his thumb, "with a New York license on your car—to a hotel like *this*." He shook his head implying that he had struggled over Amory but now gave him up.

"Well," said Amory rather impatiently, "what do you want us to do?"

"Get dressed, quick—and tell your friend not to make such a racket." Jill was sobbing noisily on the bed, but at these words she subsided sulkily and, gathering up her clothes, retired to the bathroom. As Amory slipped into Alec's B. V. D.'s he found that his attitude toward the situation was agreeably humorous. The aggrieved virtue of the burly man made him want to laugh.

"Anybody else here?" demanded Olson, trying to look keen and ferret-like.

"Fellow who had the rooms," said Amory carelessly. "He's drunk as an owl, though. Been in there asleep since six o'clock."

"I'll take a look at him presently."

"How did you find out?" asked Amory curiously.

"Night clerk saw you go upstairs with this woman."

Amory nodded; Jill reappeared from the bathroom, completely if rather untidily arrayed.

"Now then," began Olson, producing a note-book, "I want your real names—no damn John Smith or Mary Brown."

"Wait a minute," said Amory quietly. "Just drop that big-bully stuff. We merely got caught, that's all."

Olson glared at him.

"Name?" he snapped.

Amory gave his name and New York address.

"And the lady?"

"Miss Jill—"

"Say," cried Olson indignantly, "just ease up on the

nursery rhymes. What's your name? Sarah Murphy? Minnie Jackson?"

"Oh, my God!" cried the girl cupping her tear-stained face in her hands. "I don't want my mother to know. I don't want my mother to know."

"Come on now!"

"Shut up!" cried Amory at Olson.

An instant's pause.

"Stell Robbins," she faltered finally. "General Delivery, Rugway, New Hampshire."

Olson snapped his note-book shut and looked at them very ponderously.

"By rights the hotel could turn the evidence over to the police and you'd go to penitentiary, you would, for bringin' a girl from one State to 'nother f'r immoral purp'ses——" He paused to let the majesty of his words sink in. "But—the hotel is going to let you off."

"It doesn't want to get in the papers," cried Jill fiercely. "Let us off! Huh!"

A great lightness surrounded Amory. He realized that he was safe and only then did he appreciate the full enormity of what he might have incurred.

"However," continued Olson, "there's a protective association among the hotels. There's been too much of this stuff, and we got a 'rangement with the newspapers so that you get a little free publicity. Not the name of the hotel, but just a line sayin' that you had a little trouble in 'lantic City. See?"

"I see."

"You're gettin' off light—damn light—but—"

"Come on," said Amory briskly. "Let's get out of here. We don't need a valedictory."

Olson walked through the bathroom and took a cursory glance at Alec's still form. Then he extinguished the lights and motioned them to follow him. As they walked into the elevator Amory considered a piece of bravado—yielded finally. He reached out and tapped Olson on the arm.

"Would you mind taking off your hat? There's a lady in the elevator."

Olson's hat came off slowly. There was a rather embarrassing two minutes under the lights of the lobby while the night clerk and a few belated guests stared at them curiously; the loudly dressed girl with bent head, the handsome young man with his chin several points aloft; the inference was quite obvious. Then the chill outdoors—where the salt air was fresher and keener still with the first hints of morning.

"You can get one of those taxis and beat it," said Olson, pointing to the blurred outline of two machines whose drivers were presumably asleep inside.

"Good-by," said Olson. He reached in his pocket suggestively, but Amory snorted, and, taking the girl's arm, turned away.

"Where did you tell the driver to go?" she asked as they whirled along the dim street.

"The station."

"If that guy writes my mother—"

"He won't. Nobody'll ever know about this—except our friends and enemies."

Dawn was breaking over the sea.

"It's getting blue," she said.

"It does very well," agreed Amory critically, and then as an after-thought; "It's almost breakfast-time—do you want something to eat?"

"Food—" she said with a cheerful laugh. "Food is what queered the party. We ordered a big supper to be sent up to the room about two o'clock. Alec didn't give the waiter a tip, so I guess the little bastard snitched."

Jill's low spirits seemed to have gone faster than the scattering night. "Let me tell you," she said emphatically, "when you want to stage that sorta party stay away from liquor, and when you want to get tight stay away from bedrooms."

"I'll remember."

He tapped suddenly at the glass and they drew up at the door of an all-night restaurant.

"Is Alec a great friend of yours?" asked Jill as they perched themselves on high stools inside, and set their elbows on the dingy counter.

"He used to be. He probably won't want to be any more—and never understand why."

"It was sorta crazy you takin' all that blame. Is he pretty important? Kinda more important than you are?"

Amory laughed.

"That remains to be seen," he answered. "That's the question."

THE COLLAPSE OF SEVERAL PILLARS

Two days later back in New York Amory found in a newspaper what he had been searching for—a dozen lines which announced to whom it might concern that Mr. Amory Blaine, who "gave his address" as, etc., had been requested to leave his hotel in Atlantic City because of entertaining in his room a lady *not* his wife.

Then he started, and his fingers trembled, for directly above was a longer paragraph of which the first words were:

"Mr. and Mrs. Leland R. Connage are announcing the engagement of their daughter, Rosalind, to Mr. J. Dawson Ryder, of Hartford, Connecticut—"

He dropped the paper and lay down on his bed with a frightened, sinking sensation in the pit of his stomach. She was gone, definitely, finally gone. Until now he had half unconsciously cherished the hope deep in his heart that some day she would need him and send for him, cry that it had been a mistake, that her heart ached only for the pain she had caused him. Never again could he find even the sombre luxury of wanting her—not this Rosalind, harder, older—nor any beaten, broken woman that his imagination brought to the door of his forties— Amory had wanted her youth, the fresh radiance of her mind and body, the stuff that she was selling now once and for all. So far as he was concerned, young Rosalind was dead.

A day later came a crisp, terse letter from Mr. Barton in Chicago, which informed him that as three more street-car companies had gone into the hands of receivers he could expect for the present no further remittances. Last of all, on a dazed Sunday night, a telegram told him of Monsignor Darcy's sudden death in Philadelphia five days before.

He knew then what it was that he had perceived among the curtains of the room in Atlantic City.

5

The Egotist Becomes a Personage

A fathom deep in sleep I lie
　　With old desires, restrained before,
To clamor lifeward with a cry,
　　As dark flies out the greying door;
And so in quest of creeds to share
　　I seek assertive day again . . .
But old monotony is there:
　　Endless avenues of rain.

Oh, might I rise again! Might I
　　Throw off the heat of that old wine,
See the new morning mass the sky
　　With fairy towers, line on line;
Find each mirage in the high air
　　A symbol, not a dream again . . .
But old monotony is there:
　　Endless avenues of rain.

UNDER THE glass porte-cochere of a theatre Amory stood, watching the first great drops of rain splatter down and flatten to dark stains on the sidewalk. The air became gray and opalescent; a solitary light suddenly outlined a window over the way; then another light; then a hundred more danced and glimmered into vision. Under his feet a thick, iron-studded skylight turned yellow; in the street the lamps of the taxicabs sent out glistening sheens along the already black pavement. The unwelcome November rain had perversely stolen the day's last hour and pawned it with that ancient fence, the night.

The silence of the theatre behind him ended with a curious snapping sound, followed by the heavy roaring of a rising crowd and the interlaced clatter of many voices. The matinée was over.

He stood aside, edged a little into the rain to let the throng pass. A small boy rushed out, sniffed in the damp, fresh air and turned up the collar of his coat; came three or four couples in a great hurry; came a further scattering of people whose eyes as they emerged glanced invariably, first at the wet street, then at the rain-filled air, finally at the dismal sky; last a dense, strolling mass that depressed him with its heavy odor compounded of the tobacco smell of the men and the fetid sensuousness of stale powder on women. After the thick crowd came another scattering; a stray half-dozen; a man on crutches; finally the rattling bang of folding seats inside announced that the ushers were at work.

New York seemed not so much awakening as turning over in its bed. Pallid men rushed by, pinching together their coat-collars; a great swarm of tired, magpie girls from a department-store crowded along with shrieks of strident laughter, three to an umbrella; a squad of marching policemen passed, already miraculously protected by oilskin capes.

The rain gave Amory a feeling of detachment, and the numerous unpleasant aspects of city life without money occurred to him in threatening procession. There was the ghastly, stinking crush of the subway—the car cards thrusting themselves at one, leering out like dull bores who grab your arm with another story; the querulous worry as to whether some one isn't leaning on you; a man deciding not to give his seat to a woman, hating her for it; the woman hating him for not doing it; at worst a squalid phantasmagoria of breath, and old cloth on human bodies and the smells of the food men ate—at best just people—too hot or too cold, tired, worried.

He pictured the rooms where these people lived—where the patterns of the blistered wall-papers were heavy reiterated sunflowers on green and yellow backgrounds, where there were tin bathtubs and gloomy hallways and verdureless, unnamable spaces in back of the buildings; where even love dressed as seduction—a sordid murder around the corner, illicit motherhood in the

flat above. And always there was the economical stuff-
iness of indoor winter, and the long summers, night-
mares of perspiration between sticky enveloping walls
... dirty restaurants where careless, tired people helped
themselves to sugar with their own used coffee-spoons,
leaving hard brown deposits in the bowl.

It was not so bad where there were only men or else
only women; it was when they were vilely herded that it
all seemed so rotten. It was some shame that women
gave off at having men see them tired and poor—it was
some disgust that men had for women who were tired
and poor. It was dirtier than any battle-field he had seen,
harder to contemplate than any actual hardship moulded
of mire and sweat and danger, it was an atmosphere
wherein birth and marriage and death were loathsome,
secret things.

He remembered one day in the subway when a delivery boy had brought in a great funeral wreath of fresh
flowers, how the smell of it had suddenly cleared the air
and given every one in the car a momentary glow.

"I detest poor people," thought Amory suddenly. "I
hate them for being poor. Poverty may have been beautiful once, but it's rotten now. It's the ugliest thing in the
world. It's essentially cleaner to be corrupt and rich than
it is to be innocent and poor." He seemed to see again a
figure whose significance had once impressed him—a
well-dressed young man gazing from a club window on
Fifth Avenue and saying something to his companion
with a look of utter disgust. Probably, thought Amory,
what he said was: "My God! Aren't people horrible!"

Never before in his life had Amory considered poor
people. He thought cynically how completely he was
lacking in all human sympathy. O. Henry had found in
these people romance, pathos, love, hate—Amory saw
only coarseness, physical filth, and stupidity. He made
no self-accusations: never any more did he reproach
himself for feelings that were natural and sincere. He accepted all his reactions as a part of him, unchangeable,
unmoral. This problem of poverty transformed, magni-
fied, attached to some grander, more dignified attitude

might some day even be his problem; at present it roused only his profound distaste.

He walked over to Fifth Avenue, dodging the blind, black menace of umbrellas, and standing in front of Delmonico's hailed an autobus. Buttoning his coat closely around him he climbed to the roof, where he rode in solitary state through the thin, persistent rain, stung into alertness by the cool moisture perpetually reborn on his cheek. Somewhere in his mind a conversation began, rather resumed its place in his attention. It was composed not of two voices, but of one, which acted alike as questioner and answerer:

Question.—Well—what's the situation?

Answer.—That I have about twenty-four dollars to my name.

Q.—You have the Lake Geneva estate.

A.—But I intend to keep it.

Q.—Can you live?

A.—I can't imagine not being able to. People make money in books and I've found that I can always do the things that people do in books. Really they are the only things I can do.

Q.—Be definite.

A.—I don't know what I'll do—nor have I much curiosity. Tomorrow I'm going to leave New York for good. It's a bad town unless you're on top of it.

Q.—Do you want a lot of money?

A.—No. I am merely afraid of being poor.

Q.—Very afraid?

A.—Just passively afraid.

Q.—Where are you drifting?

A.—Don't ask *me*!

Q.—Don't you care?

A.—Rather. I don't want to commit moral suicide.

Q.—Have you no interests left?

A.—None. I've no more virtue to lose. Just as a cooling pot gives off heat, so all through youth and adolescence we give off calories of virtue. That's what's called ingenuousness.

Q.—An interesting idea.

A.—That's why a "good man going wrong" attracts people. They stand around and literally *warm themselves* at the calories of virtue he gives off. Sarah makes an unsophisticated remark and the faces simper in delight—"How *innocent* the poor child is!" They're warming themselves at her virtue. But Sarah sees the simper and never makes that remark again. Only she feels a little colder after that.

Q.—All your calories gone?

A.—All of them. I'm beginning to warm myself at other people's virtue.

Q.—Are you corrupt?

A.—I think so. I'm not sure. I'm not sure about good and evil at all any more.

Q.—Is that a bad sign in itself?

A.—Not necessarily.

Q.—What would be the test of corruption?

A.—Becoming really insincere—calling myself "not such a bad fellow," thinking I regretted my lost youth when I only envy the delights of losing it. Youth is like having a big plate of candy. Sentimentalists think they want to be in the pure, simple state they were in before they ate the candy. They don't. They just want the fun of eating it all over again. The matron doesn't want to repeat her girlhood—she wants to repeat her honeymoon. I don't want to repeat my innocence. I want the pleasure of losing it again.

Q.—Where are you drifting?

This dialogue merged grotesquely into his mind's most familiar state—a grotesque blending of desires, worries, exterior impressions and physical reactions.

One Hundred and Twenty-seventh Street—or One Hundred and Thirty-seventh Street. . . . Two and three look alike—no, not much. Seat damp . . . are clothes absorbing wetness from seat, or seat absorbing dryness from clothes? . . . Sitting on wet substance gave appendicitis, so Froggy Parker's mother said. Well, he'd had it—I'll sue the steamboat company, Beatrice said, and my uncle has a quarter interest—did Beatrice go to heaven? . . . probably not— He represented Beatrice's immortality, also love-affairs of numerous dead men who surely had never thought of him ... if it wasn't appendicitis, influenza maybe. What? One Hundred and Twentieth Street? That must have been One Hundred and Twelfth back there. One O Two instead of One Two Seven. Rosalind not like Beatrice, Eleanor like Beatrice, only wilder and brainier. Apartments along here expensive—probably hundred and fifty a month—maybe two hundred. Uncle had only paid hundred a month for whole great big house in Minneapolis. Question—were the stairs on the left or right as you came in? Anyway, in 12 Univee they were straight back and to the left. What a dirty river—want to go down there and see if it's dirty—French rivers all brown or black, so were Southern rivers. Twenty-four dollars meant four hundred and eighty doughnuts. He could live on it three months and sleep in the park. Wonder where Jill was—Jill Bayne, Fayne, Sayne—what the devil—neck hurts, darned uncomfortable seat. No desire to sleep with Jill, what could Alec see in her? Alec had a coarse taste in women. Own taste the best; Isabelle, Clara, Rosalind, Eleanor, were all-American. Eleanor would pitch, probably southpaw. Rosalind was outfield, wonderful hitter, Clara first base, maybe. Wonder what Humbird's body looked like now. If he himself hadn't been bayonet instructor he'd have gone up to line three months sooner, probably been killed. Where's the darned bell—

The street numbers of Riverside Drive were obscured by the mist and dripping trees from anything but the swiftest scrutiny, but Amory had finally caught sight of one—One Hundred and Twenty-seventh Street. He got off and with no distinct destination followed a winding, descending sidewalk and came out facing the river, in particular a long pier and partioned litter of shipyards for miniature craft: small launches, canoes, rowboats, and catboats. He turned northward and followed the shore, jumped a small wire fence and found himself in a great disorderly yard adjoining a dock. The hulls of many boats in various stages of repair were around him; he smelled sawdust and paint and the scarcely distinguishable flat odor of the Hudson. A man approached through the heavy gloom.

"Hello," said Amory.

"Got a pass?"

"No. Is this private?"

"This is the Hudson River Sporting and Yacht Club."

"Oh! I didn't know. I'm just resting."

"Well—" began the man dubiously.

"I'll go if you want me to."

The man made non-committal noises in his throat and passed on. Amory seated himself on an overturned boat and leaned forward thoughtfully until his chin rested in his hand.

"Misfortune is liable to make me a damn bad man," he said slowly.

IN THE DROOPING HOURS

While the rain drizzled on Amory looked futiley back at the stream of his life, all its glitterings and dirty shallows. To begin with, he was still afraid—not physically afraid any more, but afraid of people and prejudice and misery and monotony. Yet, deep in his bitter heart, he wondered if he was after all worse than this man or the next. He knew that he could sophisticate himself finally into saying that his own weakness was just the result of circumstances and environment; that often when he raged at himself as an egotist something would whisper ingratiatingly: "No. Genius!" That was one manifestation of fear, that voice which whispered that he could not be both great and good, that genius was the exact combination of those inexplicable grooves and twists in his mind, that any discipline would curb it to mediocrity. Probably more than any concrete vice or failing Amory despised his own personality—he loathed knowing that tomorrow and the thousand days after he would swell pompously at a compliment and sulk at an ill word like a third-rate musician or a first-class actor. He was ashamed of the fact that very simple and honest people usually distrusted him; that he had been cruel, often, to those who had sunk their personalities in him—several girls, and a man here and there through college, that he had been an evil influence on; people who had followed him here and there into mental adventures from which he alone rebounded unscathed.

Usually, on nights like this, for there had been many lately, he could escape from this consuming introspection by thinking of children and the infinite possibilities of children—he leaned and listened and he heard a startled baby awake in a house across the street and lend a tiny whimper to the still night. Quick as a flash he turned away, wondering with a touch of panic whether something in the brooding despair of his mood had made a darkness in its tiny soul. He shivered. What if some day the balance was overturned, and he became a thing that frightened children and crept into rooms in the dark, approached dim communion with those phantoms who whispered shadowy secrets to the mad of that dark continent upon the moon. . . .

Amory smiled a bit.

"You're too much wrapped up in yourself," he heard some one say. And again—

"Get out and do some real work—"

"Stop worrying—"

He fancied a possible future comment of his own.

"Yes—I was perhaps an egotist in youth, but I soon found it made me morbid to think too much about myself."

Suddenly he felt an overwhelming desire to let himself go to the devil—not to go violently as a gentleman should, but to sink safely and sensuously out of sight. He pictured himself in an adobe house in Mexico, half-reclining on a rug-covered couch, his slender, artistic fingers closed on a cigarette while he listened to guitars strumming melancholy undertones to an age-old dirge of Castile and an olive-skinned, carmine-lipped girl caressed his hair. Here he might live a strange litany, delivered from right and wrong and from the hound of heaven and from every God (except the exotic Mexican one who was pretty slack himself and rather addicted to Oriental scents)—delivered from success and hope and poverty into that long chute of indulgence which led, after all, only to the artificial lake of death.

There were so many places where one might deteriorate pleasantly: Port Said, Shanghai, parts of Turkestan, Constantinople, the South Seas—all lands of sad, haunting music and many odors, where lust could be a mode and expression of life, where the shades of night skies and sunsets would seem to reflect only moods of passion: the colors of lips and poppies.

STILL WEEDING

Once he had been miraculously able to scent evil as a horse detects a broken bridge at night, but the man with the queer feet in Phoebe's room had diminished to the aura over Jill. His instinct perceived the fetidness of poverty, but no longer ferreted out the deeper evils in pride and sensuality.

There were no more wise men; there were no more heroes; Burne Holiday was sunk from sight as though he had never lived; Monsignor was dead. Amory had grown up to a thousand books, a thousand lies; he had listened eagerly to people who pretended to know, who knew nothing. The mystical reveries of saints that had once filled him with awe in the still hours of night, now vaguely repelled him. The Byrons and Brookes who had defied life from mountain tops were in the end but flaneurs and poseurs, at best mistaking the shadow of courage for the substance of wisdom. The pageantry of his disillusion took shape in a world-old procession of Prophets, Athenians, Martyrs, Saints, Scientists, Don Juans, Jesuits, Puritans, Fausts, Poets, Pacifists; like costumed alumni at a college reunion they streamed before him as their dreams, personalities, and creeds had in turn thrown colored lights on his soul; each had tried to express the glory of life and the tremendous significance of man; each had boasted of synchronizing what had gone before into his own rickety generalities; each had depended after all on the set stage and the convention of the theatre, which is that man in his hunger for faith will feed his mind with the nearest and most convenient food.

Women—of whom he had expected so much; whose beauty he had hoped to transmute into modes of art; whose unfathomable instincts, marvellously incoherent and inarticulate, he had thought to perpetuate in terms of experience—had become merely consecrations to their own posterity. Isabelle, Clara, Rosalind, Eleanor, were all removed by their very beauty, around which men had swarmed, from the possibility of contributing anything but a sick heart and a page of puzzled words to write.

Amory based his loss of faith in help from others on several sweeping syllogisms. Granted that his generation, however bruised and decimated from this Victorian war, were the heirs of progress. Waving aside petty differences of conclusions which, although they might occasionally cause the deaths of several millions of young men, might be explained away—supposing that after all Bernard Shaw and Bernhardi, Bonar Law and Bethmann-Hollweg were mutual heirs of progress if only in agreeing against the ducking of witches— waiving the antitheses and approaching individually these men who seemed to be the leaders, he was repelled by the discrepancies and contradictions in the men themselves.

There was, for example, Thorton Hancock, respected by half the intellectual world as an authority on life, a man who had verified and believed the code he lived by, an educator of educators, an adviser to Presidents—yet Amory knew that this man had, in his heart, leaned on the priest of another religion.

And Monsignor, upon whom a cardinal rested, had moments of strange and horrible insecurity— inexplicable in a religion that explained even disbelief in terms of its own faith: if you doubted the devil it was the devil that made you doubt him. Amory had seen Monsignor go to the houses of stolid philistines, read popular novels furiously, saturate himself in routine, to escape from that horror.

And this priest, a little wiser, somewhat purer, had been, Amory knew, not essentially older than he.

Amory was alone—he had escaped from a small enclosure into a great labyrinth. He was where Goethe was when he began "Faust"; he was where Conrad was when he wrote "Almayer's Folly."

Amory said to himself that there were essentially two sorts of people who through natural clarity or disillusion left the enclosure and sought the labyrinth. There were men like Wells and Plato, who had, half unconsciously, a strange, hidden orthodoxy, who would accept for themselves only what could be accepted for all men— incurable romanticists who never, for all their efforts, could enter the labyrinth as stark souls; there were on the other hand sword-like pioneering personalities, Samuel Butler, Renan, Voltaire, who progressed much slower, yet eventually much further, not in the direct pessimistic line of speculative philosophy but concerned in the eternal attempt to attach a positive value to life. . . .

Amory stopped. He began for the first time in his life to have a strong distrust of all generalities and epigrams. They were too easy, too dangerous to the public mind. Yet all thought usually reached the public after thirty years in some such form: Benson and Chesterton had popularized Huysmans and Newman; Shaw had sugarcoated Nietzsche and Ibsen and Schopenhauer. The man in the street heard the conclusions of dead genius through some one else's clever paradoxes and didactic epigrams.

Life was a damned muddle . . . a football game with every one off-side and the referee gotten rid of—every one claiming the referee would have been on his side. . . .

Progress was a labyrinth . . . people plunging blindly in and then rushing wildly back, shouting that they had found it . . . the invisible king—the *élan vital*—the principle of evolution . . . writing a book, starting a war, founding a school. . . .

Amory, even had he not been a selfish man, would have started all inquiries with himself. He was his own best example—sitting in the rain, a human creature of sex and pride, foiled by chance and his own temperament of the balm of love and children, preserved to help in building up the living consciousness of the race.

In self-reproach and loneliness and disillusion he came to the entrance of the labyrinth.

Another dawn flung itself across the river; a belated taxi hurried along the street, its lamps still shining like burning eyes in a face white from a night's carouse. A melancholy siren sounded far down the river.

MONSIGNOR

Amory kept thinking how Monsignor would have enjoyed his own funeral. It was magnificently Catholic and liturgical. Cardinal O'Neil sang solemn high mass and the cardinal gave the final absolutions. Thorton Hancock, Mrs. Lawrence, the British and Italian ambassadors, the papal delegate, and a host of friends and priests were there—yet the inexorable shears had cut through all these threads that Monsignor had gathered into his hands. To Amory it was a haunting grief to see him lying in his coffin, with closed hands upon his purple vestments. His face had not changed, and, as he never knew he was dying, it showed no pain or fear. It was Amory's dear old friend, his and the others'—for the church was full of people with daft, staring faces, the most exalted seeming the most stricken.

The cardinal, like an archangel in cope and mitre, sprinkled the holy water; the organ broke into sound; the choir began to sing the *Requiem Eternam.*

All these people grieved because they had to some extent depended upon Monsignor. Their grief was more than sentiment for the "crack in his voice or a certain break in his walk," as Wells put it. These people had leaned on Monsignor's faith, his way of finding cheer, of making religion a thing of lights and shadows, making all light and shadow merely aspects of God. People felt safe when he was near.

Of Amory's attempted sacrifice had been born merely the full realization of his disillusion, but of Monsignor's funeral was born the romantic elf who was to enter the labyrinth with him. He found something that he wanted, had always wanted and always would want—not to be admired, as he had feared; not to be loved, as he had made himself believe; but to be necessary to people, to be indispensable; he remembered the sense of security he had found in Burne.

Life opened up in one of its amazing bursts of radiance and Amory suddenly and permanently rejected an old epigram that had been playing listlessly in his mind: "Very few things matter and nothing matters very much."

On the contrary, Amory felt an immense desire to give people a sense of security.

THE BIG MAN WITH GOGGLES

On the day that Amory started on his walk to Princeton the sky was a colorless vault, cool, high and barren of the threat of rain. It was a gray day, that least fleshly of all weathers; a day of dreams and far hopes and clear visions. It was a day easily associated with those abstract truths and purities that dissolve in the sunshine or fade out in mocking laughter by the light of the moon. The trees and clouds were carved in classical severity; the sounds of the countryside had harmonized to a monotone, metallic as a trumpet, breathless as the Grecian urn.

The day had put Amory in such a contemplative mood that he caused much annoyance to several motorists who were forced to slow up considerably or else run him down. So engrossed in his thoughts was he that he was scarcely surprised at that strange phenomenon— cordiality manifested within fifty miles of Manhattan—

when a passing car slowed down beside him and a voice hailed him. He looked up and saw a magnificent Locomobile in which sat two middle-aged men, one of them small and anxious looking, apparently an artificial growth on the other who was large and begoggled and imposing.

"Do you want a lift?" asked the apparently artificial growth, glancing from the corner of his eye at the imposing man as if for some habitual, silent corroboration.

"You bet I do. Thanks."

The chauffeur swung open the door, and, climbing in, Amory settled himself in the middle of the back seat. He took in his companions curiously. The chief characteristic of the big man seemed to be a great confidence in himself set off against a tremendous boredom with everything around him. That part of his face which protruded under the goggles was what is generally termed "strong"; rolls of not undignified fat had collected near his chin; somewhere above was a wide thin mouth and the rough model for a Roman nose, and, below, his shoulders collapsed without a struggle into the powerful bulk of his chest and belly. He was excellently and quietly dressed. Amory noticed that he was inclined to stare straight at the back of the chauffeur's head as if speculating steadily but hopelessly some baffling hirsute problem.

The smaller man was remarkable only for his complete submersion in the personality of the other. He was of that lower secretarial type who at forty have engraved upon their business cards: "Assistant to the President," and without a sigh consecrate the rest of their lives to second-hand mannerisms.

"Going far?" asked the smaller man in a pleasant disinterested way.

"Quite a stretch."

"Hiking for exercise?"

"No," responded Amory succinctly, "I'm walking because I can't afford to ride."

"Oh."

Then again:

"Are you looking for work? Because there's lots of

work," he continued rather testily. "All this talk of lack of work. The West is especially short of labor." He expressed the West with a sweeping, lateral gesture. Amory nodded politely.

"Have you a trade?"

No—Amory had no trade.

"Clerk, eh?"

No—Amory was not a clerk.

"Whatever your line is," said the little man, seeming to agree wisely with something Amory had said, "now is the time of opportunity and business openings." He glanced again toward the big man, as a lawyer grilling a witness glances involuntarily at the jury.

Amory decided that he must say something and for the life of him could think of only one thing to say.

"Of course I want a great deal of money—"

The little man laughed mirthlessly but conscientiously.

"That's what every one wants nowadays, but they don't want to work for it."

"A very natural, healthy desire. Almost all normal people want to be rich without great effort—except the financiers in problem plays, who want to 'crash their way through.' Don't you want easy money?"

"Of course not," said the secretary indignantly.

"But," continued Amory disregarding him, "being very poor at present I am contemplating socialism as possibly my forte."

Both men glanced at him curiously.

"These bomb throwers—" The little man ceased as words lurched ponderously from the big man's chest.

"If I thought you were a bomb thrower I'd run you over to the Newark jail. That's what I think of Socialists."

Amory laughed.

"What are you," asked the big man, "one of these parlor Bolsheviks, one of these idealists? I must say I fail to see the difference. The idealists loaf around and write the stuff that stirs up the poor immigrants."

"Well," said Amory, "if being an idealist is both safe and lucrative, I might try it."

"What's your difficulty? Lost your job?"

"Not exactly, but—well, call it that."

"What was it?"

"Writing copy for an advertising agency."

"Lots of money in advertising."

Amory smiled discreetly.

"Oh, I'll admit there's money in it eventually. Talent doesn't starve any more. Even art gets enough to eat these days. Artists draw your magazine covers, write your advertisements, hash out rag-time for your theatres. By the great commercializing of printing you've found a harmless, polite occupation for every genius who might have carved his own niche. But beware the artist who's an intellectual also. The artist who doesn't fit—the Rousseau, the Tolstoi, the Samuel Butler, the Amory Blaine—"

"Who's he?" demanded the little man suspiciously.

"Well," said Amory, "he's a—he's an intellectual personage not very well known at present."

The little man laughed his conscientious laugh, and stopped rather suddenly as Amory's burning eyes turned on him.

"What are you laughing at?"

"These *intellectual* people—"

"Do you know what it means?"

The little man's eyes twitched nervously.

"Why, it *usually* means—"

"It *always* means brainy and well-educated," interrupted Amory. "It means having an active knowledge of the race's experience." Amory decided to be very rude. He turned to the big man. "The young man," he indicated the secretary with his thumb, and said young man as one says bell-boy, with no implication of youth, "has the usual muddled connotation of all popular words."

"You object to the fact that capital controls printing?" said the big man, fixing him with his goggles.

"Yes—and I object to doing their mental work for them. It seemed to me that the root of all the business I saw around me consisted in overworking and underpaying a bunch of dubs who submitted to it."

"Here now," said the big man, "you'll have to admit

that the laboring man is certainly highly paid—five and six hour days—it's ridiculous. You can't buy an honest day's work from a man in the trade-unions."

"You've brought it on yourselves," insisted Amory. "You people never make concessions until they're wrung out of you."

"What people?"

"Your class; the class I belonged to until recently; those who by inheritance or industry or brains or dishonesty have become the moneyed class."

"Do you imagine that if the road-mender over there had the money he'd be any more willing to give it up?"

"No, but what's that got to do with it?"

The older man considered.

"No, I'll admit it hasn't. It rather sounds as if it had though."

"In fact," continued Amory, "he'd be worse. The lower classes are narrower, less pleasant and personally more selfish—certainly more stupid. But all that has nothing to do with the question."

"Just exactly what is the question?"

Here Amory had to pause to consider exactly what the question was.

Amory Coins a Phrase

"When life gets hold of a brainy man of fair education," began Amory slowly, "that is, when he marries he becomes, nine times out of ten, a conservative as far as existing social conditions are concerned. He may be unselfish, kind-hearted, even just in his own way, but his first job is to provide and to hold fast. His wife shoos him on, from ten thousand a year to twenty thousand a year, on and on, in an enclosed treadmill that hasn't any windows. He's done! Life's got him! He's no help! He's a spiritually married man."

Amory paused and decided that it wasn't such a bad phrase.

"Some men," he continued, "escape the grip. Maybe

their wives have no social ambitions; maybe they've hit a sentence or two in a 'dangerous book' that pleased them; maybe they started on the treadmill as I did and were knocked off. Anyway, they're the congressmen you can't bribe, the Presidents who aren't politicians, the writers, speakers, scientists, statesmen who aren't just popular grab-bags for a half-dozen women and children."

"He's the natural radical?"

"Yes," said Amory. "He may vary from the disillusioned critic like old Thorton Hancock, all the way to Trotsky. Now this spiritually unmarried man hasn't direct power, for unfortunately the spiritually married man, as a by-product of his money chase, has garnered in the great newspaper, the popular magazine, the influential weekly—so that Mrs. Newspaper, Mrs. Magazine, Mrs. Weekly can have a better limousine than those oil people across the street or those cement people 'round the corner."

"Why not?"

"It makes wealthy men the keepers of the world's intellectual conscience and, of course, a man who has money under one set of social institutions quite naturally can't risk his family's happiness by letting the clamor for another appear in his newspaper."

"But it appears," said the big man.

"Where?—in the discredited mediums. Rotten cheap-papered weeklies."

"All right—go on."

"Well, my first point is that through a mixture of conditions of which the family is the first, there are these two sorts of brains. One sort takes human nature as it finds it, uses its timidity, its weakness, and its strength for its own ends. Opposed is the man who, being spiritually unmarried, continually seeks for new systems that will control or counteract human nature. His problem is harder. It is not life that's complicated, it's the struggle to guide and control life. That is his struggle. He is a part of progress—the spiritually married man is not."

The big man produced three big cigars, and proffered

them on his huge palm. The little man took one, Amory shook his head and reached for a cigarette.

"Go on talking," said the big man. "I've been wanting to hear one of you fellows."

GOING FASTER

"Modern life," began Amory again, "changes no longer century by century, but year by year, ten times faster than it ever has before—populations doubling, civilizations unified more closely with other civilizations, economic interdependence, racial questions, and—we're *dawdling* along. My idea is that we've got to go very much faster." He slightly emphasized the last words and the chauffeur unconsciously increased the speed of the car. Amory and the big man laughed; the little man laughed, too, after a pause.

"Every child," said Amory, "should have an equal start. If his father can endow him with a good physique and his mother with some common sense in his early education, that should be his heritage. If the father can't give him a good physique, if the mother has spent in chasing men the years in which she should have been preparing herself to educate her children, so much the worse for the child. He shouldn't be artificially bolstered up with money, sent to these horrible tutoring schools, dragged through college . . . Every boy ought to have an equal start."

"All right," said the big man, his goggles indicating neither approval nor objection.

"Next I'd have a fair trial of government ownership of all industries."

"That's been proven a failure."

"No—it merely failed. If we had government ownership we'd have the best analytical business minds in the government working for something besides themselves. We'd have Mackays instead of Burlesons; we'd have Morgans in the Treasury Department; we'd have Hills running interstate commerce. We'd have the best lawyers in the Senate."

"They wouldn't give their best efforts for nothing. McAdoo—"

"No," said Amory, shaking his head. "Money isn't the only stimulus that brings out the best that's in a man, even in America."

"You said a while ago that it was."

"It is, right now. But if it were made illegal to have more than a certain amount the best men would all flock for the one other reward which attracts humanity—honor."

The big man made a sound that was very like *boo*.

"That's the silliest thing you've said yet."

"No, it isn't silly. It's quite plausible. If you'd gone to college you'd have been struck by the fact that the men there would work twice as hard for any one of a hundred petty honors as those other men did who were earning their way through."

"Kids—child's play!" scoffed his antagonist.

"Not by a darned sight—unless we're all children. Did you ever see a grown man when he's trying for a secret society—or a rising family whose name is up at some club? They'll jump when they hear the sound of the word. The idea that to make a man work you've got to hold gold in front of his eyes is a growth, not an axiom. We've done that for so long that we've forgotten there's any other way. We've made a world where that's necessary. Let me tell you"—Amory became emphatic—"if there were ten men insured against either wealth or starvation, and offered a green ribbon for five hours' work a day and a blue ribbon for ten hours' work a day, nine out of ten of them would be trying for the blue ribbon. That competitive instinct only wants a badge. If the size of their house is the badge they'll sweat their heads off for that. If it's only a blue ribbon, I damn near believe they'll work just as hard. They have in other ages."

"I don't agree with you."

"I know it," said Amory nodding sadly. "It doesn't

matter any more though. I think these people are going to come and take what they want pretty soon."

A fierce hiss came from the little man.

"Machine-guns!"

"Ah, but you've taught them their use."

The big man shook his head.

"In this country there are enough property owners not to permit that sort of thing."

Amory wished he knew the statistics of property owners and non-property owners; he decided to change the subject.

But the big man was aroused.

"When you talk of 'taking things away,' you're on dangerous ground.'

"How can they get it without taking it? For years people have been stalled off with promises. Socialism may not be progress, but the threat of the red flag is certainly the inspiring force of all reform. You've got to be sensational to get attention."

"Russia is your example of a beneficent violence, I suppose?"

"Quite possibly," admitted Amory. "Of course, it's overflowing just as the French Revolution did, but I've no doubt that it's really a great experiment and well worth while."

"Don't you believe in moderation?"

"You won't listen to the moderates, and it's almost too late. The truth is that the public has done one of those startling and amazing things that they do about once in a hundred years. They've seized an idea."

"What is it?"

"That however the brains and abilities of men may differ, their stomachs are essentially the same."

THE LITTLE MAN GETS HIS

"If you took all the money in the world," said the little man with much profundity, "and divided it up in equ—"

"Oh, shut up!" said Amory briskly and, paying no attention to the little man's enraged stare, he went on with his argument.

"The human stomach—" he began; but the big man interrupted rather impatiently.

"I'm letting you talk, you know," he said, "but please avoid stomachs. I've been feeling mine all day. Anyway, I don't agree with one-half you've said. Government ownership is the basis of your whole argument, and it's invariably a beehive of corruption. Men won't work for blue ribbons, that's all rot."

When he ceased the little man spoke up with a determined nod, as if resolved this time to have his say out.

"There are certain things which are human nature," he asserted with an owl-like look, "which always have been and always will be, which can't be changed."

Amory looked from the small man to the big man helplessly.

"Listen to that! *That's* what makes me discouraged with progress. *Listen* to that! I can name offhand over one hundred natural phenomena that have been changed by the will of man—a hundred instincts in man that have been wiped out or are now held in check by civilization. What this man here just said has been for thousands of years the last refuge of the associated muttonheads of the world. It negates the efforts of every scientist, statesman, physician, inventor, and philosopher that ever gave his life to humanity's service. It's a flat impeachment of all that's worth while in human nature. Every person over twenty-five years old who makes that statement in cold blood ought to be deprived of the franchise."

The little man leaned back against the seat, his face purple with rage. Amory continued, addressing his remarks to the big man.

"These quarter-educated, stale-minded men such as your friend here, who *think* they think, every question that comes up, you'll find his type in the usual ghastly muddle. One minute it's 'the brutality and inhumanity of these Prussians'—the next it's 'we ought to exterminate the whole German people.' They always believe that 'things are in a bad way now,' but they 'haven't any faith in these idealists.' One minute they call Wilson 'just a dreamer, not practical'—a year later they rail at him for making his dreams realities. They haven't clear logical ideas on one single subject except a sturdy, stolid opposition to all change. They don't think uneducated people should be highly paid, but they won't see that if they don't pay the uneducated people their children are going to be uneducated too, and we're going round and round in a circle. That—is the great middle class!"

The big man with a broad grin on his face leaned over and smiled at the little man.

"You're catching it pretty heavy, Garvin; how do you feel?"

The little man made an attempt to smile and act as if the whole matter were so ridiculous as to be beneath notice. But Amory was not through.

"The theory that people are fit to govern themselves rests on this man. If he can be educated to think clearly, concisely, and logically, freed of his habit of taking refuge in platitudes and prejudices and sentimentalisms, then I'm a militant Socialist. If he can't, then I don't think it matters much what happens to man or his systems, now or hereafter."

"I am both interested and amused," said the big man. "You are very young."

"Which may only mean that I have neither been corrupted nor made timid by contemporary experience. I possess the most valuable experience, the experience of the race, for in spite of going to college I've managed to pick up a good education."

"You talk glibly."

"It's not all rubbish," cried Amory passionately. "This is the first time in my life I've argued Socialism. It's the only panacea I know. I'm restless. My whole generation is restless. I'm sick of a system where the richest man gets the most beautiful girl if he wants her, where the artist without an income has to sell his talents to a button manufacturer. Even if I had no talents I'd not be content to work ten years, condemned either to celibacy or a furtive indulgence, to give some man's son an automobile."

"But, if you're not sure——"

"That doesn't matter," exclaimed Amory. "My position couldn't be worse. A social revolution might land me on top. Of course I'm selfish. It seems to me I've been a fish out of water in too many outworn systems. I was probably one of the two dozen men in my class at college who got a decent education; still they'd let any well-tutored flathead play football and *I* was ineligible, because some silly old men thought we should *all* profit by conic sections. I loathed the army. I loathed business. I'm in love with change and I've killed my conscience——"

"So you'll go along crying that we must go faster."

"That, at least, is true," Amory insisted. "Reform won't catch up to the needs of civilization unless it's made to. A laissez-faire policy is like spoiling a child by saying he'll turn out all right in the end. He will—if he's made to."

"But you don't believe all this Socialist patter you talk."

"I don't know. Until I talked to you I hadn't thought seriously about it. I wasn't sure of half of what I said."

"You puzzle me," said the big man, "but you're all alike. They say Bernard Shaw, in spite of his doctrines, is the most exacting of all dramatists about his royalties. To the last farthing."

"Well," said Amory, "I simply state that I'm a product of a versatile mind in a restless generation—with every reason to throw my mind and pen in with the radicals. Even if, deep in my heart, I thought we were all blind atoms in a world as limited as a stroke of a pendulum, I and my sort would struggle against tradition; try, at least, to displace old cants with new ones. I've thought I was right about life at various times, but faith is difficult. One thing I know. If living isn't a seeking for the grail it may be a damned amusing game."

For a minute neither spoke and then the big man asked:

"What was your university?"

"Princeton."

The big man became suddenly interested; the expression of his goggles altered slightly.

"I sent my son to Princeton."

"Did you?"

"Perhaps you knew him. His name was Jesse Ferrenby. He was killed last year in France."

"I knew him very well. In fact, he was one of my particular friends."

"He was—a—quite a fine boy. We were very close."

Amory began to perceive a resemblance between the father and the dead son and he told himself that there had been all along a sense of familiarity. Jesse Ferrenby, the man who in college had borne off the crown that he had aspired to. It was all so far away. What little boys they had been, working for blue ribbons—

The car slowed up at the entrance to a great estate, ringed around by a huge hedge and a tall iron fence.

"Won't you come in for lunch?"

Amory shook his head.

"Thank you, Mr. Ferrenby, but I've got to get on."

The big man held out his hand. Amory saw that the fact that he had known Jesse more than outweighed any disfavor he had created by his opinions. What ghosts were people with which to work! Even the little man insisted on shaking hands.

"Good-by!" shouted Mr. Ferrenby, as the car turned the corner and started up the drive. "Good luck to you and bad luck to your theories."

"Same to you, sir," cried Amory, smiling and waving his hand.

"OUT OF THE FIRE, OUT OF THE LITTLE ROOM"

Eight hours from Princeton Amory sat down by the Jersey roadside and looked at the frost-bitten country. Nature was a rather coarse phenomenon composed largely of flowers that, when closely inspected, appeared motheaten, and of ants that endlessly traversed blades of grass, was always disillusioning; nature represented by skies and waters and far horizons was more likeable. Frost and the promise of winter thrilled him now, made him think of a wild battle between St. Regis and Groton, ages ago, seven years ago—and of an autumn day in France twelve months before when he had lain in tall grass, his platoon flattened down close around him, waiting to tap the shoulders of a Lewis gunner. He saw the two pictures together with somewhat the same primitive exaltation—two games he had played, differing in quality of acerbity, linked in a way that differed them from Rosalind or the subject of labyrinths which were, after all, the business of life.

"I am selfish," he thought.

"This is not a quality that will change when I 'see human suffering' or 'lose my parents' or 'help others.'

"This selfishness is not only part of me. It is the most living part.

"It is by somehow transcending rather than by avoiding that selfishness that I can bring poise and balance into my life.

"There is no virtue of unselfishness that I cannot use. I can make sacrifices, be charitable, give to a friend, endure for a friend, lay down my life for a friend—all because these things may be the best possible expression of myself; yet I have not one drop of the milk of human kindness."

The problem of evil had solidified for Amory into the problem of sex. He was beginning to identify evil with the strong phallic worship in Brooke and the early Wells. Inseparably linked with evil was beauty—beauty, still a constant rising tumult; soft in Eleanor's voice, in an old song at night, rioting deliriously through life like superimposed waterfalls, half rhythm, half darkness. Amory knew that every time he had reached toward it longingly it had leered out at him with the grotesque face of evil. Beauty of great art, beauty of all joy, most of all the beauty of women.

After all, it had too many associations with license and indulgence. Weak things were often beautiful, weak things were never good. And in this new loneliness of his that had been selected for what greatness he might achieve, beauty must be relative or, itself a harmony, it would make only a discord.

In a sense this gradual renunciation of beauty was the second step after his disillusion had been made complete. He felt that he was leaving behind him his chance of being a certain type of artist. It seemed so much more important to be a certain sort of man.

His mind turned a corner suddenly and he found himself thinking of the Catholic Church. The idea was strong in him that there was a certain intrinsic lack in those to whom orthodox religion was necessary, and religion to Amory meant the Church of Rome. Quite conceivably it was an empty ritual but it was seemingly the only assimilative, traditionary bulwark against the decay of morals. Until the great mobs could be educated into a moral sense some one must cry: "Thou shalt not!" Yet any acceptance was, for the present, impossible. He wanted time and the absence of ulterior pressure. He wanted to keep the tree without ornaments, realize fully the direction and momentum of this new start.

The afternoon waned from the purging good of three o'clock to the golden beauty of four. Afterward he walked through the dull ache of a setting sun when even the clouds seemed bleeding and at twilight he came to a graveyard. There was a dusky, dreamy smell of flowers and the ghost of a new moon in the sky and shadows everywhere. On an impulse he considered trying to open the door of a rusty iron vault built into the side of a hill; a vault washed clean and covered with late-blooming, weepy watery-blue flowers that might have grown from dead eyes, sticky to the touch with a sickening odor.

Amory wanted to *feel* "William Dayfield, 1864."

He wondered that graves ever made people consider life in vain. Somehow he could find nothing hopeless in having lived. All the broken columns and clasped hands and doves and angels meant romances. He fancied that in a hundred years he would like having young people speculate as to whether his eyes were brown or blue, and he hoped quite passionately that his grave would

have about it an air of many, many years ago. It seemed
strange that out of a row of Union soldiers two or three
made him think of dead loves and dead lovers, when
they were exactly like the rest, even to the yellowish
moss.

Long after midnight the towers and spires of Princeton were visible, with here and there a late-burning
light—and suddenly out of the clear darkness the sound
of bells. As an endless dream it went on; the spirit of the
past brooding over a new generation, the chosen youth
from the muddled, unchastened world, still fed romantically on the mistakes and half-forgotten dreams of dead
statesmen and poets. Here was a new generation, shouting the old cries, learning the old creeds, through a revery of long days and nights; destined finally to go out
into that dirty gray turmoil to follow love and pride; a
new generation dedicated more than the last to the fear
of poverty and the worship of success; grown up to find
all dead, all wars fought, all faiths in man shaken. . . .

Amory, sorry for them, was still not sorry for
himself—art, politics, religion, whatever his medium
should be, he knew he was safe now, free from all
hysteria—he could accept what was acceptable, roam,
grow, rebel, sleep deep through many nights. . . .

There was no God in his heart, he knew; his ideas
were still in riot; there was ever the pain of memory; the
regret for his lost youth—yet the waters of disillusion
had left a deposit on his soul, responsibility and a love
of life, the faint stirring of old ambitions and unrealized
dreams. But—oh, Rosalind! Rosalind! . . .

"It's all a poor substitute at best," he said sadly.

And he could not tell why the struggle was worth
while, why he had determined to use to the utmost himself and his heritage from the personalities he had
passed . . . .

He stretched out his arms to the crystalline, radiant
sky.

"I know myself," he cried, "but that is all."

READ THE TOP 25 SIGNET CLASSICS

ANIMAL FARM BY GEORGE ORWELL	0-451-52634-1
1984 BY GEORGE ORWELL	0-451-52493-4
FRANKENSTEIN, DRACULA, DR. JEKYLL AND MR. HYDE	
BY MARY SHELLEY, BRAM STOKER, AND ROBERT LOUIS STEVENSON	
	0-451-52363-6
THE ADVENTURES OF HUCKLEBERRY FINN BY MARK TWAIN	0-451-52650-3
HAMLET BY WILLIAM SHAKESPEARE	0-451-52692-9
THE ODYSSEY BY HOMER	0-451-52736-4
FRANKENSTEIN BY MARY SHELLEY	0-451-52771-2
GREAT EXPECTATIONS BY CHARLES DICKENS	0-451-52671-6
THE SCARLET LETTER BY NATHANIEL HAWTHORNE	0-451-52608-2
JANE EYRE BY CHARLOTTE BRONTË	0-451-52655-4
HEART OF DARKNESS & THE SECRET SHARER	
BY JOSEPH CONRAD	0-451-52657-0
ETHAN FROME BY EDITH WHARTON	0-451-52766-6
NARRATIVE OF THE LIFE OF FREDERICK DOUGLASS	
BY FREDERICK DOUGLASS	0-451-52673-2
A TALE OF TWO CITIES BY CHARLES DICKENS	0-451-52656-2
BEOWULF (BURTON RAFFEL, TRANSLATOR)	0-451-52740-2
PRIDE AND PREJUDICE BY JANE AUSTEN	0-451-52588-4
OTHELLO BY WILLIAM SHAKESPEARE	0-451-52685-6
ROMEO AND JULIET BY WILLIAM SHAKESPEARE	0-451-52686-4
ONE DAY IN THE LIFE OF IVAN DENISOVICH	
BY ALEXANDER SOLZHENITSYN	0-451-52709-7
CYRANO DE BERGERAC BY EDMOND ROSTAND	0-451-52548-5
WUTHERING HEIGHTS BY EMILY BRONTË	0-451-52338-5
A MIDSUMMER NIGHT'S DREAM BY WILLIAM SHAKESPEARE	0-451-52696-1
MACBETH BY WILLIAM SHAKESPEARE	0-451-52677-5
THE COUNT OF MONTE CRISTO BY ALEXANDER DUMAS	0-451-52195-1
DON QUIXOTE BY MIGUEL DE CERVANTES	0-451-52786-0

TO ORDER CALL: 1-800-788-6262